*This book is dedicated to Casey,
who is the reason I smile.*

GUIDED
BY THE
WIND

LEONA BENTLEY

RIPTIDE
PUBLISHING

GUIDED
BY THE
WIND

LEONA BENTLEY

RIPTIDE
PUBLISHING

Riptide Publishing
PO Box 1537
Burnsville, NC 28714
www.riptidepublishing.com

Guided by the Wind

Cover art: L.C. Chase, lcchase.com
Editors: Stella Li, Carole-ann Galloway, Grace Stack
Layout: L.C. Chase, lcchase.com

ISBN: 978-1-62649-979-9

First edition
January, 2024

Also available in ebook:
ISBN: 978-1-62649-978-2

TABLE OF
CONTENTS

CHAPTER

✺

ONE

The old saloon was an oven. Those packed within its wooden walls—including Star—were damp with sweat and haggard from heat, spending coin as if drink could chase away the sun-damned assault. The moon's cooler touch was a long way off, but thanks to his father's blood, Star didn't feel the heat the same as those who called the hard-carved town of Standing Grave home.

They'd ridden in on scorched air gasped up from the Sun's Scar, a wraith-haunted canyon yawning long and deep just steps from the settlement. After hitting the canyon's outskirts a day earlier, they'd followed its jagged edges at a distance until it'd led them into town. After so long beneath the sun's unrelenting glare, two moons at the least, it felt good to enjoy the conversations itching at his ears.

Star's lone hope of a few days' respite sat waxing poetic a short distance down the age-scarred bar. Bill Cove, the closest thing he and his father had to family, lounged with his shirt open to show off sweat-glistening chest muscles. The man's sandy-blond head bobbed as he mimed some heart-stopping scurry for life. Exaggeration was doubtlessly involved, but that was half of Bill's charm.

The man's audience, two tow-headed twins, were as inflexible as anyone else around, and—gold or silver—they were only charmed on their terms. Judging by their matching looks of disinterest, Bill would soon either buy their attentions or lose them. Hot as it was, Bill likely didn't care either way.

"Another water?" a gruff voice asked.

Twisting back around, Star turned his grin on Sandy, taking in the owner's welcoming, grizzled brown face and steady hand brandishing a condensation-dampened pitcher of water.

"Please." Star pushed his emptied mug closer. He dug coins out of his pouch and slid them over as Sandy poured.

The lukewarm feel of the water on his tongue and throat was welcoming.

"Lost Ty fast this time," Sandy commented.

Star's mouth twitched. "I usually do." He took another gulp.

His father, Ty, was currently ensconced in one of the upstairs rooms "making nice" with Lacy, whom he always sought out when they came this way. Star—more interested in eyeing the men packed around the wobbly tables than the perfumed ones upstairs—was content to stay seated at the long, lop-sided bar. He kept watch over the stairs leading to his dad's unprotected back.

"In town long, kid?" Sandy asked, as if reading Star's mind. His old eyes scanned Star's face before he nodded to the man next to Star, accepted a few minted coins, and poured a measure of dark amber liquid into the stranger's waiting glass.

When Sandy looked back at him expectantly, Star smirked and shrugged. "We're just passing through, I think. Dad hasn't said one way or the other, but he's restless lately."

"*Lately?*"

Star chuckled at the good-natured teasing. "Fair point."

Star and his father lived on the move. Their rare stops in towns were short reprieves from sun and stars. Star enjoyed the visits, but they made his father tense and impatient. In his twenty-one years, Star could only remember one occasion when they'd spent more than a fortnight under a single roof. There had been no other option then. Star hadn't been well enough within or without to face the world, and Ty hadn't let Star far from sight.

Those memories always felt close when visiting Standing Grave. It was no fault of the settlement itself, but born of where it leaned against that bite of hell stretching leagues to the north and south. The long, curving rend split down into the sun's domain, a dry hellscape populated by winged vipers and, at night, when all became dark, slivers of memory-wraiths. Only fools entered, and almost none left. No one within Standing Grave dared stray too near the valley below, but all took a measure of pride in living above it.

Star'd entered it once, and splintered memories of that desperate rush were impossibly tangled with the horrific days that had led there. It'd been an escape he and his father had barely survived, heat and vermin vying for their lifeblood. No wraiths had joined the hunt, but he could remember their presence, silvery and distant.

"Where will you ride next, you think? South, maybe? East? West?" Sandy moved down the bar as he spoke to accept more coin and parcel out more drink. Shaking off nausea clinging to the old memory, Star watched him. Sandy added, "I assume you'll be long absent before this heatwave breaks over our heads, anyroad."

A bray of laughter from one of the regulars cut into their exchange, loud amidst the morose crowd. "Losing your memory, old man?" he jeered, dropping coin next to his emptied mug. "There's a north too. Some even say the damn place has air you can breathe, not like this scalding shit."

Sandy snorted and refilled the waiting mug. "Ty'd throw himself off his horse before going that way. Man carries grudges, that's for damn sure. Whatever he met that way, he ain't revisiting."

Star glared down at his cup, teeth set. No, his father didn't go that way. He refused to say a word about the choice, but over the years, Star had managed to deduce one thing: north was where his mother had died.

"North isn't in the dice, no," Star answered around a smile that was more teeth than joy. "Money is easier to find in other directions."

The interloper squinted at him, and for a second, Star thought the man might say something else. Instead the fellow shrugged a narrow shoulder and returned to his drink.

"As you say, kid," Sandy agreed indulgently.

Uncomfortable with the line of talk, Star cast about for a new topic. "Lacy wrote that things have been quiet." Quiet was an unusual state for a town so close to hell's guts. The type of people who chose to live near the sun's cursed lands were not a settled lot.

Sandy laughed. "You got that one, did ya, kid? She wasn't too sure you would, but you were due this way and we'd heard you and Ty had ridden east." He shook his head, then gave a sigh. "Aye, though, lad. Quiet and *too* quiet. Summer came early, and the sun is making her enjoyment known. We've had, what? Maybe five deaths total here from fights in the last moon, and maybe triple that in survived brawls. The heat's good for downstairs business, but upstairs? The girls and Davin don't like it any more than the rest of us, and with good reason."

Here he gave a wry grin, nodding to the stairs. "Well, most don't. Lacy near dragged your father up that way when he stepped through our door. Exceptions, I suppose. Anyone else would've gotten a curled lip from that one before she led the poor soul that-a-ways, and they'd have paid dearly."

"He missed her," Star answered weakly, feeling the lie as he offered it. Sandy nodded, his brown eyes not quite meeting Star's.

Disquieted, Star cast a glance Bill's way, curious to see how he was doing. The girls were gone, but that didn't seem to bother him.

Bill caught his glance with a wink and rose.

"Of course he missed her." Bill wandered over. He never missed much, so Star wasn't surprised that he'd been following their conversation. Bill dropped onto the stool next to Star, hand snaking out to ruffle his dark hair. Star glowered as the mussing knocked strands out of the loose tie, but his lips twitched all the same. Star might be an adult now, but Bill had known him since before he could walk.

"You've been drinking the town water, I noticed." Bill gestured toward the empty cup in front of Star, saying with playful criticism, "Think Sandy here can spare a drop for me?"

Sandy turned to grab a glass and a pitcher off the low table behind them. There were five more sitting, ready. "Let my girls work the room, Bill, and the first one's on me."

Bill sank back on his stool, leaning until he almost unseated himself and looking thoroughly pleased. "A cruel deal, but I'll take it." He sighed loudly, then nudged Star's slight shoulder with his meatier one. "I don't know how you take this heat, kid. I'm melting. The old crook's deal is almost a relief. Hell, I think some of those around us *have* melted."

Bill's exaggerated gape at the surrounding patrons lightened Star's mood. Busy as the bar looked, it was as Bill said. The room's bustle barely rose above a dull rumble. It was usually a far livelier place in the early evenings, but sweltering heat and no rain had dried out spirits. What would happen, Star wondered, once the heatwave broke and, feeling the moon's cooler touch on the summer air again, all that pent-up tension hit release?

While not populated by the beasts that scavenged just below them, the town was home to its own land-grown variety: people seeking to escape their pasts or avoid the Sighted Blades—relentless peacekeepers who took up post to track down those with law-approved bounties on their heads.

It made the people a difficult crowd on the best of days, and on the worst? With no appointed law-keepers, rules were few and killings common.

The saloon doors creaked. Star canted his head to watch as a pack of strangers wandered in. Where Star was tall and skinny as the bendable prairie grass, the man leading the band was lean, a strand of wire cut from a fence. He had the build and broad shoulders of a man used to hard work, with fat to soften it into a welcomingly sturdy handsomeness.

Welcome enough that Star half-considered playing at being one of the house boys to see if he could catch the man's light-green eyes.

"Well," Star muttered.

He rarely felt more than a passing interest in anyone, but looking at the dusty-brown hair and the prowl of that gait dried his mouth. The need to keep watch over his father's back was all that kept him on his stool and not playing the fool. Still, he could drink in the man's appearance, and took little shame in the doing. Any man who led two like the ones behind him had to be impressive.

The old gray-and-black-haired fellow scowling through a short beard right at his leader's heels was a compact wall of muscle, and the red-headed woman accompanying them looked more liable to shoot than smile. Star wondered what brought the three here. Once Ty returned, maybe it wouldn't hurt to wander their way and see if the younger of the group might want some conversation.

Bill leaned in close to Star's ear. "You start flirting, kid, and I'll sic your dad on that poor man the minute Ty crawls out of Lacy's clutches." There was laughter in his voice, but his eyes were sober. "That man looks like trouble, and when men travel in packs like that, they intend some."

Bill's words grated on Star's pride, but he knew they had merit and so pulled his attention back. The warning came from a good place. Even so, Star kept the strangers in the corner of his eye as he shot Bill an annoyed look that Bill answered with a smile.

"You travel with us sometimes," Star pointed out wryly. "That makes our number even with his."

"Aye." Bill drew the word out with relish before he took a long drink. "And are you two not inviting trouble when you ask me along?"

Star laughed, shaking his head. Point to Bill.

Star couldn't quite take his attention from the group. They might be trouble, he figured, but not mindless such. There was a measured watchfulness in their eyes that suggested them as being more the kind met if cornered, which he respected. Trouble wasn't something he enjoyed, although his father had raised him to be ready should it knock. He'd had enough of it five years ago, and feeling that stirring of attraction brought old fear baying on its heels.

Closing his eyes and calling himself a fool, Star reached down with his left hand to run his fingers over the handles of the two little knives and the larger dagger belted on that hip. They were there, ready, and he didn't need to check to ensure their sisters sat in their mirrored place. Feeling their steel ends and the dagger's grip calmed him, reminding him of his self-appointed duty to keep watch over his father.

Knives were his weapon. He never touched a gun. Couldn't, anymore.

He opened his eyes again, calmed, and went back to watching the handsome man and his little group. Even with ghosts plaguing the back of his mind, he wanted to try to catch those green eyes.

Bill nudged him again and grinned when Star turned to frown at him. "Are you really so bored of my company already?"

Star huffed but cracked a smile. "Never."

"I didn't expect to see either of you here till nearer fall, but I'd dropped by Bay's just as he got word you were northbound. So, since I knew you'd both be missing me, I changed my route."

"I'm glad you did," Star acknowledged, but he couldn't fight back bitterness. Star, too, had thought they'd be south longer. That he sat here in Standing Grave's saloon with the summer sun high and their pockets so empty felt wrong. Ty'd turned their heads north with a suddenness that still rankled over a moon later. Much as Star loved his father, the older he got, the harder it grew to stomach Ty's many secrets.

Their flight from the south, coupled with the desperation that'd lined his dad's face, didn't fit Ty's typical claim of a shifted wind. Pointing that out repeatedly had only received snapped impatience and evasion.

As always, Star had ended up giving in before his father, and Ty kept his newest secret.

It wasn't long before the man himself came bounding down the steps, carrying a broad-brimmed hat in one hand and his double-barrel rifle in the other. Ty looked like an older version of Star, with the same glossy black hair—only Ty's was cut to his shoulders, rather than bound down his back—and whip-thin build.

Lacy prowled behind him, her light brown hair pinned in a windy-looking upsweep and her rouged lips pursed in self-satisfaction. She wore a thin, flower-print gown and her expression was cool despite the heat flushing her skin. Star lifted a hand her way, and she mimed sending him a kiss, her eyes crinkling at the corners.

When young, Star had sometimes dreamed of his father settling with her, but years and knowledge had worn that dream to sand. His father needed the wind blowing against his back the way most needed shade and water. There'd be no home for them, just open land and the early graves that garnered. Sometimes Star wondered what it would be like to feel the wind as Ty did.

"C'mon, Star," Ty called, heading for the door. His voice carried over the other patrons, knife-sharp. He moved like there was a snake nipping his heels. "Bill, get your ass here too. We're bedding at Al's place."

Damien crossed the cramped room with a long, gliding stride. He eyed the folks gathered inside as he went, taking note of those who glanced their way versus those who paused to really look.

"A good ale would taste nice," Ostra said.

Knott, keeping close to her side, hummed in agreement. "So long as we get things settled while we have it," he added. "And keep an eye out."

The bounty on their heads might make any of those here shirk their no-law pact. None of them wanted to chance that.

The barkeep barely glanced at them as they slid into three of four empty stools along his bar. The man's attention was tied up on an impatient customer, but the look in those brown eyes had been assessing in a way that spoke of continued consideration. Damien didn't expect trouble from that quarter, but knew he'd been marked and that he'd be remembered.

"Drinks?" the barkeep demanded, finally turning to them.

"Please. Three mugs of ale."

A grunt was the answer, and soon they were served. Damien took up his own, and despite its warmth, it felt good on his parched throat. Knott hadn't taken his up yet, but by Ostra's sigh, hers was as bracing as Damien's own. It was a fine brew, even if he'd have taken pretty much any quality with thanks at this point.

"Nice to sit inside," Knott muttered, rolling his shoulders before drinking deep.

"Aye," Damien agreed, his own slow-to-relax muscles aching. He was half on his way from twenty-five to thirty, and while he still felt young enough for this life, those who followed him were leaving that time behind. Knott, the oldest of his pack, had more gray than black in his beard these days. Ostra's hair was the same, only it was bleach-bone white that shot through the still thick red she kept pinned tight to the back of her head.

Damien caught himself staring when Knott gave a sniff and raised an eyebrow. "Well?"

Ostra, seated to Knott's left and bent over a block of wood that was slowly taking the shape of a rough-featured ranch hand, snorted. "Thinking too hard, Damien?" She didn't bother looking up, knife busy and sharp eyes intent on her work.

"A bad habit," he answered.

Ostra glanced up then, one eyebrow hitched far too similarly to Knott's. "Drink and relax." Their shared strain showed on her face, but her words were light.

"I can do that."

They likely made an odd sight and would look odder again once Jonnie ambled in from putting the horses up at the stable down the road. Jonnie was a head taller than Damien, thicker-built than Knott, and as red-headed as Ostra.

If Jonnie came to join them, that was. If he had no one there to see to him, he'd sooner have his tongue go to dust than speak up and order a drink. It was a bit cruel leaving him to make their arrangements, but better he do that than help seek a guide.

"Think Jonnie will have any luck finding us a room?" Ostra asked.

Knott shrugged, answering for him. "Jonnie is exhausted. Man hasn't slept a wink, hardly, since his sister's letter. He'll want somewhere quiet to put up for the night."

The sour truth of the words settled like lead in Damien's stomach. The best they could do for the big man was to locate a guide. Trying for a smile and missing the mark, he followed Ostra's gaze as she looked around them.

"'Quiet' seems the popular theme here," he pointed out, tone lighter than he felt.

A door slammed upstairs, the noise distracting in the otherwise hushed room. Damien glanced that way and saw a slim, dark-haired man of around forty dart down the steps, spry despite the brutal heat. When the man called out, two men a short way down the bar stood. Damien perked to attention.

The blond, ruggedly handsome and all grins, was closer, but it was the man's companion who captured Damien. First was the glossy raven hair rolling down the man's back, and second the leather belt around lean, denim-clad hips, with its well-worn sides ringed in blades. The fellow's fine features, third to take Damien's breath, were similar to the spry one who'd called the man's way. But where that man looked hard and determined, the younger version was breathtaking in his road-worn cotton shirt and, beneath the belt, legs long as the plains.

Damien's mind conjured an imagine of grabbing those slim hips by that belt and pulling the man in so that he could bury his nose in all of that gorgeous hair—

An elbow caught Damien in the ribs, and he choked, catching himself on the worn wooden bar top before he could land on his ass.

"We're here for a reason," Knott hissed, annoyed.

Damien straightened, shooting Knott an apologetic grimace but unable to help a quick glance back toward the distracting fellow. Sadly, the striking man was already out the door with his companions.

"I can't help it." Damien sighed, embarrassed to be caught ogling a stranger when there were so many worries weighing them all. Even worse? He hadn't the chance to make introductions.

"Fair warning—you'll want to."

Damien twisted to face his unexpected audience. The gruff fellow manning the bar leaned their way, face hard and eyes narrowed in distrust. Damien was more curious about the words than insulted, though.

"Why is that?" Damien asked, wondering if it had to do with all the knives ringing those hips. A man like that stood out, after all.

"That kid you were eying?" The barkeep answered, motioning to the door with an empty glass. "He travels with his father. His very overprotective father."

Okay. That took some deciphering.

"First," Damien drawled, "'kid'? The lad looked like a man to me." And a man he'd very much like to get to know, at that. "And second, an overprotective parent thinks it's a good idea to take a family trip *here*? No offense, just, the reputation and all."

There was a reason, after all, that Damien had brought his little band here to look for a guide. Had they ridden into any other settlement, a peacekeeper would likely already have had a gun on their backs and nooses waiting. This place? The only sure thing was that everyone here had reason to be skulking the back trails and steering clear of more refined civilization.

The bartender snorted, nonplussed. "Star's twenty-one, so young enough." Ah, there was the man's name. It was unusual, but then so was the fellow attached to it. The other must not have liked whatever he saw on Damien's face, as his next words were sharp. "This town is likely the closest thing those two have to a regular stomping ground. They're safe enough here. They've friends and the sense to keep their noses where they belong."

"No offense or trouble meant," Damien assured, hoping to defuse any possible temper. At his side, Ostra snorted, still chiseling away. The curls of wood were building up on the counter in front of her, but the barkeep hardly gave her a frown. His vexation was, after all, visibly pointed at the man sniffing after his friend's son. "We're here to hire someone, not cause any trouble," Damien added, trying to placate the fellow.

And there came the spark of curiosity Damien needed to tend if he hoped to burn off the barman's residual distrust. Bartenders and innkeepers were the ones to seek when looking for information, as they seemed to revel in it more than pretty much any other person alive.

"I have a fair understanding of who is hanging around and their various skillsets," the barkeep offered up slowly. "What type of hiring is it, if that information isn't too sensitive for this room?"

"Not sensitive," Damien said. Knott scowled at him in disagreement, but Ostra merely arched an eyebrow. Damien took that for a win. She'd lifted her whittling knife away to watch with interest. "We need a guide."

Strangely, there came back that guarded look on the barkeep's face. "Any particular direction?"

By Moon and Sun, what had Damien done *now* to garner that expression? "Blue Roc— Ow!"

He jumped and shot Knott a glare, leaning down to rub his sore shin. Now the barman was smirking, guarded look gone and amusement blatant. Damien scowled at Knott and received a pointed look in return.

Right. Hollowood had a price on their heads. Announcing everything to the room was likely not the smartest, and curse him for the fool that pretty little backside and sea of black hair had made of him. He needed to get his head back in the situation at hand and off the appealing piece he'd missed out on. Most of the folks around them appeared too mired in overheated misery to take note, but looks could be misleading.

"I might know someone," the barman admitted. Now he looked even more amused, curse it. At least Knott's overbearing attitude was good for something. "Is the trip time sensitive?"

"Very." Ostra and Knott both let out a growl, and Damien touched their arms, placating. He understood the risk, but they had already started, and time really was against them. "We need to get there in the shortest time possible. That means we'll be traveling through the Sun's Scar, and I don't know anywhere else we'd ever even hope to find a willing guide."

It was asking for death.

The man nodded, lips pressed. "Name's Sandy." For a moment Damien had the heart-stopping hope that he meant the guide, but then realization hit. By the look on Sandy's grizzled, scruffy face, something distasteful had been decided. "There's a man. I'll talk to him for you tonight after we close. Drop by come morning and I'll let you know what he says." There returned that narrow-eyed look of warning. "And you keep your nose clean if he agrees. Remember what I said about Ty's kid, Star."

Ty. That was the dad, then. As for Star, Damien really didn't want to make any promises, despite how short a time they would be there. Especially since, if he put two and two together, it sounded like he'd be having dealings with this Ty. Or, possibly, a friend of his.

The room they'd paid for was private, with a single bed but floor space enough to make do. It was acceptably clean if stuffy, and Damien was thankful for the privacy Jonnie had spent extra to grant them. The giant of a Southerner had his back to them as he bent over his heaped belongings, already on twitching edge.

"Least we won't need bedding for warmth," Ostra muttered as she spread one of their blankets out across the worn floorboards. Knott grunted as he did the same scant steps away.

"And the floor might be the cooler of the spots," Damien commented, wishing it was easier to distract himself. His mind wouldn't let up worrying over their current problems, but their brief respite from the elements eased the tension aching at the back of his neck. It felt good to be shut away from both the sky and the strangers in the town.

Jonnie, blankets clenched in large hands and eyes clouded, wasn't paying the rest of them any mind. His thoughts were with his sister, Damien knew, just as the rest of theirs were. There was damn little that could make Jonnie smile lately, but maybe four walls and shelter would help him finally rest. The pallor beneath his tan was as marked as the bruises beneath his eyes.

Knott moved his pack closer to the back wall and away from the makeshift beds spread over the floor. He ignored Damien's eyes as he did so, and Damien made a point of looking away. Another barb, there. Knott was sensitive about his pack with its painful contents.

"Two and two," Ostra commented, drawing their attention. She looked at the bed as she, too, ignored Knott's shuffling and Jonnie's distraction. Her own pack would end up next to Knott's when he finished, but she'd still avoid the discomfort her watching would cause. Close as she and Knott were, not even she dared touch that old sun-damned pain.

Damien watched Ostra, still carefully avoiding Knott, cross the blanketed room to Jonnie's side. Presumably weary and mind elsewhere, he didn't react to her approach.

"Jonnie?" She offered what was almost a smile, hand extended.

Jonnie dutifully handed over his blankets, letting her spread them across the floor as he dug a pair of rough-hewn bone dice out of his bag, followed seconds later by a tin mug.

"Lady calls," Damien teased as he tossed his hat down on top of his own travel pack. The hat needed a good shaking off before it ever returned to his head, but that could wait. A little more dust was the least of his worn pack's problems.

Ostra pressed her lips into a line but accepted the mug and dice when Jonnie, a little less distant-eyed, handed them her way. "Suns, both, to win," she clarified. "She is in charge these days."

She rolled a sun and star.

"What do you guys make of the town?" Damien asked as he accepted his turn. The mug felt blessedly cool in his hands. He held it a second before giving it a shake and spilling the smoothed squares onto the floorboards. Two stars. No bed won yet.

"Lives up to its physical description but lacks the danger I expected," Ostra said. "That likely has more to do with the sun's current mood. Going by the look of the bar crowd, I'd say a bit of cooler air would raise spirits."

And that would mean more people ready to fight. Sweat-eating heat swept past irritability and on into lethargy. Once that broke, the sun would likely still have her way. Blood, death, and hell.

"There are more graves than people," Jonnie commented, his first words since they'd filed into the room. The ominous observation left a weighted silence as he rolled double moons.

Damien had been taken aback when riding past the long, lonely graveyard dug into the rock overlooking the yawning belly of the Sun's Scar. The bells sprinkled among the older graves were silent, the air not even able to summon a puff of breath. It was a somber and chilling sight, testament to the type of people living there.

"Aye," Damien answered, as no one else had. "We might have reason to be grateful for the sun's temper. Here's to the hope she keeps it up a little longer, lest we end up in her throat before we get to her scar."

If they could manage to convince their possible guide to help them. They'd made good time, but what they'd lose going around the Scar was out of the question. By the tone of Wendy's last letter, there wasn't that kind of time left. Their only option was to face the sun's demons, beasts told to kill any who plumbed the depths.

Knott joined them, rolling a sun and moon. Damien had half expected him to roll suns, but Knott already carried one curse from her, wrapped up carefully and tucked from sight. Why would she grant him a touch of luck after that? The damned hunk of sap had drawn most of those lines on Knott's face, after all. It might be wrapped up all nice in Knott's saddlebag, but Damien knew it rarely left his mind for long.

Old pains and new ones. The weight of ghosts was as heavy over Knott's back as the fear for family on Jonnie's, but the former was old and dated, the latter fresh and weeping blood. Jonnie's, at least, they might be able to do something about.

"Think the barkeep will come through with a guide?" Ostra never shied from a hard question. Jonnie's flinch didn't have her bat an eye.

Damien sighed, hating hearing his own worries in her words. "We'll have to hope." The cup came back to him, warmer now after so much handling. He didn't bother waiting to roll, just gave it a little shake and let loose.

The rough-hewn faces of twin suns stared up at him after the dice tumbled to a stop. It seemed he'd have something softer beneath his back than blankets over floorboards. Now to see who ended up sharing it.

"If not . . ." Ostra trailed off, apparently not willing to let go of the issue. Jonnie's face tightened, eyes losing their distance and instead all too focused on the present conversation.

Damien sighed. "If not, we try ourselves." And lose their best chance of making it through. Their bones would likely rot away under the sun long before they reached the other end.

Two more rounds and plenty of sighs passed before Jonnie finally rolled double suns glaring up at them. Tight as the fit would be, Damien was glad he'd won. Even if worries kept Jonnie awake, at least he'd be comfortable.

"You and me, then." Damien laughed.

Jonnie managed a tight smile. "Aye."

"Now that's over, I'm ready to sleep." Ostra stood, stretched, and headed for the bedding near but not nearest her and Knott's packs. Knott himself took the nearest spot, and soon the two were lying close together, Ostra curled around his greater bulk as they settled in to sleep.

Damien and Jonnie followed suit, just without the cuddles. It was close, though, between the narrow bed and Jonnie's bulk. Any other time, Damien would've whispered as much, seeking a snort that sounded more like a bull's than a man's. For such a quiet guy, his amusement could echo. They all missed it.

Damien doused the lantern, leaving them in the dark with their thoughts. Jonnie, stiff at his side, weighed down Damien's mind and kept him from drifting off. Biting back a sigh, Damien chose his words carefully.

"Wendy is tough and capable," Damien reminded Jonnie, going straight for the heart of his concern.

"All of you might die." The words were a whisper, meant only for Damien's ears.

Yeah, they might. Still.

"Wendy is one of us. She's your blood-sister, aye, but we claim her too. She rode with us. Broke bread with us. Her danger is our danger, same as yours."

And when Damien was far younger and had made the choice to strike against the man who had destroyed his chosen brother's life? She'd been there, ready with stolen horses and a calling for them to run for the corral as they fled the house.

No, he and Knott owed her their necks even as she inhabited a space in their hearts. Her face might not be alongside theirs on the bountied boards, but she was one of them.

CHAPTER

✴

TWO

Ty and Bill sat out under the black night sky, Ty trying to enjoy the weak breeze as the sweltering heat dimmed to a just-manageable burn. Next to him, Bill was obviously soaking in the relief from the sun's grip now that the moon sat high in the sky with their children. Over Bill's head, a spider crept between the sloped arch of the porch and the dipping roof, repairing a tear where some insect had proven victorious over its web.

Ty watched it struggle, bitter amusement stirring. He'd never seen the draw of a home—the closest thing he'd ever had was Bill's during his teenage years—but watching the little fellow work stirred a commiserating sympathy in his chest. His own life was unraveling more each cycle of the seasons, the life he'd fled closing its jaws on his and his son's heels the harder he fought to outrun it.

The web swayed, the spider worked, and Bill sat, by his side the same as he'd been when they were young. Still there, even though he'd had to leave behind his own family so Ty could keep his.

"You're likely not here long, eh?" Bill's eyes were closed, head tilted back. He was a few years past Ty in age, but he still looked every inch the young rascal he'd been when they'd met.

"Just long enough to let the kid visit, and for me to pick a new direction," Ty said, regretting letting them stay that long, but Star was different from him. He craved companionship, where Ty needed the freedom of the wind at his back and the plains stretched unending at his feet.

"I wouldn't mind a bit more of a visit with the lad," Bill commented, a laugh under his words, "but looks like I'll have to wait for morning. Still not one for late nights, huh? He won't even stay up to visit with his uncle!"

"Guess you aren't as charming as you think you are."

Bill chuckled, eyes still closed in content. "Guess not."

For a short time there was silence again, and Ty found the quiet of the night a welcome shroud.

"I've about exhausted my interests here for now," Bill mused, ending the peace, "and when the heat finally breaks, not one of us will want to be around for *that* special branch of hell. I've a mind to follow you for a bit."

Ty sighed, leaning his own head back. The wind teased at his hair. It didn't feel like it pointed in any particular direction, which further unsettled him. Soon it would, and he'd follow the path as he always did, but the wait was hard.

"Star and I will welcome the company, as always." Ty tried for a light tone. "Kid'll be overjoyed to have you dogging our steps."

"The two of us should be enough to keep him focused." Bill's words were light but his eyes, now open, pinned Ty where he sat. Reading too much, as always.

"Mm." Ty pointedly ignored the silent question. "Except my boy is as trouble-hungry as a rattler sunning itself, as you well know. He isn't the one I'll need to watch."

Bill nodded slowly, readily accepting the rebuke, but Ty knew it wasn't that easy.

"And what is it that needs watched?" Bill pressed. "Not only me, I'm thinking."

Ty sighed again. A quick glance through the dirty window of the cabin showed Star stretched out on the straw where old Al's mattress had been, his wide-open mouth probably catching every insect sharing his bed. No danger of an eavesdropper there.

"The older I get, the smaller these lands are," Ty said slowly, feeling out the words. "If I didn't need coin, I'd just keep to the road. We were almost caught in the south."

The flash of fear across Bill's face sliced into Ty's chest. Leaning toward the man, elbows on his knees, Ty shook his head once, hard.

"By Bears," Ty reassured him. The worst of the fear left Bill's expression, but not all. "Star didn't notice. We'd intended to pick up some travelers in a town bordering the southern desert, but when I recognized the bastard's men, I lied. Told Star the wind changed, that we needed to ride north, *hard*."

A sympathetic grimace. "And with pockets near empty?"

Ty shrugged, not bothering to answer.

"My own aren't much better," Bill offered, thankfully letting the matter drop. "We'll figure something out."

Ty let out a long breath, Bill's words easing some of the weight he carried. "Maybe we can guide some settlers through the dead springs, if you're willing?" he suggested. "That's always good for some coin."

Bill huffed, scraping up a transparent show of the happy humor he'd exhibited only minutes earlier. "By the sun, I hate that stinking hot place. Guess it'll do, but damn you for not suffering like the rest of us."

Ty managed a smirk. The dead springs were a tract of desert pocked with slow-moving pools of stagnant death. The *springs* part of its name was a cruel misnomer, but anyone with a nose would know better than to touch said pools, thick as syrup in little crags. It was the stretch of land surrounding most of the Sun's Scar and served as a stark warning to anyone foolish enough to consider passing through it and down into that hellish crack.

"It won't be fun for anyone, even if the sun doesn't bite my son or myself as hard as she does the rest of you, but you know how heat makes for desperate pockets."

Since that expanse was the only way around the Scar and on to fresher, greener farmland, guiding was a lucrative practice for anyone who grew up traveling places like that. Ty knew where to find safe water and hidden shelters, as Bill was well aware.

Bill waved the words off. "How *is* your kid doing these days? He seemed all right at Sandy's. Laughing, smiling, and with a tense room all around."

"Good," Ty assured him. "Better every day. I don't doubt he'd love to have some strangers to pester for stories."

Star was getting better with people again, had been for the last few years. Ty enjoyed seeing more and more the playful, determined lad he'd raised, and would do anything to keep that part of his son alive—even drag unwanted strangers through harsh countryside in exchange for coin. Each stranger brought the chance of danger, yes, but Ty had to trust his instincts to stay ahead there. Instinct and an old friend's deal with the monsters of Ty's past.

No wind blew as they spoke, not so much as a little stir, so it was likely not their destination. Ty said as much, and Bill sighed.

"It would be easier if the damn breeze would tell you what to do next," Bill muttered. "Save us the puzzling out."

Bill didn't suggest moving without its guidance, and he never would. He'd been there when Ty had ignored it once, when they were barely out of childhood. Mired in the dark memories, Ty closed his eyes and listened to the night rather than memories. No good could be found chasing old ghosts.

"We've nothing but time," Bill pointed out, trying for levity. "Let it blow when it wants, and we can enjoy the town until then. Maybe I'll have more luck with those blondes tomorrow."

"Charm the sun into a moment's respite and you might," Ty teased, forcing himself to focus on his friend. Hard as it was to set aside remembered pain, there were many more nights in his future to punish himself for the fault. He and Bill got too few together to let himself dwell. Far too few, truly, considering what Bill had cast aside for Ty all those years ago. Sister, nephew. Bill had left them all in another life just because his chosen brother needed him.

"The kid's getting big," Bill commented, his preoccupation apparently on the present.

Big was hardly what Ty would call his son, but he understood Bill's point. Some of the injury leaked back into Ty as he braced himself against this new line of talk.

"Leave it." Ty sighed, tired of the dig. He'd been expecting it since Star had shuffled off for bed, but that didn't make the nicks burn less.

"You know it's selfish. That box you're carrying will hurt a hell of a lot more the longer you keep it from him."

Ty had to let Star grow, but how many hurts before he became *her*?

"Star doesn't take after his mother," Ty said, "but sometimes…"

"They share a pain. That doesn't mean he's ready to point a gun to his own head."

Ty gritted his teeth, refusing to respond. That was unfair, and Bill must know it. Star's mother, Sunny, had fought against her demons as long as she could, and had been braver than anyone had right to demand.

"Ty, Star's strong. You made him that. And he's older now than we were when we left."

"Stop!" The cry tore out of him, louder than he'd meant. Desperate. Star was strong, but no one had been stronger than his Sunny.

Bill finally dropped it, though it was likely a temporary reprieve. The older Star got, the more Bill worried over Ty's continued silence. Bill hadn't been there when he'd rescued his son, so how could he know?

Bill hummed a soft tune, leaning back. Ty recognized it as one Bill's father used to favor and let himself relax, listening. The sun slept, the moon kept watch, and for the time being there was no point borrowing tomorrow's trouble.

Ty was about ready to call it a night when Bill fell quiet, body tense. Ty followed his friend's gaze to where a figure ambled their way through the dark. It was too far at first to make out the figure's face in the light from the lantern held aloft, but in a few strides, Ty made out Sandy's features.

Bill relaxed, but his own mind sharpened, the tension in his shoulders making his fingers twitch. Al's place was way out on the edge of town, nearer the graves overlooking the Scar than to Sandy's own home. If he was heading their way, he had reason.

"Clear night, boys," Sandy greeted as he lowered his lantern and closed the last of the distance. He rested his bulk on the porch rail, leaning over it to look at them.

"And a cooler one," Ty responded. "What can we do for you?"

"I figure you're looking for work." Sandy shifted, the wood groaning as he unsettled it.

"Aye." Ty sat straighter. "What type have you sniffed out?"

"A group rode in today looking for a guide. They're headed to Blue Rock territory, over east. A little farther north than you usually do, I know, but no one knows the lands leading there better than you."

Ty narrowed his eyes, studying Sandy. He'd been a good friend to them for years, and was as fond of Star as Star was of him. Ty also knew for a fact his kid wrote to him along with Lacy.

Sandy in turn sent letters that more often than not ended up in Star's hands eventually. Whether in months or a year depended on what area they traveled and where he'd guessed them to be. Sandy wouldn't be setting him up for anything beyond work, even if it took them jaw-achingly close to Bear territory.

"Are they trouble?"

"Not other than maybe being in some. I don't know them, but I know *of* them, Damien Sole in particular. Price on his head, but no innocent murders, and no cruelty to his name. The price is for stealing from a man crooked as the law will overlook. The man's kid ended up dead, along with some men, but there was something fishy about the whole matter. I'd trust him, far as the work's concerned."

Ty frowned but nodded. A burst of breeze had stirred up as Sandy spoke that felt distinctly of an easterly bent, with the littlest twist of north. Ty gritted his teeth, but as always he'd follow as was willed. "We'll talk to him come morning. Tell the man to meet us at your place before noon."

Ty read Sandy's hesitation and waited him out, the tension returning to his muscles as Sandy seemingly struggled to find words for what he had to say next.

"They're looking to cut through the Scar."

That sliced Ty, sharp and cold even in the heat. For a second his resolve wavered, but the wind picked up then, no little breeze against his skin. It fell away in a heartbeat, but it served its purpose.

"All the same," Ty gritted out. "I'll meet them."

Sandy nodded, turned. Bill gave Ty a strange look as Sandy ambled back toward his home.

"You're willingly going that close to the north?" Bill demanded, suspicious. "And through *that*?"

"The wind blows, so I follow."

Bill sighed, leaning back and shutting his eyes once more. Ty watched him, feeling the argument he was forming behind pursed lips.

"Damn your wind," Bill grumbled, his words as hard as the line of his jaw. "The memory-wraiths might not go for you or your kid, but that doesn't help the rest of us. How're you going to get us fools past them?"

Ty didn't know. "We'll figure a way. It has been done."

Bill stared at him. "Done, sure, else there'd be no stories. Shame most of those stories' sources are bone and dust. It'd be nice to meet someone in our lifetime who survived it."

Ty took his meaning, wishing he had any response that'd comfort the other.

"Guess I'd better get what sleep I can now," Bill said. "Then again, I'll have nothing but sleep soon, sounds like."

Ty sighed and stood. The ghost of a breeze traced his back as he headed in out of the clear night.

Damien wasn't surprised when he sauntered into the saloon at the appointed time and found Ty seated at the bar waiting for him. At Ty's side perched his handsome son, Star. The slim slip of beauty leaned against the counter, chatting with Sandy, and only twisted Damien's way after catching the stony look on his father's face.

Upon seeing Damien, Star shot him a large, open grin, and half lifted his hand before Ty tapped his arm and hissed something.

Damien swallowed a sigh at losing Star's attention and sat where Sandy pointed, picking up the mug of ale shoved his way. Sandy raised an impatient brow, and Damien paid for the drink he hadn't ordered. At least he'd insisted on coming alone. Knott or Ostra would have downed it *and* paid for another.

"Sandy here says you have work for me," Ty said. He had a firm voice, very no-nonsense. His son watched with interest.

Damien nodded, trying not to let his gaze linger. Business first, he reminded himself. Wendy needed him.

"I'm looking to hire a guide to Blue Rock territory," he said.

"And you want one fast," Ty pointed out. "That's what Sandy said when he sent word. I'll be bringing my son and friend into this, so I'll expect full answers. I'm also likely the best hope you have of making any sort of time." He sniffed. "And by 'best' what I mean is 'only.' You plan to head through the Sun's Scar, right?"

Damien resented speaking so plainly under such a hard gaze, but Ty had them over the proverbial barrel.

"A friend needs us, and time is tight. Her land is prime cattle territory, with good water, grazing, and plenty of trees for shade. It's large, hers, and a newcomer with a lot of backing wants it."

Ty's eyes narrowed, but his son cut in before he could say what he was thinking.

"Dad knows these lands better than anyone," Star assured him, leaning in with an easy smile at odds with the cool look Ty wore. "That's why Sandy chose to bring us here to talk with you."

Ty set his hand on his son's arm, and Star eased back, letting the older man take control again.

"If you need to make that kind of time," Ty told him, "we'll have to cut through the Sun's Scar, as you said. I've ridden through that hell before, and I can do it again." Both father and son sat stiff as they discussed the Scar, allowing Damien scant hope that Ty spoke true. "I know of a path down—nice and easy—and it'll cut weeks off the travel, but you have to listen if you want out of there alive."

"And the memory-wraiths? The flying vipers?"

Ty offered a tight shrug that was almost painful to watch. "The wraiths are death on the unwelcome, but we'll get you through."

A big claim, but one Damien desperately needed to hear. "People say it's near impossible."

"And still, you want to cross it."

"Not want, *have* to."

Another shrug. "Same ends. People *have*, but damn few. You won't have a better chance than with me."

Bold words. The certainty of Ty's claim roused the first bit of confidence Damien'd felt since Wendy's last letter.

"You'll need supplies," Ty went on. "Canteens, and quite a few. You want speed and you'll get it, but it'll be through a thin swath of the sun's hell. We have an extra horse to our names, as does our companion, but how are you looking?"

"Two extra," Damien assured them. He closed his hand over his untouched glass of ale, feeling the ache of his coin pouch. Between hiring these men and paying for all the necessary supplies, he'd do well to never buy a drink again.

"And how many of you are there?"

"Four."

"Leaving four extra between us, then," Ty mused, thinking hard. "That should be fine. Good horses?"

"The best," Damien said, and meant it. They'd spent a near fortune for one of their three mounts, and the others had been stolen from one of the best horse ranchers around. That the man, Hollowood, was also a murdering coward was a pleasant bonus.

"There'll be lean days," Ty continued. "Pack dry goods, since we won't have a fire during the nights in the Scar. Fire draws death there. Pack as light as you possibly can. It'll be hard work, and the horses will be feeling it too. It's narrower here than farther to north or south, but hell is hell, and it takes a toll."

Damien's face pinched in distaste. He wasn't used to taking orders in such a tone. Still, he'd be damned before they lost their best chance at helping Wendy.

"We'll be ready," he promised. "When will we head off?"

"Tomorrow," Ty answered, sharp. "Dawn."

Damien nodded again. Ty stood, effectively ending their discussion. His lips pressed into a thin line, his blue eyes burning into Damien's own.

"Head back and make sure our own supplies are ready," Ty ordered his son, not taking that narrow gaze off Damien until he'd finished. Obviously expecting obedience, Ty turned and stalked over to a tall, lanky woman across the bar. She was the one whose company Ty had been leaving the day before, Damien was sure.

Rather than follow his father's call, Star lingered, a curious look aimed directly Damien's way. Far be it from Damien to ignore the gifted chance. Ty was already vanishing up the steps behind his pretty lady, so there'd be no trouble from that quarter.

"Quite the blades," Damien said by opening, nodding to the ring of steel circling Star's hips.

Star tilted his head, looking at him. "I like their feel." The grin on Star's lips was fetching.

"No gun?" Damien pressed, then regretted it. There was a flash in Star's eyes, before they went forcefully blank, that looked uncomfortably like fear.

"No." Star's tone was firm. "I stick to my knives."

Point made, indeed. Topic dropped. Still, Damien wasn't about to let his chance at conversation go that easily. "It'll be a warm ride, I bet. I'm grateful for your assistance. We all are. Thank you."

The guarded look cracked, and there came that smile again, lightening the sharp lines of Star's lovely face. It was a weak smile, but better than his daddy's empty coldness. "You should save the thanks until we get you clear of the Scar. It won't be an easy journey."

Damien heaved a sigh, but his heart was soaring now that he'd gotten to see Star's infectious smile up close and directed his way. Not even noticing Sandy's sudden attention from the other end of the room could dampen his mood. "Yeah, I should get our supplies while the getting is good. How is the store down the way?"

Star paused, and Damien appreciated that he was giving actual thought to his answer. "Be polite to his daughter if she's on guard duty and you'll be treated fairly."

"I'll keep that in mind, thanks." Maybe it'd spare Damien's purse a further thrashing.

"Star!"

Damien swallowed a groan and watched Star perk up and turn to the barkeep as Sandy stalked their way.

"What is it?" Star asked.

"Your dad ran off with Lacy, and she was supposed to deliver some water to my wife. Here." He shoved the pitcher Star's way across the bar.

Star laughed as he dove forward to take it. "Will do." He grinned, standing, and raised a hand Damien's way. After offering a nod, he took off on Sandy's obviously trumped-up delivery.

Damien shot the bartender a hard look, and Sandy frowned in return.

Knott was already seated at the bar when Damien wandered in to join him. Their supplies were ready and secured at the inn, where Ostra lay sprawled on their bed, whittling away. Star's advice had indeed come in handy. The shopkeeper had been a gruff fellow, glittery-eyed and twisty-lipped as Damien strode in from the outdoors. But when Damien had smiled and nodded to his daughter, asking after her day, the man had melted into smiles.

The saloon was as quiet as ever, with many of the same people from the afternoon before haunting its wobbly tables and stained bar. The only ones moving about the room were Sandy and the women who worked for him, two blondes and an older, dark-haired woman who all drifted between the tables offering drink and light conversation. One new man, however—clean-shaven and slick-haired—stood out. The fellow was leaning at Knott's side, holding what had to be a sketch of some type.

Damn it. He didn't need Sandy's blank-faced focus on the scene to warn him it wasn't about anything good.

Damien overheard the stranger asking Knott, "Do you know this man?"

Damien held back, waiting for a sign it was safe to approach. Seeing Knott's eyes widen in obvious, unintentional surprise wasn't a comfort. Knott schooled his expression swift as a blink, but such a reaction wasn't common for Knott.

"No," Knott said. The man holding the picture narrowed his eyes, lips pressing together. He gave the sheet a little shake, drawing Knott's attention back to it.

"You always show that much surprise over unfamiliar faces?" the gentleman asked, voice wry. "Take a good look, won't you?"

"When they're that pretty, yeah." As if the loyal-hearted Knott had ever given anyone except Ostra a second look since his wife's death. And she had pressed herself on his company, steady and determined, for a long while before he'd noticed. "Man might be upstairs, come to that. I doubt it, though. I'd be up there too, damn the heat, until I had a dry purse and couldn't see straight."

Damien crept up next to them, trying to appear nonchalant as he craned over Knott's shoulder and looked at the parchment. *Pretty* wasn't the first thing to come to mind for any of his men, so it couldn't be one of them.

Damn.

There, staring back in charcoal, was the face and body of Star. It was dated, the lad probably not yet out of his teens, but there was no mistaking the likeness. Whoever drew this knew him. There was care in the lines of the face, and the eyes looked guarded enough over sweetly curled lips. A ring of knives circled slim hips, and there was the daring chin tilt that had first dried Damien's mouth.

"Quite a looker," Damien offered. His voice came out suitably empty, thank the moon and keep away the sun. "What'd he do?"

The man aimed a bland glance his way. "I'm looking for any information. He's wanted alive and unharmed so my client can have a talk with him. I've a letter to deliver into his hands, recipient only."

Yeah, *sure* there was a letter. "Have a talk" usually meant something bad enough had happened that the seekers wanted to inflict all damage themselves. If people wanted to talk, they sent the letter sans personal delivery. If the desired outcome was to make a body pay, they'd put a price on said body and send people out to bay the hunt.

Still, the man couldn't be a Sighted or he'd never have made it into the town. That meant this wasn't likely to be a law-backed search. Thank the moon for that, as Damien and his pack had their own trouble with the law. If one of the Sighted accepted coin in exchange for a law-backed manhunt, only the death of the one offering the bounty could call it off.

"Sorry we can't be a help," Damien apologized, trying to affect a polite disinterest. "It must be some letter to warrant a personal guard."

The man shrugged at the words, his eyes now dismissing Damien as a potential lead. "Too many unanswered for my client's comfort."

Damien glanced toward Sandy, nodding. Sandy's face was hard, as if he knew but couldn't quite figure out how to deal with the present problem. Damien lifted a hand, jerked his chin, and headed out the door.

Hopefully Sandy had caught his meaning.

Once outside and a few doors down, Damien hesitated. Now what? Ty and his son seemed to be pretty good friends of the saloon owner, which made it unlikely that they'd go all day without wandering back. Hell, the kid ran missions for him. He needed to find them, fast.

Someone else left the saloon, a brown-haired woman with a thin shawl over her shoulders. Sandy's worker. Damien paused and watched as, after a discreet glance around herself, she headed his way.

"You're looking for Ty," she said as soon as she reached him.

No point pretending, not if she'd come chasing after him. "You know where I can find him?"

She told him. "Make sure those two keep away from here," she added before heading back the way she'd come. Damien noted that she didn't take the front door of the saloon, instead slipping between two nearby buildings.

Her directions were easy enough to follow. Damien planned to rap on the door where he'd been told Ty and Star were staying, but found Ty sitting out on the stoop cleaning his rifle. The other two were nowhere in sight.

"Where's your kid?" Damien demanded, glancing past Ty toward the open door. He couldn't see anyone in the one-room shack, not that he could see much. Still, he craned to search the rest of the yard and the surrounding properties.

Impatient with Ty's silence, Damien glanced back. "Well?"

Blue eyes narrowed on him. "Why should I say?" Ty snapped.

"I'm here with a warning," Damien said. "There's a man carrying your son's picture and asking questions."

Ty cursed. He packed up his kit, hands flying over each piece with the speed of long practice. "He's out stretching his legs. Don't say a word to him if you still want our help." Ty stood, all long, angry fury. "How soon can you and your bunch leave?"

"Now a good time?" Damien countered, glancing back at the saloon. His people should have gathered there by now; they'd be easy enough to collect.

"You have the canteens? Supplies?"

Damien nodded. "Got 'em after we talked."

Ty grabbed his rifle and slung it over a shoulder. "Round the group up, then. It looks like we'll have an early start."

Damien quirked a brow. "Any explanation as thanks?"

"My thanks," Ty snarled, "is not taking off and leaving you. None of us would do well lingering here while bounty hunters sniff about the town."

Damien sighed. He'd expected as much, but damn he'd hoped.

Star peered over the lip of the cliff, the dead air heavy in his lungs and the past thick in his mind. Wraiths and snakes waited in the hazy depths below, cruel guardians born of the sun's anger.

Stories of them were enough to raise a chill despite any heat, and Star was one of few to have ever seen them.

It'd be a harrowing trip, daring that stretch again, but the prospect filled Star with determination. He'd prove that while memories still stung, they didn't hold dominion over him anymore, and neither did their source. He'd put that behind him cycles ago, and this? It was a chance to show that to himself as well as his father.

"Once the land here ran unbroken, the sun appeased and the people content."

Star startled, too mired in the past to have heard Bill's approach. He'd thought Bill was waiting with his father for the others. The man's voice followed the flow Ty's often took when starting one of his stories.

Letting a half smile crook his mouth, Star lifted a shoulder. "The people were never content, and the sun's sufferance of them was only temporary." It was hard to believe there was ever a time before the canyon below. Harder again to imagine the rest.

"Now *you* sound like Ty," Bill teased, his feigned outrage nudging Star from his melancholic musings.

Laughing, Star ducked his head. "And long before that, we were all the same people."

Bill didn't laugh. His hand landed on Star's shoulder. Squeezed. "C'mon, lad. Your dad is waiting on us."

Star nodded, letting remembrance die for a time. When he turned to meet Bill's eyes, there was a smile in it for him. A tilt of Bill's head urged Star away from the ledge and back to Al's.

"Why do you suppose it's the sun's fury that struck us all, not her husband's?" Bill mused as they walked, his gaze cast past where the celestial fire raged above.

Star had no idea. Ty, when asked the same, just shrugged and told a different tale. Having never been asked his own opinion, Star gathered his thoughts as his steps halted.

"The moon is the cold and the dark," Star offered slowly, unearthing beliefs born from a childhood listening to his father's. "Dad says the moon doesn't care, that since he only comes to us at night, his is a world mostly of sleep and animals. I think it's that he isn't willing to punish everyone for the cruelty of a few."

He'd told his father that once. Anger had flashed over Ty's face, but he hadn't said a word, not at first.

"If you knew what our enemies did," was the eventual response, once the sudden flush of fury had had time to fade into compressed pain, *"you wouldn't say that."*

Since Star had known only what his father had willingly shared, he couldn't dispute it. What he *could* argue had been the lack of knowledge, but as with all of Ty's other secrets, nothing more had passed his lips. Ty locked his secrets so deep that not even his son could prize most from his chest.

"Did Dad say anything about why we came back north so soon?"

Bill avoided his eyes and picked up pace. "You know Ty. Man keeps his own counsel."

Teeth clenched, Star followed. No point pressing the issue when Ty's stubbornness wasn't Bill's fault.

It took little time to find his father. Ty gave the two of them a nod as they approached Al's yard, then turned his attention to where their clients approached from the other direction.

"So this is everyone." Ty grunted, looking over Damien's small pack. Star, following his father's gaze, crossed his arms. The group hovering at Damien's back looked restless, and Star wondered what had driven them to such desperation.

"Everyone who's here," Damien answered, sounding sincere.

Ty sighed. "The end of your trail is farther north than I like, but you've done me a good turn. I'll return the favor and see about getting you there in one piece. After that, it will be your job to stay that way."

Star shot Ty a curious look, but as usual, his father offered no explanation. Damien appeared uncomfortable, his handsome face pinched. Star had noticed that trend when Damien had spoken with his father and couldn't help but find it amusing. Maybe he'd corner Damien later and see if he could get anything out of *him*.

The prospect of such an exchange excited him, more than he'd prefer to admit. Damien wasn't the first handsome man he'd seen, but there was something about him that made Star want to take a chance. That alone made him uneasy, but unsettled or no, there was a draw he didn't want to ignore.

"What about water?" the redheaded woman at Damien's side spoke up. "We didn't have a chance—"

"There's a large spring a short distance away," Ty barked. "Fresh, good water. Throw your packs on your horses and come as you are now." Offering no other words, Ty stalked off toward the stables.

Star shrugged and followed, trusting that the others would fall into step. Words might have smoothed ruffled feathers, but at that moment Star didn't care to bother. It felt wrong to not say goodbye to Lacy and Sandy before taking off, or exchange a few words with the twins and Davin, but he'd been ordered not to head inside the saloon.

The demand rankled him, especially since his father had given no reasoning for it. Bill headed to the saloon long enough to let their friends know they were leaving, but that left Star burning with irritated curiosity.

Just what had Ty so twisted up that Star wasn't allowed in a place always considered safe? Some new argument with Sandy?

"It would only take a minute," Star pointed out for the fifth time, coming up alongside Ty. His father, as expected, stiffened and didn't answer.

"Sharing your reason wouldn't hurt," Star pressed, unwilling to back down. Ty never admitted when he was being irrational, but frustration made Star push anyway.

"Keep your mind on task," Ty finally snapped.

There was no inch given there. Star knew enough to take the warning, though it stung. Shooting his father a scowl that Ty didn't acknowledge, Star marched beside him silently.

They had to pass through the town, and it was only luck that Star caught sight of Lacy standing outside the saloon. Feeling thankful that he'd get at least one goodbye despite his father's best efforts, Star lagged behind as the others moved on. She caught sight of him, and he gave her a wave while passing. She returned it with one of her winks, and he laughed.

Turning forward after, he caught sight of an unfamiliar man creeping around the corner, jittery and overeager. What . . .? The man was fixated on Damien, his whole body canted towards the object of his unbroken attention. The curled lip and fidgety hand promised nothing good. That hand groped downward for a gun.

Star moved.

His right dagger pressed against the bastard's chin before the twitchy fellow's gun made more than an inch out of its holster. Star wrapped himself around the smaller man, all sinuous grace as he fit himself close enough to detect any shifts. The knife against the would-be killer's throat was rock-steady, indenting the skin with just enough force not to draw blood. Startled shock flashed over the hired goon's face, then twisted into disgust, but Star could feel the heavy breath against his shoulder, and the curled lip was too much show.

"Drop it," Star cautioned, "or you drop."

"I have a gun." The fool growled, but shock left the words shaky. Star had seen it, yes, but a gun wasn't much good if you had a gap in your throat.

"It's very pretty," Star purred. "I don't have one myself, but my friends? They do. They're also watching us now. Maybe you want to drop it back into its house and give us a smile?"

Star felt the muscles of the man's arm flex, but then the gun was returned to its holster. Still, Star didn't pull back.

"Want to explain this little trick?" Star asked. "You were gunning for Damien there and planned to leave him a nice little hole in the back."

The others approached, watching intently. Damien stared on with narrow eyes and Knott looked murderous, but Ostra and Jonnie had a cooler look and were scanning their surroundings with guns drawn, ready should more unexpected enemies crop up behind the roadway shacks. Bill, on the other hand, stood with hands on his hips and drank it in. They all seemed content to let him have this, but never his father. Already Ty was striding his way, rifle steady in his hands.

"I have him, son," Ty called. "At ease."

Star rolled his eyes but moved back, taking up position right behind his father, where Ty always wanted him to be. That was no matter, though. Star knew that he could have one of his knives slicing through the air almost as fast as any of their bullets. At this distance it wouldn't take effort, really.

The cowardly bastard swallowed, still not answering. His face ran with nervous sweat. Lacy wasn't alone at the door to the saloon now. A small crowd gawked at them, some in the doorway and others spilling onto the narrow porch.

"You'd have shot me in the back." Damien glared at the gunman. "Think maybe I can hear why?"

The man swallowed again, looking dry-mouthed and pale despite the lake soaking into the neck of his shirt. This time he answered, eyes flicking from one of them to the other. "You've a price on your head," he managed to get out. "Two thousand gold."

Ty's scowl darkened, but Damien looked amused. Interesting.

"Yeah, that's the case," Damien drawled. "So, your plan was to shoot me right here, fair in the middle of a town full of hard-asses mostly acting outside the law, and with me surrounded by my own people?"

"An opportunistic idiot," Ostra muttered. Knott gave a snort. Despite the joking, Star didn't miss how their eyes tracked everything.

"Lift your hands nice and high," Ty ordered. The craven man hastened to do so, likely hoping to see a way out of the whole mess. Little wonder.

"Take his gun, Bill," Ty ordered. "Check that it's all this fool is packing."

In seconds, Bill held the man's gun along with a knife and money pouch.

"Now," Ty continued, "we're going to mount up and leave you here. You might want to think about relocating fast, and never mind any horse you rode in on. These people might not mind death when it comes from a fair fight, but spineless murder? Shots in the back?" A flash of teeth, sharp and white beneath the sun. "They'll run you to ground, and no one will know where to find your body."

That sparked the man. He glared back, lowering his hands and hissing, "I was doing this place a favor, taking him out! Take your whore-son and leave before someone buries you both with that bountied garbage—"

Fist, straight to the nose. Ty was half the man's bulk but still dropped him to the ground like a sack of oats, a puff of dust unsettled by his weight. Ty glared down at him. Star drank the sight in, loving it when his dad went all out and showed how strong he was. Too often, Ty was overlooked on account of his slim build, just like Star himself.

"I gave you fair warning," Ty growled. "Now, we're leaving. Enjoy the hospitality at Standing Grave."

Damien watched it all with an approving smile on his handsome face.

"Star!"

Star snapped on his heel, heading for his father. "What?"

"C'mon, we're wasting time."

"Yeah, yeah."

Bill cursed as they stomped to the stable, and Star shot him a curious look.

"A journey to a range war, they want to be there two days ago, a suicidal trip through the pit, *and* throw in a price on his head?" Bill huffed. "Better we ride off a cliff now."

Ty shot him a look that was as dry as the dust stirred under their feet. "You're welcome to stay here if you would prefer. It'll be a long, hard dash."

Bill muttered another curse. Still, he mounted up along with the rest of them when they got to the stable, and seemed eager enough when they started their ride, pack horses loaded down with supplies.

Star was intrigued. While Bill often joined them in their travels through the desert, he never showed such open doubt over their success. That he followed at all rather than try and dissuade Star's father from the job added to Star's interest. This type of trip wasn't his father's usual style of business. Never before had he considered a return to the Scar. The excitement at the saloon had his mind buzzing with curiosity, and he couldn't wait to sate some of it. Not even his dread at riding into hell could temper that.

CHAPTER

✴

THREE

"**Y**ou and your father always travel together?" Damien asked.

They were following a trail leading to the stream where they'd fill their canteens. The coming days would be long and dry, and they'd need to prepare before setting off into the Sun's Scar.

"As long as I can remember," Star said, watching Damien out of the corner of his eye. Damien rode his horse well, hands gentle and manner sure. Stretching in his own saddle, Star yawned and noticed Damien tracking his movements, same as Star had been doing to him. His interest felt heady, and Star stretched a second time, forcing the motions, carefully monitoring how Damien swallowed. Damien, seeming to finally notice his returned attention, sat straighter.

"So!" Damien said. "You two move around a lot, do you?"

Star offered a wry grin. "All we do is move. Just us, Clay here," he patted his sandy-brown horse's mane, "Dad's Shine, and our Stomper."

Damien laughed. It was a nice sound, warm and bright. "Stomper?"

"Yeah. Our pack horse, the gray? He tramped a friend's gardens when he got loose from the corral as a foal. The man—he's the one who raised him—named him that." Bay loved his horses dearly and still made a point of repeating that story whenever Star and his father wandered his way.

"Only the five of you, then? What about Bill there?"

"Bill is a friend. He comes along sometimes."

"So no home base?"

Star shrugged. The questions were prying, but it was a boring ride, and he had questions of his own to return. "A few places we stop regularly, like Standing Grave. How about you?"

"Wendy's." Damien's expression was sad. "She's the one we're going to help. Her place is the closest we have to a home. She traveled with us for years before she settled and always has beds and warm meals for us."

Star nodded, sympathy squeezing his chest. "I'm sorry. I hope we can get you there in time to help."

Damien offered up a strained smile. "Thanks. I'm holding to hope. It's hitting Jonnie hardest. She's his sister. How about you, though? Any family, or is it just you and Ty?"

Discomfort itched at Star. He didn't have many answers with this line of inquiry, a fact that bothered him more than he liked.

"Dad and Bill grew up together," Star answered, giving the only information he had. "Bill calls me his nephew sometimes, and we consider him family. We have a few friends we check in on, too, but it's mostly the three of us."

"What about your mother?"

Star lifted a shoulder. Clay snorted, and he gave her neck another distracted pat. "Gone to dust. I don't know much about her, really. Her name was Sunny, and she was a hell of a woman." A mother made of half-voiced memories, teases Star had chased since childhood.

"A lonely way to live."

"A little, but Dad gave me stories."

"*Stories*?" Damien asked, sounding confused.

A wry grin twisted Star's lips. "A family of history to replace the one I don't have. Dad raised me on tales of the skies. The sun, the moon, and all their children." The same as his father had been raised before the loss of his blood-family.

Star half watched as Damien digested the words.

"Happy stories, at least?" Damien tried.

Star sighed. "Not usually." Wanting to avoid the discomfort, Star turned the attention back onto his companion. "How about you? Are any of your companions blood related? Ostra and Jonnie?"

Damien snorted. "No. Not even them. None of us have any family to speak of save Jonnie. I've a father I haven't spoken to since I was fifteen and took off for adventure, but we were never close. Ostra is tight-lipped, but I feel safe guessing a no there." He didn't mention Knott.

Not wanting to pry, especially when he himself couldn't answer as much as he'd like, Star let it go. People tended to keep things close to their chests for reasons. Star had his own pains to bury.

"You're riding to help a friend," he said instead.

"We're all each of us have. Family." That was an end to that. Damien's voice was closing off, hinting at also wanting a break. A break Star could do.

He grinned, showing teeth. "I like when a man stands by his people." That he said as much shocked himself, but he kept his head high and his grin clear.

"Nothing is more important than your people," Damien said slowly, eyeing him. There was a flush beneath the man's hat that made Star want to grin even more. Instead, Star looked to his father and Bill, riding at the head.

"Yeah," he answered back. His mind drifted to thoughts of getting Damien alone, luring him away for a chance to taste those lips. Nerves bubbled in his stomach, but his determination rode over them. There was something about Damien that made Star want to throw his usual caution aside and pursue.

They kept their horses at the same pace, Damien's company comfortable as silence fell between them.

They came upon the spring at dusk. The water poured out of rocks and spilled to slice a path through stone and sand. Its cool blue reflection of the sky cut across the dusty landscape. A splash of green growth and a swath of thick trees sprung up along its twisty path.

Star and Damien dismounted with the others, gathering around the low-lying waterfall. A light mist sprinkled them, droplets of cooling relief from the sun's bite. While the others took drinks, Ty assuring them the water was fresh and contamination-free, Star caught Damien's arm and gave a little tug, nodding down a short distance where trees jutted between the party and the view.

Damien, curious and more than a little intrigued, followed. Star led him a short distance, and watching him, eyes on his hips, Damien's heart rate picked up. His steps, in turn, also picked up in determination.

They got to the little slice of seclusion, a dip in land and thickening of trees offering privacy, and his hopes were answered. Star dropped to his knees and pulled Damien down next to him. Once they were both on the ground, Star leaned in, pressing his knee forward enough to brush Damien's denim-clad crotch, grinning widely. Before Damien could decide how to react, Star twisted to wrap one hand around Damien's broad shoulder pull himself closer. The bony face was all smoldering eyes and confident grin.

"How badly do you want to get better acquainted?"

Damien choked out a laugh. "Too much." He swelled under the sweet-rough mix of attention.

"Not too much, but perfect, by my feel—"

"Star!" Ty stomped around the cover of the trees, face hard and voice harder. Damien started and would have jerked back but the move would have landed Star on his ass. The lad actually hung his head, whispering a curse, before whipping around and looking like a kicked dog.

"Star," Ty repeated, "I want camp set *now*."

"Yeah, comin'," Star groaned. His knee rubbed torturously against Damien's clothed length as the little minx pulled away. Then Star was striding over to his father, every inch the chastised son. As soon as he came in reach, Ty wrapped a hand around his ponytail, using it like a sort of leash.

"Get walking, brat," Ty snapped.

Damien watched in disbelief before standing and stomping around the cover and back over to his men. Jonnie shifted sideways, silently making room between himself and Knott.

"Torture." Damien grabbed one of the canteens at the man's side and slumped down to fill it in the spring. He half considered dunking himself in it too. "How'd the bastard know?"

Knott snorted and gave him a sideways look. "Way that man has been watching you, I'd be worried if his pop missed it."

Damien glared, nonplussed. Knott just went back to work, quiet. Thinking, Damien expected. It usually meant Damien wasn't going to enjoy what he'd be hearing.

Finally, Knott sat back and turned his way. The light of his eyes let Damien know he wasn't likely to get the better end of whatever point was about to be made. Knott's face could be as rock-steady as they came, but those eyes? They were talkers.

"Y'know," Knott started, "I see the draw for you. All those slim, graceful lines and fine muscles. Long neck, long legs, and a smile all welcoming. It'd make a man with that inclination, maybe even a few curious, stupid enough to fall and try getting close." There came his hard look again. "Maybe a man might forget those pretty little blades ringing his hips or the way the fellow used them in the blink of an eye."

Damien scowled. "He isn't about to use them on me."

"Yeah?" Knott asked sardonically, moving to fill their last canteen. "Maybe not. It wouldn't hurt to remember who else showed their hand on the way out of that town."

Damien remembered Ty's slim form, so like Star's, standing over the man he'd downed with a single punch. He ducked his head, but even as he forced himself to acknowledge the warning as having merit, the rest of his mind kept drifting back to the handsome, long-haired beauty who'd swallowed his sense.

Dark closed in, and most of their company slept. Dad had insisted they'd all need their rest that night, and so only one man sat watch: Knott.

Restless, Star frowned up at the branch-cut moon and his smattering of children. An itch had started beneath his skin as their descent into the Scar neared. It was easier to ignore their destination when the others were up and distractions could be had.

And distraction was exactly what he needed.

The exchange he'd shared with Damien kept teasing Star, a more welcome nipping. His was often a lonely life. Usually that was fine. Tonight, though, thoughts of broad hands and a kind, steady-eyed face stirred his blood. Made him wish for a temporary flight from loneliness and nerves.

Maybe it'd be smarter to close his eyes on the moon and try again for sleep. Instead, Star slid from his blankets and walked, whisper-soft, to where Damien lay. Kneeling, Star prepared to murmur his name, careful to keep distance between them should the other be startled upon waking. Night-darkened eyes opened as he drew breath.

Star paused. "Can I sleep here?"

Damien hesitated, and Star didn't miss the half-tilted chin aimed where Ty bedded next to Bill. Teeth set, Star kicked himself for the rash curiosity that'd spurred him into this fool's gamble.

"Never mind," he muttered, trying to ignore the creep of embarrassment threatening his chest. A strong hand wrapped around his wrist, stopping him before he could stand.

"C'mon in."

Damien lifted the blanket and, swallowing back relief, Star crawled in, settling snug against Damien's warm body. The blanket was unnecessary, but it kept the most of the bugs off them, and the heat was nowhere what it had been.

"Night," Damien whispered against his ear. "Try not to get my jaw broken." Star gave him a strange look but didn't ask, figuring he likely didn't want to know. Instead, he waited a beat, then two.

Damien didn't take the offer, likely missing the invite. Steeling himself, not entirely sure how to go about this but determined all the same, Star pressed back, not leaving any space between their bodies. Damien stirred beneath the cotton of his pants, and when he rubbed his lower body against Damien's just right the second time, the heavy flesh twitched upward, interested.

A little trace of fear sparked in his gut, but he shoved it away. It wasn't stopping him there, not this time. Instead he pressed back again, concentrating on Damien's warmth and on how the man's breathing grew heavier at his ear.

"We promised to get you there," Star murmured, tilting his head to nuzzle Damien's stubbly chin. He pushed himself backwards as he spoke, and by the grunt brushing his ear in a soft inhalation, Damien was feeling his efforts.

"I'll get nowhere if you keep it up," he grumbled, breathy. "Your dad is liable to shoot me."

Star chuckled. That explained Damien's earlier comment. "I'm a big boy. He might rage, but that'll be it."

Damien cursed but without real heat. He was fully aroused, now, by the feel of his hard, eager flesh. Then he gave a little grunt, and something switched. He slid his hand around Star's waist, arm heavy but grip gentle, and pulled him back in the next grind.

"You want it, pretty?" That voice was all surrender, but with a fire Star liked to hear. "You get me then, but not here." Lips brushed his ear, planted a kiss against the soft underside.

Hmm. Star arched again, hearing and enjoying the groan it brought out against his neck.

"We'll slip by the stream," Damien panted, voice low. He ground against Star, holding him there, and Star, feeling the waves of his arousal spiking, listened eagerly. "Away from eyes. That work?"

Star was sure those words were barely formed. The proof drove against his back in a burning brand.

"I'll go first," Star offered. "How about that?" He grinned over his shoulder, followed by a wink he knew the other man saw in the moonlight.

Damien released him, and Star crawled out from under the blanket slowly, dragging his body along Damien's larger one, then stretched on all fours, arching his back once free. The way those eyes, black in the night, followed his movement was heady.

"See you soon," he taunted, then stood and walked into the nearby trees.

The stream was close by. Star monitored the rocks and brush around its shore as he stripped. He folded his clothes and set them on a tall rock, rolling his shoulders and smirking to himself.

The fear was gone now, overpowered by the lust and excitement of what they'd do.

He hadn't thought things out past getting the other man to pursue him. Luckily, though, Damien had the presence of mind to come prepared. His rough blanket was thrown over his shoulder, which he proceeded to dump on the grass near the stream in a wrinkled makeshift bed.

"A snake bites my ass," Damien muttered, more to himself than Star, "I deserve it."

Damien cursed himself for being a fool, but there wasn't a man alive who could be blamed if he stood in Damien's boots. By the moon, the look of the other man, bare in the moonlight, with all that loose black hair glittering down the lean muscles of his back.

The younger man slunk to the blanket Damien had spread out, graceful and knowing it by the smirk on his thin lips. Damien stood, throat dry, and watched. Bordello girls showed more modesty than that minx.

As if to prove his thoughts, Star got on his hands and knees, twisting to smirk back at him. "You like me like this, right?" He purred, and Damien's face must have been answer enough even under the shade of night. "You're going to mount me. If you're any good, I'll still feel you tomorrow."

Curse him for being a fool, Damien stripped and took that challenge.

He pulled a vial from his pants before he dropped them next to Star's. Dumping the fine oil into one hand, he started slicking himself up, then knelt behind Star. It was dark, but not so dark that he couldn't see the beautiful skin.

He stroked up one long leg, starting in the dip below Star's knee and gliding damp fingers up to the dimple below his ass, watching muscles clench. "I'll be in you," he told him, "and you'll feel me, just like you want."

He poured more oil into his hand, spreading the slick over his fingers. Then pulling the cheeks of Star's ass open, he found the ring of muscle he wanted and pushed in.

Star hissed, and heat gripped Damien's finger tightly. As Damien worked Star open, Star pressed into the touch, moving with Damien and letting him know vocally as he felt each push and pull and quirk.

Damien ached, his balls full, but he planned to take his time. He'd meet that issued challenge head-on. So he continued preparation, drawing it out, enjoying it. There had been a hint of hesitancy under all that heated pursuit, but it was long gone now, leaving burning eyes and an arching, demanding body.

When Star was ready, mewling and pressing back in search of more, Damien leaned over but didn't move yet to drive home. Instead he stroked down those long, twitching thighs, feeling the soft, smooth warmth of them and wishing he could see better.

"You want me to take you," he teased, leaning over to nuzzle. Star let loose a growl, all animal need that Damien ignored. "I've never seen the like of you. Long, lean, and so damn gorgeous." He reached up to fondle those balls.

Star groaned. "I want it."

So Damien did. He surged up, curling over that long back and pressing slowly, deeply inside the heat of his channel. He slid the fingers of his left hand over top Star's own, supporting himself, his right grabbing on to Star's length and squeezing, pulling, as he rutted.

Harder, faster. Their sighs and moans threaded together. Damien pressed his mouth against Star's shoulder, straining, and Star pushed back into his thrusts, arching into him with a force that almost knocked Damien down. Everything became a tangle of sweat, heat, lust, and pleasure. Star was tight, almost painfully so, and he moved under Damien without restraint.

Damien found his hip, held it, leaving Star's dripping pillar behind. He used the hold to slow him, guiding him into a gentler rocking. This stretched somewhere between seconds and an eternity, their bodies stroking together. Then everything grew too much, and he let Star go, his own lust swelling. Damien again grabbed Star's slim, burning penis, stroking fast and hard as he drove into him. All gentleness was gone with their need to reach release.

The swell hit its peak, and Damien filled him, shooting his load deep inside and rutting it out, breathing as heavily as Star as he followed, the muscles of his ass tightening, clenching, swallowing him down before Star also spilled, come splashing onto the blanket.

Damien moved slowly, exhausted now, waiting till Star was done. Then they sank down together, barely missing the wet puddle. Star rolled against him, chuckling, and Damien had to edge off the blanket to make more room. Then they lay in a tangle, panting, coming down.

Those night-darkened green eyes narrowed, self-satisfied, as they looked into his own. Even in the moonlight Damien could read Star's satisfaction and, under it, a sort of awe.

"I might just feel that in the saddle tomorrow," Star gasped, voice hoarse and strangely wondering.

He should, the little bastard. He'd pretty near ridden Damien into the sun's clutches.

Damien just closed his eyes on his own sigh.

CHAPTER

✹

FOUR

Her eyes were cool as stone, blue as the sky. He knew and loved her face as he knew and hated his own, seeing in it the absence of hers. But there was a gauntness to her pale cheeks that he'd never known before that night, and there were no tears in her stony eyes to soften their resolve.

The gun muzzle pressing against her breast glinted in the candlelight. It lined up perfectly with her heart. Tangles of her loose black hair draped its length, long and windswept since childhood.

"Take him and run, Ty," she ordered. "It'll be too late any second."

Pitiless, the muzzle stayed in place, steady as the grave it intended for her.

He didn't move, heart frozen with desperate fear.

"Sunny," he begged, her name a cry of pain and sorrow on his tongue.

"He cannot be here!" The first emotion to crack from her lips, so fast he might not have seen it: a flicker of fear shivered in her eyes. A glint of firelight, he told himself later, for the eyes that burned him still had been as stone.

Ty woke with a curse, his heart pounding to escape his rib cage. He lurched up, searching the dark camp for his son in the scant light of the moon. Star was always the first thing he sought after that dream. This time, though, the boy's bedroll was empty. So, Ty noted next, was the one of the bold bountied who had hired them.

That wasn't a surprise. Ty had no doubt that his son had led the other man off to play. He'd known what would happen the moment he'd seen Star's face watching Damien in Standing Grave. When Damien had looked back, all was sealed.

It was good to see his son interested in someone, but that didn't stop his fear. That it was in a man with a price on his head, and one riding off to face some unknown danger, made it all the damn worse.

The problem of Damien Sole coupled with the hell he was going to be dragging his boy back into that next day, and no wonder his own sleep was filled with past horrors. Twice Ty had traveled through the Sun's Scar, and both times he had felt the braying of hounds on his heels. Both, he had almost lost his son.

He shot a hard look Bill's way and, annoyingly, Bill was still awake and gazing at him with an amused but wry grin just discernible in the moonlight. Knott, Damien's own watchdog, looked resigned.

Ty knew he was acting wrongly. He smothered Star, guided his every step and policed each breath, whether he did the policing on his own or through another, like Bill. Twenty-one years since his birth, but Ty still saw only his child.

Bill, ever the peacekeeper between Ty and Star, offered, "Let the moon travel a bit more, then one of us will herd the missing ones back."

The quiet night was still warm but had lost the cruel bite that would return when the sun rose. Ty should let his son be and give them a measure of stolen privacy. Star needed all the comfort he could get before they rode into bad memories.

Ty stood and beat at the soles of his boots before pulling them on, comfortable that nothing had crept in for a nap.

"Which way are they?"

"Do you really want to do this?" The strained note in Bill's voice betrayed that he already knew the answer.

Ty didn't bother giving one. Bill sighed, raised his hand in the asked-for direction, and Ty went.

Star groaned as a leather boot dug in just below his ribs and *pushed.* He opened one eye to glare at his scowling father. Damien, waking when Star shifted, took it a lot harder, scrambling for his pants. He yanked them up over those lovely muscled legs of his without checking first for critters, which was a good way to be bit. Still, it seemed he'd be surviving. Nice luck, there.

Star huffed but knew when he was beat. He sat, still glaring, but more resigned now. It wasn't like his dad hadn't seen it all before, so he didn't bother trying to cover himself. "Yeah?"

Ty scowled down, but Damien, holding his boots and standing around in awkward uncertainty, made the situation funnier than it should have been. Damn it, but he was a grown man, and he'd never felt so drawn to another before, not after what pain he'd known could be born of lust. His father really didn't need to pull this.

"If you're both done," Ty drawled, pitiless, "think you can come back to the group and stop acting the tomcat?"

"Maybe," Star answered sweetly. "Hand me my pants?" He still wore his boots, so no trouble there. Poor Damien.

Dad rolled his eyes but stalked over to collect them. Star's lips twitched as he glanced from his annoyed father to their awkward, uncertain company. Hearing material flap as Ty checked for stowaways, Star's eyes lingered on Damien's chest, remembering how soft he was over muscle, and how—

Spluttering, Star fell backward, making a grab for the pants that had smacked him in the face. "Hey!"

"You have better reflexes than that. I won't feel sorry for you. Get moving!"

Muttering, Star stood and pulled his pants back on, buckling them over his hips. He took a moment to stretch, feeling sore and *good.* He'd figured it would be. Damien's looks had caught his eye first, his careful control and polite front second.

Searching, he found his hair tie on the ground and bound it back before stalking off ahead of both men, enjoying the way his body ached just right while he purred over the memory of gentle, sure movements and a sweet, kind voice.

Too agitated to bother going back to sleep, Ty took over the next stretch of watch and dragged Bill along with him.

"I told you he's growing up," Bill pointed out, sounding all too much like he was defending Star.

The others were mostly asleep, Star stretched out on that bastard's blanket. Or, now that Ty looked more closely, on his own. The other blanket lay away from them, soaked and forgotten.

Deciding he didn't want to know, Ty returned his attention to Bill. "You've made yourself clear already."

Bill, as always, refused to back down. Ty'd known this was coming since the other night on Al's sagging porch. "Did I? You still seem intent on keeping your mouth shut. What happened to the promise you made when we first ran? Kid's long past sixteen. By the look of tonight, he's long past a lot of things you've been using as new excuses."

That was a sore point, and Bill knew better than to voice it. Turning from the man he considered his brother, Ty focused his scowl on the surrounding tree line.

"We were young idiots ourselves then. What did I know about raising a boy when I picked that age to dump everything on his head? Star knows as much as he needs to." Ty kept his eyes trained on the periphery of their camp, refusing to meet Bill's intent gaze. "I've taught him how to live, how to listen to the wind and follow."

And he'd stressed that it needed to be followed. If Star ever did feel that push, he knew to listen. Ty had warned there were consequences to not, though he'd never given specifics. Star had listened to him with a careful focus Ty appreciated, and though Star had asked for more information, he hadn't fought Ty's refusals. That time, at least.

"You haven't taught him enough to realize he should be scared."

Monsters still lived, even if an old man's threats kept them leashed. Bill voiced a cold truth Ty shied from but couldn't deny.

"I'll keep him safe enough," Ty managed through gritted teeth, voice a low hiss, "and I'll thank you to mind your own business. I told him our people were hunted and killed. That's enough."

Ty's answer, of course, wasn't enough. Once Bill sank his teeth into something, he loathed to give it up. "He isn't her, damn it, Ty." Knott shifted nearby, and Bill softened his tone even as his intent sliced deep. "Star isn't her, and you can't expect him to live accepting all your secrets. He's grown now and has a right to answers."

Ty looked Knott over carefully, decided he slept still, and fully faced his friend. Much as he wanted to glare, instead he met Bill's narrow gaze with the calmest he could muster.

"He isn't me, either, Bill." Ty wouldn't budge this time. "I know my son. There are things he doesn't need to hear yet, and some he never should."

Ty had been the one to hold on to his son after that monster had hurt him. He'd seen the scared, reticent remains of a strong, curious youth, and he'd spent the last five years doing everything in his power to help his boy relearn himself.

His were necessary secrets. Star didn't need any new pressures, not when he was doing so well.

"It's a mistake."

"Then it's mine to make."

Bill grunted, making his belief on *that* clear, and Ty ignored him.

"The sooner we finish this job the better," Ty grumbled, aiming their talk to new ground. The dark of the night pressed in closer than he liked. Memory and threat whispered over sand and stone, mocking the choices he'd made and those he hadn't. With the past so close, Bill's arguments were a battle he had little strength to wage. "I'll be happier when it's just us three. Sole makes me uneasy."

"Is it so bad that Star's taking an interest in someone?" Bill pressed, returning to their earlier line of contention. Always one hard battle or another. "Don't you want him to find other people besides us old men?"

There was sense there, but all Ty wanted was for his son—her son—to be safe. Damien Sole, while seemingly honorable, didn't strike him as a safe choice.

"I'm not going to make any more mistakes that take family from me. I'll be there to protect him even if it's from himself."

Bill sighed, long and slow, looking out over the dark with a hard twist to his face that made Ty stiffen well before he spoke. "What happened to Sunny wasn't on you."

Damn him thrice.

"She was my responsibility and I left. I turned my back on all of it." A fool move, cowardly and childish in equal measure.

"You tried to live. She made her own choices."

"What they let her."

Bill raised his same old argument. "It was well out of all control."

Ty shook his head. "I let it be. I knew they hated her there. I should have stayed. Should have let her know there were still options, that she didn't need to . . ."

"She knew her own mind enough to fuck up everyone else. Don't take that on yourself."

"She was mine," Ty answered, forcing himself past the pained remembrance.

"No." The twist of Bill's lips, caught between sneer and sympathy, tainted the hard line of his words. "You were hers, but she was no one's."

CHAPTER

※

FIVE

"*All that blood, pretty blood, just for me.*" Slicing pain over already torn skin. *The cold touch of metal gathering what spilt, and the threat of a gun against his aching temple each time he fought.*

Star cursed as he rolled, kicking and shivering, out of his blankets. His dream pounded through his mind as he blinked in the predawn morning. His mind was slow to drift back into the memories where it belonged. He felt the belt bite into his skin again where scars had long gone to silver, and felt those hands—

He leapt to his feet, grabbing his boots, and beat them hard a few times before shoving them onto his otherwise bare feet. Someone called his name, but he didn't look their way, barely able to function beyond getting from point A to point B. He needed space.

Turning on his heel, he stalked toward the clearing and its rocks. It was far enough away that the voices of camp wouldn't reach him clearly, but close enough he could find his father if needed.

Star scrambled up the small embankment, with its pebbled base. That hateful, too-loving voice purred in the back of his mind, telling him they were meant to be together, that his blood called the man to him.

"*With you I can make my own tie to the earth. Feed it and win it.*"

Fighting shaking pain, Star perched on top of the largest rock. Gripping his fists over top his pants, he closed his eyes and felt for the wind. Then he searched for himself, delving under layers of fear and sense-memory to find the core of strength at his center. He brushed his fingers over the hilts of his knives and daggers, both hands reaching, feeling their comfort and listening to the wind promise its own.

The breeze was strong, and it was blowing the way they would be traveling. Fortunate, Star mused. His father had taught him to use it as a touchstone. That served him well now. It didn't come to him as it did his father, guiding and firm, but it was there when he reached.

Keeping his eyes closed, Star let himself be, the minute tremble in his fingers easing. His father would come for him when it was time to go, and not before then. Given a bit longer, he could lock his emotions down again and remember how to be.

"Give the lad space," Ty ordered, looking up from his work only long enough to scowl at the rest of them.

Damien stared after Star, wondering at the change in him between night and morning. The confidence had fled, leaving a shaky, hiding fellow.

Judging by Ty's face, Damien would find no answers there. Ty was preparing the rabbits that'd wandered into his snares. While thankful—otherwise it'd be a bland breakfast what with most of their supplies being saved for the trek ahead—Damien would've liked to shove them aside and get the bastard's attention.

Hissing out a long, irritated breath, he shared a look with Knott over Ty's back. He didn't miss how Bill stared off in the opposite direction, avoiding all of their faces. No good choice but to let this one go for now, Damien figured, hoping doubtfully that it had nothing to do with the night before. It had been amazing—right up, that is, until he'd been chased out of their postcoitus cuddle by his partner's angry father.

Ostra, likely sensing that things would get more awkward if someone didn't step up, came out with a question Damien himself should have asked. "I don't know this country." Her whittling knife was in one hand while a mostly finished man was in the other. "How long, roughly, do you think it'll take to get us in Blue Rock territory?"

Ty paused, his frown thoughtful rather than annoyed. "I'm hoping less than two weeks. If we hit trouble, maybe two and a half."

Bill's lips pressed together tightly. "The canyon we'll be crossing—you sure it's necessary? Going around it adds weeks but the place is deadly. There's no shelter, no safe water but what you bring, and with the ground the way it is, we might not all make it."

Ostra stepped in, voice firm and eyes steely. "Jonnie's sister might not have that kind of time."

Bill sighed but backed down. "Then be ready." He took the first rabbit and set it to cook. "We'll be walking most of the next three days, and if you think this is hot, you'll soon change your tune."

Hard as it was to imagine, Damien didn't doubt him. There were legends aplenty about folks riding unawares into the upper reaches of the canyon only for their companions to be swallowed up, and about riders who went in and were found, years later, as dried husks picked over by enterprising scavengers. Bugs were said to sometimes roast alive on the rocks, easy pickings for the winged vipers snaking through the shaded walls to try their hand at higher altitude.

It was the opening to the underbelly of the world. Death walked in the land no one dared, one full of the sun's will and its own amusements. The only ones ever said to travel there unbothered were supposed to be the Wind-whispers, but they were all hunted down now, dead for almost fifty years.

"Make sure every canteen is full before we leave," Ty spoke up finally, turning and glancing toward where his son perched on the far-off rocks. "Drink as much as is comfortable. After our next stop this afternoon, the water has to be rationed, part for us and part for our mounts."

Ty sighed, eyes still on Star. Worried, Damien thought.

"This time of year, any water down in that hell-pit has dried to sand. It'll be at least another moon before a trickle starts. Rain just dampens the steaming dirt and evaporates before an hour in daylight. Damn well keep an eye on your water. Say something if you're running low."

Much as he hoped it was all an exaggeration, it lined up well with the little Damien had heard. He could scarcely believe they'd managed to find a guide, and couldn't help but wonder at their folly even as he steeled himself. It was the last place he'd ever expected to go.

Ty wandered off, and Damien found himself kneeling next to Bill as they bent to their tasks. The question of the gentleman with the picture in the bar kept teasing his mind, and while Ty was a danger to ask, Bill might be willing to grant some insight. From what Damien had seen, Bill was far more open to conversation.

"I've a question," Damien started off, tucking his first filled canteen away and continuing with the next.

Bill glanced up from his work with a quick, friendly smile. "Ask away." He was far easier to get along with than Ty, but Damien still picked his words carefully.

"Back at Standing Grave there was a fellow with a drawing of Star," he began. "Said he carried a letter for him. When I told Ty as much, he ran us out of town before nightfall."

Bill stared at him, his already-full canteen held uselessly in the flow of water. Damien read the discarded responses in the intent narrowing of his eyes, and more again in his furrowed brow.

"What have you said to Star?" Bill eventually asked.

"Nothing. Ty gave explicit orders that way, and we need your help too much to jeopardize that."

Bill pressed his lips together. "It's a private matter. The lad has done nothing wrong, if that's your worry. Best keep your nose out of it." There was little of the friendly openness in the response, but Bill's wan expression at the end was at least kind. "You won't get any thanks for stirring up trouble."

Damien shrugged, feigning an accepted indifference he didn't feel. He never liked leaving riddles on the ground.

"As you say," he agreed vocally. Bill frowned at him, then finally removed his canteen and got back to the task at hand.

Damien could bide his time. They had days of travel, after all.

The land leading up to the Sun's Scar stretched for an eternity. Scattered patches of blue sage added a trace of color to what was otherwise a painfully dry-looking expanse of cliff, crag, and looming chasm. Making the trek more difficult were the patched cracks opening out of nowhere, purple-bellied maws ready to swallow the unwary. In time, they would come to the path Ty had told them about, and the whole procession would be slowed to a death-crawl.

"Any other way," Ty sighed, "and we'd be better off."

Now that they were on the road, the weight Star'd woken with began to erode. Sitting atop Clay, watching the twisting, gradual path unfold before them, he shoved back the nipping strands of unwanted memory by focusing on closer, pleasanter things. Thinking of his tryst with Damien helped, and he wrapped himself in the recollection of the man's calloused hands and hot breath. The feel of his skin, present and real so short a time ago.

"What should we do if we face the wraiths?" Ostra said, startling him back to the present. Her voice steady and eyes narrowed, he could see her mind hard at work. Planning, no doubt. She had a strong hand on the reins of her chestnut mare, and the other rested on her knee close to her gun.

"They're not true ghosts," Star assured her, repeating from his father's lessons. "They're reflections given form by beasts trying to mimic what they've seen. They use it to get close enough to feed."

Ostra, lips pulled back in distaste, shot him a doubtful look. "Feed?"

"Their bite, like the flying vipers, paralyzes their prey. Then they feed on blood and muscle." A grisly thing, but Star only knew of it through stories. As little as he could remember of that horrible flight through the northern end of the Scar, he only recalled the silvery forms at great distance. The vipers had been their true concern.

Those around him grimaced but didn't appear surprised by his warnings. Stories of the wraiths were common even as survivors were not. For every ten who told of them, his father liked to say, there were ten liars. Hopefully their group would put a little bit of a lie in *those* words.

"And you've seen them?" Damien asked, his voice sending a pleasant shiver down Star's spine. If all went well there would be time again for another slip into trees and distance once the Scar fell to their backs.

Star twisted to face him, knowing the smile curling over his lips to be at odds with their topic but not caring. "They look silvery and night-washed, and they're hollowed at the core."

Ty cut in, his words matter-of-fact. "They only seem real under the moonlight until they get close enough that you can see their eyes, and then you realize what you really face. Their eyes are too empty." He heaved a heavy breath, and pity washed through Star at his father's wary expression. Leather creaked as Ty shifted in his saddle, eyes distant. "Aim only for the head. Shots to the body won't stop them, and if they get close enough, you won't get a second chance. They travel mostly in small groups, so don't expect much warning."

The others took the time to digest the words.

"You know a lot about them," Ostra said, her words casual but her eyes sharp.

"A fact that's a boon to you," Ty bit back.

She grimaced and Knott spoke up, likely to keep tempers even.

"When do the creatures come out? I hear they're night-spooks, but I'd rather hear it from someone with experience."

Jonnie, next to the older man, gave an agreeing grunt.

Ty nodded. "Fair. They escape during the sun's rest to play in the night, and are limited, like the flying vipers, to the confines of her scar. Unlike the vipers, they cannot ever stray beyond its floor. We shouldn't have any trouble until the sun goes down, and even then I doubt they'll come right away."

The discussion fell off, each left to their own thoughts. They rode for a stretch, watching the ground and keeping an eye on the progress of the sun. Trying to distract his mind from the pending return to his own hell, Star eyed Damien as they went. He looked gorgeous on the back of his gray horse, as in control as he seemed in every other instance.

For all of his determination to feel Damien, Star hadn't known he'd be able to go so far before he'd issued his challenge. He'd touched others before, and certainly let them touch him, but that? Not for five years, and never once by choice.

Why now? He'd sated his lust before on visits to towns, where he could taste and leave without danger of attachment. Out here that wasn't an option, something that should have stayed his hand but hadn't. Worse, instead of being satisfied, Star wanted more: to feel Damien's skin against his own again, and to see if memory painted their exchange prettier than fact.

Yet, it'd also be a lie if he denied his want to push them all the faster. To chivy the group along until he could be shut of them and these newly woken feelings, that curiosity and interest all roiling around Damien, pricking through Star's carefully maintained control.

Luring Damien off had been a chance at escape. Not understanding why he and Ty had ridden north as they had, recognizing fear haunting his father's eyes but being refused the why of it, and capping it all with their return to this sun-damned hell? He'd just wanted something to feel *good*. *Right*. To not think but feel. Drawn as he felt to Damien's warm eyes and sure steadiness, he hadn't expected the trap of leaving their exchange wanting more.

Star shook his head, forcing his mind away from that line of thought. They were worries for later. Looking for another distraction, he found one in Damien's hulking friend, Jonnie. The fellow stared straight ahead, face distant, as they finally came up on the narrow little slope they'd been seeking. The grade at the top was gradual, so riding was fine for the time being, as long as they took things slow and steady in the rockier patches and gave the horses their heads.

Clay, always pleased to have new places to explore, needed to be held in check time and again when she wanted to move on ahead, but she gave in with fine grace when Star pulled her back to carefully match step with Jonnie's own mount. There was space for two abreast, but no more.

Star nodded to the red-headed man and received a wan grimace for the trouble. The hat tied to Jonnie's head bobbed with the move.

"What can you tell us about your sister's situation?" Star asked, seeing no point in mincing words. Jonnie was a man who spoke little, but Star hadn't missed the deep feelings roiling behind the giant's eyes.

"Not much." Jonnie squinted through the sweat-damp strands of his red hair. The hat was keeping the sun back, but the heat washing over them came straight from the sun's hand. "I know Ram hired a dangerous pack masquerading as cowhands— gunmen, cutthroats, and rustlers, Wendy says."

Star winced. No wonder the man rode as if to a hanging, and his fellows looked on him with poorly masked sympathy. Curiosity, that damn nuisance, pricked at Star.

"How does her side look?"

Jonnie grunted, reaching forward to pat his horse's mane. She was a thick roan, smoky and well able to bear his weight. The lady had a similar enough look to Damien's own that Star bet they sprung from the same line. "Wendy's a good hand with a gun or rifle, but Coy don't shoot much and they've little'uns."

The big man paused when a warm breeze drifted against their backs, daring somehow to run with them into this mouth of hell. Star took comfort in its brush, hoping that it meant they traveled where they should.

"How about their hands? They have a ranch, right?" Star wondered at himself for asking. What did that matter to him? They'd split from Damien's group before coming up on that trouble.

"My sister-in-law might be around, along with their dad, and they're both fair shots. Tough, those two. Wen and Coy's hands are all strong, good people, last I met, but not a one is a trained killer. Still, life made them hard enough to live there, so."

Hopefully they'd be up to the challenge when the time came. Guilt ate at Star. Jonnie's face showed a deeper worry now than it had when he'd first rode up. Still, there was another question, and once he had its answer, he vowed he'd let Jonnie return to his thoughts.

"Who is this Ram?"

"That's the question." Jonnie sighed, then clammed up. Star waited, but it seemed there was nothing more coming.

Ostra, likely seeing he wanted more, lifted a hand to catch his attention and motioned for him to join her. Star nodded to Jonnie, gave Clay's reins a little tug, and they slowed back to where Ostra trailed their small group.

"Ram Gaines," she said. "All we really know is his brand, the Speared Ram. We'd never heard of him before Wendy first mentioned him in a letter a bit over a year ago. Her comment was all complaint, and at the start those were slight enough. He was mouthy and pushing weight. Not a rare type in these lands, except that the money he threw around with that weight could really talk."

Jonnie spoke up again, voice pained, "I should've thought more about it. Wendy, she don't complain until it's for good reason."

And good reason she must have, considering this mad dash through certain death in the hopes of making it to her in time. What, Star worried, did this group plan to ride into in the Blue Rock territory?

And why did he feel guilty for his part in bringing them there?

Damien had expected hell and wasn't disappointed. He'd ridden through barren lands before, but none like this.

For Wendy, he reminded himself again. The words kept him focused.

The white sand was a powder beneath their horses' hooves now that they'd reached the bottom of the path, and it rose in a dusty cloud to coat everything. It painted the horses' legs and sides like a clinging mist, along with their own legs and clothing.

Ty insisted they wear strips of cloth over their mouths, saying they'd need it more once they started leading the horses. Damien kept his hat low. It was a hot, miserable ride, and would have still been one without the sun burning them alive.

The sea of sand was only broken by outcroppings of red rock rising from it like the skeletal remains of some behemoth, and by the dry scrub, a handful of the bushes leafless but most with a few tattered little hangers-on. Those lucky enough to have leaves usually sat close to the murky, foul-smelling pools of thick water peppering the otherwise dry landscape.

A fog of insects hovered above each of them, and many lay in the syrup-thick, soupy surface. The horses shied back when they rode too close. Thirsty as he was, the smell of spoil wafting from the pools turned his stomach.

"Set a watch," Ty ordered when they finally stopped for the night. "Bill and I will take the first two marks. What we're watching for will be hard to see by moonlight, so eyes peeled. Scorpions. Wraiths. Snakes, flying and otherwise. Anything seeking a snack now that the sun has gone to bed and the moon has cooled the night." He gave them all a hard stare, his son included. "Shoot and yell. There's no time for more. To hesitate is to die.

"As for the horses, hobble them and *watch* them. Vipers they'll react to, though those travel in small groups if not alone, so aren't likely to try for us. The wraiths, though, won't garner much from our mounts. Their draw works on them too. We're more likely to lose a horse first than find out danger from them."

They searched the rocks where they planned to spend the night. Cutting off a dry branch from a wiry, leafless bush, Star stuck it down various crags and shaded cubbies. A few of the others joined him, including Damien. Ostra was taking particular delight in the hunt while Knott just scowled and seemed to follow her motions by rote.

"If you find it, you eat it!" Star teased when Damien came up close to stick his branch into one particularly deep-looking crack. Thankfully, nothing came out other than a few disturbed insects, and not the problematic kind. His poor stick was already marked by webbing and guts from those less fortunate.

Still nervous about how Star had been acting, Damien shifted to rub along his side, staring into the next hole but also watching how Star reacted. No fear, thank the moon. The dark-haired beauty blinked once, slowly, then brushed full-length against Damien before moving off. That gave Damien hope it might not have been a one-time deal. Maybe there'd be time to explore once free.

Finding themselves relatively safe of critters for the time being, they made camp. The horses were unburdened, then given a thorough brushing and feed.

When setting up his bed, Star further solidified Damien's hope by stretching his blanket close enough to where Damien had laid his that their edges overlapped. Star, Damien was finding, lacked any lick of subtlety.

As happy as Damien was with the turnabout, he wasn't sure he'd survive Ty if Star didn't show some decorum. Damien shot him a look and, of course, up went that bony chin. Damned proud bastard, Damien reflected, amused despite himself.

Ty was glaring at him. Lovely.

Damien had never felt so much like a ranchman trying to slip the boss's virgin child into the barn for a feel-up, not even when he'd *been* the rancher's teenage son chasing after the village blacksmith's eldest boy.

Damien loved his life and loved the people he traveled with. Still, until that tall slip of pride and fire had curled around him and started purring, he hadn't realized how alone he was. Rather than leave their tangle with contentment—itch scratched and pleasant memories had—Damien wanted more. He wanted the quiet, natural intimacy Knott and Ostra shared. Someone who was his, as no one else could be.

What had bitten him, he couldn't say. Damien liked pretty men, sure, and Star was the prettiest he'd ever seen, but he'd never experienced any stir beyond lust to be sated before. Actual interest was dangerous. The waking desire to find someone, somewhere, to call his own? Deadly. It was no time to let such inklings seed.

Even so, Damien smiled as he watched Star give his father a pointed look. Bill rolled his eyes while Ty narrowed his own and puffed up like a disgruntled cat.

They all settled in, drinking water and giving some to the horses before hobbling them and bedding down. They dug a dry supper out of their packs. Star sat next to Damien when he dropped onto his bedroll. Star, holding his own bit of dried meat, leaned close when Damien caught his eye.

"Why not share a story?" Damien said without thinking.

Rather than pull away, Star straightened up, visibly eager. Then he hesitated, meeting Ty's stony expression with a questioning one. Ty gave no visible condemnation nor encouragement. Up to Star, then. Jonnie, for his part, was watching with more interest than he'd showed most days, and Damien hoped Star would choose to go along with it.

"I guess it can't hurt," Star decided, and Damien fought back a grin. "How about something tied to where we are?"

"Could be interesting," Knott commented.

"Especially since we know precious little about this stretch barring its dangers," Ostra agreed.

Damien could see Star digest the words.

Star frowned, then nodded. "Okay. How about the birth of the wraiths?"

Damien had expected something more along the lines of the men's last visit there. He leaned in, curious. "That's something I'd like to hear."

Star offered them a weak smile. "That's what I'll tell, then. You all know the favorite of the sun's children?"

A hesitant question showed in the surrounding faces. Ty snorted, making clear his opinion. Star visibly ignored his father, focusing instead on Damien and his crew. Damien lifted a shoulder, ruefully acknowledging his lack there. The sun was fury, the moon cold disdain, and that was the extent of his knowledge.

Star took his time reading their faces before nodding. "Okay. An explanation first. Her favorite is her son, the land where we live, whose own blood fills the rivers, lakes, and oceans, but whose mother's gifted blood trickles in the deep chambers within his chest."

Damien felt a nibble of recognition there and thought he might see the same guarded acknowledgment in Ostra. Knott, next to her, appeared carved from stone. Damien shivered to see that closed-off part of the man whom he'd known longer than the others. Damien had missed something, and Knott hadn't.

"There was a deep crack in the earth, as deep as this scar but long before it existed," Star continued. He shot another quick glance his father's way.

Ty watched, a frown on his lips and the eyes above it as cool as Knott's. Ty's hands closed into fists, a twitch in the line of his jaw showing he felt as uncomfortable with the coming tale as Knott. Why, Damien wondered but didn't dare ask.

"Within the crack flowed that very blood, and at the shore were bits of amber solidified around droplets thrown from where the waterfall beat against the rocks. Those were the relics, which gave people abilities directly from the sun's hands. Some used them to see the present, far from where they lived. Some could see into possibilities of the future, and so were given a chance to act before it became engraved into life."

Star lifted a shoulder, a wry, apologetic smile touching those gorgeous lips. "Other things too." His voice lost the musical, storytelling lilt of seconds before, not that it stopped the cool shiver that sliced down Damien's spine. "But they don't matter here. Just the water."

Star had won all of their attention now, Jonnie present in a way that was rare these days. Ostra's pinched face looked almost as pale as Knott's, who stared on, expression closed and eyes sharp. Knott had known where the talk was heading, Damien reflected, trying to steel himself.

Pressing his lips together, he leaned closer to Star, catching their storyteller's attention. "I'd never heard tell of this water. The relics and the sun's blood, sure, but not that."

Ostra grunted her agreement.

"It's an old story," Ty acknowledged, offering support. "Most probably don't remember it. Go on, son."

Star nodded thanks. He hesitated for a second, obviously uneasy with the response he'd garnered. Damien offered up a gentle nudge, lips curling at how Star's tension eased at his touch. Maybe it would've been kinder to Knott to let the story die, but they were on the path now. Best to see it through.

"The sun guided her still nomadic people to that rocky shore, and they in turn traded the amber away to old allies and once-family. Until enemies, why I don't know, slaughtered the nomadic people and in turn angered the sun."

Star hesitated again.

"Foolish move, I expect," Damien offered into the silence, hoping to spur the tale on.

Star tried a laugh, failed. Was his discomfort from the tense response? Damien chewed on the question as Star retook the trail.

"It was. Furious, the land reacted, splitting open and swallowing the pool. That's when the wraiths were born. The sun formed them out of her blood, giving them life from it just as the droplets in the amber gave the relics their abilities. The relics were a gift, a gentle show of her favor; the wraiths are a curse, punishment for crimes known and, possibly, unknown."

Star stopped there, chin high and eyes on every face except, tellingly, his father's. The awkward silence held for a beat.

"I wonder if that's truly what they are," Ostra mused, watching Star. "I've never heard any of that before tonight."

"That's what they say," Star answered, and didn't sound put-out by the question.

"It's more explanation for both the wraiths and the relics than I've ever been given," Damien countered, grinning at the thankful look he received. "Where did you unearth this story?"

"It hardly matters," Ty barked, ending their discussion. "If you're done sharing stories, those not on watch need to get to sleep."

Star grimaced and settled down into his bedding as bid, but Damien didn't miss how he pressed against Damien's side.

Exhausted from the long day, Damien slid in next to Star, willing himself to relax.

At least until he heard the shifting of blankets and felt warm breath tickle his cheek.

"You've all been traveling together a long time," Star whispered, tone carrying a touch of question.

Damien opened his eyes and found himself almost nose to nose with Star. "We have." His words were as soft as the smile curling over his lips.

"How did you meet?"

Damien chuckled despite himself, thinking about his first introduction to Knott. Chastising himself for likely drawing attention, he leaned closer and smirked. "I had a hankering to take off not long after I turned fifteen. A cattle-drive drifted by, and it seemed a good way to experience the world. I offered myself up as a worker, and the boss accepted."

It ended up harder work than he'd expected, but the reward had been great. Seeing the back of his town had been nerve-racking, not that he'd recognized the gut-dropping emotion of the time as anything but excitement.

Damien continued, "Knott, having signed on for the trip, took me under his wing."

Star lit up, curiosity clear even in the dark. "He was a cattleman?"

"Aye. And has quite a bit of experience, not that he gets much use of it now. He told me that he often helped as new ranchers traveled, fattening up fresh livestock and bringing them to wherever they hang their hats. I liked the idea of travel more than I liked the thought of following the lot of them home and hanging my own hat, so when the drive ended, I hitched myself to Knott's side and followed *him*."

Green eyes held his. "You must have gotten along fast."

Damien choked back a snort. "I think he was more worried about the others murdering me if he left me in their care." He grimaced, remembering what an ass he'd been. "I was young and overconfident, even after Knott proved how little I knew about my new job. He was likely the only one patient enough to deal with me back then."

That put a smile on Star's lips. "You?"

"My father was a rancher—is still, probably, not that I've kept in touch. I was a hard, headstrong kid to raise and he was as happy as I to have my back to our town."

"Did Knott introduce you to the others, then?"

Damien shook his head. "No. We met them together, later. Knott and I found Jonnie, Wendy, and Ostra traveling, oh, years back, the girls striding short and squat next to his lanky giant-height. Ostra's the one who cornered me, offering their hands to help Knott and I take care of a difficult piece of revenge. I've no idea how she knew what we'd been about, but when the whole mess went shit-end-up, we fled together. That was that."

Damien watched the play of thoughts over Star's expressive face. "What about your mother?"

An old pain twisted in his chest. "She died when I was small. It was just my father and I, but we weren't like the two of you. There was respect but little love." Painful as it was, this gave him an opening to ask questions. "How about Bill? How did you all meet?"

Star lifted the shoulder not pressed against his bedding. "He grew up with my father."

That wasn't much information. "He must have known your mother too, then?"

Star grimaced, looking away. "He did."

Star didn't like that question. Damien thought back to the picture in the bar, with the would-be messenger and Ty's reaction upon learning about him. There was a mystery there, if he could just find a way to approach it. But not tonight.

Damien stretched out, then grunted as a weight settled half on top of him, bony and determined. He opened one eye to find Star, elbow in Damien's side and head on his shoulder, shutting his own eyes and burrowing in comfortably.

Moon preserve him. He'd be stabbed in his sleep, but whether by that elbow or by Ty was anyone's guess.

CHAPTER

✹

SIX

Bill and Ty sat in silence, scanning the camp and beyond it. The horses dozed on their feet as the deepening shadows closed around the fire's reach. Jonnie, farthest from the others, shifted in uneasy sleep. Damien and Star appeared especially comfortable, although Ostra and Knott weren't too far off. The latter were lying close enough to touch, guns in reach and Ostra's loosened hair spread over Knott's arm.

The other two? By the moon, Ty wanted to murder someone. His son was determinedly coiled about Damien, like a snake with its next meal. Ty didn't know whether to take Star aside and talk sense into him or wait to get Damien alone and let him taste both barrels of his rifle.

"How're you doing?" Bill asked, voice pitched low.

Ty shot him a bland look. "Last time I came through here, Star was all but catatonic."

Between forcing water down his injured kid's throat and keeping the damned beasts away from what they'd marked as an easy meal, it was a miracle Ty'd gotten them through at all. And if they hadn't been close enough to a friend's land after stumbling out of those damn shallows—half-dead and bone-weary—they might not have survived past it.

"It's hell being back here," he told Bill bluntly, taking the silence as Bill waiting for more. "The only good point is that Star seems to have enough of a distraction that he isn't suffering for the choice."

Bill followed his gaze to where his son was stretched over top Damien. He'd rolled over until he wasn't even partially on his own blanket anymore. Bill's lips twitched, and Ty glared at him, not that it stopped him.

"Think you and Star will be enough to keep the memory-wraiths away?" Bill asked hurriedly, a half laugh caught beneath his words that Ty was only too happy to ignore.

That was a question. He'd never had cause to fear the wraiths before. As Star'd told the others, they were perversions of the silvered water that flowed deep in the earth's veins, born for the sun's vengeance when those to whom she had entrusted fragments of those "gifts"—if they were such, and Ty had never believed that—were turned against.

"We'll see," Ty finally muttered, bitter.

Bill digested that quietly, and Ty thought it might be the end. It wasn't, of course, what with this being Bill. "Never thought I'd be daring this insanity."

No. They'd peered down into this hell time and again from the land above, both as young men together and older men on pursuits of their own, but only Ty had ever braved the madness, and that only out of true, gut-deep desperation. The hollow wraiths were no threat to him, creatures of the sun's intent, but the winged vipers were only born of her. Their desires were their own, and all blood called to their thirst.

"Why do you think you're supposed to take this job, anyway?" Bill questioned, tactful. When Ty didn't offer any answer, his eyes narrowed. "Your damned wind. You got a look on your face when Sandy mentioned this mess. Said you felt it then. Figure it means anything?"

Ty took a careful glance around. Sleep appeared to hold dominion over the others and so it seemed safe enough, but a thread of threat twisted his gut at being so open. "Aye."

Bill nodded, accepting that as he always did. "I wonder what it is about them. Especially Damien Sole. Star has taken to him in a way I've never seen. He seems honorable, sure, but there has to be more behind it."

Ty shrugged at hearing his own concerns, eyes once again combing the dark and seeking out any possible threats. If he kept his gaze pointedly turned away from where his son slept, who could blame him?

"I stopped asking questions of the wind twenty-three years ago," Ty whispered. "I follow where it leads, and only ask that it keeps my son safe."

Knott's holler tore out alongside the sound of gunfire. Star woke scrambling across the blankets for his blades, accidentally elbowing Damien as he mirrored the move.

Wraiths. He'd only seen them at a distance but knew them on sight. Their humanoid forms glistened, distortions of the targets they'd chosen that night.

One of Star's slim throwing knives took the closest woman-form in the eye. Inhuman screeches raised his neck hair as their kills shriveled into puddles of silver. The others were firing, taking the wraiths down almost one per shot. The creatures weren't fast, thankfully—their strength was in their number.

Seven fell. Then eight.

The next to take Star's blade took a gunshot alongside it. They were moonlight gray, their human forms too real in the monochrome of night. Only their dead eyes, images without function, gave them away. His knife sliced through clean as a bullet, melting the enemy even as his eyes sought a new target. The members of his camp were all on their feet now; several of the creatures still lumbered in their sight.

Ostra made a dash for where the horses stirred, shaken up by the gunfire. As she ran, she took two more down in a heartbeat. She upset her and Knott's packs in her haste but was quickly kicked off the spilled clothing that caught beneath her boot.

Five left.

The others continued working, guns as steady as their cursing. Star stood back, next blade in hand, and searched the darkness for missed threats. No other flash of gray showed itself in the pale light, and as the gunshots stilled, his clenched muscles eased.

Around them were the pools left by the wraiths. A cool breeze rose from each, welcoming in the heat. Jonnie took a step closer to the nearest pool, peering down at it.

Star grabbed his arm. "Don't touch. Don't drink from them, either."

Their company turned to stare, questioning, and Ty nodded, taking over for him. "Some poor creature will, and it'll become one of them. It's how wraiths reproduce."

Knott grunted. "Shouldn't we bury it, then?" He looked ready to do just that too. Jonnie, for his part, backed up and grimaced.

Ty shook his head. "The sun gives allowance to those strong enough to survive her land. Destroying her hands would wake her rage."

"It's night, now," Damien argued. "Shouldn't it be the moon to say and judge?"

Ty snorted. It lacked any humor. "This is her domain, night or day. All such places—deep rends in earth down into the core—are. Respect her."

Damien's expression didn't soften. "I thought you said small groups."

Ty scowled. "This *was* small. The well they spring from runs deep."

Damien looked away, frowning. The rest settled back, likely not wanting to continue the topic. Star wondered at how little they knew of the Scar they were so determined to travel. He doubted knowing would have changed anything, anyroad.

Sighing, Star wandered to the nearest bit of brush and cut off a branch. He used it to edge his blades out of their pools, taking care not to get too close. When they were freed, he drove the stick into the sand, tainted-end down, and returned to the others. Hopefully, by the time they broke camp he'd be able to pick up the damn things.

Knott and Ostra, kneeling by their spilled packs and gathering the mess, drew his attention. His interest flared when he caught a flash of moonlight from the cloth Knott was collecting. He handled the bundle gingerly.

What could have the gruff man so tentative?

He turned their way but didn't make it far before Damien sidled alongside him.

"Think we're good to catch some sleep?" Damien asked.

A grin stretched over Star's lips. Curiosity forgotten, he fell into step.

"Knott carries a relic in his saddlebag."

Ty watched Bill startle, though his curse was soft as a breath. No one in the camp stirred, though the sun was soon to rise. Already a gray predawn eased the work of his eyes as he and Bill kept their watch. *Their*, they called it, though it was only theirs by long habit. Ty's had been the first, Knott's second, and this was Bill's. It was their own fool selves who chose to sit with each other.

That, and Ty's need to share what he'd discovered.

Bill turned a sharp look to where Knott lay sleeping, his brow furrowed. "Trouble from that quarter?"

Ty thought about it. Those bits of amber had, long ago, been items of trade by his now-dead people: gifts of the sun's blood used to reforge connections and show favor. That was before the relics had soured. Still, Knott wasn't wearing it. Without use, there was no slight and so nothing was likely to strike at them for it.

Ty shook his head. "Not immediate, I think. We were convenient targets for the wraiths in the night—I guess that answers whether Star and I are enough to shelter you—I don't think it was anything more."

Bill seemed to consider his answer. Ty waited, knowing that wouldn't be the end of it. "Should we mention it to the lad anyway?"

Ty had taught Star about those little slips of captured power, yes, but not like he himself had been. Some information might be armor but other was gunpowder. Ty would never arm Star with anything so volatile.

"No."

Bill's gray-cast face took on a familiar mulish look. When he didn't speak, Ty figured he'd have to drag it out of the man.

"Well?" Ty demanded softly, already expecting what he'd hear.

Bill never disappointed. "How many secrets until there are too damned many?"

"You heard him last night. These things are stories to him. He didn't live our life."

"And you're doing a fine job trying to keep him from living *any*." Bill's hissed words seared like fire down Ty's spine.

Ty swallowed the blade lodging in his throat. "I'm keeping him safe. What would you have me do? Fill his head with truths and watch them either tear him apart like his mother or drive him back to a place where enemies wait? Which should I hope for? Star destroying himself or him throwing himself into the maw of monsters?"

The image of Star, dead and left to rot just as his own people had been, sent a wash of panic through Ty.

Bill, squinting at him through the lightening dark, softened and sighed. "He's a good, strong lad, Ty."

If only that were enough. "Sunny was strong too."

Bill made as if to speak, but Ty glared and saw the moment the words withered on his tongue. It would have been a lie, and even Bill, much as he'd hated her, had to know it. Sunny had been stronger than anyone.

Bill let it drop. He glanced instead toward where Star lay curled against Damien, as shameless as he'd been before the wraiths attacked.

Ty wanted to find his earlier frustrations but instead kept falling back into the past. Relics. He wondered at the chance these strangers carried one with them. Was that what had driven the wind to guide him on their paths? Looking at Star, his claim on Damien stated even in sleep, Ty wasn't sure that was completely it. He hoped, prayed it was all mere chance and the need for them to be on the road. Moving.

But everything always tied back to those sun-damned curses—"gifts," but he knew better. So, he thought, had Sunny, and probably with greater understanding. She'd wrapped herself tightly in the stories they'd been raised on, ingraining them so deep within her core that he'd expected their etchings on her very bones.

Memories moved in, guiding Ty further away from the present, back to the days of sun, home, and a waiting he hadn't understood.

Ty leaned over his knees, sitting in the grass and watching Sunny as she stared across the field from their cabin. Her eyes were on a distant form on horseback. Ty wished she would hunt with him, ride with him, anything but stare after that damn blond man.

"You said they dug relics from a pool deep in the ground." Bill nudged Ty in a demand for attention. He sat next to him, waiting patiently for Ty to give up and come ride.

Ty had shared the story earlier that day, corrected time and again by Sunny's sharp memory. Back when he and Sunny had first heard it and others, she'd drunk down the tales thirstily while he'd perched, listened, and done his best to escape as soon as he could. Some were beautiful, woven from happy memories and carried proudly. Others were ugly, colder, and he'd fled from both into sun and grass each chance that came.

"A long time ago, yes." Ty didn't want to revisit the tale.

Bill's blue eyes narrowed under hanging blond hair. He needed it cut but wouldn't let his sister Mae do it, and not even Ty would let Bill's father near him with anything sharp enough to cut skin. The man had been deep in ale since his wife's death, and little captured his full attention.

"Why start murdering for them, then?" Bill rarely let things lie. "Why didn't people gather their own before the hole in the earth was swallowed? The work?"

Ty let his eyes drift back to Sunny. She still watched the field, one hand curled over the hilt of a knife on her belt. The other was clenched at her side, nails dug deep into the meat of her palm. There was another figure. Ty could see Mae's long hair caught in the breeze, dark with distance but in truth as golden as the sun.

Bill's head shifted out of the corner of Ty's eye. Then his elbow dug into Ty's gut. He'd seen too, Ty figured, but didn't care. His interest was on the story, not his sister. "Well?" Bill needled. "Why not?"

"Their location was a secret," Ty snapped, annoyed.

Sunny whirled around, her black hair glittering in the sunlight. Her rolling eyes made Ty want to grit his teeth.

"If you're going to tell stories, then do it right." She crouched across from them. The tall grass scraped her bare skin, and she scratched an elbow, her smirk aimed straight at Bill's carefully blank face. She knew he didn't like her; Ty knew that if Sunny wanted it, she could have Bill spitting acid and shaking in anger within very few sentences.

It was a game of hers.

"Tell it right, then," Ty challenged, hoping to stall the inevitable. She wasn't wrong, after all, about his ability.

"The chasm down into the earth's heart wasn't found until the days after our people started breaking apart, many choosing their lands and building these cities out of wood and dirt."

"Rock and cement, not dirt," Bill grumbled. Ty clenched his teeth, not enjoying the sharp line of Sunny's teeth as she grinned. It reminded him of a sun-bleached skull leering at the sky. She wanted Bill's anger, and Ty had no idea what he could do to calm her. This new frustration she carried was one he didn't understand.

"And what makes those?" A laugh in her words. Bill twitched, obviously wanting to snap something back, but when Sunny kept talking, he listened. "Those who still traveled grew smaller in number but were thick and wind-blown as pollen in spring. The wind's demands grew weaker at their backs. It went with the settlers, some thought, and believed maybe all of our people should give up traveling. Pick a place on the land, take its name, and become like the rest."

Bill didn't ask the question trapped behind clenched lips. Ty could read the torn emotions on his face, need to ask vying against disgruntlement over asking her. The poor attempt caught Sunny's eye too; she never missed anything.

"What?" she demanded, and Ty braced himself. "Ask."

"Why didn't they have family names before they settled? Wouldn't that make more sense?"

A lifted shoulder. A small dribble of blood where she'd picked a scratch on her elbow. Ty winced, expecting words sharp as knives, but though her eyes were hard, her delivery was not. "We knew who we were. One people, and each with our one name. It's all we needed."

Bill frowned. Had more questions, likely. Sunny narrowed her eyes, waiting. A cloud rolled over the sun, throwing shadow over the long grass, and Ty wondered if he'd soon have to break them up.

By some miracle, Bill didn't set Sunny off. "Okay." An annoyed giving of ground, curiosity not sated, but there wasn't any better answer. "What kept them from giving in? Then they'd have needed other names, I bet."

Ty watched the play of thoughts behind her familiar eyes. Waited to see if she'd take the invitation back to the abandoned strand of the tale or dig her teeth into the latter part of Bill's comment. When she chose her story, Ty's breath hissed between his teeth. For that second, at least, he could breathe easy.

"The wind came back," she answered, falling into step, "strong and demanding. Insistent when some thought of giving up. It refused to let them. There were still a handful of groups, ones who traded a scattering of times each cycle, who traveled north when the others went south. All met where the wind took them, riding with it, excited and anxious in equal measure.

"There they found the fissure, old even where they'd never seen it before in all their years. Roots held the ground around the drop from collapsing, borrowed ladders and netting. Born from generations of the determined trees and brush, all keeping that hole there."

She had Bill leaning in, his animosity forgotten as he followed the trail she purposefully laid. For that moment he was in her thrall, and the glitter in Sunny's eyes told Ty she reveled in it.

"Partway down spilled a great waterfall of silver laden with gifts from the sun's veins. The amber was easy to find at the shores of its pool. The relics. They'd collect it from beneath the water's edge, down deep and mixed with rocks. The gathered treasures held everything from plants to bugs, but it was the pieces with water that they worked smooth."

She told it beautifully, the same as they'd been taught. It was a tale he'd always loved, but a sad one too, for it seeded their people's end. The swallowed emotion in Sunny's voice during those last lines, the tremor of her fingers . . . Ty knew she felt the same. Ty knew, too, what Bill would say before he spoke.

"So Ty was right when he said it was a secret." Bill actually sounded civil. Annoyed, but he managed a strained politeness. He didn't know Sunny enough to recognize the danger just then. "Why keep it one?"

Her teeth again, shown in a grin that made Ty want to throw back his head and sigh. They'd been so close to her true self, but there, with those few words, Bill raised in her again that false face, same as all those she showed the others. "You wouldn't understand the answer anyway. Why should I bother?"

Emotions twisted over Bill's face. Frustration. Anger. Injured pride. Bill was on his feet before they finally settled into rage. Ty prepared to jump up and separate the two, but Bill spun on his heel instead, leaving.

It was for the best, Ty supposed. As for Sunny's story, pieces were left out, even Ty knew that. "Why didn't you tell him everything?" He watched Bill, spine straight and shoulders square, stomp off into the distance. "Or actually tell him the part he wanted to hear?"

"What would you have told him, then?" Her sneer was turned on him. It hurt, always hurt, but Ty met her gaze straight-on.

"You said nothing about why we were hunted." Not why those little bits of solidified sap also seeded his and Sunny's own people's end. Their ancestors had gathered, polished, and traded the relics, and in doing so had soaked in that same pool. It didn't mark them, didn't give their people myriad gifts as it did the relics, but it changed their blood. Something their people learned far later.

Her face had settled back into a sad semblance of a smile.

"Why should I?" She shrugged, then shifted back to watch the field. The two figures were gone, but Ty expected she continued to see them in her mind. "You might foolishly call him yours, but I never will."

That was the problem with everything, Ty knew.

And still knew all these years later. She'd kept so much of herself apart from everyone else, only trusting Ty even as time stretched along.

Ty had told Bill the rest eventually, once Bill's pride had softened enough that he would listen.

Why think of all that now, Ty wondered. Were the memories stirred by being so close to a relic again, seen or not? By trudging through the sun's hell, pushed by wind and mired in recollection? Or was it because she felt so close to him these days, her ghost seemingly watching them?

"Are you confident that hunk of amber won't bite our asses?" Bill asked, bringing Ty back from his remembered childhood.

Ty was sure of nothing, and so he kept his silence.

CHAPTER
✳
SEVEN

"**J**onnie is worried about how much time Wendy has," Star pointed out, leaning closer to Damien. The sun burned down on them as they led their horses through the barren stretch with its dry, chalky sand and rusty shoots of rock.

"All of us are," Damien answered.

Overhead, hopeful vultures circled for a stretch, then wandered off, only to return and circle again in a patient but macabre expectation.

Star's skin spurned the sun's assault as always, same as his father's did, but the others kept their hands close to the shade of their bodies and their hatted heads tipped down.

"We'll move faster once we leave the sun's mouth," Star offered, wanting to cheer them up.

"*If,*" Ty snapped, never one to look away from the ugly.

Star rolled his eyes. He patted Clay's head as she pushed her nose into his back. The only real sounds were the horse's hooves against sand and rock and the vultures' cries.

A shifting shadow behind a rock caught Star's eye, and he reacted without thought, his blade finding its target. A second blade in hand, he craned forward, silent and ready. Knott leapt back from the unexpected beast as its tubular body fell, stumbled, then cursed again.

The knife had pierced the neck of a winged snake. Defending its territory or just desperate enough, Star wondered, eyeing its corpse. He'd caught it on the rise, either way. Its layered opaque wings brushed against the rocky ground as its body, a dull brown that matched the dessert around them, twitched into a loose coil.

"One bite from this and you'd drop," he reminded them. "The acid in its bite softens you up to make you easier to swallow. They usually spend the day in the walls or in shade, but don't trust to that."

Placing a foot on the serpent's head to ensure safety even in its death, he pulled his knife free and wiped it before returning it to his belt. "Watch the shadows," he added, passing Knott and continuing.

It was hard, slow travel that morning. They took a break as the sun hit its highest peak in the starched sky. With no better option for shade, they grouped below a red outcropping. Star helped Bill and Ostra chase down the cracks for unwanted company.

"A meal, should I find the brush," Ostra said with an exhausted chuckle. Star glanced over to see her lift a snake-speared blade.

"No fire," Damien reminded from where he was inspecting the horses. He gave the impression of being no more overheated than Star felt, though the others showed strain.

Everything else was easy to root out, and soon they turned their attention to watering themselves and their mounts. They were all a tired, dusty mess, the sand coating clothes and hair and once-glossy coats. Star's mouth tasted of chalk, and the water he drank helped little. The bite of dried meat he took with it brought to mind the Scar's floor.

Sooner than any of them liked, it was time again to press forward.

"Two, three more days of this," Ty muttered, taking the lead.

"An eternity to us mere humans," Ostra threw out there. Star could imagine her dry lips twisted in a sardonic grin and fought down a smile. Miserable as the others looked, he didn't want to tempt tempers.

In no time they were marching off in silence, the horses stirring up another cloud of dust to cake their clothes and catch in drying sweat.

"Keep drinking, else you're dead," Ty called out again after they'd walked a ways. "Remember to save enough for three more days, just in case."

Star, having drifted farther to the side than the others to inspect the waves of color rising in nearby rock, disagreed. "I doubt it'll take us—"

The ground beneath his feet crumbed. He dropped hold of Clay's reins with a shout. Sliding, scraping, it was a steep slope of purple stone worn smooth in parts and jagged in others. Catching himself before braining himself was a lucky break—all that saved his life—but the first snap of his arm when it bashed against a rock choked the breath from his lungs, and the second, when he landed, threatened to take his senses.

He slowly drifted back from the dizzying edge of consciousness and stared at the jutting boulder he'd caught himself against, aghast. There was still farther he could have rolled. He was damn fortunate to be hanging there, but how the hell was he to get out?

"Star!" he heard several voices call. Looking up, he found the party, pale beneath their tans and burns, peering down at him.

"Alive," he ground out, sounding more doubtful than he'd intended.

"Stay there, son," Ty yelled. "We'll get you." His face vanished from the light. All but Knott and Ostra followed. Tense conversation carried down to Star where he lay, the words impossible to make out over the rushing in his ears.

The pain was growing worse. He glanced down at the torn, aching mess that was his arm and grimaced. Blood and bone, ugly to see. The first break was all beneath the skin, but the second had split bone. Looking at it, a hysterical laugh bubbled unvoiced in his throat. It seemed the Scar was still after his life, and this time it might take it.

Arguing above him caught Star's attention as his anxiety settled. His father was demanding to be the one lowered to him, but that would never happen. Ty was the only one who could guide them, and they couldn't chance it. Damien was equally demanding to go down, and using that same logic.

"Are we just letting him bleed out?" Bill snapped.

That got them moving.

It was Damien who ended up being lowered. Star gave him a strained grimace as he used the rope around his waist to join Star on the narrow ledge inside an otherwise mostly smooth, tunnel-like cave.

Damien proceeded carefully, taking a second rope and edging closer until he could crouch next to Star. "How bad is it?"

Star smiled weakly. "I've been worse." He motioned to the grisly, blood-soaking mess with his good hand. At least the bone was stoppering the bulk of the bleeding.

Damien winced. "Can you lift it?"

Star did, gritting his teeth. Then Damien moved, tying the second rope around Star's own waist. Then, gently, Damien stood and lifted Star up, pulling him tight against his larger body.

"This isn't going to be fun," Damien warned.

"No?" Star teased around a grunt.

"Ready?" Ostra called.

Ty leaned next to her, face set. Star knew him well enough to see the lines of terror there.

"Ready as I'll be," Star called, and looked challengingly to Damien.

Damien grimaced but called back his own assent. He held Star steady as they were raised, and Star clung to Damien instead of the rope, not wanting to bloody it. Even his good hand was damp, both from his arm and from scrapes and cuts.

When they made it to safety, Damien let Ty pull Star away. Star leaned against his father as Ty pulled him close, careful of his injured arm.

"I'll be fine," Star assured him. "Thanks, Damien. All."

The others had gathered as much wood as they could find among the scrub. Some of their precious water was heating in the bottom of a cookpot over a fire. Star winced to see it, cursing himself and his luck.

Ty tapped his chin. "Let me see."

Star held his arm out, and Ty looked it over, scowling. "It'll need to be set. Then I'll stitch it up."

The water came to a boil and the bones—top and bottom—had to be lined back up. Star almost fainted, a hiss tearing from his lips and his vision going out. It lasted all of a second, and it was done, thank the moon and keep away the sun. Then, it was a matter of sewing and wrapping. The needle and thread had been sterilized already, so right on the heel of the bone setting came the fun part.

A softer hiss slipped from his lips as Ty pierced his skin with the round bone needle. It took Ty little time, though, and the hole was patched. After that, Star was bandaged, stuffed into a makeshift sling, and free of their doctoring.

"We should rest," Bill worried. "And give you time to catch yourself."

Both Ty and Star shook their heads.

"Can't take the time," Star snapped. "I can keep going."

The sun was heading down and riding was agony, but the more time they wasted, the longer they'd be in hell.

Vultures glided patiently overhead, constant reminders of both where they were and the expected outcome.

They settled into camp that night tired and ornery. Damien watched Ty hover over Star like an overgrown partridge, ready to drive off anyone who might drift closer. He'd shuffled his son up against a dead-looking sapling, and Star sat with his back against the tree and his eyes closed.

Ty's glare worked to keep away most of the others. Even Damien couldn't bring himself to dare that snapping beast, but Bill was proving to be pretty lacking in common sense. How, Damien wondered, had the irreverent, sandy-brown haired man with his quick grin and quicker mouth ever ended up friends with serious, swift-tempered Ty?

Bill ambled over. "Let's see the broken wing."

Star opened his eyes with a sigh and a faint smile, but it was his dad who did the answering. "He's leaving his arm still, Bill, and you'll stop egging him if you don't want a matching sling."

"Yeah, sounds about right." Bill chuckled and slumped down closer than Damien would have dared. Star was fully up now and leaned over to let Bill fuss over him.

Damien left them to it, heading over to where Ostra was digging some food out of their extra packs. She passed him jerky and bits of sun-dried apple as he squatted next to her.

"Supper," she said.

"Thanks." He took a bite of the meat first, tasting only sand. It took a good mouthful of water before he could get it down.

"Those men meant it when they said this is hell," Knott commented, taking his own share. "I've half a mind to just lay down here and not bother going tomorrow."

Ostra snorted. Shoving the last into her mouth, she grabbed Knott's beard and gave it a yank. The yowl Knott let loose was at least good to keep any suicidal predators away.

"Damn it," Knott muttered, rubbing his chin. "Hurt, wench."

She smirked, showing a row of teeth impressively clear of dried beef or apple.

As she dug out her whittling, Star slipped free of Ty and wandered their way. Wondering how he'd managed it, Damien glanced toward the dead saplings. There, Ty was busy in a low, hissing argument with Bill.

"What's that for?" Star asked Ostra as he sank onto the ground next to them. He looked pale, his arm tucked close in a makeshift sling. Still, he seemed healthy enough. Scrapes and bruises, mostly. Star was damn lucky, and Damien felt lucky himself to still have him with them.

Ostra gave a half smile. "I'm carving it for Jonnie's niece and nephew." She held it up for him to see. The little wooden fellow had a face now under his hat, but still needed work before he'd have a left leg. "I always make sure to have a new one for them to play with when we visit." The sadness in her speech betrayed her worry. She'd only be able to give it to the children if they still lived.

"I bet they'll love it," Star offered, tone gentle. He was a perceptive one and sweet under all that bravado. "How old are they?"

"Five and three," she answered, going back to carving again. Star watched, shifting until he was propped against Damien's shoulder. Damien, for his part, just smirked and held still. Maybe he'd get a slip of the hell Bill was experiencing when Ty caught sight of them, but with Star pressed against him, it was hard to care.

Damien took his spell on the watch that night with Ty, their group having switched to double watches after the wraiths attacked, and he found himself sitting in uncomfortable silence. It almost made him wish for flying snakes or gray-lit false phantoms. The sun had set, and with it too dangerous for a fire, they had nothing to look at besides the barren, night-black surroundings and each other.

"Star's mom must have been a beauty," he said, then flinched. Great. Remind the man about the woman he'd obviously lost, and make himself look a heartless cad.

Ty surprised him, though. Instead of snapping, he glanced toward where his son slept. "Yes. She was the strongest, most beautiful woman to ever live."

The earnest loss in Ty's voice rent Damien's chest. The same could be said for Star, he bet, though he looked far too much like his father to resemble his mother much. "Sweet and kind with her family, I bet?" Like Star, under all that fire and determination, had a kind core.

"Never." Ty's answer shocked him. Worse was Ty's somber smile. It was the truest emotion outside of anger or annoyance that he'd ever shown Damien. Ty's pain couldn't be missed.

"Star told me you lost her. I can't imagine how hard it must have been."

Ty looked toward his son again and Damien followed. Ty sighed, blue eyes distant and wistful. "I'd give almost anything to see her again. Just not my son."

"You loved her," Damien said, then cringed again. Of course Ty had. She was the mother of his son, and despite the cruel bent of Ty's first answer, it rang with longing.

"Aye," Ty answered. "I don't think it's in me not to. Star's mother made a life of getting what she wanted. My life was spent giving it to her."

Silence closed over them again. Damien, leaving Ty with his thoughts, worried over the bones of what Ty had shared. He wanted to ask about the letter the gentleman had carried in Standing Grave, to press for more, but after his last blunders, Damien worried how much worse he could do.

Another night, he promised himself.

Star stirred, likely feeling the weight of their eyes, but he didn't wake. Knott, however, did. Damien saw him shifting in the shadow and glanced his way. He received a snort for his trouble, Knott's expression one of exasperation.

Yeah. Damien was falling hard, and he knew it.

CHAPTER

※

EIGHT

They approached the lip of the canyon not long past dawn, the end to their trek through hell thankfully in sight.

"It's a long, hard walk," Ty called back. "Step easy."

His father was always barking ;things, and to Damien's credit he no longer pulled a face each time. Mostly. Star had been checking.

His arm ached, a reminder to keep his ear tuned to their surroundings. The cloudy distraction of his mind warned of an infection that he didn't dare poke at yet, not until there was water and safety. Their constant motion wasn't good for a clean healing either, but he did his best to keep the arm steady.

"We got turned around—" Ty sighed, picking his own path in the lead. "—but we can make up the time by going through the valley up ahead. I know this area well."

Star considered his father's words and realized with some surprise what he meant.

"This is leading into Bay Coyoteye's territory." Damien scowled as if he expected the man to ride up from behind the scrub. "He isn't keen on strangers coming through this way. Better to take the mountain route, isn't it?"

Ty scoffed.

Star grinned, his chest lightening. "Bay is fine. We're all old friends."

"Friends? With *him*?" Damien demanded. Even Knott looked somewhere between impressed and wary.

Star shrugged. "He's a bit intense, yeah, but he's a good man. Dad says he'd have killed a man for a frown when he was younger but that if he liked you, then you were safe enough. I've known him as long as I can remember."

"He might know you, but that doesn't mean a whole lot for us."

"He'll let us bring you through," Star assured Damien. "Make sure to not piss him off."

"We'll save at least five days cutting through Bay's lands," Ty threw in. "He'll want a visit, but we can spare a night as payment. Fair, I'd wager."

There wasn't an argument to be made, so visit they would.

When they reached the top of their climb, they stood in an exhausted clump, catching their breath and letting the horses rest. Star shoved the stiffened bandana down from his mouth, breathing deep to taste the cleaner air. Behind them lay the bodies of the flying serpents who'd made a last gamble for blood, but now they were free of the Scar and all her cursed ilk. Even so, Star kept a careful eye on the rocky stretch they'd finally left, not ruling out any pursuit.

"See those trees?" Ty motioned ahead of them. Star turned his head and squinted, sighting the thin slips rendered indistinct with distance.

"Aye," Damien answered for his group, all of them but Knott now covering their eyes against the sun to better see. Knott instead glared back at the trail they'd climbed, brow furrowed in annoyed expectation. He searched for another shadow over rock and sand, Star reflected, appreciating having the steady man at their side.

"There's a spring up ahead," Ty continued. "We'll refill our canteens, though there is water in plenty after we get moving."

It was, as claimed, a short trip there. Soon the smoky trees grew body, and as the sun rose, Star could see the downward slide of the land beyond them. That, he expected, was where they'd find the spring. His chest beat hard at the thought of fresh water, but none of them had the heart to push their mounts.

It was a relief to reach the downgrade. Up ahead, he could see the spring break from rock, a thick run of water that poured down the hill and on to a river that curled into the distance.

"Ain't that a sight." Damien sighed.

Jonnie grunted, taking over for Knott, who still carried a pensive look. They all practically fell by the water's side to sate their thirst, releasing the horses to drink and feed on the lush grasses. It tasted like life, clean and good.

"Thank the moon for something to drink not out of a damned canteen," Knott muttered, water drops glistening in his beard. He looked more relaxed now that they'd made it safely, though the corded muscles of his neck still stood out.

"Thank sun and moon both we made it out," Damien threw in, ignoring the huff Ty gave.

"Maybe thank our guides?" Ostra suggested blandly before taking another drink.

Star shot her a grateful look.

Bill, for his part, winked. "Happy to help."

Damien's lips thinned. Not even the taste of fresh water had eased the hard lines Ty's words had left on his face. "I'd thank them more if they weren't going to lose us a day."

Star swallowed a curse, sitting straight and watching. His father's hand didn't move for a weapon, didn't clench in threat, but Star knew the danger in the way Ty stood. The forced ease in his shoulders and the cant of his head was a danger Star had seen before, and he hoped it wouldn't be turned on Damien now.

"A day lost for far more gained," Ty answered, cool and deceptively calm. "Rest for horses taken to their limits, a chance to regain our own strength, and, *yes*, damn you, some courtesy and fellowship in exchange for more days saved."

Damien's tension lessened, but Star could tell Ty wasn't done. Damn it, was he a fool to ignore how Ty looked at him?

The sound of horses drifted to them, and thankfully Ty's attention was now on those approaching from a distance. Relief there'd be no fighting warred with unease over his father's restlessness.

"Dad?" Star asked lowly, rising next to him along with the others.

Ty stood from where he'd crouched, chin up and hand still loose. Ty's face clouded for a second, then he relaxed, and Star let out a breath.

"No danger," Ty assured them. Damien frowned, narrow-eyed, but Star knew his father enough to know that when he said no danger, there was none.

"It's fine," Star assured Damien, moving closer now that the dangerous mood had blown free. "It's likely Bay's men."

Star was proven right, a grin stretching his lips as a group of three men and two women rode up. The man in the lead, older than the others but as spry in the saddle as any, tore off his hat and waved excitedly. "Hello! Boys!" Two loose folds of skin sagged like sails as he talked, old muscle that had gone first to fat, then fat lost to age.

"There're my boys!" Bay cried as he hopped down from the saddle and stomped their way. First he clapped Star's cheek, second Ty's arm as the two men came to meet him halfway. "Who are the extras? They look like more trouble." He nodded past Star's shoulder toward Damien. "That one? I've seen his mug. Wanted for robbery and murder, eh?"

The joviality never left Bay's face, though the lines around his eyes hardened.

"I like him." Star smirked and caught Damien's eye. Damien, edging toward the group, stopped and blinked, likely trying to figure out how to respond to that. Star loved seeing him wrong-footed. He choked back a laugh.

Ty closed his eyes on an offensively pained groan, but Bay chuckled.

"Then bring them along, lad," Bay ordered, the hard lines vanishing. "I'll take a reference from you any day, even if the man stole the sun and killed the moon." Bay's companions snickered as Bay himself laughed aloud, enjoying his own words.

"Thank you," Star said, meaning it. Bay's constant welcome made his lands and company a comfort.

Bay shrugged his great shoulders, eyes warm. "Come along now, all. We'll have some drinks and catch up before you fools head on your way." Bay waited while they got their horses ready and mounted up. "Will you and the little pack be staying long?"

"Wish we could," Ty said. The strain from before was missing. "We've promised to get them to Blue Rock before the new moon. Sorry for the brief visit this time."

Bay chuckled. "Sorry isn't something you feel, Ty. Well, if you have plans, you have plans. Try to follow your whiskers back this way before my gray head goes to dry old earth, won't you?"

He clapped their shoulders again, taking care to only lightly clap Star on his uninjured side, and then shook Damien's hand. Star brightened, liking the sight. If he had his way, Bay and Damien would have plenty of future chances to meet and mingle. Maybe one day he'd be able to snare Damien one of Bay's horses, the best there were.

"Come, come, lads and ladies. We'll get you settled, fed, and rested up before dawn drags your company away again."

Teeth gritted, Star held himself still, arm stretched out across the table at Bay's as his father fussed. Bill and Bay, looking on, were no help. The wound, once bared and carefully cleaned, looked about how Star had expected, the flesh swelling around the stitches and the skin patched in feverish color.

"The skin is hot," Ty grumbled, scowling beneath his worry. "Infected, by the look. Damn it. Bay, what do you have we can use?"

Bay eyed the raised flesh and frowned. "Not too far gone, thankfully. No worries, lad, we'll get that cleaned and redone properly."

Ty made an annoyed sound. "We were down in that hell, Bay. What more do you think I could've done?"

Bay waved a hand. Damien, leaning in the doorway at a safe distance, offered Star a grimace before ducking back out to rejoin his crew in the yard.

Star made it through the thorough washing, salving, and restitching with minimal hissing. He was light-headed and sweating by the time they finally let up and he could sit back.

"Keep your head where it should be and take it easy," Ty ordered, a hard look accompanying his words.

Star rolled his eyes as the others crept in, called to the table for a bite. Bay's crew cleared away the water and rags, replacing them with thick, hastily gathered platters of food that no doubt had been meant for their own supper. None of them complained, nodding and shuffling off to wait for the next round.

"Well?" Bay barked, gesturing at the table. "Dig in."

He didn't need to ask twice. After the hard, lean days, it felt good to have something substantial in their stomachs. Star was more thirsty than hungry, but still kept up with the others.

As soon as they'd had their fill, the platters were removed and Bay leaned forward, eyeing them. "You all might want to take this chance to rest up. You've free rein on my lands, so long as you cause no trouble. I'll trust my boys to keep an eye on you."

Ty snorted. "And they'd better not make that necessary."

Damien, lips pinched, didn't rise to the bait. Star sighed and started to stand. "C'mon, Damien, I'll show you guys around."

Ty's hand closed over his good wrist, halting him. "Not so fast. I need to see what you can still do with that injured arm."

Star narrowed his eyes. "I'd say I've shown you."

Ty didn't budge. "In an emergency, yes. I want to see how you can move. Or do you want to stay here while Bill and I finish this job?"

Star's jaw snapped shut. He recognized the warning in his father's eyes. He meant the words.

"Fine."

Ty led him out into the sun, heading to where they'd once spent hours each day practicing. The spot was much the same, with just a little silvering of old wood to show for the passing years.

Star pulled a knife off his belt, stealing a second to breathe and prepare himself. Then he started, taking care not to show any weakness his father could seize upon and use. There was no doubt in his mind that Ty would leave him there if given any excuse. The muscles in his left arm were tight and cramped, making movement difficult, especially when each throw jarred his wound. Ty leaned against the fence, watching.

From the corner of his eye, he saw Damien and Knott heading their way. Damien, gaze following where he'd sent his last throw, whistled. "Terrifying."

Star leered over one shoulder. "Want to taste the next one?" He purred. "No?"

"Keep on, danger." Damien laughed.

Star threw three knives in quick succession, right down the trunk. His infected arm gave an angry ache for the show.

"Keep going, Star," his dad snapped, "but stop moving your whole body. It's pulling on your arm. Two more sets, then we're done."

He rolled his eyes as Ty collected the blades, but he did as ordered.

"His ma could throw too," Bill shared, coming up to join their group. "She preferred guns, but liked both."

Star resented Bill sharing those things, although he liked hearing them himself. He gritted his teeth as he continued on with the practice, ignoring the twinge of pain as his arm strained to keep up.

"She teach him?" It was Knott asking, this time. Damien knew otherwise.

Ty sighed and answered that one himself. "No." His voice was worn.

"Star never knew her," Bill explained, chatty as always. "She died shortly after he was born."

They were quiet for a time, but Star knew they were still standing there watching the show. He kept up the work, taking each blade as his father passed it to him and throwing it true.

"You plan to practice too?" he called over his shoulder, just to let them know he was aware of his audience.

"Not today," Ty answered. "One more set. You're looking tired."

Took. Threw. Took. Threw. Star continued the cycle beneath the heat. Sweat ran down his face and neck, his shirt soaked and his eyes narrowed on the target.

"Enough," Ty said eventually.

Star had one knife left, so he threw it, then dropped his hand, letting out a long breath. "Fine." Tossing his head back, he stomped away to wash in the stream.

"He's good," Damien commented to Knott as he passed the stream. "Amazingly good."

Star perked up, a grin curling over his lips as he thought of how to reward Damien's praise later. Those simple words left a warmth in his chest that thrilled as much as scared him. Something about Damien burrowed into Star's marrow and left him desperate for more.

"Are you looking for some company?" he called hopefully, but Damien was already past hearing. Star pouted and received a stern glare from his father, who had followed him. Swallowing his chuckle, Star headed off for a patch of sun where he could rest his muscles and enjoy the warmth. His mind, however, followed after Damien.

It was terrifying to want someone so much. It was also heady.

Damien sat in a patch of sunlight on the steps to Bay's front porch, nursing a mug of ale and breathing in the taste of the warm summer evening. From his vantage point he could keep an eye on the shade beneath a tall cypress tree where Star had stretched out in the long grass for a nap. Likely tuckered himself out. As expected, Ty was perched at his son's feet, his old rifle stretched out across his lap and his hat tucked down to keep the sun from his eyes.

It was a beautiful home, small enough to be quaint but large enough that there were extra rooms. Ty and Star would be sleeping indoors with Bay and his foreman, while Damien and the rest would room in the longhouse with Bay's hands and other workers. Their horses, grazing in a small corral built for the use of guests and customers, had been brushed to gleaming, manes now dust-free.

One day, he wanted a place like this. A place where his people could hang their hats next to his, no posse on their heels or price on their heads. Knott and Ostra were getting older, and they deserved to find some peace before meeting their makers.

They were his, though, and he'd never insult them by leaving them behind.

His mind kept running over the conversation he'd shared with Ty. It was a challenge to reconcile the new information with the man he was learning.

Bay wandered his way, a floppy hat pulled low over his eyes and the cotton of his shirt marked by dirt and sweat. He joined Damien on the step, resting his large hands on his knees and looking Damien over thoughtfully. Damien gazed back, waiting. He'd let Bay make whatever decisions Bay was intending to form, then see where that took them.

"Good stock," Bay commented, nodding to where Damien and his group's horses mingled in the corral. "I've never done business with the man, but I recognize good breeding. Guess his family name can be known for more than just their sheep now."

A roundabout way of stating he knew the price on their heads. Still, Bay's tone was mild. No threat yet, or at least not a blatant one.

"They've saved our necks more than once."

An acknowledging grunt, then silence again. Damien waited, knowing there was more.

"You're keeping a mighty close eye on the kid," Bay said at last.

"I am," Damien answered, keeping his tone smooth and calm.

Bay nodded slowly. "I take it you plan to keep on this way. I'm thinking rightly?"

It took a second for Damien to take his meaning. "It's a thought."

"Yeah." A sigh. "I figured as much."

That was a curious response. Damien wondered over it as they sat in silence for a time. A breeze had started, stirring dust and worrying the grass. The flies kept up their soft hum, and the steady sounds of ranch life carried on around them. Still Star slept, an arm thrown over his face and his father sitting guard. The sun traced the line of the shotgun, sending a sharp blinding glare into Damien's eyes. He squinted, looking back to the corral and horses.

Bay's voice, soft enough it barely carried, startled him into turning. "You ever find yourselves in that narrow, hilly territory over northeast, you keep both of those eyes on the lad, not just the one."

He took in Bay's serious expression and pursed lips. He didn't like the pain in Bay's eyes. "Trouble there?"

"Trouble, aye." He sneered, showing yellow teeth that still had a lot of bite. "It's not for me to tell, but you upset him? I might have to run the lot of you off."

"You'd have Ty for help there." Damien snorted.

"I would at that. So I've your word? Both to keep an eye and to give him any space he needs?"

"Yeah. You've my word."

Bay nodded. Then he tilted his head, an old dog scenting something on a new wind. "Honestly, son? I'm amazed Ty is letting you anywhere near his boy."

Damien groaned, unable to help himself. "He doesn't seem to like the idea."

"Lad? This? This is not him disliking the idea. This is him accepting. Him not liking would be you being eaten by carrion hunters after they dug you from a too-shallow grave. One that, just in case you missed my direction—"

"He put me in," Damien supplied, letting his eyes drift back to Ty.

Bay snorted again. Staring at Star, sleeping seemingly without a care in the world, Damien wondered what he kept bottled up inside.

Jonnie wandered their way from where he'd been talking to Ostra over by the corral. He slid his hat off and stood there awkwardly. Bay studied him for a moment, then rose and stretched, his back creaking. "I'm moving to a chair up there. You're a mighty big lad—Jon, was it? Why not come sit with me and leave the kid the ground."

Damien was happy to see Jonnie's lips kick up into a small smile. It had been ages since he'd done more than look melancholy. Damien patted his leg as he walked past, and Jonnie even shot *him* a smile before taking the offered chair.

"You must be feeling restless," Bay came right out and said as he took the seat beside Jonnie. Times like this, it was easy to see his influence in Star.

"I'll feel a mite better once I see my sister and her family," Jonnie responded, ever polite. The same worry that filled his voice creased his face.

"We'll set out again as soon as dawn lights our path," Damien assured him. "You've my word."

"Aye," Bay spoke up. "Ty said as much to me earlier. I'll have packs made with supplies and have a few of my people escort you to the edge of my territory. That'll save some trouble, at least on my range."

"Thank you," Jonnie said, beating Damien to it.

Bay shrugged, speaking to Damien as if he'd been the one to offer thanks. "Watch over my boys and we're even."

CHAPTER

✳

NINE

Star kicked the door shut as soon as Damien walked through behind him. Damien gave a little start, and all Star could do was smirk, then slide the bolt into place.

"Locking me in, then?" Damien was relaxing, finally, from whatever bee had stung him while Star had napped. Damien eyed the room appreciatively, and Star grinned.

He joined Damien in inspecting the dark stain of the walls and the brightly dyed blankets on the bed. He'd spent a lot of nights here, and it felt a bit like home. Some he didn't want to remember, but others had been nice. Peaceful.

He backed up a step toward the bed, dropping his useable hand to his jeans and unsnapping the belt buckle. He let the ends hang, open, waiting, as he set his hand on his slim hip and gave Damien a challenging look.

A feral light entered those green eyes, but there was a wariness that Star would need to drive away if he planned to get what he wanted.

"You do know you're sharing this room with your dad, right?" Damien pointed out, not yet taking the bait.

Star hummed, twisting a finger around the button on his jeans. "That was the plan, but plans change." There was a very nice bed, and an actual window with sunlight pouring through. His only taste of Damien had been in moonlight, and that, for one, wasn't going to be the case this time. Star planned to get a good, clear view.

"And your dad'll like that change, huh?" came the answering drawl.

Damien still wasn't reaching for his own belt, or Star's, and that was a problem. Star slinked back another step, fumbling with his shirt next. With his other arm pinned in its splint, it was harder to get the damn thing open, but he managed. "He'll be fine. He'll likely just sit up drinking with Bay and Bill half the night, anyway."

Damien snorted. He still didn't take the bait. "Or he'll come in, a few marks from now, and kick me off the bed."

That, sadly, was possible, not that he wanted Damien entertaining such ideas. They were likely to keep things from progressing.

Star sank onto the edge of the bed, legs splayed and shirt hanging open, revealing the splint. He leaned back, resting his good hand on the quilted bedspread and showing off pale skin for Damien's enjoyment, should he just stop worrying and *move*.

"You don't have to be scared of him." This time Star got the reaction he wanted: a feral burn, igniting and taking out the last of Damien's wariness. He stalked across the room, and Star's lips twisted into a self-satisfied grin as he drank in the prowling sight.

Damien stopped between Star's splayed knees and just stood there for a minute, looking. Evening light was pouring through the windows, and Star used that to his advantage, stretching further and showing himself off. There were at least two marks before dusk, and he'd enjoy Damien fully before that time was up.

Damien reached down and ran his calloused fingers over Star's stomach, shoving the faded material of Star's open shirt out of his way. Star's breath caught as Damien's fingers scraped past a scar to graze the tip of his nipple.

"Kick those jeans off, won't you?" Damien leaned over him. "And the shirt can go too."

Damien took back his hand and started stripping off his shirt. Star, forgetting the orders in light of this new development, watched all that tan skin being bared. Damien knew how interested he was too, the bastard, and was enjoying it, judging by how he slowed down.

Damien took his time digging a small vial of oil out of his pocket and then gave a little mock throw before actually tossing it onto the bed, and all that before even starting on his belt. For a second, Star felt a shiver of nerves. He forced it away, biting his cheek until he tasted blood, and then drove his tongue against the cut. Damien, he reminded himself. Damien, who he himself had pursued and had won.

Damien's hands were back then, pushing Star's shirt over his shoulders, Damien's belt long discarded. Star kicked himself. He twisted to help, pulling his good arm free and watching as Damien chucked it to join the clothing on the floor. Then Star yanked his own pants off, likely appearing a fool for how he had to roll to get any purchase. Damn it, but Damien was in the way of him standing, and he only had the one arm. He was doing the best he could for being bed-bound and one-handed.

Finally, after far more work than it should have been, he had his jeans kicked off. Damien, the jerk, was staring down at him with one eyebrow crooked, half-laughing. It was not the predatory look Star was striving to earn.

"I got them off," he pointed out, dry. "Not that you were any help there."

Damien chuckled, then climbed onto the bed to stretch over top him. "That you did." He planted a kiss on Star's stomach above the trail of dark hair leading to his groin. "Impressive."

Star rolled his eyes, yanking on a few strands of Damien's hair when he started scattering light, chaste kisses up from that trail. Damien licked his stomach, then lifted his head, grinning. "Yes?"

"Come up here," Star ordered.

Damien slid up, careful not to hit Star's injured arm, and they kissed for a few minutes, slow and sweet.

"This is nice," Star panted when they separated, "but if you sit up, I'd like to ride you. How about that?"

Damien gave a breathy laugh and pulled back. "Sounds good."

Star rolled onto his side, getting into position to lever himself up. Damien's hand came to rest on his back.

For a second Star was paralyzed, caught wrong-footed and scrambling to figure out what was wrong. Then Damien's fingers pressed alongside what Star knew to be a scar. He closed his eyes, silently cursing the light he'd so enjoyed moments ago, and cursing the past that refused to stay out of his way.

"Star." The cold fury and pain in that one word erased any of Star's doubts that Damien understood what he saw.

"His name was Finn," he answered slowly, the name hard to force from his lips. "It was five years ago."

Gently, Damien ran his fingers from scar to scar, tracing the visible rends in Star's soul. Then he shifted closer, leaning until his warmth closed over Star's back.

"How old were you?" Damien breathed the question against the nape of Star's neck.

"Sixteen," he whispered, hating that he answered but not seeming able to stop. "He had me for four days."

Four days of hell and torture. He'd been drugged, abused, beaten, and when he'd fallen to begging for it to end, Finn had just licked his tears and kept going. Star was his, he'd told him over and over again. His blood had been made for him, and so what he did was right. He'd been guided to him, and why else but to keep him?

Those words haunted Star. He refused to believe them, but when his dad drank some nights and started talking about rot taking root, begging Star not to let it settle inside him, Star felt fear.

Four days, and five years later it could still cripple him. After the first year, he could stand to look in a mirror again. He'd slept pressed next to his dad for most of it, only to wake from nightmares and flinch from any other person's touch, including Bill's and Bay's. Most of that old terror was gone, beaten down by time, but the nightmares? He'd had to accept that they would probably never go.

Damien's hands left the scars, trailing over his skin to find his shoulders. The left hand stroked up and down Star's good arm. Chasing gooseflesh, Star realized and felt shame flush him as he shivered, pressing into the light touch.

"Do you know if he still lives?" Damien asked, voice low. There was something strange there, but Star couldn't begin to guess. Didn't want to.

"He doesn't," he answered, facing away, "but he had men who do."

Damien pulled on him, and Star moved with it, twisting to climb onto thick thighs, all too glad to get back to where they'd been headed. He wanted this to be fun, and he was going to get what he desired.

"Let me focus on you," Star demanded, narrowing his eyes at Damien's concerned face. He'd chase that expression away before they finished, he vowed. "I changed my mind. Think you can pin me down and keep me there, or am I too much for you?"

Damien gave a quick jerk and gently pinned Star down, his good arm lifted high over his head.

"I think I can manage." Damien smirked, and then pushed down enough to rub his attentive length against Star, letting him feel how he'd risen to attention. "Know what's better? I can do it with one hand."

Star blinked, then huffed. Damien grabbed the vial he'd flung onto the bed. He used his teeth to uncork it, then stopped again and actually laughed, spitting the cork out onto the quilt.

"All right, new plan." Damien grinned. "Keep your hand right where I have it, Star. If you want this, you'll have to be a good boy and not agitate your splinted arm."

Star glared, but then Damien let him go. Grumbling, Star lay back and watched Damien pour a generous amount of the oil into his palm, spreading it up over three of his fingers. He briefly considered shifting his arm, if only to see what Damien would do, but he wanted what was coming too much to jeopardize it. Maybe next time.

Fingers oiled, Damien still didn't continue. Star frowned, confused, and found those gorgeous eyes trained on his.

"This *is* what you want?" Damien checked.

The soft words and searching eyes, so at odds with the taunting of seconds before, startled Star into stillness. Damien didn't move, waiting on him.

Star met him eye to eye. "I want you."

Damien leaned over Star again, one hand closing over his wrist and the other nudging between his thighs.

"Open up?" Damien suggested, playful, though the tender care didn't leave. Star squinted at him but parted his legs wider, wincing slightly when one finger eased inside. The oil helped, and the finger explored for a moment before there were two. Then three.

Star was clenching his teeth, growling, by the time those damn fingers were replaced with what he actually wanted. Damien, pressing their foreheads together, held Star down with a careful strength as he settled between Star's thighs. Star could feel his length there, as hard and eager as his own, but rather than fill him, Damien laid a chaste kiss to his lips.

"Are you ready?" Damien asked.

Star lifted his chin, hearing the question Damien really needed answered. "More than."

Damien's smirk returned, all teeth. He slowly pushed his way inside, his hair shining in the sunlight pouring through the breeze-blown curtains.

"Harder," Star ordered, moving into the burning length filling him, still so slowly.

Damien pulled out, then slid back in. Once, twice, faster each time, and on the fourth and fifth entries, Star threw back his head, giving a sharp, strangled sound. On the sixth, he choked on the thrust of Damien's tongue as he caught their lips together.

"Shh." Damien grunted, and the roll of his hips had Star letting out a second cry. Again Damien kissed him, shoving tongue deep and letting them do battle there as he slowed his thrusts to a snail's torturous pace.

"Careful," Damien teased, touching the arm splinted across Star's chest. "You jar this, we're done."

"Then—"

Damien didn't give him time to talk, driving in again with more force than he'd shown that night by the stream. Star was broken down to mere animal cries, and Damien chuckled in his ear as he worked fast.

"So gorgeous," Damien moaned, losing rhythm as he neared his end. Star came first, back arching and fingers digging into the bedding so hard he almost ripped it. Then he was slumping down, beat, and Damien slid his arm under his slim hips, angling them to where he could just—hit—right—

Afterward they lay together, sharing each other's breaths as their bodies came down from the rush.

CHAPTER

✺

TEN

"That man, Damien," Bay commented as he dropped next to Ty on the shaded veranda and tipped his hat back, "I think I could like him."

Ty leaned his own head back against the house, letting loose a sigh from his very soul. "He's a good man," Ty muttered, hating to admit as much. "Unfortunately."

His son had woken from his nap not long before, and in seconds the rascal was crawling over Damien, hinting that it was "nice upstairs." Ty was proud of himself for not running both of the fools off. Instead, he'd gritted his teeth and stood back until Damien had given in.

Ty had taken Damien's spot on the porch and stewed until Bay had wandered over.

Bay snickered at him, the old bastard. "'Unfortunately,' Ty? I cannot wait to hear this."

Well, then. Hear it Bay would. "Anything else I could run off, but Star is stubborn and determined, and the bountied is completely smitten."

"And you have run anything else off, I bet." The weight of Bay's eyes didn't ease, no matter how light his words were. "Tell me this, though: When has your son ever shown an ounce of interest in someone for more than a quick tumble?"

Ty had to give that ground. Rarely, and never more than twice. There'd been scattered rendezvous in their past that'd had Ty gritting his teeth and waiting on edge until Star ambled back. This, though? This was unchartered territory, an interest growing more than carnal, and it raised Ty's hackles.

"Damien is honorable," he managed, determined to admit the virtues of the man he wanted to strangle. Star had good taste in this, it seemed, even if Ty wanted to scream. "His people love him, and he seems ready to stand his ground over one he claims as his own. Kid's no coward."

"And," Bay spoke up, seeing right to the heart of it, "Star likes all that."

Ty sighed but agreed. "Too much."

Bay gazed across the yard, quiet. The gravity in his next statement further roused Ty's unease. "Ty, do you know who put that bounty on Sole's head?"

"No," Ty answered, narrow-eyed.

Bay breathed out. "Sam Hollowood."

The name stabbed Ty. A guttural sound rumbled from his chest as he lurched to his feet, muscles screaming to move, to collar Star and ride as hard and fast as he could. Only the wind, rousing and making intent clear, kept him rooted where he stood.

"*Damn it*," Ty hissed, fighting to calm his heart. "*Why?*" He whirled on Bay, meeting sharp eyes and wishing he could see the mind beneath them.

"A dead son and stolen horses, according to the bounty sheet." The hard note under Bay's words reminded Ty who sat there. "Whatever else there was, no one is sharing."

But there was always more with the Hollowoods involved. The family that'd killed his own all because of a blood-gutted tree. The men who'd hurt Sunny and the madman who'd stolen his son all stemmed from that same rotted line.

The Hollowoods weren't allowed any farther south than Beresford's lands to the north, an agreement written in the Hollowoods' blood at Bay's hands, but Ty wasn't fool enough to trust in old agreements. They were a pack he'd fled before, leaving as little trail as he possibly could.

And now this? Damn the wind, damn Sole, and damn this whole rotting land.

"Then I've put my son right where those bastards are searching, and this with the law behind them!" Ty snapped.

The Blades wouldn't touch the Hollowoods for massacring Ty's people, claiming it a blood-feud, but they'd take bounties from the sick bastards without batting an eye. The Hollowoods had money, both from centuries spent farming and so many homesteads invaded and gutted. It wasn't just Ty's people they'd killed, but his were the only ones they sought.

"For Sole and his people, not you."

Ty clenched his teeth, trembling with rage and an inability to act. "I don't know what to do about it."

Bay sighed. "I imagine not. Would you be able to turn the kid's head?"

No, Star was as stubborn a bastard as he was. But it was Ty who had to follow where he was led, not his son. Ty faced Bay, his chin high and jaw set. "I can't turn off this path, but I can force him to stay here."

"At his age?"

Ty scowled, another howl rising in his throat, but Bay didn't give him the chance to respond.

"Son, sometimes you can't change facts. Moon knows, sun accepts, you just have to accept too. If your son plans to follow Sole, the best you can do is tell him why it's a bad idea and give him a chance to choose."

"Moon knows, sun damns, more like," Ty snarled. "You know what choice he'll make!"

Bay stared back, waiting on him. Ty seethed, taking a step away from the porch and then whirling around again, dizzy with crashing thoughts.

"What am I to do? Sole's likely to get Star killed. My son hasn't come out and said it yet, but he'll be following that man into trouble. They've a brewing range war, and Star is going to plant himself right in it. Now you tell me that even if he gets through that mess, it'll bring Hollowood eyes down on him?"

Bay met his gaze with a hard one, the lines on his face deep as cracks in the earth. "If that's the kid's choice, then he'll have you there too, along with Bill, to protect his back. That seems like fine odds to me." Bay's words were measured, but a rumble under the calm let Ty know the surface was a lie. "Even knowing you're there, the Hollowoods can do damn little without leaving their territory. I didn't tell you this to scare you; I just wanted to be sure you knew."

Ty sank back down onto the step. Leaning his hands on his knees, he glared between his feet. "I hate this."

"I'd worry if you didn't." Bay sighed, and Ty waited. "It isn't just the Hollowoods you should be thinking about, or even the coming fight."

Ty grimaced. "What, then?"

"Damien Sole has a whole pack at his back. I think, a few years down the way, that he's going to want to settle. Quite a few of his pals are long in the tooth, and the way he was looking at my spread? And at your boy napping in it, content as any old sated tom?" Bay quirked a brow, waiting, but when Ty refused to speak, he went on. "Man liked what he saw."

Ty gritted his teeth, the truth of it nails in his coffin.

"You like the open fields and a sky as far as the sea. Your kid? He writes me letters."

Yeah. There was that too, and it made the whole damn thing worse. Star clung to their connections, digging in and holding on with almost manic desperation. Since most of the towns they frequented were tucked-back, hidey-hole locales, the bulk of the letters went to Bay. He could use his men to deliver them. He had business in Standing Grave, so it was the easiest way for Star.

Star's mother had never desired connections. She'd spit on anyone who tried to press her, and almost nothing would have stopped her leaving anyone other than Ty. She never wanted to stay with their people as a child and hadn't changed as she'd aged. Star, though, wasn't like her. He had in him a quiet shoot that wanted to find soil and take root. Ty, not so unlike her in the end, didn't have that in him.

"I love him."

Bay nodded. "Do you love him enough to settle down if that time comes?"

Damn the man. "I've done right by him. Kept him safe."

Bay didn't argue. Ty could give any arguments himself, so why should Bay bother?

"More right than I have," Bay said after a time. "Mayhap, if I'd done more, you wouldn't fear Damien drawing eyes to your boy."

Ty held back his flinch, Bay cutting deep. "You can't take responsibility for what your family has done."

Bay raised a shaggy eyebrow, voice steady. "If not me, then who?"

Ty thought of Bill's arguments and his own inability to accept his past. Ty knew the burden of guilt's weight and that his next words were useless even as he offered them.

"Your family. They hold the blame." Ty stood, putting his back to Bay. "You chucked that name when you left the bastards behind. Helped Sunny and I when you had no reason to stick out your neck. Damn them for worshiping a fucking tree that does nothing but lead them to murder, not yourself for having a fucking lick of sense."

"And Finn?"

Ty did flinch this time.

"My men missed his cross through my territory. He'd never have gotten your kid if we'd done our job."

"Bay," Ty barked, tense. There was a hard look on Bay's face, warning he wouldn't back down, and Ty steeled himself against his next words. They always came back to this, every visit.

"Finn succeeded because of my pity." Bay wore the guilt like shackles. "I let a handful of kids barely younger than your boy is now enter my territory and did nothing but run them back to their sheep-herding bastard family."

Ty couldn't strike him. Couldn't blame Bay for what he hadn't known any more than he could blame him for the crimes of his forefathers. That didn't change the stretch of pain between them, something neither could forget.

"My son is alive, and so are we. The Hollowood who hurt Star rots in the ground same as those who hurt my sister. Neither of us can afford to borrow their blame."

Ty stalked off before Bay could speak, putting distance between himself and the memories he'd rather forget. Bay, for his part, kept his seat and let him escape.

Damien lay on his back with Star sleeping stretched against him. Star's body was twisted so he could press his face practically in Damien's armpit, baring the top of his thin back.

Lying in the sunlight, Damien stared at the thick silver scars marking the lean muscles. Bay had hinted about them, and Star had filled in the blanks. Or, at least, some of the blanks.

Sixteen.

Star was playful when it suited him, dangerous when needed, and, somehow, so sweet at his core. Knowing now about the monster of his childhood made things much clearer. The flashes of fear—incongruous with his fierce spirit—had been learned. That he'd said anything at all, and not bottled it up, was gift enough to convince Damien he wasn't alone in falling.

Damien gently moved soft hair away from Star's face. He stroked fingers down the slight stubble Star hadn't bothered to shave, admiring the strong beauty in his chiseled features.

Damien ached to be able to take that pain away, and what that meant was sobering. He wanted this. He wanted them in bed with wind and sun blowing through large windows and hours to enjoy each other. He wanted this prickly, gorgeous man to stay a part of his makeshift family. Lastly, he wanted to keep any madman from ever touching what was his.

Half-lidded green eyes peered at him. "You're thinking hard."

Damien snorted, scratching Star's chin like he would a cat's. Star purred as nicely, stretching to offer more skin. "It'd be nice to be able to lie in, no danger at our backs or threat to hunt." Star gave a little *mmm*, and Damien went on. "A bed of our own, one no one else claims."

Gorgeous eyes crinkled. "It sounds nice. Why not find it, then?"

Damien's lips twisted in a wry smile. "There's the bounty for one, but I have many reasons, and there are always more stacking up. A home is one of those dreams, Star, that men die still dreaming."

Star closed his eyes, snorting. "If you tried for a ranch, Knott would fire you as boss in half a moon, you know."

Likely, yes. "That's why he'd need to be foreman," Damien countered, accepting the attempt at levity.

"Hm. Ostra would listen to him, and Jonnie listens to her. Sound plan."

It was a lovely, if terrifying, thought. Damien held the image in mind for a beat of his heart, then sighed. "I'm not sure I'd want that, though. I might just like to sit back, farm a little patch of land, and be content."

Star didn't comment, apparently himself content to continue lying there. Damien gave a last stroke to that gorgeous neck before sliding down to touch where he'd left a mark on Star's shoulder.

He let his hand fall. "I should get up before your father *gets* me up."

That inspired a smirk. "He knows why I brought you up here."

"More reason."

Now those half-lidded eyes were narrowed. "It's still light out."

Yeah. Barely.

Damien sighed and slumped, cursing himself for being a fool. A fool growing dangerously attached, too late to stop if he'd ever had a chance.

Dawn streaked the sky with a splatter of gold and red paint. It looked bright and dark and altogether beautiful over the distant craggy hills. Star led Clay out of the corral. Their pack horse, Stomper, nipped at his hair while he passed. The horses could feel in the air that it was time to be off, and they seemed restless to get started.

"They're familiar with this place, huh," Damien commented, leading his own horse over to be saddled and readied.

"Bay gave me Clay," Star said with a small smile. He'd been a wreck, shaken and unable to find his way, but Bay had been patient. When Star had finally started leaving his room—wandering out onto the grounds and watching the corral—Bay had ordered Ty to stay back. Bay had then guided Star over to where a foal had been playing.

"This little lass is gonna be yours, kid," he'd told him. "She's a baby now and a lump of clay. You'll have to raise her up."

And then he'd set about showing Star how to do just that.

"He's the one who raised Stomper too," Star continued, shaking his head to dispel the old memories. "She's five now, and Stomper is seven, but they remember their first home."

Ty wandered their way. Star smiled, watching him collect the rest of their horses. He could feel Damien's eyes on him and shot a quick grin his way before focusing on his task.

The others arrived as he worked, and before long everyone was saddled, packed, and itching for the path.

Bay, standing and watching them mount, laughed. "Off again, I see. I hope the wind blows you back my way soon, lads. Feel free to bring your friends along again too." He winked, but there was a strange sadness in his eyes.

Ty sat stiff in the saddle, his face strangely blank. Bill, next to him, didn't look much better. Star wondered at that but shrugged internally, too used to their odd ways.

"Thank you," he said to Bay. If they were going to be weird, he'd have to take point. "We appreciate everything you've done for us."

"Aye," Damien added. "We appreciate everything."

His father was watching Damien now, and Star flashed a smile at Damien, hoping to cheer him a bit, before looking back to Bay. "I'll try and drag Dad back soon, Bay, and stay long enough that you can put us to work. You've my word. Damien, too."

Then he nodded and urged Clay forward, figuring one of them might as well set their party off.

"Ty?" Bill said behind him.

Star glanced back in time to see his father turn also, eyebrow arched.

"Sometimes he's the very picture of Sunny," Bill said. "She'd be proud."

His mother. A shiver went up Star's spine. His father, in turn, only looked sad.

"Aye," Ty agreed. "I wish she'd lived to see him."

Bill pressed his lips together and didn't respond, but Star felt a thrill of warmth. It was rare for Ty to speak about his mother, and the exchange left him with hope to hear more soon.

They rode off.

CHAPTER

✺

ELEVEN

That night, after Bay's men had split from them, they camped next to a stream that they followed the next morning. As they were riding in a loose line, they veered off on a worn trail.

"This will take us to the river crossing," Ty assured them.

Trees dotted the path, scattered markers in an almost straight line. Ostra commented on it.

Star grinned. "Planted to keep the route originally, before the path we're following was worn by travel."

His father nodded. "When you see trees in even rows like that, there's a reason."

They crested the hill and the river stretched out into the distance, wide and glistening under the summer sky.

A little house and a worn old barn sat beside it, with a pier stabbing into the waterline like a fishing pole trying to reel in a big catch.

They dismounted and led their horses the rest of the way, stretching their legs and watching. There was no sign of anyone else, though as they neared, a stooped figure came out and raised a hand in greeting.

"Well met," the fellow called, hobbling their way. He was young, his build thick and strong, but a twist in his leg made the cane in his hand necessary.

"Good day," Ty answered, and the others echoed him.

"We're looking for the boat," Damien said, patting Ink's black nose and giving the man a nod.

The fellow sighed. "I'm afraid there'll be a wait. Still, give me a bit and I'll have you crossing in no time. I just need to patch a hole."

There was an old draw-well with a metal trough in front of the barn, and Star wandered that way while the others talked to the boat's master. They could figure it out. He'd rather get a taste of water and explore.

There were no animals in the field or any smell that would suggest their presence, so they must have been long gone and the barn only for show.

The pump moved easily beneath his grip, but when he bent to lift the bucket, he heard the barn door open. It wasn't so empty after all.

"Well, well." The man at the head of the group whistled, raking his eyes up-down Star's dusty body, lingering at his hips. "Seems we have some entertainment while we wait."

A prickle of disgust and nerves ran up Star's spine, his body tensing, his hand curled but frozen. The next of the three smirked, resting his hands on his belt buckle. "Water might cost ya, pretty thing." His companions snickered. The man's closest partner had a gun trained on Star's stomach. A bad way to go.

Star tensed further as the first man adjusted himself in his pants, and panic reared in Star's breast. Then anger overtook it, and he tucked his chin down, meeting their gaze straight on with his own.

"Careful," he warned, all teeth. "I'm likely not the company you want."

"A pretty piece like you?" The leader ambled closer. The men behind him kept pace. "We only want to talk a bit. Come along with us and we can have a nice chat in that cool barn. Too hot out here, you see, and a mite too crowded. Maybe we can find a saddle for you."

Star clenched a fist, knowing that grabbing a knife would mean his death. He cursed his useless broken arm. Fear prickled at the back of his mind, his old friend ready to crash over him, but he shoved it back with brutal ferocity.

"Drop the gun, stranger," said a welcome voice from behind him, "or we'll drop the three of you."

Star's rising terror eased back. Turning his head, he spotted Damien, Ostra, and his father. Damien's guns were in hand, and

Ty's rifle was aimed straight at the leader. Ostra, in turn, had her gun pointed a little lower, and the smirk on her lips wasn't lost on the leader. Knowing he was beat, he sneered and shoved his companion's gun down.

"We just wanted company," he said. "Didn't realize this lad belonged to you. Seeing as you have a pretty lady right there, I don't suppose you'd be sympathetic? Especially since we come bearing a message for Damien Sole—you, right?"

Damien's face darkened. "Spit it out, then give me a good reason not to drop you here and now."

The spokesman shrugged. "Reason is you're said to be an honorable man. We have our guns away, don't we? We never planned to hurt the pretty fellow. We wanted to tuck him away, maybe use him as a bargaining chip. You are so fond of him and all."

A lie, clear as a sunny blue sky. Even if Damien might have fallen for it, which Star doubted, his father's cold face never changed.

"I thought you didn't know he was with us," Damien growled.

"Slip of the tongue! Kill me and you won't get the message. Isn't that worth our lives?"

"Say the message, then we'll see," Ty rumbled. It was a dangerous sound, and the man picked up on the warning quickly.

"Ram sent us," he spat out. "He wants Andy Knott and Damien Sole. Says he'll let the whole pack go if those two bring him back his property."

Damien scowled, confused. "Why the hell does this Ram think we have anything of his?" Then, something entered his eyes, and he looked sick. "Who," he repeated, "is Ram." Not a question, but a demand.

"You took his trinket and he wants it back. We lucked out, being here to catch you. We had to pick from three crossings. Maybe it's a sign, and you should give yourselves up and come along. Wouldn't want to cause a lady to lose her land and family, would you?"

"Then she's still alive," Jonnie said, coming toward them.

"Boss wants to make Sole and Knott sweat. He won't finish the fight till they're there to see it."

"What else do you have to say?" Damien snapped.

"Nothing, honest, just that." The man's bravado was long gone, his eyes now trained on Star's father. Few could hold a gun so long without wavering, but the double-barrel rifle hadn't budged an inch the entire exchange. What had changed was the look on Ty's face. Star hadn't seen that level of fury in years, and a chill set into his bones.

"Done, then?" Ty growled.

"Done."

Two shots ripped the air. When the third man, tucked at the back, lurched and went for his gun, bullets tore through him and sent him down with his companions. Star loosed a blade into the man's throat for good measure.

After, Star sagged back, closing his eyes. He was finally able to breathe easier with the leering men put to the ground.

"Son?" Star heard his father reload the rifle, then Ty's hand pressed to the back of his neck, cool against sweaty skin. Star leaned into the gentle hold.

"I'm sorry," he answered, shamed that he'd let the men unsettle him.

"I'll get your knife. You take a seat."

"I'm fine," he argued, but without energy.

"You haven't been in five years." Cruel, but true. The hardness hadn't left Ty's face, but it wasn't for Star. "Get moving, or I'll call Bill over. He was with the boat-master right, but he'll have heard the shots."

Star nodded and went as bid. He slumped down on a stump outside the dock shack, leaning his elbow on his knee and dipping his head. He worked at catching his breath, still shaken. The distance from the others helped, a semblance of privacy without being out of eyeshot.

Damien headed his way after a minute, a tin mug in one hand and Star's knife in the other. "Here." He squatted and passed him the mug.

Star took the mug, downing it in four scalding mouthfuls and letting the heat shock his system.

"Thanks," Star told Damien, then took the knife next, sliding it back with its brothers. Maybe his father was softening on Damien.

"That was quite a throw. You're damned fast."

Star quirked a brow. "Good shooting too."

Damien snorted. "Your dad doesn't take threats to you lightly or leave them to chance. I wanted to shoot them and am glad he started it."

Damien looked like he wanted to keep going, but Star refused to rehash that conversation. He'd said enough at Bay's. Instead, he turned the talk back. "You know who Ram actually is, now, I take it?" He directed the last to Knott as well, noticing him headed their way.

Damien gave a pained nod. "A sick bastard is what he is." Star waited, and Damien didn't disappoint. "His true name is Sam Hollowood. He killed Knott's wife fifteen years ago on the same night he stole her family's relic. A necklace, and Knott says it could tap into the sun's fire."

"A *relic*?" Star winced. "I'm sorry." It explained Knott's suffering, but not why Hollowood hunted them *now*. Narrowing his eyes, Star straightened. "What haven't you said yet?"

Damien shrugged. "Madmen hunt and steal them, mostly in the northern sheep country. Knott was raised there, and that's where he met his wife. The thing was supposed to be a big family secret, her pap's treasure, but somehow that insane bastard found out."

It was a picture Star'd heard painted a million times by his father. "And killed them for it," he finished, the thought chilling.

"Aye."

Knott held his face forcefully blank. This would have been before Damien met him, Star realized. How many years had he been grieving?

Spine stiffening, Star looked from Knott's craggy face to Damien's smoothly sad one. "He killed for it. Took it. Why is he still chasing you?"

Knott reached into his saddlebag and pulled out a torn strip of what might have been a woman's dress. The sight of the faded material gave Star a pang of sadness. Pain lay stark on Knott's face, and Star worried that he knew where this was going.

Knott pulled back a fold, revealing a small orb—golden with clear crystal drops in the center, circles of hollow-looking paleness trapped in a yellow sleep.

"*Truly?*" Star demanded, staring at the bauble. Needles pricked down his neck and back, the shock hitting hard. Star's instincts couldn't decide between fascination and revulsion.

"Damn it, and damn *him*," Knott said. "This thing was my wife's. Don't touch."

Knott's snap hurt for the second it took Star to remember himself and what sat there.

"A stolen relic is a curse," he reminded them, lost. "If it was hers, then it was tied to her blood. Better to bury it in the earth's bowels and live without. Why would you chase such madness?"

"Revenge," Knott said. "Even curses can't overpower a man's blood-price. I didn't care, but she and her father did. Foolish, they refused to give it up when Sam Hollowood came issuing threats." He swallowed. "Hollowood stole this in the night and set fire to our house. His people drove the cattle into a stampede, killing some and doing damage. They burned our barn and shot us as we ran out. They left me for dead."

Damien spoke next. "Hollowood knows Jonnie is mine, same as Knott. And he's pissed because, two years ago, we stole it back for Knott."

"So it's Knott and the relic he's after," Star summed up, mind churning with the new information. "And the rest of you for riding with him."

A smile, small and without humor, traced Damien's lips. "Not completely."

Star narrowed his eyes. "What else?"

"The night we retook that, I killed Hollowood's son," Damien admitted. "Shot the bastard in the head when he tried to shoot Ostra."

Knott threw the cloth back over the cursed thing and stuck the bundle back into his bags.

By sun and moon both, no wonder Hollowood wanted their blood.

He wanted to demand why they'd taken it back. What good was that over just killing the enemy and being done? All this trouble, all this pain, for a hunk of sap hardened around a drop of the sun's blood.

But he did know. Revenge. To give the lost blood of Knott's wife a purpose. Wasn't that what Star heard in his father's voice when he spoke of those who'd killed his family? A wish for vengeance? The relic itself was useless, and by some miracle Knott recognized that, but as a piece of his revenge?

At least Star knew, now, why Damien had no hope of his enemy ever tiring of the hunt.

"Why not chuck it into some pit?" Star asked.

"It was hers," Knott answered, the words a rumbled mix of anger and pain. "I hate the damn thing, but she died for it. I'm not throwing it away like some rock."

Star shivered. Better to do so and forget it, he thought, but didn't give the opinion voice.

"I had no idea Hollowood was behind the threat to Wendy," Damien continued. "We didn't know he tied her to any of it. She was never named like us, though she was there in the fields waiting. He must have learned she was Jonnie's sister, or maybe the bastard knew about her all along. He's using her to lure the rest of us into his trap. I'm sorry. I understand if the three of you want to leave us here. You've done your job, and no shame for leaving now. I'll pay, you've my word."

Star stiffened, struck as if slapped. "You think I'd leave you here like this? After everything?"

But how could Damien have known? Star himself hadn't realized his own intent until that moment. Staring down the loss of Damien, Star knew a clarity of purpose. Was this what his father felt when the wind breathed at his back? There was no guiding touch for him, just that hard, handsome face and exhausted eyes looking into his own.

"You've my word, Star. I'll come find you after we finish, so long as I survive."

Glaring, Star grabbed Damien by his shirt and yanked him forward, face to face. "I'm coming with you," he growled, "and I'll be at your back when you take that man down." His hair, having come lose from the tie, swung into his face, and he glared through it at the other.

Star had realized at Bay's that theirs wasn't going to be a quickly sated tryst, and Star would be damned before he let the bastard treat him like it was.

Damien reached out, as if sensing Star's thoughts, and slid his hand through the tangles of hair, getting his fingers caught when he stroked downward. Damien made no move to pull away, letting Star's grip keep him there the same as his own at the back of Star's head.

"I'm sorry," Damien said. "That wasn't what I meant." He sighed. "I want you safe, no lie, but we need all the help we can get. More even, now that I know Hollowood is at the head of this."

"You better be sorry," Star grumbled, but the sting was out. He eased off, and Damien rocked back on his heels, a slow smile spreading across his face.

"I guess you'll be coming, then." Damien cast an uneasy glance over to Ty.

"Aye," Star challenged, scowling.

"And your dad? He'll just let you?" No glance this time, but it was close. Star let it go.

"I'm old enough to decide." The weak pang in his chest was harder to force down, but Star wasn't going to back down on this. Cruel, maybe, knowing how it'd hurt his father. He knew how Ty felt about the relics. Instead of going down that path, he narrowed his eyes on Damien, waiting.

Damien shot him a thin grin. "I bet, now that particular problem has been dealt with, we'll find the boat isn't in such disrepair. The way the man kept talking about the barn—needing supplies from the barn, worrying he might not be able to carry it all—he laid it on pretty thick."

"Thankfully," Star muttered.

Damien poked him in the nose, and Star scowled again but had to fight to keep his lips from twitching.

"Thankfully, yeah. Maybe don't wander off on your own?"

Star rolled his eyes. They went back to the others, who shifted to make room for them in their small circle.

"We need to be honest," Damien started, looking to his group. Star watched them process Damien's words, each looking to Knott in an obvious attempt to gauge his reaction.

"Honest?" Ty demanded, his voice chillingly quiet.

Bill set his hand on Ty's arm. "What is it?"

Damien shared the basics with Bill and Ty—that the whole thing had started over a relic. It was a brief, condensed tale, touching on Knott's pain without baring his bones. Star watched his father throughout the telling, dreading what the end would bring.

Ty's face was as furious as Star had ever seen it, and on the last words of the story, he lunged toward Damien, snarling. Star slid between them before Ty could grab Damien. Back straight and chin up, Star stared Ty down as Ty glared straight through him at Damien.

"We'd seen one in Knott's things," Ty snapped, his words daggers, "but had we known it to have any part of this . . ."

Knott stood next to Star, his lips pressed thin. "This is on me, not the others."

Ty snarled again and paced three steps. Star's back hit Damien's chest, his eyes never leaving his father's shaking form. The circle broken, the others clustered closer, watching as Ty glared into the distance.

When Ty came back, tremors shook him. "They cause nothing but rot and death." He was nose to nose with Knott. Star, still in front of Damien, hovered uncertainly. "The Hollowoods have wiped entire histories from the land over those trinkets."

Star stiffened, pieces fitting into place. He'd never heard the name Hollowood before, but he recognized that fury on his father's face, and knew, too, what history Ty meant.

"We had no idea it was Hollowood behind Wendy's trouble," Damien snapped. Knott's face flushed fast, anger rising. "And we didn't start this fight."

Ty flicked a look at Damien, sneered, and turned his attention back onto Knott. "You lost your wife because of it? Her family? It could have been everyone you ever knew."

"They were all I cared about!" Knott roared, his muscles clenched. Anger crashed against anger, neither giving ground. "What, damn you, do you think you know about this?"

"More than you," Ty fired back, the cold of his voice like blades of ice. "They're madmen who use blood and those thrice-damned *gifts* to water their beliefs. When this is over, I suggest you take that cursed thing and chuck it into the deepest, darkest pit you can find. If it lost its intended bloodline, it'll bring nothing but trouble. Until you do, even if you kill *this* Hollowood, the rest will keep coming. Apparently deals mean nothing to those bastards anymore."

Damien and Jonnie grabbed Knott's arms, holding him back. Ostra stood near them, her face a blank mask. Would she stop Knott if he broke away, or would she stand there and let him?

Ty stormed away without waiting to see. After casting a desperate look at the others, Star took off after him, words ringing in his ears. Secrets were all Ty ever wanted to give him, but after that, Star wouldn't be left without answers.

Ty eventually stopped and Star came to his side.

"The Hollowoods." The name fell awkwardly from his lips. Ty's back, already so stiff it could have been a sheet of glass, didn't move. "Dad, I have to ask. Are they the ones who killed your people? And what *beliefs*?"

Ty turned slowly. Anger still burned in his blue eyes, but his face was again one Star knew. "They are madmen, Star, and ones I won't discuss."

Star tensed, hating those familiar words. Ty started walking again, but this time he wouldn't have his way. Star caught his arm, clinging.

"I need to understand," Star begged, hating the plea in his voice. There had been something desperate in Ty's words, and, try as he might, Star couldn't get the burn of them out of his ears. "You said you know those monsters, that entire histories were destroyed. I'm tired of all your half answers and refusals. You meant *your* history, I know it!"

"You don't need to understand," Ty said, and in his words Star heard years of loss. "Leave it, son. You know they died. Isn't that enough?"

Hurt, Star dropped his hand. "Fine." A bitter curl in his breast spurred him to add, "I should've known I wasn't worth an answer to you. I never am."

Ty stopped him with a grip that startled him more than hurt. Turning and finding pain twisted behind his father's eyes, Star swallowed hard.

"Dad?"

Ty loosened his hold but didn't let go. "It isn't a happy story."

Nothing could be that left so deep a hurt. "Holding in poison lets rot set deep. You told me that." Star saw Ty wavering and pressed forward; seconds could grant him time to shut Star out anew. "Are you going to let yours keep eating at you?"

Uncertainty danced behind Ty's eyes. Star wasn't sure which of them was more surprised when he started speaking.

"Hollowood comes from a family of monsters, ones that hunted me long before I knew Bill. Sunny and I lived as we do, always on the move at the whims of the wind, but we were young and surrounded by family who listened for us. Just like I do for you. These madmen who covet the relics hated us with passion equal to their greed, and hunted our people with the same hunger. My family carried no relics, but our people had been the source of them, and the Hollowoods believed some of the sun's blood ran through ours. When they attacked, your mother and I were the only two who survived."

A tremor caught in Star's chest and ran through his good hand. He'd known there was a horror in his father's past, but that?

"Because of their beliefs?"

"In a sun-damned tree." A flicker of hesitation showed on Ty's face, and Star moved closer as if it'd keep the man talking. By some miracle, Ty did. "They used it somehow to hunt us and decided that meant the earth wanted it done. Murderers, birthed on a septic homestead that should've been razed centuries ago, before we were dead and their bloodline swelled."

"I'm sorry," Star choked out, his frustration dying as horror seeped into his soul. He hated that his father had kept this from him, but how could he blame Ty for not wanting to speak of it? What if it'd been him alone, his father and Bill dead?

"Our bloodline is a secret, Star. Bill knows because his family found and took care of us, but no one else can, not even that bountied of yours. I need your word, son. Even after this matter finishes."

They hate us. The meaning of those words crept over Star slowly. He wanted to ask more but knew by his father's face that nothing else would be shared. Not yet.

"You have it."

Ty searched his expression again, eyes narrowed. Star could see the moisture gathering there and didn't speak, just met his eyes and tried to hide how the truth shook him.

"Thank you." Ty released him. Sighed. "I know you won't, but I don't care. I'm sending you back to Bay's with Bill. This is a matter for me to deal with, not you."

Star started. "What? No!" This time he grabbed his father's arm, holding on until burning blue eyes met his. "I'm not some kid anymore. I'm following Damien. If this man is one of the ones who destroyed your family, then we both have reason to help them."

Ty's fury rekindled. "*I* do, not you."

Star lifted his chin, glaring. "You're my family. My only family. They took the rest from us."

A muscle worked on Ty's jaw. Fury and pain roiled together as Star stared, unrelenting, back.

"I never should've opened my damn mouth. Curse Sunny for giving you her stubbornness." Ty jerked his arm free. When his father started off again Star didn't follow, instead watching the man put distance between them.

He'd known that madmen from the north had killed his parents' people, but never in so much detail. The horror of it, coupled with the knowledge that those men still carried on their hunts, explained Ty's refusal to travel there. Men lived who coveted the sun's blood and hated Star's own. *Why?*

When this was done and Hollowood dead, Star promised himself, he would make his father tell him. Ty was hurting and Star would give him more time but not forever. Shaking his head, wishing he could forget but knowing the words would haunt him, Star headed back for the others and left his father to gather himself.

"What, by the sun, was that about?" Damien demanded as soon as Star came close. Knott stood a short distance off with Ostra, his head bent low to hers. There was still an angry flush on his face but her hand, curled over his forearm, seemed to calm him.

"I've no idea," Star said, the admission thick and clumsy on his tongue. Ty had never tried to send him away before, and that he'd wanted to now shook Star.

Damien stared at him. Star looked away, the information he'd learned churning like acid in his stomach. He expected Damien to speak, but instead, he clapped a hand to Star's shoulder and let the matter drop.

They had barely ridden into the thick trees closing over Blue Rock territory when they came across a spring bubbling down from a rocky hill. Damien, still tense from before, was the slowest to dismount and head for the water.

"Dad won't stay mad long," Star offered, though his eyes betrayed his actual thoughts.

"He's worried," Damien pointed out, words stilted. He was furious over how Ty refused to see Knott's pain. Ty couldn't be blamed for his concern, but neither could he blame them for their silence. How could they have known Hollowood and that damn relic were behind this all? And how the hell did Ty know so much about the Hollowoods—things Damien himself had no idea of?

"Let the horses rest," Ty snapped, moving for the water with his own Shine and two of the pack horses. Star, with an apologetic grimace, joined him.

"They've a right to be worried," Knott said, joining Damien in watching their guides water the horses and drink. "This is a sun-damned mess and you know it."

Damien sighed, looking sideways to meet Knott's eyes. Ostra, clapping Knott's arm and giving Damien a wry look, left them.

"This isn't your fault."

Knott shrugged, neither agreeing nor disagreeing. His anger had dimmed, leaving behind a weary guilt that Damien didn't like. Before he could come up with something else to say, Knott led his horse over to the others.

Damien sighed again and, shoulders slumping, gave up. He went to the end of the line and wasn't that surprised when Star joined him. Damien rinsed his face in the fresh water, had a drink finally, and turned when Star stared at him. "Yes?"

"Dad doesn't actually blame you," Star said. "Not really. It's mostly the matter about the relics. They attached themselves to bloodlines and don't release that bond even for death. Those who steal them usually try to use them, and that's when things turn. They lash out unpredictably, tricking or injuring. Being near one makes him leery."

There had to be more to Ty's temper than that, but Damien was too damn tired to possibly start a new fight. "Don't worry about it."

Star appeared to chew over his words. There was no give in those gorgeous green eyes, so Damien waited him out.

"What does Knott's do?" Star finally asked.

Damien snorted. "Besides bring heartache?"

Star scowled and Damien surrendered. "It lit fires. He doesn't know much more than that. Says his wife's people were tight-lipped even after he married, and he hadn't cared enough to poke about."

They sat in silence, Star obviously chasing some new thought. Damien, having questions of his own, spoke up. "Has Ty told you about Hollowood and his ties to those hunters?" Damien didn't mean to sound so challenging, but the expression Star had worn left him sure of the answer.

Star pressed his lips together, eyes narrowing at a point past Damien's nose. "Yes. He knows of them. Says the whole family is in on the hunts."

"Damien, come here," Ty barked. Bill shushed Ty as Star pushed forward, not one to be left out of any conversation. Damien fought a weak smile and followed.

"Ram, Hollowood, however he styles himself," Ty said, "sounds like the problem. He's the one in the wrong, and you and yours were just trying to right things. Blood for blood."

His admission had all the sound of an apology with none of the words. Damien tried to think how to answer but never got the chance.

"Well!" a voice crowed. "Steady, steady—we've guns on the lot of you, and ammo to waste."

Shocked, Damien shifted slowly to face the voices. Three men were striding toward them, guns aimed and smirks wide.

"No one moves," the smallest of the fellows ordered, all crooked teeth under dirty white-blond hair. "We want the horses and the money."

They approached slowly. The little one edged closer to toe at one of their bags on the ground, soon joined in his search by his companions. While he and another man remained intent on the packs, the third flicked his eyes over Ostra, curling his lip. Before he could speak, Knott had the man on the ground, blood pouring from what had been his face.

Damien bit back a curse, diving to his stomach and grabbing his gun as a rifle cracked and more shots followed. A bullet cut through where his head would've been seconds before, close enough he felt the burn. A second crack sounded, but as Damien twisted, firearm in hand, the man was already dropping, a blade in his throat and a bullet in his chest. Blood bubbled from a gaping mouth as the dying man's gun hit the ground before he did.

Gritting his teeth, Damien ran his eyes over the rest of the scene, his weapon ready but not apparently needed. The attacker who'd leered at Ostra lay motionless in the dirt. The third man quaked where he stood, hands thrown over his head and splattered with his companions' blood.

"No fight!" the coward hollered. Damien could see that. Star, already at the man's side, patted him down for weapons.

"That's his gun." Star nodded to where it lay off the path. "He threw it as soon as Knott downed his pal." He whistled as he collected a long knife, the only other weapon to their prisoner's name.

Damien stalked over to the quaking bastard.

"Fine," he growled. "You don't want to fight? Make it worth your hide. First, what's your name?"

"Slate," the would-be thief answered, almost too fast. By the sun, had he never met with opposition before? "I'll tell you anything you want." His eyes—terrified, calculating—were too wild to trust.

"Make yourself useful, Slate, and maybe we'll let you go."

"Anything!"

Damien shared a look with Knott, who stood wiping blood off his knuckles, then raised a brow to Ty, Bill, and Ostra. All three were fine; he'd apparently drawn the only bullet fired from the other side.

"Bill and I can see if they've any horses," Ostra offered, turning on her heel and striding off.

Bill, blinking, watched her. "Guess I'm under orders." He headed in a different direction.

Jonnie, face pinched, looked away. Damien gave a hard nod to himself, then turned back to Slate.

"What is going on in this part of Blue Rock?" he demanded.

The fellow grimaced, eyes roving over their faces again. "Nothing, nothing of worth."

"Then I guess you aren't of use, are you?" Ty drawled, coming to stand at Damien's shoulder and keeping his doubtless reloaded rifle trained on its target. Despite his annoyance, Damien enjoyed the cool tone and the reaction it garnered. Their thief flinched, paling even more. "I want to know about the town and anyone of import. *Well?*"

"Last I was there, this man Ram was strutting around, claiming he had big plans for the place."

"Plans?" Jonnie demanded. Damien jumped, not expecting him to speak. Jonnie pushed past, and Damien stepped back to watch.

Their thief took in Jonnie's large, angry face, and empty, clenched fists, and shook hard. "I don't know! I don't know the man, don't want any part of this mess!"

Jonnie leaned forward, eyes burning and fists clenched. Even with his gun stowed, the thief edged away from him. "Is anyone from town dead? You know that much?"

The rapid blinking hurt Damien's eyes, but Slate's next words eased the gnats gnawing on his guts. "No one. Not to hear. He don't like the cattle ranchers, especially old Vin's family, but no killings I've heard!"

That was some comfort, at least.

"Vin is Wendy's father-in-law," Damien explained to Ty, keeping sight of Jonnie out of the corner of his eye as he whirled about and stalked a few steps away.

"And does this *Ram* have any family in town?" Ty demanded, turning back to their captive.

The man hastily shook his head. "Not a soul. Just a bunch of hires who don't seem to know him all that well."

"Nothing else to add?" Ty pressed.

"By the moon, man, I won't be trouble!"

Not if they kept a gun on him, but Damien had no doubt he'd shoot them all if given half a turn. Ostra and Bill, apparently having met up in their loop, came back leading five rangy-looking horses, saddled and lightly packed, the smallest of them with a rifle still on its back.

"No one else was with them," Ostra informed them. "Not that Bill or I saw."

Bill, still looking bemused, shrugged when Ty's narrow eyes turned on him.

"We'll let him go, then," Damien decided, and sighed, just plain tired, when Ty turned annoyed eyes on him. "We've his gun, knife, and horses. He's alone and on foot. What threat is left?"

Ty scowled. "Better to kill him."

"We beat him once. His friends are dead. Craven bastard isn't worth the bullet."

Later, Damien would wish he'd killed *all* of them.

CHAPTER

✺

TWELVE

Gut-deep unease spread through Star as they neared a thick pocket of flies and carrion eaters a short distance ahead of their horses. Before he could point it out, his father stilled and called, "Easy. There ahead."

One of the ranch's stock, Star wondered, squinting. The others had assured them they were close to Wendy's ranch. Had one of the cattle wandered off and gotten itself killed, possibly having taken a tumble from the cliff only a short crawl away? Surely if it was the work of Hollowood, there'd be more than one.

They fell silent, easing their horses into a trot. As they got closer, Ty's face became stony and Star's unease took on a distinct chill as he realized that it was no animal beneath the swarm.

The flies weren't disturbed by their presence enough to leave. The larger carrion eaters, however, were less brave. Blackbirds shrilled their dissent but didn't return, and vultures hovered, impatient, overhead.

Jonnie turned as pale as bleached bone. "A woman."

Star wasn't imagining the fear in his voice. As they drew closer he relaxed marginally. Still, the paleness never quite faded beneath his dark tan, and neither did the pain in his eyes.

Jonnie dismounted and knelt next to the woman's body, studying her torn features. "She was one of my sister's hands. Olivia. Hollowood's men shot her in the chest."

Star pulled one of his blankets from a saddlebag. He passed it to Ostra, and she walked over to Jonnie, giving him a gentle nod before spreading it out over the scavenged woman.

"We need to send someone to get the lay of the land," Ty ordered, and Star didn't miss how he eyed their surroundings with thinly veiled suspicion. "We can't lose our heads now, especially because we're so close."

A muscle twitched on Jonnie's jaw, but he didn't raise an argument.

"I'll go," Knott volunteered, cutting across anyone else. Ostra bristled and Knott frowned at her. "You're a better fighter when it comes to guns," he pointed out. "Watch the boss's back. The work I plan, up close is best."

"And your back?" Ostra asked, voice pointed.

"Knott can watch himself," Jonnie returned, words rough. He pulled his shovel off the pack horse, hands steady and face closed off. Worried, no doubt, about his sister and her family but practical enough to acknowledge they had to learn more before riding up.

"The more time we argue, the longer before there are answers," Damien cut in.

"Billy and I will head to town, get a measure of this place. Someone is always ready to spill gossip."

Damien turned to Ty now, frowning. Star braced himself for a fight. "What should the four of us do?"

"Don't make a fire, for a start." Damien gave Ty a dirty look as Star let out the breath he'd held. "Keep your eyes open and your weapons close." Then it was Ty's turn to scowl. "And keep your damn eyes on my idiot kid."

Star glowered.

Bill and Ty rode off easterly and Knott walked his horse south, not mounting until the others were out of sight. If he'd wanted to say something, he'd changed his mind.

The rest of them hobbled the horses and remained close to the blue-gray cliff, listening to the birds and beasts carrying on their business in the surrounding forest. The steady sound of Jonnie digging maintained a constant reminder of possible of danger.

"So long as they're chatting—" Damien sighed. "—we should be mostly fine."

Star snorted. "Maybe."

"Or they'll creep up on us, shoot, and *then* nature will take its quiet time," Ostra muttered, reaching over to pet Damien's knee. She glanced Jonnie's way with a guilty grimace. "We'll know when we know," she added.

The grimace twisted into a sad, slow smile, before she went back to watching the tree line. Jonnie wasn't saying a word, his work on Olivia's grave stalled as his eyes trained in the direction Star bet they'd find his sister's homestead.

Ty walked through the streets of the town slowly, leading Shine and feeling eyes and guns on his back. Knowing he was a stranger there deepened his unease. The saloon was easy to spot, its door propped open by a large hunk of red-black rock and its old steps sloping, half-sunk into the dry dirt below. He tied Shine's reins around a post, gave her neck a pat, and headed inside.

The saloon was the same as most: a low-lit, packed room smelling of sweat and libations. He paused just inside, looking it over with a critical eye, then stiffened at an all-too-familiar face at a corner table.

For the space between heartbeats, Ty considered stepping backward. He could take Shine at a run, grab Star, and be away before the past could seep into their present. Leave this whole mess behind, fast as the wind could carry. But no wind blew its warning to urge him down that path, and wind or no, Star would not leave his lover's side.

Charles Bearson stared back at him, green eyes hard in his craggy old face and lips pressed thin beneath a short-trimmed gray beard. He was older, the last of the brown faded from his hair over the twenty long years stretched between their meetings, but those eyes were as sharp as ever. He kept them right on Ty's blue ones as he kicked out a chair and waited.

Swallowing acid, Ty walked over and took the seat, keeping track of where those gnarled hands rested atop the table.

"Beresford didn't appreciate hearing that his son warms a bountied's bedroll," Charles said by way of greeting and in a tone that cut through bone. Age might've softened the bulk of his muscle to fat, but he remained as large and commanding as ever.

"*My* son," Ty corrected him sharply, fire roaring through his veins, but lowered his voice when those at the tables nearest them shot over curious looks. "And your nephew's opinions can choke him. Star makes his own choices, and Damien Sole is one. Mae's damn dreams don't give any of you a right to pry."

It didn't matter that Star's choice aggravated him. Ty would die before he let that damn Bear, Beresford, think he had any say. Same for Charles.

Charles just hummed, fingers tapping the stained tabletop. He could play all he wanted at the benign old man. Ty knew him and his family too well to buy it.

"What type of man is he?" Charles asked next.

Ty bristled, his anger soaring higher at the affront. "He's my son. *Her* son. He's a damn good man, and you have no right to even ask it."

The look Charles sent his way was insulting. "The bountied, you stubborn, proud fool."

Chagrined, Ty turned away, eyeing the bar and the satin-and-lace-clad woman manning it. A drink would make that answer easier to give. Feeling the rage simmer down to a low boil, and one not just a little tainted by shame, Ty wished he dared have a drink and numb the senses he'd likely soon need.

The words, when they came, were painful to force out past his pride.

"Damien is honorable," he admitted slowly. "His people follow him through hell, and they trust him to be at their backs. Sun curse it, I trusted him at mine."

And he would again if given the choice. For all his faults, Sole had crossed the Sun's Scar, all for a woman who he considered his. Not only that, but he'd proven himself time and again on the trip, both firm under danger and quick-thinking when needed.

"You'd call him an honorable criminal, then?" And there was the sarcasm Ty knew to expect. It lay thick and bitter atop each of Charles's words. "You, the child-stealer?"

Ty clenched his fists to keep himself from throwing a punch into that lined face. "Sunny was never going to belong to your nephew, Charles, and neither was Star." Certainty weighted his heavy words. "He belonged with me then and still does now. Beresford would smother him as he did *her*, and how could I trust any of you to keep him safe when you failed to keep Sunny so?"

The benign look vanished. "What message did she send that brought you to her so quickly, those twenty years ago? You crossed the world in a leap."

Memory of that terrible dash and its horrific conclusion still haunted Ty's dreams. Damn Charles for thinking he had any right to know.

Ty told him anyway. "She wrote she was dying."

Charles didn't so much as blink. "So a lie."

Cold, cruel, and spoken by a man who had no idea who Sunny had been or the horrors that had made her that way even before the ones Charles knew. Knowledge, truth under the pretty, could seed a rot impossible to dig out when watered only with pain.

"She died, didn't she?" Ty's words came out a choked growl. He wanted to seize that old, brick-thick neck and squeeze. The cool regard in Charles's eyes assured Ty that he saw that desire and found it amusing.

"She *is* dead." There was always a *but* with these people, and Charles never disappointed. "Her son isn't." And, because that whole damn family never knew when to quit, "Come back when this sorry mess is over, lad. Everything will be forgotten. We just—"

"Save it," Ty interrupted. "You know I'll kill before I betray her."

A sigh came as answer. Charles shook his head. "What of the kid?"

"What of the danger there? The same danger that drove Sunny mad? Sneered at by the people around her, a prisoner on your lands? You want me to take my son back to that kind of life? A place where enemies know to find us? Those bastards have broken their agreement with Bay twice now, and I refuse to chance it happening again after we dispatch this newest Hollowood."

"Neither of you ever tried to fit in," Charles snapped back, ignoring the last part of Ty's speech. "She ostracized herself, that high-headed way of hers and her refusal to associate with anyone except you and my nephew. Then you, clinging to Bill and twisting away from anyone else who might offer you a new life. And your enemies? I was here to fight them before you even knew a Hollowood was in this land. Leave here and they can always find you. Better to have protection at your back than be alone in the world. Or is that what you want for the kid?"

"Protection? You're here, yeah, but only you, and the local bastard Hollowood is still alive."

"Any more of us drop down on this place, every Hollowood eye'd be on it. That any good for the boy?"

Ty leaned forward, sneering. "None of you ever took the threat seriously. You think I believe you'll start now? Had you back then, they never would have gotten to Sunny in the first place. Then you made her a prisoner, destroying what those sick bastards left of her spirit. You think I'm going to let any of you close to her son?"

Charles sneered back. "I think you want him safe. Or am I wrong? Do you not care if he comes out of this sun-be-damned shit-show alive?"

Ty glared, tired of humoring him. "Will you tell me what's happening here, or do I need to chance my son's head on the words of some stranger likely to be an enemy?"

"Keep your skinny ass in that chair," Charles growled, every inch the bear his family took after. "My eldest great-nephew Aric has already attached himself to that hulking bountied's sister, claiming—rightly—to help. You'll collaborate our story if you don't want your kid to learn some uncomfortable truths."

Ty bristled. "You expect me to trust the Bear's son to keep his mouth shut when Star's right there on the same ranch?"

Charles leveled a look that would have melted sterner spirits. "If it means Star's safety, you're damned right I do. Aric and I are gonna be your friends, as far as the whole pack is concerned. We'll sort the rest later. Now shut your damned mouth and listen to what's what."

Ty stiffened, but by the strain in Charles's voice there was more unpleasantness to hear.

"This Hollowood calling himself Ram is waiting. He makes threats and killed the local Blade. Put his own man the Blade's place, claiming him to be one of the Sighted even if he hasn't the tattoos, and not a thing anyone could do. The only reason a message got out to your *friends* is that he wants the kid's man, near as I can tell."

"It fits with what we've learned on the way," Ty gritted out, the admission dry on his tongue. The entire mess was an elaborate setup for blood revenge.

Charles raised a brow but let that go. "I've sent for more help from some friends in the area, but it'll do damn little good. This whole situation doesn't add up."

Ty would choke on his own tongue before he filled in Bearson's holes. "Why are you here at all?" Then Ty's eyes narrowed and he answered that himself, voice hard. "Mae."

Beresford's wife. A quiet, determined woman. He'd have thought she'd keep mum rather than help them, even if her relic played a thousand dreams through her nights. Hadn't she done so before, after all? When those dreams had concerned Sunny? She'd admitted as much *after*, right in the first and only letter she'd ever sent Bill after Ty tore them both out of the Bearsons' lands permanently.

"Only Aric and I could come from our family. She was resolute on that. So, here the two of us are to meet you in this shit-show."

"This is none of her business," Ty snapped. "Or yours."

Charles grinned. It was a chilling sight, his teeth bared in obvious threat. The green eyes over that grin were hard. "If you're really that willing to let pride keep Star from having backup, maybe it should be our business and not *yours*."

"How can I trust you aren't here to steal Star away?"

"You do or you don't." And he kept right on, not giving Ty a chance to speak. "Mae says he is bound up tight in the bountied. If the price on that man isn't removed, it's just another danger on the lad. We get rid of Hollowood, the bounty goes. So, here we are."

Ty scowled. "She could have helped before everything else happened. *Now* she wants to stick her nose in our lives?"

Charles scowled right back, the look close to a sneer. "You know what your sister and my nephew did to Mae. Now, shouldn't we be getting back so you can introduce me to our new friends?"

Ostra and Damien flitted between hovering around Jonnie and granting him a wide berth. Since Star had no idea how to comfort him except by offering what they couldn't—to ride in, blind, to Wendy's ranch—he kept his distance, instead watching for the others' return. The questions that'd bothered him since his father's tale about the Hollowoods roiled in his gut, adding unease to a tense situation.

Knott came back first, carrying the good news that the path to Wendy's was clear enough. Star, sitting next to Damien as he finished applying salve and redressing his arm, nodded thanks to Knott and shot Jonnie a weak grin. "Looks like we'll see your sister soon."

Damien finished with the bandages and Star leaned against him, catching his eye. The furrowed brow and expectant look Star received in turn should have made him laugh but, instead, the hollow feeling in his gut deepened. This was his best chance to get his question answered. Ty gone and nothing immediately pressing on them until the last of their group returned.

Now or never, he told himself.

It was Ty's own fault. Had he not wanted Star to look elsewhere for answers, then he should have given them himself.

"What do you know of Hollowood's family?" Star grimaced. His question had come out a whisper. Foolish. It wasn't like Ty could hear.

Damien huffed. "Not much, apparently. Your dad seems more familiar with my enemy than I."

Damien wasn't wrong. Star shrugged. "But you might know something he doesn't."

It wasn't Damien who answered.

"They aren't social, but there are rumors enough of them being bloodthirsty and unstable." Knott's gruff words reflected his cutting scowl. "They've the largest flock in the north, and coin enough for ten families. Most in the area have some business with them. Even my family did."

Star met Knott's sneer and waited out the short silence.

"Sam had the name but raised only horses, no sheep. I figured him for a distant connection. Didn't like him—no one did—but not one of us saw that murderous side until too late."

Star flinched. "I'm sorry to pry." Guilt pricked down his back. They knew only their issues with this Hollowood, not others'. All they knew was that he poked at their wounds.

"You're riding into this mess at our sides. You've a right to ask."

More right than they knew, really, but it was obvious the answers he wanted couldn't be found there. What had he expected?

No, they weren't the ones he needed to press. When this was over, Star promised himself, he'd have answers from his father.

He heard the horses first. His free hand on the hilt of a blade, Star slid to his feet seconds before the others found their own. When Ty broke through the tree line, Star loosed a half laugh. It wasn't Bill who rode up with Ty, however, but a gray-headed grizzly of a man.

The others held their silence, watching curiously and letting Star take point. Star lifted his head high. The frown on his father's face left unease in his gut. "Glad you're finally back," Star greeted his father, "but where's Bill?"

"Still gathering information."

Not much of an explanation but Star held back questions, not sure how to get around the prickly mood his father was in. Instead, he turned to watch the stranger slide from the saddle with the ease of a younger man. Star half lifted one hand in greeting only to drop it as the fellow let out a loud snort. Ignoring the rest of the company, the stranger studied Star with a critical eye. Star didn't like the way thin lips twitched around probably rude comments.

"Star," he introduced himself, and couldn't stop his frown. "You are?"

His question was met with a toothy grin behind a short white beard, and the expression transformed the fellow's face from dour unpleasantness to bright merriment.

"Call me Uncle Chuck, kid." Mirth filled his words. "That's what they all call me over home. I'm an old friend of Ty's."

A friend who Star'd never met before. Ty answered his wary look with a stiff nod and a strained expression that left Star hesitant. Maybe an acquaintance, but there didn't seem much friendly between the two.

Star forced a smile. "Well, we could use all the company we can get. Dad told you where we're headed?"

Damien stood at Star's side. Not the most subtle guard, Star knew, but it was a nice thought. He bumped his hip into Damien's gently, careful of the belted gun, and shot him a grin.

"Uncle Chuck" fixed green eyes on Damien, one shaggy eyebrow arched. "You're a bold fellow."

It was Ty who sighed this time. Damien just blinked. "I— Yes?"

What?

Before Star managed to voice his confusion, Chuck grabbed his arm and pulled him over to their horses. The others, slowly trailing them, seemed to mean nothing to him.

"Well, lad," Chuck declared, "mount up. Wendy is waiting, and no reason to keep her pacing when the news is this good."

A little wrong-footed but charmed despite himself, Star followed. He still wondered at his father's scowl but didn't have much chance to question it. Chuck took up most of his attention as they rode back, keeping up a constant litany of information and questions.

"My eldest grand-nephew and I were passing through on our way to Ameson when we heard there was trouble hereabouts. Figured we'd help, seeing as I'd gotten a telegram that you and Ty were heading here. Good thing too. Not a one in Wendy and Coy's house knew that bastard Ram's actual name."

Star was desperately curious about said telegram, but the angry look Ty wore at Chuck's words convinced him it was better not to ask. He knew what he'd be told, anyway—that it was none of his damn business.

"Lucky chance," Damien pointed out stiffly, and Star appreciated the question in his voice.

Chuck shrugged. "Everything's a chance, kid, and seeing as those two wouldn't leave anyone stranded, how could I not offer?"

Ty hadn't spoken since they'd started riding. Star wished Bill was here. Not only because he was good at whittling away Ty's sour moods, but Star was curious if he also knew Chuck.

"Good of you to stay," Star offered.

"Eh, we're happy to help, my grand-nephew and I. Aric's about your age." Chuck threw Star an easy grin. It was hard to hold on to his unease. "A bit hard-headed, but he gets that honestly enough. You'll meet him soon. Maybe the two of you will get on."

Star offered his own shrug. "I'm sure we will."

Chuck nodded, then turned the talk to the situation at the ranch. By the time they arrived, Star knew more about what they were riding into than he'd ever thought possible.

At first, the couple had lost scores of livestock but no men. Then, months ago, one had been shot in the arm while riding guard, so he and four others took off, forgoing their last pay for what they called the sake of their lives. Vin—Coy's father—and his sister Andrea had come to stay with the couple to help out.

Jonnie livened up as they spoke, firing eager questions that their new guide seemed happy to answer. The more smug Uncle Charles got, the surlier Ty's expression.

It was almost a relief to ride into the little ranch's yard. The naked fear and hope in Jonnie's eyes switched to joy as a woman came tearing out of the house. Red hair flying in her haste, there was no question who she was.

"Jonnie!"

Jonnie leaped down and swept her into his arms in hardly a breath.

"Wen," he sighed, setting her down only to crush her in his big arms. She stayed close when he let her go.

"How is everything, Jon?" She leaned against her brother. "Coy and I were worried."

Relief showed on every line of his broad face as he smiled at her. "Better now."

Star's chest tightened at the affection the two shared.

"Good to hear," a large blond woman cut in, drawing their attention away from the heartwarming reunion. "I'm Andrea, Coy's sister. That old twig looming back there in the doorway is our dad, Vin."

"Nice to meet you," Damien greeted, following where she pointed. Sure enough, Star saw a man near Uncle Chuck's age standing with arms crossed and a rifle at his feet.

"Not nice to meet anyone in this situation," Andrea snapped. "Still, come along inside. We'll get you fed."

Vin vanished back inside, not waiting for them. They followed, Wendy and Jonnie not letting go of each other. Star fell to the back, taking time to look over Wendy's place. His father took up one side of him, Chuck the other.

Wendy's house, two stories and wide-built, sat surrounded by land that showed care. It was a beautiful home, and Star didn't blame their unwillingness to give it up. Knowing what he did now, he had to wonder what Hollowood would have done if they'd actually accepted his deal.

A rough-looking fellow met them inside the doorway, gun raised and eyes questioning. No one had bothered filling him it, it seemed.

"Just my brother and some friends come to help," Wendy assured the man, Andrea having continued past. "No worries."

The fellow nodded and holstered his gun. "Glad to have help."

The interior showed the same care as the outside, the rooms and their furnishings worn but tidy. Two little brown-haired children peered down at them, wide-eyed, from the central stairs.

"And there," Wendy grinned, "are your niece and nephew, Jonnie."

Jonnie's face softened as he headed their way. "Look how big you two are." They let him tousle their hair, hardly needing to reach to get to them.

Ostra joined him, digging out the wooden man she'd carved and rising to the tips of her boots to hand it to the eldest. The boy took it, wide-eyed again.

"What do you say?" Wendy called, grinning.

"Thank you," the child said in a rush, tugging the little man close and then holding him out for his toddling sister. She touched it carefully, and Ostra's face was a mix of pride and sweetness Star rarely saw from her.

"They still keep the others upstairs in Andy's room. Well, except the dog you gave them on your last visit," a new voice commented. Another man joined them from the other room, blond and average height. By the lines of his face, similar enough to Andrea's, Star took him to be Wendy's husband. "Candice stole that one, and poor Andy has given up on getting it back with the rest."

Ostra grinned, wicked and more herself. "I'm glad they still like them. It's good to see you again, Coy."

Coy snorted. "*Love* them, Ostra. Candy is still learning her words, but she knows 'dog' and she knows 'aunty.'"

Ostra flushed.

"Anyway, mind coming to the kitchen? Dad went to collect the rest of our crew, and we should soon all be set there. You can fill your stomachs while we fill you in."

The table where they gathered was a sturdy, well-worn wooden testament to more than one generation of gatherings. Star sank into a waiting chair gratefully, his father on one side and Damien the other. The ache in his arm lessened as the salve from Bay did its job, but he could definitely use some rest.

Others joined them, greeting their bosses with nods and the rest with grunts or a raised hand. It was easy to pick out Chuck's actual grand-nephew from the crew. The young man shared not only Chuck's height and musculature, but those same sharp green eyes swept over their faces.

Star nodded politely when they landed on him, not expecting the furrowed brow or crooked frown.

"Get over here, Aric," Chuck barked. Sure enough, the frown turned Chuck's way and he did as bid.

"Help yourselves," Vin ordered, dragging Star's attention back.

"There were more of us," Wendy told them over a cold spread of beef and bread. They'd all tucked in close around the homey kitchen, some at the table and others leaning against the walls. The bunkhouse table was longer, they'd been told, but everyone had taken to staying together as much as possible around the ranch.

"Cowards," a big ranch hand sneered from where he sat. Slamming his water down, he shoved back from the table, the legs of his spindled chair scraping over the boards of the floor. The door to the yard slammed shut behind his back.

"He's taking it hard." Vin sighed. "They left us in a lurch, no mistake, but no soul can truly blame them."

"Except you can," Uncle Chuck countered, his bushy eyebrows bunched together in a hard line. "The world needs cowards like it needs the brave. Someone has to live when the fools all die. Doesn't mean we have to smile about their spinelessness."

Vin gave a wry snort. "Aye." Star felt the weight of those eyes once they moved his way. "What brings you boys on with this lot, anyway?"

"Damien is a friend of mine," Star answered, lifting his chin.

Chuck snorted. "Must be a damn good friend."

Ty shot him a glare at the same time Star did. Damien snorted. The blond next to Charles wrinkled his nose at the three of them, expression not quite a sneer.

"There've been murdered cattle," Vin reminded the room, glowering them back into focus. "We'd hoped you were Olivia coming back. She's been gone for several marks now. Not that we don't appreciate the extra hands."

Damien and Knott shared a look, but it was Jonnie who spoke up.

"If we guess right, she won't be coming back," he told them gravely.

Their hosts' faces darkened as they heard about their finding a body on their way there.

"Damn it," Vin cursed. Coy slid his hand around Wendy's as the group digested the news. "Hell of a woman."

"Looks like we're nearing the end," the hand who'd met them at the door pointed out. The set of his jaw promised blood.

Uncle Chuck snorted. Star frowned at him.

"It's always the end," Chuck explained, the twist of his lips out of place in the grieving crowd. "Keep your guns close, all the same."

It was a long evening. Star let his father poke the healing stitches on his arm, glad to see the infection easing. The break itself, finally given a chance to rest, felt better.

Bill wandered in near dusk, smelling of ale and full of rumors. Star didn't miss how Bill jerked back, startled, at the sight of Chuck among Wendy's crowd, and intended to put the screws to Bill as soon as he got him alone.

"Good to see you, Bill," Chuck greeted, a leer beneath the words.

"Charles," Bill muttered, throwing Ty a frown. Aric, who hadn't strayed far from his uncle's side, turned his back and left the room.

"Is Uncle Chuck an old friend of yours too?" Star asked Bill. He earned a wide-eyed look from the usually calm man. "*What?*"

"I told the lad that's what I'm called," Charles said, the smirk on his lips as sharp as his gaze. Star shared a puzzled frown with Damien but didn't speak. It wasn't the place or time to press. Not under so many eyes.

The strange confrontation ended there, Bill sticking close to Ty's side and neither of them willing to cave to Star's curious prods once the room's attention shifted. Soon enough, night fell and it came time to spread their blankets out in the parlor.

Frustrated, Star left his father and Bill to their secrets and headed out on Damien's heels to get his bedding. He'd have his answers, he reminded himself. He just had to wait this out.

"Chuck," Bill muttered.

"Chuck," Ty agreed blandly. He leaned against the wall, gaze keeping steady watch over the moonlit grounds. He'd taken his watch in the kitchen, as far from the others' ears as he could manage without actually heading outside. As expected, Bill sat next to him, his own watch not due until dawn.

"Of all the damned Bears."

"Of all the damned Bears *and* their grand-nephews."

Bill's frustration didn't mirror his own, not even close, but Ty felt good hearing the echoed aggravation. Nothing moved outside the house save the wind-stirred trees. The sky was overcast, the moon and his children hidden in thick cover.

"What are you going to do?" Bill asked.

What indeed. Ty breathed out, knowing the answer and hating it. "I tell my son what I can once this mess finishes."

Ty saw the sharp twist of Bill's head in his periphery. Annoyed, Ty turned back to the window, lips pressed.

"Truly?"

"Not until this mess is over and I know he's safe. Then, yes. You're right, and so is that old bastard when he says I'm keeping my kid from his best protection, sun-damn him. The Bears knew before I did that a Hollowood stood this far south. If we survive, I'll tell Star about *her* and *him*, and let my boy decide what we do next."

His son. Damn them all for saying Star was anyone else's. Ty seethed as Bill digested his words. When Bill hummed, Ty finally looked back.

"And if the wind disagrees?"

Ty flinched, closing his eyes on the next three beats of his heart. Could Bill never leave anything alone? When he opened them again, he stared back outside, seeing but not seeing the dark-lit tree line. Instead he pictured Star alone, trying to navigate a world without him. Could Ty ignore the call again?

"Then I try to explain and hope he's still willing to listen. Star doesn't hear it like I do. Not like Sunny did or any of our people. Maybe because I've always heard it for him."

"He'll take it hard. I'll tell him with you. It's my blame too. And we'll follow whatever path he chooses."

Side by side, as always.

"Bill . . ."

"I chose you over my own sister, Ty, and I'd choose you again. You're my brother, and that isn't going to change. Still, it'll be a damned difficult story to tell."

It was a painful enough one to live. How was he supposed to find the words, ones that would tell it all without breaking his son's heart? Knowing that Bill would be at his side as he told it took some of the weight away. Maybe, somehow, his son could forgive them.

CHAPTER

✷

THIRTEEN

Ty woke Star when it was time for his watch. Stretching his good arm and rolling away from Damien, Star rose to his feet. Chin high, he met his father's questioning eyes with a look he hoped said what was needed.

By the downward tilt of Ty's lips, it did.

Ty followed on his heels as Star took the chair by the kitchen window, but he didn't take the seat next to him. Instead, he stood at Star's side and gazed over the moonlit yard.

"What's going on?" Star demanded quietly so as to not wake the others.

"That isn't much to go on, son."

Star fought back a sigh. The moon's light promised no threat yet, so there was time to talk. "Who are Charles and Aric?"

He saw the press of his father's lips out of the corner of his eye and waited out the play of thoughts behind his scowl. "They aren't a concern, Star."

"Dad."

That earned a sigh. "After we finish here."

Startled, Star nearly turned from his post before catching himself. The defeat in Ty's voice roused an ache in his chest.

"Then you and I will talk. I promise, you'll have your answers. All of them."

No matter how much he wanted Ty to stop with the half answers, it hurt to make *him* hurt. Curling his good hand around his father's wrist, he squeezed once, thankful.

"I'm sorry," he told him, meaning it but unwilling to drop the demand. Thoughts of finally getting those long-sought truths occupied his mind as, left to his vigil, he stared out at the night. Hope and fear circled each other, welcome distractions from his guilt.

Even so, once he'd traded places with Damien, it took only seconds for sleep to find him.

Morning brought its own diversions. After a quick breakfast, Andrea, Jonnie, and Vin headed out with a handful of hands to check the cattle while the rest held down the house. Things would move quickly now, they were sure. Once Hollowood found out Damien and his crew were present, he wouldn't hold back.

Star perched next to Damien on the old, thread-bare couch that took up the bulk of the small parlor. From there, he watched Ostra whittle where she sat, legs crossed, by their feet, as had become his habit. It was fascinating to see the forms slowly wear down into recognizable shapes.

This one was a long, very non-human shape. A cow, if he had his bet. It was still more block than figurine, and he eagerly anticipated seeing the start-to-finish work.

Ostra threw him a quick smile. "Maybe, once you've a second hand, I'll get you to help make them their little army?"

Star grinned, warmed by her offer. "I'd love that."

She nodded, then set back to work, her knife once more shedding curls of wood into the pile.

"What will you carve first?" Aric asked from where he leaned near the window, startling Star. He was a riddle Star couldn't quite grasp. Aric had rarely left Star's presence since they'd risen, and while he'd politely reply to anyone, it was Star who kept his attention.

Star shook off his unease and considered the question. "A horse." In his mind's eye, he could see a carving of Clay coming to shape at his hands.

Ostra snorted. Surprised, Star glanced down and found her gazing back at him, eyes glinting.

"Maybe something easier first," she suggested lightly.

He laughed, accepting the advice. "I'll think some more about it, I guess."

Bullets cut through his last words. Shattered glass sprayed the air, carpeting the floor where everyone dropped with startled curses.

Star crouched where he and Damien had pulled each other. His lover had a gun already in hand, returning blind fire as curses fell from his snarling lips.

Knott and the remaining hands took to the stairs, their bodies low. Coy grabbed a rifle from the wall rack and ran after them, but hesitated at the foot of the stairs, throwing a concerned glance his wife's way.

More bullets sang, a blind volley no less dangerous for it.

"Go," Wendy mouthed, barely saying the word.

Blood dripping down her chin from a scrape, she kept her children pressed to the hardwood floor as she tugged them toward the carpet. She kicked it out of the way and then peeled the boards up, one after another, revealing a hidden pit. Carefully, she lowered each down into the crawl space.

"Stay there," she ordered them sharply. "Andy, hold on to your sister and don't you let her go." Then she replaced the boards and the carpet, jaw clenched tight.

Star watched it all, mind racing. A hand caught his arm. Star jerked, startled, and looked at Ty. His father had been near the wall seconds before. When had he moved?

Ty snatched his gun out of its holster, only to press it, grip-first, into Star's hand. Star's heart lurched. Ty closed Star's fingers over it when they started to shake. Squeezed, then tugged him along toward the front corner of the parlor.

Knives would be useless. There was no other choice.

The third rush of bullets slowed.

"We don't need to include anyone else," Damien yelled. "You and me, Hollowood. I know you're out there."

The bullets stopped outright.

Uncle Chuck's growl drew Star's eye just in time to see him point at Aric. "Stay down here with the kid." Not waiting for an answer, Chuck took to the stairs while Aric scowled.

Star leaned close to his father, hand gripping the gun and head throbbing with his pulse. Angry fear made him want to yell at Damien for offering himself up. It took strength to hold his tongue.

"I want that bastard Knott too," Hollowood yelled back, obviously done with whatever counsel he'd been doling out. "And Jonnie, his sister, and that other bitch redhead."

Damien growled. "The table," he hissed to Bill and Ostra, then raised his voice to call out to Hollowood, "You know we can't do that." He darted for the kitchen, Ostra and Bill at his heels.

Wendy and Aric, taking Damien's cue, grabbed the couch and shoved it, getting it between the closed front door and the entrances to the parlor and kitchen. Ostra and Bill took positions by the windows.

"Keep your focus," Ty ordered Star, dragging his attention from the others' movements, "and watch the back yard. It's open on your side, so you should be able to see. And keep your head down."

So saying, Ty lurched up and yanked the blind down before taking cover again. Star, dropping the gun next to him, mirrored the action with the side window as the other blinds were pulled down as well. His injured arm, already throbbing, almost screamed at the tension traveling down from his shoulder.

Hollowood laughed loudly, calling, "Go ahead, then, and try to crawl out of this. We have you surrounded. What say you, Sole? Should I start my count, or are you reconsidering?"

Wendy took the place by Ty. Watching her, Star missed Aric's movements until he brushed his side. Star twisted a look Aric's way that went ignored. Ducking behind Star and gun in hand, Aric canted slightly to see as well as he could through the slit of the blind.

What, by the sun, did he think he was doing?

"Count away," Damien called, kneeling in the far corner of the kitchen, Ostra at the other side of the window. The table stretched between them and the entryway, a second barrier if they were stormed. "You'll get your answer."

"Breathe, Star, and focus," Ty ordered. He already had his gun trained outside. Something must have caught his eye; seconds later, the first barrel of his gun exploded. A cry went up, then pandemonium. There was no time to do more than hope that luck was not with the enemy.

Bullets whistled through the walls. Ty threw himself backward and slid into the corner, reloading as swiftly as possible. Then he lined up a shot again. Star, adrenaline shooting through him and chasing away the horror of what he held, focused on his own shots, ducking and firing as best he could. Bullets tore through walls as the enemy fired blindly.

Aric remained at their side, near enough Star could hear him grunt as a large splinter drove into his arm. It didn't slow Aric.

The children were screaming below the floorboards, their cries barely audible over the explosions. Star cursed and fired, ducking to the floor to reload only to get up and do it all over again. Splinters tore his right cheek. Twice bullets passed close enough to draw blood. He barely noticed the burn over the pump of his heart and the scream of the fight.

Blood splattered from his father's ear, but Ty was otherwise unharmed, still shooting, ducking. More poured down Wendy's arm, but she was relentless.

Aric aimed over Ty and Wendy's shoulders, no longer bothering to fire out his own window. Star followed suit, kneeling to shoot through the freshest hole next to them, then pressing against the wall when three bullets clipped where he had been. One caught his knee, little more than a scratch.

Seconds, minutes—time was a stretch of fire, screams, and whistles. When he paused to reload, he saw Damien still going strong and clung to the hope he'd stay that way.

A rapid-fire explosion echoed, followed by an answering flurry of shots, but none came their way. Star jerked, looking to his father. Ty's face went stony as he continued shucking shells and reloading.

"Thank the moon and keep off the sun." Wendy sighed, daring to peek through the blinds. She fell back seconds later, lips pressed but eyes hopeful.

"What?" Damien hissed.

"The others," she answered.

Damien dove to the window, shoving the blind up and daring a new round. Star and the others followed his cue, and a few rounds went off from the floor above them, though too few to be comforting.

It was silent soon after that. Long, empty silence, made more horrible by the sobbing beneath them. They didn't dare go to the children, waiting in case someone came along.

Star looked to those closest, then slid to Wendy and tugged off the sling with his free hand to press it against her shoulder. His father took over a second later, having two free hands. Star nodded thanks, then called, "Damien? Your side?" Realizing his mistake, Star flinched, waiting. No shots came.

"Hands full. Ostra is out but— Yeah, she should be all right, just need to stop the bleeding. She took a pretty deep graze against the top of her head. No broken bone, thankfully. Everyone else? Yours?"

"Wendy took one to the arm but we're all good. Bleeding but not enough to kill."

Damien's side had been the only one to call out. Star stood, a wave of terror seizing his chest. Aric rose with him.

"Upstairs," Star gasped out. How bad were their injuries?

"I have Wendy in hand, son," Ty assured him. "Go check."

Star rushed to the stairs, Aric on his heels. Damien joined them at the foot.

"Ostra?" Star asked, taking the stairs two at a time, gun still in hand.

"Bill has her," Damien assured him. Star hadn't seen Bill, and the second, surer confirmation of his safety eased his tension.

Star headed for the closest bedroom only to stop in the doorway when Coy, looking up, shook his head. The largest of the ranch hands was spread out under a cotton throw, blood soaking through the thin material. Coy himself seemed scratched up but not needing any help. Star nodded sharply and stepped back, heading for the next. It was empty, the little crib fallen but no blood.

"Damien?" he called, heading for the last.

Damien and Knott were bent over Uncle Chuck. A fissure of worry, startling in its intensity, clenched his gut. He'd only just met the man, but his rough ways had grown on him.

Aric ran from where he'd been keeping place with Star. "How bad?"

"Shoulder, arm, and leg," Damien answered, voice strained. Their shirts were already pressed against the wounds. Aric, kneeling behind them, ripped apart the bed's quilt with his knife, handing over strips.

"Find out from Wendy where the bandages are," Damien ordered Star, "and make sure everyone has some."

"On it." Choking back his fear, Star did as bid.

"Don't shoot!" called Wendy's father-in-law from outside. Vin sounded weary and out of breath but still alive.

The children were tucked away upstairs, which had been cleaned as best they could before they'd closed the little ones away with toys and stern orders to stay. Everyone else was rushing about, taking care of the wounded.

Star hurried outside to meet him, leaving the newest pot of water on the woodstove to work its way to a boil. Vin was all but carrying Andrea, and while he was covered in blood, it looked like most of it was hers.

"They were cocky," Andrea wheezed from where she was propped up against her father. Vin shifted so Star could wrap his arm around her, taking some of her weight off him.

"Jonnie? The others?" Star asked, hating to push. Their silence said everything. His chest clenched, a flash of mourning hitting along with concern for Damien and the others. Forcing the emotion back to focus on the immediate, Star gritted his teeth and set to work.

They carried her inside, and Damien met them at the door. Damien took over for Vin, leaving the older man to follow. Even knowing it was coming, Damien's glance behind them sent a wave of sympathy through Star. Then Damien's eyes met his. By the way his face closed off, Star knew he'd put things together.

"I'm sorry," Star told him.

Andrea started talking again as they lowered her to the kitchen floor. Her voice was weak, but determination pushed her. "Outclassed us, they thought. Took risks. Both sides mostly shot blind, and we took them from behind. Jonnie, he saved us."

She closed her eyes on a shuddery breath. Damien, grabbing up the bandages thrown on the table, turned to Vin. Vin shook his head slowly but picked up the story.

"We're the only ones who survived. We had to leave Robert and Jonnie there to get Andrea back. I'm sorry."

Star threw a needle and thread into the water, then walked over to Damien, resting his hand on Damien's shoulder. Damien cupped his hand and Star felt the minute tremble in Damien's fingers. Star squeezed, pressed a kiss to Damien's head, and headed back to the stove.

Star used tongs to pluck the needle out of the boiling water, then, seeing Damien ready, he released it onto a cloth. Damien barely waited before grabbing it. He winced, no doubt feeling the burn, but wasted no time leaning over. Andrea's father untied where he'd bound his shirt tight over her blood-soaked arm. Star dipped a fresh cloth in the water and washed away the blood so Damien could close the wound.

"The bullets went through, right?" Damien demanded.

"Aye."

He quickly stitched the arm and started on the leg next, where Andrea's own shirt had been used as a temporary bandage.

"Jonnie stepped out ahead of us," Vin told them gravely as he wrapped Andrea's freshly stitched arm. "Three of the bastards aimed their shots on him, and that's the only reason we're still breathing. Hell of a man."

Star rubbed Damien's arm as he swallowed hard, eyes filling with tears.

"Hell of a man," Damien repeated, voice thick. He broke off the string and sat back on his heels to watch Vin bind the wound. "Who killed Hollowood?"

Vin flinched. Dread ached in Star's guts before the next words left his lips. "He got away. His bastards covered for him and he made a break for it."

The sound Damien made was more hiss than growl. Star leapt after him as Damien whirled and rushed for the door.

"What are you thinking?" Star demanded, keeping stride. He heard cursing behind them but didn't check to see what the others were doing.

"Ending the bastard before he lands here with more hired guns!"

He'd get himself killed if he went alone.

Star gritted his teeth. "Fine. We'll chase him down."

That made Damien slow. They were in the yard by then, out in plain shot should the enemy already be returning. "This is my fight. Jonnie was mine. Wendy is mine."

Yeah, but Damien was *his*. "And I'm following."

"Not by yourself."

They turned. Knott stood a few steps away, Ostra at his side. Ty and Bill, not bothering to glance their way, swept past and headed for the horses.

Damien gaped, stunned. Star followed after the others, only half-listening as Damien grappled for a semblance of control.

"We can't all go," Damien choked out. "Wendy and the others need someone watching their backs in case I don't stop him!"

"Then I'll stay," Ostra threw out.

Star, knowing what Damien had really meant, clenched his jaw in annoyance as he saddled Clay.

Damien rushed to follow suit, his face clouded with displeasure. "Knott and I—"

"I'm coming." Star swung into his saddle and glared down at Damien, daring him to argue.

"Star—"

"My kid is going, lad, and that means we are too. You can stand there arguing or you can start riding. Or do you want us to get shot here with our tongues wagging?"

Vin's voice cut through their chatter. "And I'll show you the way. Unless the lot of you planned to guess?"

Star, twisting to Vin and Aric at his side, cursed himself for not noticing yet more followers.

Damien, for his part, just appeared tired. "Then saddle up fast."

It was a quiet and tense ride to where the others had faced down Hollowood and his gunmen. Star could see the dampness in Damien's eyes when his glance slid to where Jonnie's hulking form sprawled with the fallen. He didn't hesitate, however, before turning his horse in the direction where Hollowood had fled.

"How many went with him?" Damien asked.

"None. We fired after him, but no killing hits. Not unless we were luckier than it looked," Vin answered.

"Luckier?" Damien pressed.

"Leg. It might slow him down, but he doesn't have far to ride. If we hit the meat, he'll make it back with little trouble."

And if there were more gunmen left behind at his ranch, they'd have hell waiting for them.

Ty's jaw clenched and color rose on his skin. Anger blazed in Ty's every line. A need for revenge, Star knew, one that vied with Damien's. Would his own blood burn the same after Star finally knew everything that'd been done to his father's line?

Star caught movement in the corner of his eye and whipped around, releasing the reins to grab for a knife. His father beat him to it. The sound of his rifle echoed as one of the thought-dead figures sprawl back down, his own gunshot going wide.

Knott cursed.

"Best to ride before any more of these corpses start shooting," Bill muttered.

The path was wide, torn by hasty hooves. Star hoped they would meet Ram before reaching his ranch.

"How many more do you figure he has?" Ty demanded, clipped. Damien flushed, likely at the lack of his own forethought.

"Enough to make it a fight," Vin gritted out. "Best to ride hard and hope like hell he fell out of the saddle on the way."

"Not enough blood," Knott pointed out unhelpfully. "There'd be spray marking our way."

The words were punctured by a bullet, followed by cursing as the one who'd shot it saw he'd missed. Blood ran from Knott's forehead. Star dropped down from his saddle and crouched, gun ready. Peering past Clay, he saw where his father's narrowed gaze had landed: an old, well-rooted pine.

There was no horse. Hollowood had lost his seat, it seemed, and been left behind.

"We have you pinned," Damien growled, easing around his horse with his gun raised and sighted. "You can't shoot us through dirt and root, and as soon as you stand, one of us will end you. Give yourself up and you can come to the Sighted Blades. Give it to them straight."

"The one in town?" Hollowood's voice, while weaker than it had been before, was just as cruelly mocking.

"Your man will be ousted now that you're done throwing your weight."

"Think, then, I'll go out my way and take you with me!"

Damien's lip pulled back, finger on the trigger and ready. Star knew what would happen, that Hollowood planned to rise and aim straight for Damien's voice. He lurched toward Damien, desperate to get between Damien and death.

His father got there first. Damien's bullet fired off-course as Ty's shoulder drove into Damien's aiming arm, but Ty's rifle shot true as he loosed both barrels into the rising bastard's chest.

Bullets hit Hollowood, but the man's shot sent Ty to the dirt.

Star scrambled to where his father had landed, uncaring that it exposed his back. He threw himself over top him, grabbing for where blood seeped out of his father's chest. A shot fired. Undeterred, Star pressed harder, trying to keep the blood from escaping.

"Ty, shh, Ty," Bill crooned as he fell next to them. He leaned in close. "Hold still, man."

"Star?" Damien's voice.

Star gave his head a hard shake, eyes locked on his dad. Emotions raged under his smothering terror, threatening but distant.

"Too late there," Ty muttered, eyes half-open. A thin line of blood trickled from his mouth as he forced out the words. "Not too late . . . everything." He fumbled, weak, at the neck of his shirt.

"Be still," Star begged, wanting to pin that hand but too scared to take his grip off the leaking hole. Some distant part of Star registered the blood at Ty's mouth and knew what it meant. The rest of him shivered it off, refusing the knowledge.

Bill caught Ty's hand and squeezed it.

"I have it, Ty," Bill assured him.

He didn't look at Star, eyes still sharp on Bill. "Protect . . . to the Bear . . ."

"I will," Bill promised, voice thick. "I'm sorry, Ty. So damned sorry."

Star choked back a sob, still pressing tight to the wound even as he knew it was too late. His hand and legs were drenched, the thick blood soaking the ground.

"I'm sorry, Dad," Star told him, no longer able to deny what was happening. "So sorry . . ."

Finally, his father looked at him. Blue eyes, blood-stained lips, and love even beneath the fog. "M'sorry," Ty managed before releasing his breath, and Star trembled as he knew his father was gone.

Bill silently closed his brother's eyes, his tears joining Star's own.

Then Damien was there, pulling Star to his feet and tucking him close. Star closed his eyes, his chest an aching mess of pain that had nothing to do with splinters and bullet burns.

"I'm sorry," Damien told him. Star bet it was not for the first or last time.

He gripped Damien's arm, centering his aching self on the warmth that proved Damien was alive. His father had saved him. Horror and agony twisted in Star's chest. Ty had been the one constant he'd always been able to depend upon. His father's firm love and tough care had backed every step Star ever took.

"Fuck," Bill sighed, his voice cracking under the strain of his own grief. "Fuck the sun, the moon, and all their thrice-damned children. And at the hands of that bastard family."

Star pressed his face against Damien's shoulder, hiding his tears. He hadn't the strength to face his feelings. How *stupid* he'd been, spending so much energy during the last twelve hours obsessing over answers promised. How *reckless*, chasing after Damien's heels without truly considering their chances of loss.

"Hollowood is dead," Damien said, voice flat with shock. Your dad took care of him and saved my life in the doing."

The words echoed in Star's head, biting. "I heard a shot, after?"

"Me," Knott answered, more growl than speech. "Hollowood looked dead, but I wasn't taking any chances."

"He's rotting right where he fell," Bill promised. "No rites, just insects and carrion hunters."

"We'll bring your father's body," Aric cut in, likely to stop Bill from saying anything more macabre. "And we'll get the rest."

"Shush!" Knott ordered, but Star was already looking up. He glanced from Bill's red-rimmed eyes over to Aric's determined face.

"I want to help," Star said, not bothering to hide his tears anymore.

Damien sighed, muscles clenching under Star's grip. "Why don't you let us take care of it?"

Star couldn't face Damien. His choice had led them here. Knowing he wasn't the only one stinging from loss, that losing Jonnie must have torn a hole in Damien's chest, didn't lessen the growing ache of guilt and blame.

"He's mine," Star answered instead, eyes locked on Bill. If he focused on this one thing, he didn't have to face the rest yet.

Bill smiled gently, then grabbed a blanket and led the way back to Ty. Star, releasing Damien, followed, dogged.

"You can't dig with one arm," Bill told him softly, voice pitched for his ears alone. "Find a place for him, Star. That's what you can do. I'll help the others dig their graves, but when you get me, I'll come and dig his."

Star swallowed hard but had to agree. Feeling the tears once more welling in his eyes, he turned and headed into the trees.

Damien, Wendy, Knott, and Ostra gathered in a small field a short distance from a tall copse of oak and flowering crab. It had taken most of the afternoon to wrap the bodies and prepare them for the ground. Their enemies would be dealt with later. First, they'd honor their own.

Bill remained with Star, helping to lay his father to rest. That left the rest of them to take care of the other fallen. Wendy and Damien dug Jonnie's grave, with Ostra and Knott working nearby. They bent to the task, careful not to hit each other as they dug deep. The scent of earth filled Damien's nose, and his muscles burned as they worked through the rocky soil.

At last, sure of the depth, Damien threw his shovel out and climbed after it. Kneeling, he reached for Wendy and, when she gave her his hand, pulled.

"Thank you," she told him, catching her balance. He heard what she meant in the thickness of her voice, and nodded once, hard. Together they carried Jonnie's wrapped body to his bed, where Damien hopped down into the dark depths to guide him to his rest.

Covering him was harder than preparing the grave. Damien had to stop twice to catch himself, but at last they finished. Knott and Ostra, seeing this, set their shovels down and joined them. Each laid a hand on Wendy's shoulder as they said their silent goodbyes.

"He'll be missed," Ostra promised as Knott, nodding agreement, squeezed Wendy. Then he turned away, Ostra falling into step.

Damien rested his own hand where Knott's had been. "I'm so damn sorry for all of this, Wendy."

She shook her head, tears in her eyes but a hard look on her face. "Don't be. We joined up with you. Jonnie loved all of you, same as I do. We made this bed."

Damien sighed, the words heavy. Sliding his hand away, he picked up his shovel and went to help the others. Wendy, without another word, accompanied him.

Too many graves, all for one man's greed. Damien's mind worked over the hell they'd walked as his muscles burned beneath their labor. Star's face kept rising to the forefront: his pain, tears, and naked desperation. Damien had chosen to pursue Hollowood. It was his choice that led to the rest. It had been the right decision, he stood by that, but damn it, Star and the others never should have followed. That, too, was on him.

Once their own were buried, they worked together to dig a large, shallow pit farther from the individually marked graves. There they dumped the bodies of those who'd attacked them. Damien dragged the last corpse himself and felt a bitter satisfaction as he rolled it into place.

"Don't cover it yet," Knott snapped, startling him.

They watched as he stalked up to the lip of the grave, reached into his pocket, and pulled out a bundle: his lost wife's relic.

Damien wasn't so tired that he didn't feel a chill of recognition. "Knott?"

Knott didn't glance his way. It was Ostra who came to Damien's side, resting her dirt-caked hand on his elbow. Ostra, Damien knew, wished to be next to Knott at that moment but couldn't.

Knott looked down into the knot of rough-wrapped bodies. Then he chucked his small bundle into their midst. Only after did his damp eyes meet Damien's.

"You sure?" Damien asked, eyebrow arched but tone gentle.

"She and her family are dead now, have been for fifteen years. No one needs the trouble. The damn thing is cursed, which is why I never touch the bastard rock, and he's dead. Carrying it around like this, for her, *no*. I've got to end it."

Ostra moved from Damien's side then, throwing herself against Knott. He took her weight easily, bending to bury his heavily lined face into her graying red hair.

Damien bent to work alongside the others, giving them their moment. They'd been lucky, all said and done, to have lost as few as they did, but losing Jonnie hurt, and no death was luck.

Cowardly or no, Damien was glad to have something at hand to bury himself in the doing.

After a short walk, Star and Bill entered a clearing. At the top of the small rise in the ground was the place Star had chosen. The blanket-wrapped bundle on Clay's back would soon be at rest there, and thinking of it had Star blinking back more tears.

"Here is where I want him," he told Bill.

Bill nodded, resting a hand on Star's shoulder. "It's a perfect spot, lad. We'll lay him down deep." Bill avoided glancing to where Ty was.

Star tried to thank him but couldn't manage the words. He pulled away, pressing a hand on Bill's chest when he tried to follow, then walked toward the body.

He peeled back the blanket to see his father.

"This was because of me," Star said at last.

Bill growled softly. "He lived because of you, and don't you dare say otherwise. Without you, the stubborn bastard would have died twenty years ago."

Star didn't bother wiping his eyes again, just leaned over and let them fall on his father's face. "I let myself get tied up, and the both of you with me, in a mess that never should have killed him. I should have stopped Damien. Or, baring that, shouldn't have followed him."

"That isn't you, kid. Standing back and letting Damien go would've never been your choice. And Ty, damn him, couldn't have let that Hollowood bastard live any more than he could've let you ride off without him."

And Damien, seeing such a clear path to his quarry, could no sooner have stood down than any of the rest of them. Knowing was a damn poor comfort and couldn't touch the bitter pain curling beneath his heart.

"Let them take you to her," he whispered to his father, twisting his fingers into that hair so like his own and pressing his forehead against the cold one. "I'll listen for you on the wind, like you taught me. Maybe it'll talk to me if you ask."

Bill let him cry. Only once he'd emptied himself of tears did he pull back, giving one last kiss to his father's forehead and tucking the blanket over him.

"He'll have his wind here, Star," Bill assured him, edging closer.

"Thank you," he said, voice hoarse. Star closed his eyes as Bill removed Ty from Clay's back, and then he headed toward the spot he'd chosen. Bill followed, setting Ty down a few steps away, then taking the shovel and digging the grave himself. Star, unable to help, sat next to his father and watched.

At last, Bill climbed out and wiped his dirt-stained hands on his just as filthy pants. "It's done, lad."

Star pressed his lips into a thin line. "I want his rifle."

Bill stared, everything about his manner screaming he was unsure. Then his shoulders slumped and, kneeling, he reached into the blankets, pulled the gun from where it rested, and pressed it to Star's chest, hand shaking but eyes firm. He held it there until Star took it.

"It's yours." He stood with a groan, Ty in his arms, and carried him to his bed. Star held the rifle in his hands, staring past it into the memory of his father's own hands.

At last the final shovelful went in, and Bill came back to his side. Together they sat, staring at the fresh grave.

That was where, finally, Damien found them, worry in his red-rimmed eyes. "I'm sorry."

Star looked away, chest swollen with words he couldn't form. Looking at Damien hurt. There was a heavy silence.

When Damien spoke again, his speech came slower. "We should pay our final respects. We need to leave come morning, before the fake Blade is replaced and the new bastard rides out to show a better face than his predecessor."

Star flinched when Damien reached for him. He scrambled to his feet, heart in his throat. "Not yet. Give Bill and me another day."

"We can't wait. I'm sorry." Damien sounded it too, damn him. "The one who charged us is lying dead, but our names will take time to clear. Believed or not, three bountied would likely strain any Blade's ability to plead ignorance. We'd be held here until it was removed, and even without Hollowood's money, the new Blade might execute us before the bounty order is overturned if he feels the need to prove himself."

But Star and Bill could stay. The offer, left unspoken, was shattered glass scattered in the space between them. Ty's death, Jonnie's, this twisted tangle of lust and growing affection—it all lay sharp in the silence.

If Star didn't ride with Damien, would he come to regret it? The ache in his chest answered that.

"I'll be ready," Star promised around the lodged weight in his throat, tired. "Just let me say goodbye."

Once Star was done, he joined the others in front of the graves. Damien met his eyes with a drawn look. Star tried to smile, failed, and glanced away.

Footsteps, quick and heavy, turned their heads. Aric strode their way from the direction of the house, where he'd been checking on the wounded. His sleeves were darkened by blood, and Star wondered whose injuries had opened again. Damien stepped out to meet him, but Aric ignored him.

"I want to talk to you a minute, Star."

Bill made a noise of complaint, but Aric, lip curling for half a tick, didn't look away.

"This can wait," Bill argued. Star, exhausted, cast him a questioning look. Bill ignored him, eyes fixed on Aric.

"It'll just take a minute," Aric refuted. "Then I'll have a few words with you too, Bill. How does that sound?"

Bill's jaw clenched. Star felt a fissure of curiosity crack beneath his pain. That had sounded almost like a threat.

Swallowing, Star stepped forward, away from Damien and Bill. "I'll be back," he promised, still avoiding Damien's gaze. "I'd like to hear what Aric has to say." And to clear his head.

Aric nodded, green eyes hard, then put his back to them.

They headed into the trees. As they drifted closer to where Star's father lay, Star slowed, dreading that was where they were headed. Perhaps it had been worse to follow. As it came within sight, Star stopped.

Aric also halted, the lines of his face tight. "I'm sorry about Ty. I mean that."

"Dad was your friend," Star said, wincing at how much it sounded like a question. Hours ago, the greatest of Star's worries had been wrangling answers out of his father. What did it matter now how he'd known Aric and Chuck? What did *any* of it matter?

Neither of them said anything for a moment, Star waiting and Aric reading something into the unintentional query.

As the silence stretched, Star's eyes wandered back to the grave. He'd pour his own blood out to sun and moon both for a chance to make different decisions. He'd always known their time would be short, but never that his could stretch beyond Ty's.

"Your father," Aric said carefully, "used to have a sister."

Star jerked his head sideways, gaze torn away from the gravesite. Aric remained calm, as if he had no idea how destabilizing those words were to Star.

"He *what?*" Star demanded.

Aric's jaw tightened. He looked like a man facing down a gun. "My father loved her more than anything, my mother included. She burned him like a wildfire, and he never got over it."

Star struggled, cold and hot and *lost*. Aric looked at him patiently, his green eyes kind. They were at odds with the harsh lines of his face and the pained grimace on his lips.

"What happened to her?" Star managed at last. An aunt, and he'd never so much as heard her name. Why hadn't his father ever said anything? Why was Star only hearing about this woman now, with the dirt of his father's grave still beneath his nails? Betrayed pain churned his chest, eating at his exhaustion and fueling his uncertainty.

Aric's lips twisted in sympathy but his words came blunt and hard. "She was shot. My father didn't blame Ty, but Ty blamed himself, I think. You must know he doesn't goes north?"

Never. "I thought I knew why." Star stumbled, mind racing ahead of his tongue. An aunt who had lured away Aric's father, and still he'd called Ty a friend. "You must have hated her." How deeply hurt had his father been, he wondered, to not once breathe his sister's name?

"No," Aric answered, terse but not cruel. "Mom couldn't forgive her, but she never hated her." Not an answer, but Star didn't pursue it.

"Your father, though?" he asked instead.

"Ma gave Dad two sons. He hurt her, yeah, when he stepped out on her, but he never hurt her again."

Stepped out. The words were hard to hear.

"How can you be sure?" Star demanded, then wanted to kick himself. It wasn't his business, not really.

Still strangely gentle, Aric shook his head. "Because no other woman like her exists, and neither does any like my mother." The way he said it, looking straight at him, made Star's skin feel too tight. There was something in those words that he couldn't place, leaving him wary.

Aric, accepting his silence, reached over and set his large hand on Star's shoulder. "Ride with me to my father's ranch. If you and your friends come, my family can offer protection until things are straightened out and their bounties lifted. You know they can't stay here."

The offer didn't make sense. Star was the nephew of a woman who'd apparently torn Aric's family apart, or near to, yet still he offered safety? Chuck had named himself a friend, but more and more Star doubted the truth of that.

He swallowed, his mind humming with questions that he couldn't ask his father. How many of them would have been answered if things had been different? "Why offer so much?"

Aric lifted a shoulder, lips pressed together in a hard line. For a second it didn't seem like he would answer. "I'd like to learn more about you, and I can answer some questions too."

Answers. Rare, in his life. Guilt nipped at him for wanting so badly to take that deal.

"I'd like that," Star admitted, ignoring the drop in his stomach. "I'll have to ask the others."

Aric grimaced, gave Star's shoulder a squeeze, and dropped his hand. "Thank you."

They turned back, no more words passing between them.

CHAPTER

✴

FOURTEEN

D amien sat next to where Star lay napping. The sun was far along in the sky, warning that day would soon be over. He stroked the sweaty, dirty hair away from Star's face. Star didn't react, dead to the world. It was probably better that way. Damien hadn't missed the way his eyes skirted around him, and the reason was easy enough to guess.

"Poor lad," Damien whispered, feeling every one of the six years between them. He wondered what had passed between Star and Aric to bring about the invitation, but hadn't felt comfortable pressing. Something about the new pain and confusion on Star's face suggested it was a conversation best had alone. There was a lot to discuss, and that talk, once it came, would be rough on them both.

It'd been a hard day for everyone. Sadly, dawn wouldn't make things easier. They'd have to ride, and early, to give time for the Blades to straighten out the real guilty party. Wendy had offered her home again, but Damien felt better outdoors. He still wanted to lick his wounds, same as Star, and the others felt similarly.

With Hollowood dead the bounty would die. No one to pay meant no temptation. Unless the Blades themselves took damage, the crime only had to be outlived. All they had left was to wait for word to spread. But was it right to follow Aric, a practical stranger, into unfamiliar territory?

Ty'd claimed to know Charles, and Charles in turn had named Ty a friend, but Damien hadn't forgotten the tense air between the two. With Ty dead, the only tie left to uncle and nephew was Bill, and Damien remembered how the other man had reacted when first seeing Charles. More than that, until that offer, Damien had the idea Aric didn't think much of them.

Having promised to sup with Wendy, they'd made their camp a short distance away. They'd piled their belongings together, ready to be added to their mounts once the sun opened her eyes and glared her morning greeting.

A sigh drew Damien from his thoughts. Bill pressed his lips together, pensive, and hunched over the bottle he'd been nursing. His weary, red-rimmed gaze slid to Star, and already-slumped shoulders fell further.

Damien's look caught Bill's attention. "Bill?"

Bill made to speak, stopped, then heaved another deep sigh. Sliding to his feet, he motioned Damien to follow him.

Damien stared a moment, worn muscles and weary spirit dragging his reaction. He'd been the one to offer conversation, and sitting there would only disturb the others. Damien slid to his feet. The worry in his gut grew as Bill, leading him to where he'd dumped Ty's things, started digging in Ty's saddlebags.

"What are you looking for?" Damien asked quietly.

"Shh." Bill continued to dig. A moment later he held out an old, dented metal tin.

The sun was setting, casting everything in a bloody orange glow, and looking at its reflection in the dull metal, hesitation creeped through him. What was so important that Ty kept it hidden, or that Bill insisted it be studied at this time?

When Damien didn't move, Bill waved his bottle, impatient. "You still want in this horse show, you take the damn thing and follow me."

Seeing no other path, Damien took it and fell into step. Knott and Ostra threw him tired looks, questioning, and he shook his head, waving them off. Bill didn't take him far, but with a copse of trees between them and the others, they had privacy.

Bill slumped to the ground in a miserable lump, arms on his knees and the bottle against his chest. Pity and grief stayed the hard words Damien wanted to voice. Instead he knelt and opened the lid.

Letters were the first things he saw, but not all. Digging through the contents and reading the letters, he wished he could chuck the thing into the campfire. He wished, too, that Knott was at his side to make sense of it all.

"Why are you showing this to me?" Damien demanded. "Does Star know?"

"I gave Ty my word I'd never tell Star without his say, and now he's dead." Bill's bitter words echoed the twist of his lips. "We planned to tell him together when he was sixteen, but before we met up, something . . . happened. I never expected to be the one telling, and I'm too much of a damn coward."

Damien understood, finally, the slick man back in Standing Grave who'd shoved that picture of Star under Knott's nose. There was a Bear out there who still wanted his lost kid. The question was—why? To kill a claim on their riches? Star was out of wedlock, and no Blade would rule for him unless every other viable option were dead.

Jealousy? Did the wife want the stain wiped out? It didn't fit with any of the stories about their family, but then no stories had ever hinted at a stolen child. The Bears were supposed to be a strong, rich, honor-bound family. Large-bodied, straight-backed, and proud.

Shame, then? But if so, why grant credence at all to Star's existence? It would have been easier to claim him a liar and laugh it off should issues of paternity be raised. Star looked every inch his self-styled father and, judging by the picture, his mother. Any blood of a Bear was buried beneath leanly muscled, fine-boned delicacy.

Damien picked up the topmost of the letters addressed to Ty from a woman named Sunny. It was too light for the weight it carried.

Typhoon,

The fields have grown loud and Starlight and I need you. I'm dying, and my little one will be unprotected without me. The Bears hear nothing and see less. You have lived in the sound while I've kept to silence. Would you refuse me this?

If you care for me, come.

"Ty stole him," he said aloud, wondering.

"At gunpoint."

Damien whipped his head up. *What?*

"Not his gun," Bill clarified, "and the muzzle wasn't pointed at him."

Struggling to digest that, Damien looked back at the letter. *Starlight and I need you. I'm dying.*

"Explain this, then." He brandished the note.

"Ty's sister never accepted no. It wasn't in her. Sunny was a cold, determined asshole, terrifying and driven. Best thing that ever happened to Star was being raised by Ty. She'd have destroyed him."

The contained fury in Bill's voice startled Damien. Bill hated Sunny. She'd been dead all these years and that emotion still blazed strong. What kind of person could birth such passion in another?

"What do you want from me? To be the one to tell him? He's already upset with me." He'd make that same choice again even knowing the outcome. To do otherwise was to chance everyone's lives anew, but guilt ached deep in his very bones.

"I need you to do what I can't," Bill answered. "Star isn't going to have me at his side when we get where we're going—the Bears will let me stay, but I'm not fool enough to think they'll make me welcome—and he'll need you."

Damien stared, wondering what the hell he was supposed to make of that. "Where, by the sun, will you be?" Bill had seemed to love Star like his own. To desert him like that shocked Damien.

Bill, it seemed, wasn't ready to answer. He picked up the story again. "You know of the Wind-whispers?"

They had been a nomadic people who were said to read the voices in the wind and ride with its whims. They'd been killed off, feared and hated by the rest of the world. They'd vanished within the last century. What did they have to do with this?

Bill's ghastly smile promised nothing comforting. "I have a little story. Not a fun one, but a good one."

Damien scowled. "Tell it, then." Already blood thumped in his temples with fear at what he'd be hearing.

"Twins. Barely in their teens. Their clan butchered around them. They're the only two children in the entire group, and their people protect them with all the fierceness their deaths allow. They lose; they haven't numbers to win.

"The men in the attacking party are monsters. They intend, like many monsters, to rape them both and leave their bodies to bleed out and rot with their people. The end to what was once a large, peaceful people. Only, the children are ready. They watched as their families died. They took in everything they could through the slits in the tent walls, pressed tight enough to peer through cracks.

"The little girl has a knife, their grandmother's, tucked down her shirt against her chest. The boy, huddled in the furred bedding that had belonged to their uncle, hides a loaded rifle. Double-barrel, I am sure you understand."

He did. Horrified, he understood all too well.

"The enemies tear open the tent, knowing by the way the last of the people stood their ground that the children would be hidden there. One man grabs for the girl's hair. Two men, instead, fall dead. A third has his throat slit seconds later, just like the first, while a fourth falls, screaming, to a gut shot."

Bill seemed to have forgotten he was drinking. He sat instead, staring down at the tin in Damien's hands, no matter that the darkening sky made its contents impossible to see with any clarity.

"The twins take their enemy by surprise, the men drunk on stolen wine and victory. The little ones escape out the back of the tent. The boy had worried a hole in it while watching the fight. No one catches them because they are the wind. Their people were close to Bear territory, a family known for its wealth and strength in those parts, so the twins run that way. The girl says, later, the wind told her to do that. The boy says he ran the way it blew."

Sickened and caught enthralled, Damien stared at Bill. "How do you know all that? From Ty?" And had they truly kept it all from Star? *Why?*

"From Sunshine, called Sunny by some. Typhoon—Ty—was huddled behind her in my grandfather's barn when my sister sent me to find them. Sunny told it all to me. Believe me, I never forgot a word." Bill shivered. "Her words were the deadest things I've ever heard. Cold, clear, and she told it plain. If Ty hadn't been behind her, red-eyed and clinging to that gun . . ."

"It's a wonder they survived." Damien had wanted his curiosity sated but wished he'd known what he desired.

"Sunny and Ty were survivors, same as Ty's kid. And he is Ty's, no matter who sired or carried him. The Bear already had a son at the time Star was born, damn the man, but when Sunny gave chase, twenty years old and as beautiful as she was cold, he let her catch him. Likely out there under the prairie sky."

Damien remembered how Star had chased him, proud and demanding. He tried to transfer that onto the woman Bill was describing. Someone driven, but cold where Star was warm, and uncaring where her son felt so damn much.

It all made a terrible sense. He'd never met anyone like Ty and Star, able to stand beneath sun and wind and never show a sign of strain. She would have been like them. Had Star's mother caught the Bear's blood on fire like Star did Damien's? Had she faced all the blame when he, the great man of the territory, turned his face from his wife's to chase someone else.

Damien was reminded of how Ty had spoken of Sunny with such loss and love. They'd met in the womb. Then Ty had become mother and father both to the boy she wouldn't parent, maybe couldn't if Bill was to be believed. A sister Ty had loved so deeply he'd mourned her until his own death. That, combined with the letters, drew someone hurt, beautiful, and sad beyond measure.

He picked up another, earlier missive, needing to think.

Typhoon,

The fields are so quiet now. Starlight grows within me by the day, and soon I will know if I am to have a son or daughter. You will likely learn by letter, but I hope to be wrong. Thrice I tried to escape to you. Each time they caught me and brought me back. Beresford has his own child, but still he wants what is mine.

Bill carried me news that you are well. At least he has some use. He promised to put this letter in your hand before my child's birth, and this once I will trust his word.

Come see us, Typhoon.

"You said gunpoint," Damien reminded Bill weakly.

"Sunny was mad in the end." Bill seemed to remember the bottle and tipped it back, swallowing the last dregs and then shaking it to be sure it was empty. That much drink should have had him on his ass, but he barely seemed drunk. "The poisoned stories her people poured into her from childhood, the shock after the same bastards who killed their people violated her, slitting her skin and planning to kill her, no one could have withstood it all. The desperation and pain she built up while trapped afterward, the Bears refusing to let her leave their lands for her own sake?" Bill shuddered. "Star can't know, but how do I keep it from him now when they are ready to collect?"

Curses to the sun. A sick chill churned in Damien's guts as he digested the revelations. "What did she do?" He was sure he knew. Hoped he didn't.

Bill gave another pull on the bottle, but it was empty and there was nothing for him.

"Shot herself." Another try for a mouthful. Damien wondered if he even noticed it was empty. "Held the muzzle to her breast and demanded Ty take the kid and run. So they ran. And she waited."

"Star's father—" Bill curled a lip and Damien amended, "This Beresford, I mean. He was so terrible?"

"Losing her freedom was so terrible. The people on his land resented her, and still the Bear ordered her to stay. Ty rode hard and fast to escape the place, sometimes with me and sometimes without. I can still see her as she was. That chin, pointy like her son's, but skeletal, jutting up in pride; wide blue eyes burning with insanity and demand. She'd given me the letter, threatened me if I opened it, and then carried the babe off in a proud stride. Star was so small against her chest then. Kid looked even smaller when Ty showed up at my door days later, wild-eyed and shaking like a fox put to the hounds. We ran, all three of us, and knew that man was on our heels."

As would any man whose son had been stolen. Damn it. "What did you do with a baby?"

"Goat's milk. Cow's milk. Anything we could find." A wet laugh. "Hell, the child was a long-haired, green-eyed terror once he started to walk. If it moved, he pounced. Thought he was a cat. That we kept him away from snakes, scorpions, or any other number of killers is a miracle."

"Why didn't she go with you?"

Bill shook his head. Guilt twisted his face. "She didn't have it left, I don't think, for a long fight. It was her way for freedom. Woman was a walking wraith, hair tangled and mostly skin over bones. I *know* I should've questioned what I saw that day. Stayed, maybe, and tried to talk to her, but Sunny hated me." He sighed. "That's one regret I can't kick away. Hell, I don't know how she carried the kid, looking as she did."

"She was sick?"

Bill lifted a shoulder, the non-answer explanation enough: he hadn't asked.

Damien's mind went back to where he'd been worrying over the bones of the Bear family hunt. No rumors of missing a stolen child, no, but there were equally no rumors of a surviving Windwhisper. How, by the sun, had they managed *that*?

Questions swamped Damien, so many his head ached. What had driven Sunny to shoot herself? To demand her brother steal her child? What monsters were the Bears to make her so desperate? Or was it, as Bill said, about freedom? There was no freedom, after all, with the Bearsons' blood. Instead of living and letting her son grow alongside others of his blood, she'd forced on him a different life. Cold and cruel, Bill had called her, but such a one would not have cared what became of their child.

The fields are quiet; the fields are loud. You have lived in the sound while I've kept to silence.

I'm dying, and my little one will be unprotected without me. The Bears hear nothing and see less.

It read like madness. Or like a message not meant for his eyes. One that a brother would see and answer. Usually he could act on the fly, but this? Here? His thoughts tangled in on themselves, doubt and uncertainty twisting around horror.

"What do you intend to do?" Damien demanded, looking from the thrice-damned metal tin box to Bill. He was as close as Star had left to known family. What was the next move?

"I guess we start by talking to Star before his brother beats us there."

"*Brother*?" Damien snapped.

"Aric."

Sun-damn it, what a kick in the teeth. That glaring, mistrustful, condescending jackass was Star's brother? It should have been unthinkable, except Damien had known the green of Aric's eyes.

"How do we know he hasn't already told him?"

Before Bill shook his head, Damien knew it couldn't have been. "If that kind of information had gotten passed on, we'd know. Aric told Star something but not everything. All I could get out of the bastard was his confidence we'd be following him to Black Falls and his word he'll leave the telling to me so long as it's done tomorrow."

Damien winced. "And Star?"

Bill stared into the empty bottle with a wary frown. No. There'd been a strange quiet between the two. Having heard this poison now, Damien felt he had a good idea what ate at Bill. That wasn't fair to Star, but then what about this damn situation was?

Damien shook his head. "And now you want us going there and talking to Aric. Wasn't everything to keep Star from them?"

"It was never about safety." Bill scowled, tearing up. "It was Sunny's damned pride. She'd have burned the world before anything of hers looked tame, and that? A family for her babe? That looked like being tamed to her. She was mad, surrounded by distrust and full of her own mistrust."

"But Ty—"

"Would have walked through ten leagues of hell for that woman." Bill glanced back to camp. They were far enough away that their voices wouldn't carry, but close enough Damien could see Ostra carving away, leaning against Knott. "Ty's dead. I don't intend to see the same happen to his son, and if you have any care for the boy, you'll listen."

He excused the words on account of grief and drink, but Damien would be damned before he let anyone accuse him of leading Star on.

"I'll help you tell him, but you'd best tell *me* if there is any more to this. Any more secrets crop up and I'm packing him up and riding off. You and that Bear-pack can search every inch of moon's earth and sun's hell, but you won't find us."

Bill snorted, smiling weakly. "Good man."

"What of the threat you said attacked Sunny? You said it isn't about safety, but then said his mother was surrounded by distrust. Is that what Star looks forward to if he goes there?" That line about Star being unprotected kept teasing at Damien. The desperation in the notes wouldn't leave Damien alone.

"Sunny made it hard to like her. Star is different. As for the threat . . ." Bill grimaced. "It wasn't just for Star that Ty came here to kill Hollowood."

Damien stiffened.

"The Hollowoods killed every family member Ty had except Sunny. Bay, on hearing of the massacre, sent his men to decimate their clan. Told them if they ever came south again, he'd do worse. They did, but then so did he. Whittled them to bone, and left with a blood-bought vow they'd never come again."

The worst part was the terrible clarity Bill's tale granted. Ty's burning words to Knott, *"Her family? It could have been everyone you ever knew,"* reached back from the grave to close around his heart.

"But Sam Hollowood did," Damien managed.

Bill breathed out. "He did." The bottle dropped to the grass. Damien didn't take his eyes off Bill's face. "I considered convincing Star to ride back to Bay's. His hold on the vermin up north is slipping, but at least the old coyote has some grip on the nest." A rough shrug. "Bay's one man, and his people are loyal to him. He falls, that's it. Ty said to take Star to the Bears, so that's what I'm going to do."

"His mother seemed to think it wasn't safe there," Damien pointed out, still trying to shake off the newest horror. "You claim it changed?"

Bill shook his head hard. "I don't know a damn thing. I'm too tired to fight this mess on my own." Loss echoed beneath the weak admission. "Isn't it better to have help watching him? Or to at least, if you both choose not to stay, let him have a chance at meeting family?"

Damien thought it would be better to cart Star off to the other side of the world, but he let that go. He'd watch Star's back, as would Ostra and Knott. As for the rest?

"Why won't you be there with him? Do you expect him to hate you after all this?" Damien wouldn't blame Star if he did, but couldn't see it. Bill could probably burn Star's world and still have him.

As that was what Bill intended them to do, they'd soon test his theory.

"It'll be my sister who does the hating."

By sun and moon both, Damien wanted to throttle Bill. "Your sister?"

Not even a grimace this time. "Beresford's wife."

Damien closed his eyes, breathed in through his teeth with a whistle that almost hurt. "Anything else?"

Bill shook his head. "If there is any more, death sealed Ty's lips."

Damien sat by the fire long after his conversation with Bill. Uncertainties ran through his head, chasing every idea he started forming about what to do. Part of him wanted to keep Star as far from the Bears as possible, knowing that his ancestors had been destroyed on or near those lands. A threat might still be hidden there. The other part wanted to give Star every option to know his kin, and to let him change some of the choices his *family* had made for him.

Leaning closer to the flames, Damien picked up the tin Bill had left and opened it. He picked through the letters and pictures, his heart growing heavier as he did. It was the picture of the twins that cut him the most.

Ty had said there was no woman like her, and that in her pain she preferred death over being tamed. Those words were made terrible by the knowledge of how deeply she'd meant them. How many lives had she destroyed to achieve that goal? How many hurts had she suffered to drive her there?

Her eyes in the picture were stony. They all looked serious, as was the norm in such photos, but there was a coldness there that wasn't present in the calm face of her brother. He could see Star in young Ty, but there was nothing of him beyond the surface in the girl's face.

Knott sat next to him, eyeing the picture in his hands. Damien sighed and handed it over, then took out that damning stack of letters and handed it to him too. Knott scanned both, then cursed softly.

"Tell Ostra," Damien told him, "but not where Star might hear. Not until I've had a chance to talk to him."

Knott, still reading one of the letters, nodded slowly. "Things are already strained between you. Think talking to us instead of him is the right approach?"

Damien gnashed his teeth. "I think there is no right here, just wrongs."

Knott's snort sounded like agreement.

"Bill says Ty wanted it a secret," Damien whispered. Star slept, he was sure, but better to be safe.

"And you?" Knott pressed, tone bland. Damien knew him well enough to know he shared Damien's opinion.

"He needs to know, especially before dawn brings him face-to-face with a sun-damned older brother."

Knott's narrowed eyes were question enough.

Damien gritted his teeth. "Aric. The man who offered us shelter until our names clear. Turns out that's his reason for such generosity."

Another curse fell from Knott's lips. Ostra was watching them, now, but Knott shook his head and she stayed back.

"I'll tell her," Knott promised. "By the sun's madness, I'll tell, but you'd best tell your own part."

"It wasn't the sun's madness," Damien muttered unflatteringly.

Instead, he thought of a pair of twins with Star's hair: a girl with eyes that glittered cold as ice and a boy who grew into a man with too many secrets.

CHAPTER

※

FIFTEEN

Star woke, thrashing, to the feeling that he was being smothered. Half-remembered words chased him, crooning about his blood and the gift it'd give. A man grabbed him, ordering him to breathe, and for a moment the hands around his arms were bony, nails digging into skin like daggers. He lashed out, kicking and coughing. His foot caught the phantom in the chest, and he coughed, doubling over before scooting away.

"Stay back," a voice choked out. "Give him space." Then, stronger, "Damn it, Star, breathe! There's no danger."

Damien's voice. That, finally, broke through to him, chasing away the phantom. Shadows lay thick over his surroundings, but there was something familiar about them. The figures hovering at the edges of his narrowed perception no longer loomed so threatening. Blackness ate at his vision until he realized he had to breathe out. He did, a shuddering, gasping thing, and suddenly had room for air again. His free arm, when he looked down, showed no marks from gouging nails.

Memory crept in through the cracks of his crumbling panic.

"I'm sorry," he muttered at last, voice as shaky as his legs as he stumbled to his feet. Avoiding the camp's eyes, he slinked off to where they'd buried his father. It had been so long since he'd last dreamed such horror. Why now?

Standing at the foot of the fresh-dug grave, he stared at where the split-open branch that served as its marker had been stabbed into the ground. Ostra'd carved his father's name,

Typhoon, deep against the grain, the letters running down. It truly was a beautiful spot.

They couldn't stay there, but how could Star ever leave him?

Damien had followed him, but he stood back. There were roughly five feet between them. The span of a man, Star mused. He wanted Damien close, but damned if he knew how to close the space. He felt raw and hollow inside.

"We need to put some distance between us and Wendy," Damien finally said. "We can't be sure that we won't be followed. Hollowood's guns were all hired, but that doesn't mean one of them might not come anyway. Pride is a damn thing."

"I know." Star knew the man had a family up in the north. There was no guessing how those madmen might react.

Still, he stared toward his father's bed and kept silent.

"I talked to Knott and Ostra," Damien continued. "They agree our best bet is to take Aric's offer."

Damn him for not letting Star have a minute, and damn himself for knowing why he couldn't. There was no time. They'd all lost people, and every second he held them back spit in the face of their pain.

North to Black Falls. He'd never traveled so far, but it was a large town, and it would get them out of easy target range should Hollowood's leftover men strike for revenge. It was a good destination, and while he didn't understand Aric's offer, could they really afford not to take it?

There would be messenger routes there too, which he could use to write to Lacy and Bay. Maybe they would hear the news from him rather than another source.

Star closed his eyes, listening for a moment to the wind in the trees and the birds overhead. It was a good place. He wished it could be a mountain overlooking a swath of prairie field, where the currents blew hardest and carried the loudest stories. Here, though, there was a peaceful little glen and leaves to sigh at the stories the air told.

It was nice.

"Okay," he answered at last around a lump in his throat. "I need a drink first, then I'm ready."

Damien gave a laugh that was too forced to be real. "If Bill left anything, it's yours."

Their goodbyes were hard. Damien's surviving crew and Wendy stood almost on top of each other as they exchanged their last words. The kids, no doubt sensing the somber mood, hung back with wide eyes and nervous looks. Star pitied them, knowing it must be hard and confusing.

Aric hadn't said much that morning but stopped next to Star as he passed from the house to the corral. "Uncle Charles wants to see you before we head out."

Star hesitated, then turned to Bill. "I'm going to say goodbye to the old fellow."

Bill pressed his lips into a hard line but nodded. "I'll wait here."

Having thought Bill would want to come along, Star paused. An offer hovered on his lips, but instead, he returned the nod. "I'll be quick."

Star slipped by the others and headed inside. He took the stairs slowly, not wanting to wake any of the injured. At the door to Uncle Chuck's room he hesitated a third time.

A peek around the door showed Chuck squinting up at him, a grizzled brow up over his deathly pallor.

Star swallowed and stepped in, removing his hat. "Aric told me you were up and wanted to say goodbye."

Chuck grunted. "You'll be following my nephew to Black Falls, aye?"

"Aye," Star agreed. The spread of Chuck's smile was impossible not to meet with a weak one of his own.

"Then I'm sure we'll meet up eventually, if I ever get out of this thrice-damned bed."

Star laughed despite himself. "I guess we will." As short a time as he'd had to get to know Chuck, Star couldn't see him staying abed longer than it took a man half his years to heal.

Uncle Chuck blinked, slow, and Star took it as cue to leave. "I'll let you rest. I just wanted to thank you and say goodbye."

"Not yet, lad."

Star hesitated, torn between repeating his excuse and waiting to hear what else Chuck wanted. "As you said, we'll likely meet up eventually." Those glittering eyes held an intensity beneath blood-deep exhaustion that made Star's already heavy spirit shiver.

"You go careful," Chuck ordered. "Keep an eye at your back and weapons handy."

Chuck's strange fervor increased Star's discomfort. "We'll leave before the Blade gets here. Damien and the others will be fine."

Chuck scowled, scruffy brows lowering over his eyes. "I'm worried about you, you damn fool. Let that bastard take care of his own mess. You get to Black Falls and don't dawdle."

The intensity of the words was as startling as the venom beneath them. Star wavered in the doorway, wrong-footed. "Things have settled."

"They'll never be settled enough to keep your head on those bony shoulders." A yawn split the words, the intensity failing as Chuck blinked. Consciousness was taking serious effort. "No man's threats can hold rabid creatures at bay. Their minds will go too far to care."

"I'll be careful," Star promised, throat thick with nervous tension. What threats and what creatures? The *Hollowoods*, his mind supplied, and a shiver traced his back. "What has you worried?"

Chuck didn't seem to hear that question. "Tell that big bastard of yours I'll have his head if he doesn't keep an eye out."

Star took a careful step back, wishing he knew what Chuck meant. "I will." Questions pressed on his tongue, but Chuck nodded and closed his eyes. Star made his escape.

What, by the sun, had brought on *that*? Questions would need to be put to Bill as soon as he got him alone.

Outside, those of Wendy's family who were still standing had gathered at her side as Damien and the others sat in their saddles, waiting on him. Star wavered a second, then turned to Wendy.

"I'm sorry about your brother," he told her. "And the others you lost."

Her red-rimmed eyes met his, clear and kind. "I'm sorry about your father too. Thank you for coming here. We owe you and yours a debt."

Swallowing hard, Star nodded. "You're welcome." He forced a small smile before joining the others.

"Hurry up," Aric ordered as soon as he closed the distance. "We should've been gone already. Better to be long shot of here before anyone comes snooping."

Star muttered an apology and hastened to mount. They turned their horses into the direction of Black Falls, and Damien gave a final wave. He and the others never looked back. Star himself wasn't so strong and glanced over his shoulder before they crossed into the tree line. Wendy gave a sharp nod, and that was that.

It was a quiet ride. They were approaching the last legs to Ameson, a town they planned to skirt around on the route to Black Falls, when Damien called for a stop. They'd been following a well-traveled path for several marks, so it wasn't a surprise they'd be turning off as the already worn ground showed more use. Otherwise, they'd plod straight into the town itself.

Star looked toward Damien, waiting to hear what he'd say. The frown Aric aimed at Damien showed how little he liked the other's calling, but he didn't voice a complaint.

"I want to have a little talk with Star," Damien told them.

Star's trepidation stirred at the pronouncement. The unease between them had been thick, but Star wasn't sure he could face it yet. Still, he slid down and waited, the double-barrel rifle slung painfully over his aching shoulder.

When Bill dismounted too, Star paused. Watching Bill dig a familiar tin box out of the pack bags on Lacy-Lee, his trepidation rose. Damien's arm sliding around his back startled him. He looked from his lover to Bill, uneasy, but let Damien guide him, Bill's footstep soft at their back.

They stopped a short distance from the others, within sight but not hearing. Star threw a glance back at them, grouped together in the wind-blown grass and beneath the bright, late-morning sun, then faced Damien and Bill. "What is it?"

Damien's expression was a study in concern and sympathy, and Bill's creased with pain and guilt.

"We have to tell you some hard truths before we get to Black Falls," Damien answered him.

Bill held out the box, a fine tremor in hands Star had always known to be rock-steady. Carefully slipping the rifle under his broken arm, Star reached for the box, dread winning out over the vacant ache that had swallowed him since his father fell. Bill pulled it back closer to his body, shaking his head.

"Sit first, please?"

Star studied him carefully, then nodded and sank down. Damien mirrored his movement across from him, tucked so close Star could almost feel the heat from his skin. The hum of insects and cries of birds would have been soothing if not for the way Damien looked at him.

Bill knelt, the box a poisoned blade between them. His eyes remained locked on it, dry lips tight over whatever it was Bill wanted to say.

The scraping sound when the box opened cut through the peace. Bill stared into it like a man gazing into the sun's fiery face, then pulled out a slip of paper.

"This first, lad." Still Bill didn't meet his eyes.

Star took it. Two solemn and beautiful faces stared out of the old photograph, both achingly familiar. He knew his father even in youth, and knew her because she was nearly the image of them both. Tears prickled at his eyes. He closed them, took a breath, then opened them again. "My father and his sister. Aric told me about her in Blue Rock. I think Dad planned to tell me once . . ." He lifted a shoulder, letting the words die.

She appeared cold, but Ty was so perfectly himself. He held that same stubborn jut to his jaw that Star had loved and hated in equal measure, the one Bill assured him often that he shared. Her nose was sharper than his, his chin longer. The stare in Ty's eyes as he faced down the camera was determined. Star set the photo on his knee, refusing to give it back yet. Damien rested a hand on his other knee, loose and comforting.

Next Bill passed him a thin sheet of paper. A letter.

"No, Star," he said softly.

Confused about what he meant, Star shot Bill a questioning look, but it was Damien who nodded to the letter, face sad.

Star started reading and had his explanation.

The wave of loss was quieter than the first. No, that hadn't been a picture of his father and aunt. It was one of his mother and her brother. Star wondered if, were his father—*always* his father—still alive, this information would have left him feeling anger instead of an aching, terrible emptiness.

"How long have you known?" he managed to ask Damien around the lump in his throat. Why was Damien aware when he himself wasn't? Bill would have known from the start.

"Only since your father died," Damien said. Star hated how gentle his voice was. "Bill brought this to me yesterday evening while you napped."

Bill. The cut of that left ice in its wake.

Star watched the man he called family and finally, slowly, those blue eyes rose to his. "*Why.*"

It wasn't a question but a demand. Bill's strain increased but Star didn't care.

"If you ask why I told your man, lad, it's because I'm too much a coward to tell you alone. If the why is about Ty, then you know."

More letters were handed over. Star wanted to throw them out almost as strongly as he wanted to bury them in his heart. His name was Starlight. He hadn't known that.

"I can answer your questions. I can also give you time to think and grieve first, if that'd help."

Star stared at the pile of letters on his lap, pinned there by his hand. Damn the wind, trying to steal even this from him. "Why am I being told this now?"

Damien answered. "Aric is your sire's eldest, and the lands offering us shelter belong to his family."

A brother. He'd thought it strange how determinedly Aric had pressed himself on his company during the firefight. Aric hadn't left his side until the bullets had stopped. The sudden offer of shelter coming hand-in-hand with the airing of bad blood between their families hadn't sat right, but Star had been so desperate for a respite that he'd seized it. Another thing he should have questioned, it seemed.

"That's why he offered to shelter you." Star shivered, forced himself to ask. "My family. Is it just him?"

"The man you met with him at Wendy's? He—"

"My own great-uncle, then." Star choked on a hollow laugh. Uncle Chuck, he'd insisted Star call him. That, at least, had been honest.

"Aye," Bill told him. "He'll be holed up with Wendy for a while, but I've no doubt the old bastard will soon be on the mend. Since he couldn't bring you back to the Bears, that falls to Aric."

The brother he hadn't known, and now didn't know how to accept.

"What does Aric actually want?" And that was the real question. Not to be friends, that had been a line.

"They've been hunting for you a long time."

Chuck's orders for him to watch his back echoed in Star's mind. "Hunting me?"

Bill kept silent, and Damien spoke. "The day after we met, a man came into the saloon with your picture. He wanted to talk to you. I went to warn you and found your father instead." Star stared at the ground, holding a blade of grass as those words crashed over him. "When I told him, Ty was furious. He had us leave that minute."

Star had wondered at the change, but his father truly went with the wind. He'd accepted the order like he'd always accepted them.

A sigh escaping, Star squeezed his hand, the dry blade digging into his palm. Looking up, he stared Bill in the face. "I want to talk."

Bill raised his gaze to meet Star's like a man facing execution, but Star couldn't muster pity for him.

"How did she die?" he demanded.

"Star—"

"How did my mother die? Was it him, the man in the letter? Beresford?" Star hated how his voice trembled. Still, when no answer came, he made himself speak again. "Aric said she was shot. Was it because of me?"

That broke the silence. "It wasn't you, Star, and it wasn't the Bear. It was sudden, that's all."

Star swallowed air, his throat thick. At least Bill's avoidance wasn't a lie. He'd get that answer, but there were more he could push for first. "What was she like?"

Bill sighed. "She wasn't like your father. She had a coldness that burnt harsher than any fire, and a fiery determination that was as cold as a desert night. She killed herself to force your father to raise you alone, all because she thought that was how you should be raised."

Killed herself. Staring, Star tried to understand. "*Why?*"

"Your people were old. Ty never said much about them, and I'm sorry I never really asked much. I doubt he said anything to you about them beyond his stories, did he?"

Star shook his head, tightening his hand over his father's rifle. "Just that they died, leaving him and Sunny alone, and then he found you." Nothing more. Not one word about a sister, or about being his uncle, or even about the north beyond that his people had been killed there.

Bill nodded, confirming he'd known as much. "At least he told you that." After it was obvious Star planned to say nothing, Bill spoke on. "They had enemies, and some of those enemies hurt her. Bad." A wince, and Star heard the name of those enemies without needing it said: Hollowoods. "Maybe that left her seeing threats where none existed. It'd been years earlier, well before you, but that's all I have. I can't explain the why, lad, only the how."

A bullet from her own hand. The cold truth of it left a shiver in Star's blood. He'd spent so many cycles wondering what had taken her from him. Now he knew.

"Did she hear the wind and follow it like Dad?" Star asked, not caring if that name for Ty was now a lie.

"As she could."

She'd claimed to be forced to live in silence. Then that the fields were growing loud, Star wondered if she'd been hearing the wind then. How much worse would it be to hear it and be unable to answer than to never hear it at all?

"It doesn't speak to me. Not like it did to Dad." The admission tumbled from his lips, truth from an old, mostly ignored wound that now felt new.

Bill pressed his lips. "It's in your blood, Star. Whether or not it makes demands of you changes nothing."

Star knew Bill meant it to be a comfort, but the words still felt sour to him. Damien, hand gentle and eyes steady on his face, didn't offer any platitudes.

"I don't know what that means," Star admitted, tired of it all.

"Ty said that he told you of your people." Bill spoke with gentle uncertainty that frustrated Star more than anything else.

His father's warning not to speak of any of it before Damien flashed through his mind, but Ty was dead and Bill was a liar. Damien was at least honest.

"Dad never told me anything even when he tried," Star countered, anger leaking into his hurt. Bill flinched but didn't dispute it. How could he? Bill had known Ty too, and better because he'd lived what Star had only heard of in bits and starts. "Why are we really going to Black Falls?"

"They want to meet you, lad. It's one of the only safe options left."

"What about what I want?" But Star didn't know what he wanted. The world, already crumbling around him, was too much.

"Tell me, and I'll do my best to make sure you get it."

Star looked down. His hand drifted to his side, running over the handles of his blades.

"I'm sorry, Star, about all of it," Bill told him. "The secrets were wrong, but Ty loved you. He only ever wanted for you to be safe and happy. After Sunny was hurt, Bay and his pack killed most of the Hollowoods and kept the rest in the north by threat, but Sam Hollowood didn't come for you. He came for Damien and the others."

It was a cold, hard truth that sliced deep.

"I don't know that Bay would justify attacking the Hollowoods for one man's act, even with Ty killed at that bastard's hands." Bill's voice shook, and Star squeezed his eyes shut, forcing back tears. "What Sam Hollowood has shown, though, is that Bay's word isn't enough to keep them all north anymore. Ty must have decided the same. He told me he wanted you to go to Beresford with his last breath."

Star suddenly understood the nonsensical ramble seared into his brain the same as the feel of Ty's warm blood.

"What do you think they'll want?" Star asked. "I don't want any more surprises."

Bill sighed. "Honestly? I think they want to bring you home with them." Damien cleared his throat, wearing a sharp expression. Bill looked away, swallowed, and continued slowly, "Bear's wife? I should tell you, Star. She's my sister."

Star jerked at that, the fingers of his free hand fumbling to find Damien's. He squeezed his fingers as Bill's pained expression seared to the bone.

"They were already married, with one son, when you were born."

Star slotted those new pieces into the half-made image. It was a cold, cruel picture. "And you helped Dad take me," he answered. "From your brother-in-law."

Bill grimaced. "Aye."

Star released Damien's hand and stood, hefting his father's rifle onto his shoulder and stalking back to the horses. As Star remounted, Aric stared at him from the head of their pack, expression closed. Shoulders bowed, lips pressed thin, Star kept his eyes straight ahead and nudged Clay forward before the other two regained their saddles.

They continued on.

Threats. They haunted Star, nipping at him from too many directions. Uncle Chuck had hinted they existed while Bill had said they were old and buried, driven away by spilled blood. Grateful for the time to think, Star wondered at Bay's part in it all. He'd ask Bill eventually, but the questions wouldn't cross his tongue yet.

Too much had happened, too fast: Ty dead, Star and Damien the cause. The lie of his life, a bitter one. And the mother he'd only known in broken bits of memories now lived in his mind. By the sun, she'd put *herself* into her grave, but why? That was the largest question of them all.

The others busied themselves settling their horses and preparing for the night. All but Damien, who moved next to Star and stood there like a stone carving. Damien, who had to feel the strain between them, yet still offered support. Star felt as though a gun were leveled at his back as he dismounted and met Aric's intent gaze.

"Bill spoke to you."

Knott and Ostra put their heads down and moved farther away with a haste that spoke of foreknowledge. While thankful for the measure of privacy, Star resented that Bill followed their lead.

"He did."

Star read relief on Aric's broad face, but all he felt was dread.

"Your friend there wants to stay straight," Aric finally stated, probably realizing Star wasn't going to break the silence. "If you come home, we can give him that chance."

Star's tense muscles unclenched as curiosity ate his fear and distrust. "They've the law on their side now."

"Aye, but memories are long-lived. How easy will it be for Damien and his pack to find a safe place? They can take their pick of land off our ranch and settle there. We'll give you cattle, horses, whatever it is you need to start. Just come home, Star."

"You haven't a clue who he is," Damien stepped in, voice hard and carrying an echo of distrust.

"He's my brother," Aric snapped. "And now he's bloodless out here."

"He's ours," Damien argued.

Aric's green eyes—the same as his own, Star realized unhappily—narrowed. "But he was ours first."

Star pressed against Damien's side, struggling to break the tension. He didn't want to be there, watching two idiots fight in a show of "I am top dog."

"That skinny ass belongs with me," Damien growled, and Star could hear anger building up.

"And that *right there* is why you should be as far from him as—"

No matter how uncertain Star felt about everything else, he knew one thing for certain.

Stalking closer to his self-declared brother, Star leveled his best glare at him. "You want me? I'll bite, but only *if* you keep your word and grant Damien and his crew shelter."

Aric fell silent, the anger on his face melting into hesitant hope. Star's own glare died, replaced by confusion. How could a man he had barely met feel so much for him?

"You have my word, Star," Aric assured him. "You're all welcome. Just, please, say you'll come and meet us."

Star paused, but he'd already said he would. "Aye. You've my word, so long as your family keeps theirs."

Aric puffed up like he wanted to correct him, but Damien, giving Clay a soothing pat, shot Aric a hard look. Whatever it was Aric wanted to say, it subsided. "Thank you," he said again.

Uncomfortable under that intent, eager face, Star let his shoulders drop and shuffled back a step. "Well," he stuttered, then forced his voice firm. "It's time we helped with camp."

"I'll take first watch and wake you for second," Aric told Damien as they sat around a small fire, the sun sleeping and the moon creeping across his dark plain. Only half-listening, Star leaned against his knees and let his mind wander.

It was a relief to crawl into his bedroll. He'd stretched it out alongside Damien's, not willing to give up the comfort of his presence. Aric remained at the fire, eyes on the trees and brush surrounding them. Sounds of the others settling to rest—Knott and Ostra's soft exchange of words, Bill's restless shuffling—drifted on the air.

Star rolled against Damien, finding him easily in the low light of the fire's coals. Damien stiffened as their bodies touched, and Star cursed himself for being a weak fool. Before he could shift away, Damien's fingers slid into the tangled mess of his hair. They caught on the snarls he hadn't cared enough to tend, but rather than worry them away, Damien started rubbing his scalp. Leaning into the gentle ministrations, Star sighed.

"Can't sleep?" Damien whispered.

"I don't want to." Dreams waited. The feel of Damien's fingers digging lightly into his skin soothed the ache in his chest. Star pressed his face against Damien's chest, letting loose a soft hum of contentment.

If only he could capture this sleepy comfort and carry it with him, an accessible wave of peace filled with the clean smell of the summer night and Damien himself. His father's loss burned like the sun, searing him with its wrongness.

Damien shifted, wedging his other arm beneath Star, and Star let himself be wrapped in that careful embrace. He pushed closer as Damien pulled him up.

A question rose in his mind, and he couldn't stop himself from asking. "How do I live with him gone?"

Damien kissed the top of his head. "You keep us with you. We'll be here, and you'll find your feet again."

The words soothed Star when almost nothing else had. It was a huge admission from Damien, and he held to it with everything he had left. He wanted to keep this moment, cling to it even as his chest burned with guilt and blame.

He kissed Damien's throat, then curled against Damien's shoulder. There he could only smell him. Damien's chest rose and fell with each breath. Star rubbed his face in deeper, snaking his hand beneath the shirt under his chin to feel warm, living flesh.

Damien had lost weight, he recognized, worry chasing the thought. There was less fat atop the muscle now. Then, they'd both lost weight since leaving Standing Grave. Lost it, but gained more of a different type. It lay raw and untreated, but there'd be time to tend it when the world stopped spinning away from him.

He prayed there would be.

A rough nudge to Damien's ribs startled him into waking. Aric, crouched beside him, glowered in the low light of the freshly fed fire.

Damien rolled to his feet, careful not to disturb Star. He should've known Star'd never budge. He was a creature of habit no matter the circumstances, wanting to sleep as soon as the moon tipped his hat. Knott already sat by the fire like a poorly mannered shadow, hunched forward and scowling into the distance. No doubt distrusting Damien's ability to make nice with their newest guide.

"You played dirty," Damien told Aric as he settled by the fire, one gun on his lap and the other holstered. Knott heaved a loud sigh that he ignored.

Aric shrugged, showing no shame. "That sick bastard Finn got Star years ago, and we didn't hear until it was over. Not even Mom with a dream. Then Ty got himself killed by one of the very bastards who made him an orphan. I'll play any game needed to get Star safe within our borders."

"Star's stronger than you give him credit for," Damien snapped, fighting back shame.

"He's still my little brother," Aric growled, narrowing his eyes, and Damien felt sure that here was finally the meat. "What is he to you but a lay?"

The insinuation sliced through the tattered cords of Damien's restraint. Anger stirring, he reminded himself that Aric knew damn little about Star and was only trying to protect him. "It's none of your business, but I give him exactly what he wants, and how."

"As I'm sure Finn thought too," came Aric's snarled response.

Knott seized Damien before he could throw himself past the fire. Unable to land a punch on that too-deserving face, Damien bared his teeth. "If you weren't his blood, I'd kill you for that."

Aric stood, fists clenched and eyes hard as tainted emeralds. Those eyes might share Star's coloring but they could never be mistaken for his. "I want to kill you for touching him, but I can't because for some damned reason the fool loves you."

The anger in Damien banked. In truth, Aric wasn't who he really wanted to fight. That man was in the ground, and yet still could cause terror. "And I love the fool. He'll be safest in your territory. Give me your word no one will try and take him from us and I'll support you."

Aric searched his eyes and Damien waited, knowing he would find nothing but honesty there. "Until he wants free, no one will drive you off."

Knott's grip on his arm tightened, almost bruising. "How will he be welcomed? He's your married father's bastard."

"He's his second youngest son, who we've been trying to bring home since he was a baby." Aric either meant it or was giving a good show. "He'll be made more than welcome. None of what happened was his fault."

Pretty words. "Your mother really thinks so, then?"

Aric's face hardened. "Bringing him home can't worsen the air. Dad's obsession won't end until given closure, and Mom desperately wants that." Chin high, like the stubborn bastard Damien loved, Aric's expression didn't waver. "She told me to use you in her last letter. 'Give the fox a well-hidden den,' she said, 'and his mate will follow.' She told Dad to declare you off-limits in our county before the bounty died. Is she happy? No. But that doesn't mean she'll hold any of this against him."

With a flash of teeth, Aric met Damien's glare with his own. When he turned, heading for his own bedroll, Damien slumped back onto his seat, suddenly exhausted.

"Feel better?" Knott muttered sarcastically, releasing him.

"Not in the least."

Knott sighed again and patted his shoulder. "Wake me for my watch. I'm trusting you not to murder Aric in his sleep. Don't make me regret it."

Damien watched with sour longing as Knott rejoined Ostra, curling together in long familiarity. Left alone by the fire, he leaned forward and stared into the night, wishing it could be that easy for him.

CHAPTER

※

SIXTEEN

The stars spread across the sky in a wild sea broken by rolling clouds. All day, Aric had ridden by Star's side as fields gave way to forest. He'd even had the gall to try to take Clay's reins when they'd forded a shallow river cutting across their route.

"I have her," Star snapped, only to be laughed at, Aric proceeding to hover as they crossed. Worse, he kept almost as much an eye on Star's mount as he did his own, as if Star were a child incapable of keeping control of his damn horse. Then, when Star had gone back to help his pack horse cross, Aric had come too, under the pretense of ensuring no one had forgotten anything.

Bitter and on-edge, Star'd given way and let Damien lead Shine, shoving the reins into his hands with a warning glare. Damien must have taken his meaning, as the reins remained with him, not Aric.

Now, sun sleeping and moon awake, Star tried to will himself calm as they took their time riding through the night's shadows. Aric insisted there was a cabin where they could all bed down, and the promise of a roof over their heads helped ease his aggravation. The clouds were heavy with the promise of rain, but the well-worn trail made for an easy trek.

In time, the cabin showed itself through the tight press of trees surrounding their path. The building was small but had a good roof, four walls and, Aric promised, a stone fire-pit within. A pile of weathered wood sat beneath the cover of a fat oak for firewood.

"Our family uses this as a hunting camp," Aric said. "The woods are rich, and this is the start of our family lands. See the shed?" Star did see it peeking through the trees a short distance from the camp. "We skin and hang the meat there, and there's a smokehouse a short ways behind that again."

"We're on your lands already?" Star spoke up, surprising himself.

"*Ours*, yeah, but there's a lot of it. It'll take the morning to get to the house. We'll be going through the back, so there won't be a lot to see other than gardens, cattle, and more road. This is the trail we take to do trade in Ameson."

"Open range, then?" Knott asked.

"It is. Our hands keep a weather eye on them, herd them nearer if they wander too far, but they've all been branded, and we've the largest number of livestock. The Crowsfields have the next, but since we're neighbors, our people work together. We watch our side and they watch theirs to keep them from getting too lost."

"And the others?" Ostra inquired.

"And the others, but that's just a handful of small-timers. We all do our part and work together."

It felt good to set up camp that night. Aric stretched out snoring not far from where Star slept, having surrendered first watch to Knott. Damien tried not to acknowledge his flicker of amusement at the two brothers falling face-first into sleep with the rising of the moon beneath the night's clouds. The last thing he wanted was to think fondly of Aric.

Unable to find his own sleep, Damien slid from the cabin, closing the door quietly.

Knott looked up from where he and Ostra sat together on the low porch, and the flickering light from an oil lamp caught on the haggard lines of his aging face. "Can't sleep?"

Damien shrugged.

Ostra stood and came to his side. The same light that traced Knott's face betrayed the strain of the last few weeks on hers, but still her mouth pursed in that amused line Damien knew well.

"Want to take a walk?" she asked.

He hesitated.

Knott huffed. "I have the watch. Your lad is safe. You two go and talk."

Knott always saw through him. Holding out his arm, Damien tried for a smile as Ostra took it, leaning against his side. The feel of her there, steady and strong, comforted him.

Knott lit a second lamp and held it up for Ostra. "To keep you from breaking your necks in the dark. Douse the thing if you see anyone."

Ostra rolled her eyes and tugged on Damien, leading him away from Knott, who'd already turned back to his task. The flame lit their way through the high grass as the threat of rain on the air turned to mist.

"You're a hard man to get alone these days," she commented, expression closed-off.

He sighed. "Knott filled you in, then."

"What he knew." Firelight caught the flecks of silver in her red hair. Her eyes, when they met his, reflected that same flame. "Now it'll be my turn to fill *him* in after you spill the rest."

They were apparently far enough now from the cabin. Ostra turned, expectant, her arms loose at her sides. Damien's heart was heavy, but he spilled the story in all its ugly detail, including what he guessed, based on theories both firm and tenuous.

Ostra's eyes never left his, and when he'd finished, she nodded once. "We don't know enough about the situation, but we won't learn more by leaving here. The Hollowoods have more to them than Sam showed." Heaving a sigh, she shook her head. "Ty's people are remembered in the south. They were good folk. I knew Sam Hollowood to be rotten, but to be part of what was done to them?"

Damien still struggled to swallow it too. "Aric wants to protect Star from us, you know."

She snorted. Her fire lessened a bit, tempered with humor. "From you, I bet. Knott and I hardly register, the fools."

"I think it'll do Star good to go somewhere he can rest. If we return to Wendy, she'll still be dealing with the attack. Cleaning, sorting out the herd, and hiring more workers. If we go north . . ."

That was the unknown.

"The Bear territory is large. Beresford and his family are known to be fierce. Hell, there was a reason Wendy took on Chuck with no real questions asked."

Oh. He stumbled a step, dread wafting through him. Ostra, ever able to follow his thoughts, howled out a shrill laugh that cut through his ear.

"Oh, Damien, *Oh*," she crowed. "Uncle Chuck. That makes so, so much sense now."

Aric. Charles. Would all the Bears look at him like they did? Damien could feel a headache growing behind his eyes, and Ostra's continued snickering didn't help.

"When they get to know you," she told him gently, voice still choked with laughter, "I'm sure they'll like you as we do."

At least one of them was confident.

"The offer buys us time to regroup." She shrugged. "Knott and I both agree that it's too good to refuse. Bay's might be another possible choice, seeing how involved he is with all this, but Black Falls is only a short ride now. Where is your head?"

Damien grimaced. "Too many places to do us any real good." It felt like his moves since hitting Blue Rock were all reactionary. The others looked to him, and he knew he wasn't holding up under that weight.

Ostra must have read some of that on his face. "Keep to the trail for now. Knott and I are watching your back. We've both worked cattle ranches before and know the general lay of that land. You focus on your lad and these Bears."

The crisp words were a warm comfort.

Light rain picked up as they turned back, moving from a dusting of mist to a steady downpour. He pulled his hat off, tucking it under an arm and tilting his head back to catch the cool moisture on his face.

Ostra tilted her own head back with a little laugh. The rain had already soaked her hair. "We needed this."

"Aye." It had been too dry for too long.

Ostra took his arm again as they silently walked through the growing mud. Damien let his mind wander, thinking about what was to come and what they'd be doing. The Bears had offered them land but who knew the cost. Star, exhausted and hurting, would likely see it as a chance at safety. Maybe it was too. Damien just wasn't sure he liked it.

Ostra slipped free as they came back to the cabin's porch, rising on her tiptoes to plant a kiss on his cheek. "We have your back," she reminded him before retaking her spot at Knott's side. Knott nodded before his and Ostra's heads tipped together. Probably already sharing the new information, their soft words lost under the beat of rain.

They rode out of the sparse forest and onto the next stretch of plain. As they broke the tree line, a misty bluff rose into the sky, hazy as a puff of smoke against the horizon. It was a lone giant among the grass stretched out in front of them. Damien, close to Star's side, reined Ink to a slower pace and whistled.

"Aye," Star agreed. "It's beautiful."

"You'll see it better once we get closer," Aric said, voice full of proprietary pride. "It's what gave our town its name—Black Falls. In the city you can make out the falls too, and with a day's ride, you can visit them."

For the first time in days, Star's fear and pain drifted away, replaced by curiosity. One day he'd ride out there and see what he'd find.

Bill pulled up his horse and Star hastened to follow suit, scanning for a threat but finding nothing. When Star tried to catch his eye, Bill avoided his gaze.

"Best I'm not around when you arrive," Bill muttered.

Startled, Star leaned forward. "Where are you going, then?" Angry or not, he'd counted on Bill being there when he met the rest of Aric's family.

"Ty's cabin." Bill finally met his gaze. His lip twitched in an attempt at a smile. "I'll be easy enough to find, lad, once you're settled. You all should keep riding."

Gritting his teeth, Star lifted his chin and urged Clay on. He felt Bill's eyes on his back but didn't say another word, and neither did Bill. The others came up alongside him, Aric pulling ahead to lead.

Around midmorning, a reedy little man, wiry and large-handed, met them as they rode through the low, rolling hills. He'd been riding his horse at a walk, watching a wandering herd of grazing longhorn, when they caught sight of him. His head tilted their way as they closed the distance. Aric dismounted and the others followed his lead.

The stranger did the same in turn and led his horse their way. He reached up to clap Aric on one of his large shoulders. "Good to have you back, son. Your parents will be thrilled." Then he looked them over, eyes assessing. "Any of these fellows coming my way later?"

"I've worked on ranches before," Knott said. "I've a good memory for that work."

"And I go where he goes," Ostra threw in after.

"Thanks," Aric said. "Gavin here's the foreman and will welcome your help."

The reedy man, Gavin, looked Knott over, then Ostra, and nodded. "You seem like a good and tough son of a bitch. I'd say the lady looks about the same."

"And us?" Star asked, pride twinging.

"You've one arm and are healing," Aric answered.

Star's face hardened. "I can work."

But, truly, could he? He didn't have the first idea what to do with the cattle. Without Ty, the choice to ride here was his own, and how could he know it was the right one? They would all be strangers in this place he'd been born but never known.

Memories of lying abed in a wash of sunlight, listening to Damien's quiet wish for a home of his own . . . those were what kept Star from turning back. There had to be a way for them to build something together, and this was their best chance. Ty was gone, but at least Star could protect the rest of them. Theirs was not a life for the long-lived.

But Star knew deep down, where his good intentions ended and the truth crouched, why he really kept to this path. It was a chance to shake off a world shaped by lies and to face truths his father and Bill had never been willing to give.

"You should hurry along," Gavin suggested, voice knifing through the uncomfortable silence following Star's words. "Bear is home, and they'll be glad to see you."

Eyes flicked his way, then back to Aric. Star swallowed hard and fell into step.

It was a large, sprawling property, covered in green grass, flowering fields, and fence-enclosed gardens filled with growth. Apple trees speckled the path, some ripe and others not yet hitting their prime. In the distance loomed a large, black butte, a lonely giant against a beautiful summer sky.

The house, when it came into sight, was larger than Bay's and glowed with fresh whitewash. It had wide, curtained windows, a gentle slope to the roof, and the charm of it took the breath.

"We're coming up on the opposite side from town," Aric said, face bright with pride. Star couldn't even fake a smile, dread coiling like a serpent in his stomach, ready to lash out.

A large figure ran their way from the side. At first Star took it for a man, but soon he could see limbs that held the gangly lines of a body quickly growing. The lad couldn't be a day over sixteen summers. He was as tall as Aric, putting him a good few inches over Star, and had the same sandy-brown hair.

Aric laughed, twisting in his saddle. "Looking for us, Cal?"

Cal, who had to be Aric's brother, grinned. "I'd hoped it was you! C'mon, Ma is waiting at the house."

"How has everyone been?" Aric asked, urging his mount to a walk. The horse nosed Cal, content to amble along.

"Great! We've gotten your old room ready, and Ma has been cooking and running us all ragged cleaning."

The words didn't help Star's nerves, but Aric said, "Sounds about right."

"And you avoided it, as usual," Cal sang back. The jovial play between the two made the air heavy in Star's lungs.

They left their horses in the corral and headed for the door. Cal kept shooting Star curious glances that he did his best to ignore. He only wanted to find somewhere quiet to sort his feelings but that choice wasn't on the table.

Star's guts twisted further as he stepped through the painted doorway. Bill's sister waited inside, and he wanted nothing more than to flee. How could she bear to look at him, physical proof of her husband's betrayal? A quick check Damien's way showed a closed-off nervousness, and when he glanced at Knott and Ostra, their expressions were solemn stone.

Mae—for it could be no one else—met them in the wide, homely entryway leading to either kitchen or lounge. Her blonde hair was the same shade as Bill's, her eyes slightly darker. She didn't smile, but neither did she grimace.

"I'm pleased that you made it safely," she said. "You can get cleaned up at the pump in the yard. Then I'll get you all something warm and hearty to eat."

"Thank you," Damien answered for them. Star couldn't get a word past his swollen-feeling tongue.

"I've made up a room for you and Star, Sole," she continued, her focus on Damien. Star leaned closer to Knott, not wanting to draw her eye. "You two will be right upstairs."

"Damien, please."

Mae offered a strained smile. "Damien, then." Star didn't miss the quick glance she cast him before she turned to her son. "Before you wash up, we'll get everyone settled. Aric, please take . . .?"

"Knott, ma'am," Knott introduced himself. "And the lady is Ostra."

"Knott and Ostra." She smiled again, the expression still stiff though her eyes were kind. "Please take them to get settled in the bunkhouse. Star and Damien, I'll bring you to your room."

Knott shrugged, his hand sliding over Star's shoulder in a rough but comforting pat before he trailed after Aric. Ostra, keeping pace with a firm rigidity in her step, slanted him and Damien a half smile.

It was just them now. Star edged closer to Damien, pride stopping him from grabbing his arm. They followed Mae's back up the stairs past the kitchen. There was a small hallway at its landing. She led them down it to a corner room, resting a hand on its painted latch.

"This will be yours," she told them. "Please, don't feel you have to rush. Bear should be in by the time you join us downstairs. He can't wait to meet you, Star."

She left them, her words rousing an anxious flutter in Star's stomach. Bear, the father who would replace Ty if he could but was years too late, remained a mystery he wasn't sure how to face.

Star stood, uncertain, taking in the room as Damien pulled the door shut behind them. The windows were open, letting in a warm breeze through gauzy blue curtains. It smelled of the tall lilac bushes below and summer itself, sweet and fresh.

A patchwork quilt stretched invitingly over the bed in the corner, flowers embroidered on each patch in soft, neutral colors. A bowl of crushed cedar and rose-petals sat next to the bed, and when Star managed a step closer, the scent joined the rest. It was welcoming, awakening a feeling he couldn't quite place, aching and yearning all in one.

"I guess we should wash up and then bring our packs up here." In contrast to his words, Damien leaned back against the door, staring at him.

Star swallowed, a minute tremble in his fingers making him clench his fists. This wasn't a life he knew. Why did he think he could manage it?

In two steps Damien's hand closed over his good arm, his warmth cutting through the cold of Star's fear. That loose, easy grip was enough to stall Star's panic.

"I don't want to meet him," Star admitted. "Why did I come here?"

Damien pulled him closer, and Star wrapped his arm around him, holding him there. Damien gave in without a fight, letting Star cling.

"Are you sure you don't want to?" Damien asked. Star rested his chin on Damien's shoulder as he spoke, feeling the words as much as hearing them. "Or is it that things are happening too fast?"

Star gritted his teeth against an argument he knew would be a lie.

"C'mon, Star," Damien suggested, voice gentle. He slid out of Star's hold, and Star missed the feel of him there, solid and real. "Think of the steps and don't let your mind chase you."

Star ducked his head, face flaming at being caught off-balance. It felt like he lived that way lately, and he hated it. Firming his resolve, Star grabbed the throat of Damien's shirt and pulled him in for a quick kiss. The press of dry lips calmed him, the familiarity a welcome respite from so much *difference*.

He released Damien and led the way out of the room, his head high and shoulders loose by force. Damien was at his back this time, and Star resolved not to hesitate in front of him.

Bear was indeed inside once they came downstairs, and he surged out of his seat the second he saw them on the stairs. There would be no quick escape, it seemed.

"You look like your mother" were the first words out of his mouth. Star flinched, but Mae just stood there, a little pained smile on her lips.

"I've been told so, sir," he answered uncertainly, continuing down the steps.

Beresford started to say something else only to have his wife catch his arm.

"Why don't you boys wash up?" By Bear's expression, her grip wasn't kind.

Star couldn't get outside fast enough.

The water from the yard pump splashed, cold and fresh, into a dark metal trough. Star rolled back his sleeves and took his time, capturing the liquid in his hands and burying his face into it before it could all slip between his fingers. Damien did the same at his side, his sun-darkened forearms gleaming above his dusty sleeves.

Cleaned, he pumped a little more, cupping it in his hand and drinking. Its taste washed away the dryness. The task took far too little time, even as he tried to stretch it out, his mind worrying over what he'd seen between husband and wife. He finally stood back from the trough with a sigh, frowning.

"How are you doing?" Damien gave his hands a shake. Droplets of water glistened on his face as they caught the sun.

How was he doing? Uncomfortably. The strained air made his skin itch. "Should I be here?"

Damien grimaced. "You aren't at fault. You know that, right? It was your mother and Beresford. Only them."

And his father for stealing him. Bill for letting it happen.

"That isn't an answer," Star pointed out, taking another step back from the hand-pump but not yet turning for the house. Damien stood next to him, staring at the white-washed walls.

"If you want to leave, then we can. For now, though? Maybe taking a bit of time to learn these people isn't so bad an idea. They *are* your blood, and they want you here. Staying tonight doesn't mean staying tomorrow, or a moon from now."

Knowing Damien stood beside him, that he'd support him here, was comforting and made it easier to start back for the front doors.

Inside, they found the large bear of a man waiting with his sons, Mae tucked back and almost out of sight behind them. All three carried a strong resemblance, another reminder that Star didn't really belong.

"Let me see your arm," Beresford demanded, apparently not one for small talk.

Star stiffened, the desire to refuse rushing through him. He swallowed the urge back, not willing to risk insulting the man who offered Damien sanctuary. "It isn't necessary, sir. I'm about healed."

Ignoring his words, Beresford, his father, carried a chair out from the kitchen and set it down in the middle of the parlor. "Son," he ordered Aric, "get us some bandages from upstairs."

The man went as bid, returning swiftly with a clean roll of bandages. Beresford nodded thanks as he took them, and his large hands were gentle as he helped Star first out of the sling, then out of his shirt.

"How did you get hurt?" Cal asked, jarring the table as he hastened around it to get a closer look.

"You have work to do," Beresford interrupted, not giving Star a chance to answer. He took his time unwrapping the bandages around Star's arm as Aric dragged Cal out of the house. Star barely winced as Beresford bared the wound. Damien, hovering at this side, watched with careful eyes but didn't say a word.

"This is a good job," Beresford commented, glancing Damien's way. "You do this, son?"

"Aye."

Beresford nodded slowly. "Well done. I'd say it's healing nicely. You can leave off the sling soon, long as you take it easy. The stitches I'd give another day, maybe two."

As he spoke, his eyes drifted to Star's back, eyes running from silvery line to silvery line. Watching over his shoulder, Star swallowed at the pain growing on Beresford's face but kept his own expression neutral. He hated the prickle that always came when anyone stared at proof of his time with Finn.

He didn't try to say anything, throat too dry to talk. Beresford gave him a look full of sympathy. Star wanted to dislike that offering, but Beresford's green eyes were mirrors of his own, no matter how different they were in every other way, and the look was comforting, somehow.

Beresford, finally ducking back to his task, wrapped the arm up again. Star sighed with relief when Beresford finally patted his good shoulder, finished.

"You need rest so you can heal," Beresford announced, as if Star hadn't the sense to rest and look after himself. Then his eyes flicked to Damien, and Star tensed all over again. "There wouldn't have been much opportunity for that on the way, but maybe, now that you're safely here, that'll be easier."

Damien's face was closed off, but, to his credit, his nod was hardly as stiff as it could have been.

CHAPTER

※

SEVENTEEN

"**S**tar!"

Star almost missed the last step on the staircase. Blinking back sleep, he found Cal darting to him with a toothy, excited grin. Startled by his excitement, it took Star a moment to realize Aric was at his heels.

"Good morning, Cal," he greeted, then nodded to Aric.

"We thought we could take you for a tour around the grounds," Cal chattered "How about it?"

Had they been ready to spring at first sight? Star cursed himself for not waiting for Damien before venturing out, but with the tense air between them, he'd wanted quiet time alone to think. "It might be nice."

"We'll introduce you around," Aric added.

Mae emerged through the doorway to the parlor, a glass of water in her hand and a frown on her lips. "Let him have a drink first, boys. And I want to look at his arm before you drag him after you. Go get some fresh air and wait."

At the chorus of apologies, she straightened and approached. When she held out the glass, he took it slowly. If she read how nervous he was, she didn't show it.

"Thank you," he told her.

Some of the hardness left her face, and for a moment, he could see a soft melancholy stain her eyes. "You're welcome, dear. Sit with me?" He followed her to the table, slipping his arm free of its sling. She worked quietly, humming at what she saw. "The stitches will need to go soon, but not today."

He thanked her once she finished replacing the bandages, and she managed a wan smile. "Please, let the boys take you outside," she said in place of an acceptance. "I'll let your young man know where you are when he gets up."

Not seeing a way free, Star surrendered with a small nod.

Cal practically flew to his side once Star stepped out into the clear, sunny morning. The rain a few nights back had slit open the heat's belly, and the air felt lighter for it. Aric, waiting a few steps away from them, just nodded and waited for them to join him.

They led him straight to the barn, where two men stood alongside Gavin, who they'd met in the fields the previous day. The foreman, Star remembered. His brothers joined the crowd, and he trailed after them, feeling a little twist of amusement in his gut at the sight the group presented. Those big bears that called themselves his brothers made the others look like bushes next to trees.

They said something to Gavin, and he twisted to look Star's way, a grin crossing narrow lips. "Ah, decided to come visit, have you?"

Star nodded. "Aye. They want to introduce me to everyone."

Gavin grunted, glancing to the barn. "Well, everyone is out and about but the three of us. These are Roy and Hender." He nodded to the two men standing at his side. "We've dropped by to check in with the Bear before heading to town."

Roy grimaced an approximation of a smile. Hender met Star's eyes with a cool gaze that prickled the back of his neck. He was barely taller than Gavin, but there was a thickness at his shoulders that suggested a raw strength. Roy, while not much taller, lacked that same presence.

"Nice to meet you." Star hesitated briefly before taking each offered hand. Roy's handshake was quicker than strictly polite, his grip sliding away swift as a blink. Hender squeezed harder than expected, sending a shot of pain up Star's good arm.

Instincts screaming, Star took a full step backward after he was released. He maintained a polite expression through force of will, angry at himself for letting his nerves get to him. Cal and Aric traded a look but, thankfully, didn't comment on his cowardice. Hender's and Roy's lips twitched at the corners but that was all. Asses, both of them. Nothing more than that.

"We want to show Star around the grounds," Cal explained to Gavin, as if needing the wiry man's permission. Maybe they did, since Gavin immediately turned to study Star. The frown Gavin turned on them, centering particularly on Aric, didn't make Star feel better about the whole situation.

Aric, Star was beginning to suspect, was largely considered the responsible one of the pack. He wondered how that had come about, or if it was the price of being the eldest.

"Not the whole grounds," Gavin drawled. "Right, boys?"

Roy, watching from behind him, snickered. Hender frowned and shifted impatiently.

"Just the area around the house," Aric assured. "I want to show him where I've built my place in case he needs me."

Star gritted his teeth, disliking the implications in that statement, but none of them seemed to care about his pride.

"And maybe the old cabin where our uncle Bill is staying," Cal added. "He hasn't been by yet, but he'll be around more once he's settled in, Ma says. I want to meet him."

The words woke hope in Star that swiftly died as Gavin shook his head.

"Your home only, lad," Gavin ordered. "Then the two of you bring him back. He can see that old tom another time."

"I'd like the visit," Star spoke up, voice firm. He gave Gavin a narrow-eyed look.

Gavin, in response, snorted. "Ty raised you, all right. Still, lad, sorry. You'll be needed back sooner rather than later. The Bear would likely set to roaring otherwise, once he found out his cubs ran off with you, and those same cubs would soon be on latrine-cleaning duty—among other, more wonderful tasks."

Taken aback, Star stared first at Gavin and then at the brothers. Their wrinkled, pained-looking faces suggested experience with what Gavin said. He sighed, disappointed. It seemed theirs would be a short walk.

"We'll be quick about it," Aric promised.

Annoyance burrowed in Star's chest. Why should they have their steps curtailed? Only the amused light in Gavin's eyes as he'd compared Star to Ty kept him from arguing. Instead of giving Gavin more ammunition, he fell into step with his brothers, vowing silently to see Bill later. He missed him, though he understood Bill's reluctance.

"You grew up traveling, right?" Cal asked as they waded through grass and flowers. "Was it lonely?"

"I had my father," Star said. "Bill, too." It sounded like a weak defense to his own ears.

"Still," Cal pointed out, "that's not many people."

Aric shot him a sharp look that Cal ignored. And why not? Cal had a point. What might it have been like to have others around that were his age? Star felt a flicker of envy that he swiftly doused. He'd had a wonderful life. His father had always been there and had taught him how to look after himself in case he someday wasn't.

And now he wasn't.

Tears prickled the corners of his eyes. He stared stonily ahead, tired of these unexpected bursts of mourning and fear. Aric pulled Cal back, saying something, but Star hardly gave it a thought.

Striding forward without any mind to direction, he tried to outdistance the twisting in his gut. Shame and frustration were a slow poison that joined too easily with the emotions he already carried.

Rushing was foolish. Star heaved forward off-balance, his foot tangled in grass. Cal, having pulled away from Aric, caught him before he could fall flat.

"Thanks," Star muttered, his face on fire. His splinted arm panged in rebuke as he found his feet.

Grinning, Cal let him go. "You tripped on *grass*." As if it was a delightful turnabout.

"We're a little off our route, but we should probably head back anyway," Aric suggested gently. "I'm sure Damien is up by now and looking for you."

Star accepted the weak excuse with no complaint and followed their lead back the way they'd come. He wouldn't relish latrine duty, either. Ashamed at how rudely he'd been treating them, he asked, "What do you have for livestock?" he asked, trying to make up for his rudeness.

Cal instantly perked up. "Cattle over that ridge. Our neighbor keeps sheep, but he's good about keeping them off our land, and we do the same."

"No horses?" Star asked, curious and a little surprised. "The ones by the corral are beautiful, and I'd thought you might breed them."

"No," Aric said, visibly relieved at the new conversation. "We get our horses from Bay Coyoteye, whose lands are to the south a fair piece. He's worth the travel. He doesn't like visitors, but he'll let buyers pass if he has word of their coming."

"Bay? You get your horses from him?" No wonder they were so lovely.

"You know him?" Aric asked, eyes narrowed.

"He's a friend to my—" Star caught himself. "He's a friend." He hadn't missed their discomfort the last time he'd named Ty father. "My own horses are from his herd, and there are none better."

Aric gave him a look mixed with pain and sympathy. "I really am sorry. If you'd like, next time you can come along. I bet he'd be glad to see a friendly face."

"I'd like that."

And he would, though it'd be hard. Bay had known things about Star that Ty had kept from him, same as Bill. But it was Bay's threats that'd kept them from being hunted by the Hollowoods. As much as Star looked forward to seeing him again, there were questions that couldn't lie silent. He was done with that.

"Is that why Bay struck at the Hollowoods after your mom's family found Ty and my mother? He protected them because of ties to you?" Star asked.

Aric flinched. "That's a question for Dad, and not for out here."

"We're not allowed to talk about any of that," Cal hastened to add. "But no one ever said why."

"Cal!"

Star gritted his teeth, wanting to press but seeing no point. Aric had made it pretty clear they couldn't answer. Star wasn't about to ask if he didn't have to, but *Bill* would know. Ty'd told him everything.

Star turned his attention back to the fields ahead of them, but he couldn't force the thoughts to stop churning even as his newfound brothers started talking again. Bill would be answering more questions as soon as Star managed to slip free of the shackles.

Damien, waking to the news that Star was out exploring with the Bearson brothers, decided to track down his own family and check in on them. An older hand gave a rough description of where he might find them. So, saddling Ink, Damien rode out. Eventually he spotted two familiar figures on horseback in the distance.

Knott greeted him with a grin. Ostra, following his gaze, smirked.

"I didn't know if I'd be finding you. Sneaking away?" Damien teased, bringing his horse alongside theirs.

Knott snorted. "Just getting the lay of the land. The foreman, Gavin, wants us to know our way about before he sets us to work."

"How about Star?" Ostra threw back. "He try to escape yet?"

Damien, reading the concern beneath her question, shook his head. "Star is fine. Out with his brothers, actually. Mae isn't happy but she is kind. The others are overwhelming him with attention, and I think it scares him, but he's handling it."

And Star wanted family. Desperately. Losing Ty had shaken him to his core and knowing he had others besides Bill to call his own might help soothe some of that pain. Not enough, by the sun, never enough, but maybe . . .

"How are *you* doing?" Ostra asked, interrupting his morbid train of thought.

How, indeed. Damien wanted to say he was fine, but the words refused to leave his tongue.

"Worried," he finally answered.

Knott and Ostra looked at him without censure, their expressions twin understanding. For all that Damien had wanted a place to settle for the last few years, their lives weren't sedentary ones. Now all three of them were staying here and with no idea for how long.

Would it be for a moon? Two? *Longer*? Was it borrowing trouble to worry over how the three of them would manage the change? Would Ostra and Knott stay if it ended up being longer? Would he, himself, be able to adapt?

"Keep one foot ahead." Knott turned his gaze back to the distant herd milling around. "You know we'll always have your back. That fear you're choking on isn't gonna help anything."

Those rough words eased the growing knot in Damien's chest. Aye, they were a family, and he was being foolish. Wendy had left, but she wasn't Knott and Ostra. He'd always have a place to go with Wendy, but where one of their final three went, the other two would follow. He suddenly felt Jonnie's loss all the keener, knowing that his hulking form would have been seated right beside them had things gone differently.

"Thank you," Damien managed to choke out past his thick throat.

Knott shrugged, Ostra snorted, and that was it.

"It's a nice ranch," Knott commented, changing the topic.

Yeah. Riding to find them had given him a chance to look over the lands, and they were rich in water, good ground, and plenty of growth. No wonder the Bears did so well. Land, a large family, and open arms—those things should have made him comfortable. Why, then, did Damien feel as if some threat curdled the air? He wanted to tell himself it was leftover nerves from everything that had gone wrong, but he'd never been one to ignore his instincts.

"Keep your eyes open for me," he said instead, turning to glance in the opposite direction. A bluff loomed large and beautiful, but it was a reminder that there was more in the distance than could be easily seen.

"Someone has to," Knott teased, "since you're liable to forget and watch that pretty lad of yours."

Damien laughed, feeling more of that melancholic unease splinter away. Still, he couldn't let it go completely.

CHAPTER

✸

EIGHTEEN

Star wished he could just slip out the back door, but he doubted he could escape without drawing notice. So instead he milled around the yard, answering Cal's questions and trying to ignore the sharp watch Aric kept over them both. Eventually Gavin came to collect Cal, chiding him for neglected work, and Star retreated to his room.

Damien had left, no doubt seeking his own people. Hating his relief, Star paced the floor and chewed on anxieties he couldn't shed. Gavin hadn't wanted him to see Bill, an order that grated against him.

Aric and Cal fell to the foreman's words with an ease that betrayed practice, but Star had only ever given one man that kind of loyalty. Knowing they were there on the Bearsons' suffrage wouldn't keep him from seeking out his original family. Finding Bill shouldn't be too hard. He'd learned the direction of his cabin, and once night settled, he'd ride.

So Star bided his time. He went down for lunch and exchanged light words with Damien once he'd returned, both of them careful to avoid anything that might touch too deep on the space between them.

Dark fell, and he slipped away to saddle Clay. A few of the hands glanced his way, idly curious, but Gavin was thankfully elsewhere and none of those present attempted any conversation. Focusing on the direction Aric had given for Bill's, Star rode out into the evening, Clay's hooves a soothing clod against the ground.

A voice interrupted the quiet. "Out here alone? I would've thought the Bears would have you tucked up at the house."

Star pulled up Clay and twisted to face the voice. The shadows cast over the man's face made it hard to place at first, but as he neared, Star recognized Hender. He was on foot, explaining how he'd slipped by Star's attention.

"No one clipped my steps," Star fired back, remembering Hender's harsh grip and cold eyes.

"Prideful as your mom, I take it."

There was no missing the sneer in the words. Star gritted his teeth. "I'm sorry if I've given offense."

Unwelcome unease prickled over his skin as Hender's glittering gaze sliced into him. "I'm sure."

Star clenched his fist around Clay's reins. "Am I the one who offended you? Or are you angry at a dead woman?"

That got a reaction. Hender's lip curled back, cutting into a snarl. "You're a damn fool for coming back here, you little—"

The sound of hooves on soil took them both by surprise.

"Hender!" A stranger, but Star was relieved to have that uncomfortable confrontation end. The snarl was gone from Hender's face.

"If you'll excuse me." Star urged Clay on before the new arrival could waylay him further. Smarter, probably, to stay and press for answers, but Star didn't want to lose the chance to see Bill.

What was Hender's problem, anyway? He didn't look old enough to have worked for the Bears while Star's mother still lived. But he must have known Sunny to speak of her so coldly. That was something he'd ask Beresford, Star decided, scowling into the shadows. It'd make it easier not to step on any toes.

The cabin came into view, and Star slowed Clay, his heart rising into his throat at the age-silvered wood of its walls and the old tin of its roof. This was the cabin they'd given his parents. It was a lonely little shack off the beaten path, its sloped stoop sitting in a pool of moonlight. Three wooden chairs were shoved back, away from each other and the opening door.

"Lad."

Star held back for a second, then threw himself from the saddle. Mounting the porch steps, he grabbed Bill with all the strength he had. Bill smelled of drink, but Star didn't care, holding harder as his arms came up to embrace him.

"Easy, Star," Bill said. "Don't go snapping my back. Or rebreaking your arm. One night with the Bears and you're already one?"

Star laughed into Bill's shoulder and eased his grip, swallowing hard and blinking back the moisture forming in his eyes. He hadn't known until he'd seen him how much he'd needed this.

Bill dropped his arms.

Star forced himself to take a step away and meet those familiar eyes. "It's good to see you." Leaning back, Star's gaze roved over the interior of the wooden walls. The corner where two bedframes sat, only one holding a mattress. The crooked table where two empty bottles of drink had been abandoned and a third, almost empty, waited with a dirty stack of bowls. The rifle-stand, its antlered single shelf dusted over and unused.

Star saw, too, the newer floorboards near the cabin's entrance, the wood aged but not yet as worn as the rest despite its placement. Star heard Bill swallow as he gazed at the spot. He knew the answer and didn't bother asking. Blood had soaked into the floor there. It'd stained the wood and been sawed out as if the removal could replace the act.

"Have you seen Mae since you got here?" Star asked instead, startling himself with the question as much as he did Bill.

After a beat, Bill shook his head. "No, lad, but I doubt she'll let me get by with that much longer."

Star glanced at the bottles again, then away, worry gnawing at his guts. "It's strange here."

Bill forced a laugh and shook his head, giving no sign he'd noticed Star's distraction. "Strange for me too, being back. I never thought I'd see these lands again. These once belonged to my family. Still do, I suppose, but they're Bear lands now, not Cove."

The fields where he'd grown up. A home he'd lost when he'd chosen Ty. "It must be hard." Hard enough for him, and he'd never known this place.

"Late for you to be prowling," Bill commented, pushing past the words.

Star shrugged, letting the subject change. "Easier to slip away."

Bill snorted. "No doubt."

Star took his time going over the cabin again, chewing on the things he wasn't quite ready to say. "This is where Dad lived."

"And where you were born."

But now it was where Bill hid with their ghosts.

Star took a breath. "The Bears. They're all strangers but they keep pretending I'm not one."

Bill sighed and sagged, taking a few steps out the door to sink onto the deck. "Have you decided what you want yet?"

That question again. Even half-drunk, Bill came back to it. "I don't know," Star admitted, taking a step closer.

"Ty isn't here to make that choice for you. It's all you now."

Grimacing, Star sank next to him close enough that their legs brushed. Bill was running hot. Drink, most likely. Under the full moon, Star could see the flush on his skin. He'd been too deep in his own grief on the last leg of their ride to notice, but now, seeing Bill like this, Star regretted giving him so much space.

They sat in silence.

It was unfair, taking advantage like this, but Star had questions and he'd ridden out to ask them. "What age did they start living here?"

"Fifteen." Bill laughed, a terrible and aching sound. "Their first few years were in my father's house—which no one uses anymore, now that the man is dead. People wanted them dead, lad. We changed their linens for our clothes, but we couldn't change their nature. All my parents could do was offer them a refuge."

Star couldn't imagine being on his own so young. "Did they spend a lot of time here?"

"Not Ty. Not if he could help it. But Sunny wasn't allowed to leave after the attack. Too many dangers *out there*, apparently." Bill's eyes narrowed on him, suddenly clearer. "This ain't what's bugging you."

Star shrugged. "It doesn't matter."

"You actually want to talk something out? It matters. Spill."

Star met Bill's gaze. "If you share some of your drink."

Eyes slipping away, Bill waved a hand behind them. "Find any left, feast away."

Star stood. The door creaked open on a room that ached with loneliness. Ignoring the mostly empty bottle on the table, he found one abandoned beneath a shirt that needed washing. Using the material to wipe the filth off, he carried it outside and passed it over. Bill popped the cork and took a swig, grimacing at the taste.

Reclaiming it and throwing back his own mouthful, Star closed his eyes and let the burn swallow his worries. The second's reprieve hardly touched them.

"Aric told me that Beresford knows Bay." He took another mouthful, swallowed, and pushed ahead. "Is that why the old coyote helped Dad?"

Bill sucked in a breath, and Star clenched his fingers around the bottle, reading the panic in his eyes.

"No." Another breath. Bill took the next turn and drank deep. Just when Star had braced himself to take it away, Bill finally put the damn thing down. "It isn't something you'll like hearing."

Picking up the drink, more to keep it from Bill than to have it himself, Star shrugged. "I don't like hearing much anymore."

Bill avoided Star's eyes, finding something else in the darkening night. "My family didn't have any part in Bay's decision, and neither did the Bears. Striking at the Hollowoods after they massacred Ty's people so close to Bay's own land was all the old man's choice and came down to his blood.

"Bay left his name in the north when he left that sheep country and set stakes in his own territory. He didn't agree with the rest of his blood and threw the name away. Took Coyoteye instead, after who his family had been long before that damn tree sucked blood into its roots and convinced a bunch of madmen that the earth wanted the owners of that blood dead."

The weight in Bill's adverted eyes had warned that the new knowledge would be hard, but he hadn't been prepared for the truth. Another piece of his family's story, Star reflected, and when he'd thought there could be no more. All those years of secrets finally dead, but unearthing the truths didn't come with the joy he'd always imagined. It'd been childish of him to ever think there would be.

"Bay was one of the Hollowoods," he finally made himself say. Would it have hurt more or less to have gotten this newest piece from his father, not Bill?

"Aye. Back before either of us were born, that was his name. But he threw it away and made something better of himself."

"That's why Bay didn't kill them all that first time."

"Blood is blood, no matter if you hate every lick of it in your veins. He felt like he needed to give them a chance. Thought more kids might grow up to follow his steps, but none did."

"And the second attack, the one on my mother?"

"He killed most of the bastards. I wish he'd killed them all, but he'd thought his point made. They did stop coming for you, even if that monster Sam Hollowood did come south."

Star leaned over his knees, a fist clenched in his throat. When would he hit the bottom of the horrible truths? Was there one?

"Kid?" Worry in Bill's voice. "How are ya?"

A stupid question. Star fought back a laugh that'd ring as hollow as he felt. "Tired."

Bill hesitated a moment. "I think that's enough for tonight. There isn't anything more to tell, anyway. Get me some water, lad, from the house. I'll need a good drink before I can ride, and you won't be going back on your own."

An argument rose in his throat, but Star forced it down. His meeting with Hender kept him silent as he stood and did as bid. There was something else he'd realized during Bill's confession.

"You don't trust it here," Star said, one foot in the cabin and his back to Bill. "Even with Bay's grip on the sick bastards up north."

There was a bucket of water on the floor, full almost to the rim. Two more steps and he'd filled one of the tin mugs sitting next to it.

"Bay is old and a deal three times broken is breakable again."

Star bowed his head, wishing for once he could have a break. That they could have a chance to heal before this new mess fell onto their heads. Why hadn't he just stayed at the house and tried to talk to Damien? But that wouldn't have gotten him answers.

Beresford and Mae wouldn't appreciate seeing Bill at their door, and it was already later than Star liked. "You don't have to come back with me. I won't be talking to anyone tonight anyway."

Bill's scowl answered.

They were saddled and riding before realization hit home sharp enough to draw blood. Star pulled Clay up short, heart pounding in his chest.

"Kid?" Bill squawked, turning his own mount around and walking her back.

Star glared at Bill, frustration and desperation coiling in the pit of his stomach. "You said three times."

"Star?" But Star saw Bill's flinch, read his panic and regret as plain as the moon and stars that surrounded them.

"First, they killed my mother and father's people," Star listed, words sharp as his knives. "Second, they attacked my mother. What third deal possibly lies broken between them? Sam Hollowood coming south to seek my lover? But why would that affect Bay?"

Bill's soft cursing didn't move Star to let the matter drop. Bill ran out of steam and slumped forward, hat obscuring most of his twisted-up face. "Kid," he choked out, expression stricken.

"I'm not a kid anymore," Star fired back. "I haven't been in years, not that *either* of you ever accepted it." He didn't feel any pleasure at Bill's wince, just a guilty ache dulled by exhausted impatience.

"No." Bill ducked his head. "You've the truth of it." Star gritted his teeth, waiting, and Bill gave a shuddering breath. "Five years ago, Finn Hollowood came south and took you. That's when Bay killed almost all of them. Not for Sunny, lad, though he did kill a great many that day. For you."

Star tried to speak. Couldn't, not at first. Instead he heard words that haunted his dreams, clearer than they'd been in years, claiming his blood and praising what gifts it'd give.

"Every horror visited to my life has a root leading back to them, doesn't it?" Star forced out through his thick throat. "Dad saw the whole tree but didn't want me to see it."

A small hesitation. "Aye."

Ignoring the tremor in his hand, Star urged Clay forward. They finished the ride in silence.

CHAPTER

✳

NINETEEN

Mae was mending clothing by lantern light with a small, melancholic smile, an untouched tin mug of lavender tea by her elbow. Damien perched at the kitchen table across from her husband, nursing his own mug and waiting out the heavy silence. With Cal in bed and the others gone, the house was still as a grave.

When Beresford had asked Damien to come down, he hadn't expected they'd spend so long swilling tea and avoiding one another's eyes. Twice he'd considered escaping to the couch with an offer to help with Mae's mending. Only the nervous hope on Beresford's face kept him at the table.

Beresford leaned over, lengthening the wick of the lantern between them, and Damien tensed. The light flickered over the scarred tabletop as the fire flared and then settled.

Beresford finally lifted grave eyes. "I don't know my son."

The words came without blame or anger. Factual. Pity wasn't what he wanted, and Damien forced that reaction out of his voice. "Star is a good, strong man."

"I've no doubt of that." Beresford sighed. "I need to know how to make him comfortable here. Show him he can trust me."

Damien grimaced. That wasn't so easily answered. His attempts to be a solid, comforting presence as Star worked through everything had felt ineffectual. How was he supposed to help someone else? "That'll take patience. And time."

The response earned him a wry smile. "Those I know. Is there anything he needs? *Wants?*"

"Safety. A chance to rest." He searched Beresford's face. Hoping he wasn't misreading it, Damien asked, "Is it safe here for him?"

Unease ran down Damien's spine as Beresford looked away again, expression distant. "It should be. You know of Bay's involvement with the Hollowoods?"

Damien hid his discomfort. "I'd like to hear your take on it."

Beresford nodded, staring at the moonlit fields outside the nearby window. "I took Bill and Ty to Coyoteye's lands not long after Mae and I married. The lads were eager for the trip, and good company. I needed the help bringing back new horseflesh."

One shoulder lifted, a great mountain shifting in the firelight. "Can't say how Bay knew the lad's history, but he stood there staring when we dismounted, gray as the belly of an old stone. Didn't seem to see the rest of us anymore. Just started swearing to Ty he'd keep the hounds from the lad's neck. Vowed Ty would live, and that had he known any of Ty's blood still walked, then he'd have made sure the slaughter never happened."

An ill wind brushed a chill down Damien's back. He hadn't questioned Bay's involvement before, thinking it tied to their friendship. This? It made no sense.

"Why?" Damien demanded, harder than he'd meant.

Another lift of a heavy shoulder. "He never would say. Glared when I asked. I tried questioning Ty too, but he was always a close-mouthed bastard." Beresford looked like he regretted that insult after it left his mouth.

Damien couldn't blame him, not after knowing what else Ty had kept unsaid. Maybe Beresford hadn't deserved answers, but Star sure had. "They found them here. Bay's threats, whatever they were, hadn't been enough that time." Bill had said as much.

"And Bay rode here himself not three moons later. Vowed to Sunny and Ty he'd exacted blood vengeance and a new vow from the head of the Hollowoods."

But that meant someone at least lived who'd known to find Ty and his late sister there. And if Bay had known Ty's descent by sight, how many others might have managed the same? They'd been so focused on the present—Star eager for a place to call home—Damien had never thought much beyond Star's newfound family.

"You truly believe he's safe," Damien pressed, needing to hear it.

"Aye," Beresford promised. "And we'll keep a close eye on him."

Very well. But if things weren't safe, Damien would do his sun-damned best to ensure they left. He kept that behind his teeth.

"Is there anything else Star might want? Either of you?"

"As I said, somewhere to rest and safety for our friends."

Beresford's face was wide and open. He'd missed his son's growing years, Damien mused, and now chased Star as if he could reclaim the loss. "Thank you. Do you think he's happy here?"

"I do," Damien said slowly.

Green eyes brightened with a hope that made Damien's chest ache. The poor man wanted so badly to please the son he didn't know. How had Damien ever thought Beresford might want Star dead? It was hard to distrust him. Still, Damien didn't know if remaining here was the right path.

He debated his next question, but he had to ask it. Clearing his throat, he waited until first Beresford, then Mae looked to him.

"Is it painful for either of you, having Star here?"

Beresford shook his head, and his face was clear of any lie. "This was my greatest wish for over twenty years. Star might be grown now, but we can get to know the man he grew up to be. That'll have to be enough."

Damien focused on Mae, and she lowered the shirt she held, her smile fading. "He belongs here."

It wasn't an answer, not truly, but there was no anger on her face. Damien wanted to pry, but instead he nodded and resolved to keep careful watch. One more question, then, though this was far less difficult. "Have you heard from Chuck?"

Beresford laughed aloud, brightening as Mae went back to her work. His sudden delight was impossible not to enjoy. "Yeah, my uncle is doing fine. Your friends are apparently refusing to let him push himself, thank the moon. He'll be on the mend soon, and then he'll land with both feet on our doorstep. Just you wait."

Damien scratched his chin. Chuck was a lot to take, and there were already several people pressing in around Star. Still, Chuck obviously liked Star, so it couldn't hurt. More people to draw Star out of his shell would likely be more useful than not.

A soft voice drifted through the open window as someone approached. Mae, faster than both of them, dropped her work and practically ran for the door as it opened.

Star entered first, head down and fist clenched, but he wasn't who they'd heard. Bill hung back as Star, not sparing any of them a glance, vanished up the stairs.

"Mae," Bill greeted, his awkwardness not helping the hard clench of Mae's jaw.

Beresford, finally over his shock, leapt to his feet with a force that knocked his chair to the ground. Damien stood too, but didn't pursue Star yet. The dangerous glint in Beresford's eyes held Damien in check. Beresford, however, wasn't the one to speak.

"I see you're still alive," Mae snapped, and *there* was the anger Damien had expected. "Funny. Seemed twenty-one years was enough for you to forget where your sister lives, but I guess you did know."

Bill shuffled uneasily. "I didn't want Star riding back alone this late. He doesn't know the grounds." He avoided Mae's eye and took a careful step away from the door. Too late for that, Damien figured.

"You're going back?" Mae demanded, stalking to the door even as Bill retreated.

"Aye. For the best, I think."

"Fine." Mae shoved past him. "I'm coming with you."

Damien took in Beresford's icy glare as Bill, flushed and wild-eyed, shut the door behind himself. There was nothing Damien could say that'd ease Beresford's temper, and he had worries enough.

"I'll go check on Star," Damien said, leaving while he had the chance. The room behind their closed door was silent. Taking a moment to steel himself, Damien pushed inside and found his lover staring out the window. "That good a visit?"

He got no answer. Sinking onto the bed, he set about pulling off his boots. He'd shed his shirt and unbuckled his guns before Star finally spoke.

"Finn was a Hollowood."

Damn it.

Gritting his teeth, Damien swallowed the worst of his sparked anger. "Bill told you that tonight?"

Star's handsome face twisted into a bitter, tired sneer. "Not on purpose. Not at first, anyway." *That* Damien could believe. "I don't remember things. Not really. But I remember Finn's obsession with my blood. How he told me I'd been created just for him."

Damien hesitated, sickened. He wanted desperately to pull Star close but couldn't be sure that it'd be the right move. Setting his guns on the bedside table, he stood slowly, letting the creak of the floorboards announce his steps as he closed the distance between them.

"I'm sorry," Damien muttered uselessly. Damn Bill for holding this back. Hadn't he promised all the secrets to be aired? That all else died with Ty?

"I didn't know a damn thing about my own life," Star continued. "There isn't an end to the secrets, is there?"

Damien stopped when there was barely an inch between his chest and Star's back. "My money'd be against it."

Star answered by turning and burying his face in Damien's neck, slender fingers digging into his shirt with a grip tight enough to tear. "It shouldn't matter." His hot words were muffled.

Rubbing his back, Damien let Star keep that lie. "Should we even stay here?" They'd all believed Sam Hollowood was the first and only one to break Bay's pact in over twenty, twenty-five years. What did it mean that Finn had too, only five years ago? Beresford claimed Star safe, and Bill claimed the Bearson land safe, but what other near misses were buried under still standing lies?

Star pulled back, and his stubborn expression wasn't reassuring. "They've offered shelter."

"I know." Damien fought the urge to sigh. "But we don't know these people. Only Bill does, and you see what they think of him."

Star's expression didn't change. It'd be a mistake to keep pushing, but it was hard to drop the line of talk. Another night, Damien reassured himself. There'd be more chance of talk when Star wasn't reeling beneath new shocks.

Pressing their foreheads together, he took a breath. Released it. "I'm sorry. We're both tired and frustrated. A night's sleep would do us good."

Star's face softened. "Aye."

But Damien lay awake in bed long into the night, Star stretched out next to him and smelling faintly of rum. No amount of exhaustion could turn off his thoughts. Beresford was far beyond welcoming, desperate to keep Star on the ranch. Could his decisions be trusted?

Star held to Damien with the same grip Damien kept on him, but it wouldn't last if they didn't clear the air. They needed to talk about Ty's death, lance out what poison they could, but *how* when every day dug the wound deeper? Damien had never known himself to be a coward before, and it was a sobering, gut-wearying thing to suddenly face.

They had time, he told himself firmly, needing to believe he was right.

CHAPTER

✳

TWENTY

hree blocks of wood balanced precariously atop the empty corral's weathered fence. Star took up his stance a shorter distance from them than he would have two moons ago. His left arm panged as muscles clenched in preparation.

He threw.

His knife clipped the bottom of the first block and sent it falling, but not the way he'd wanted. He glared at where it lay in the tall grass, his teeth clenched. Would he do any better if he grabbed his father's rifle? Doubtful. Too long unusable, his arm was rusty.

Less than a week had passed since the revelations, and Star had been too restless to stay indoors. His arm spurred on the current attempt at distraction. He'd intended to practice alone, but Cal had noticed him in the yard and invited himself along. The kid had chattered at him incessantly when he'd first started practicing, but in time the sun's strengthening glare and the quiet—broken only by the distant voices of the ranch workers— had lulled Cal into a nap, his gold-brown hair, so like his mother's, mixing with the grass.

Star was about to collect the traitorous blade when he heard his name. Turning, he raised his hand in the voice's direction.

Damien was a shadowed figure against the bright backdrop, but Star well knew his shape and stride. "Training?" Damien asked as he made it to his side.

Star sighed, lifting his rebellious arm to point to where the target lay on the ground. The dagger hadn't even embedded itself into it. The few scars on the rest showed how poorly the morning had gone. He'd considered switching to his right arm but had decided against it for the sole reason that, were he to miss with *that* hand, he'd likely start screaming.

"Well." Damien coughed, and Star appreciated the attempt at levity. "Maybe it's a good time to take a break? Beresford is looking for you."

Nerves bubbled in Star's chest. Only Damien's presence seemed able to quell his fears and keep him from spinning into the empty well yawning in his breast.

Damien who, even now, was picking up the dagger and carrying it back to him. "Your arm was broken, Star, and not just a little. The bone tore muscle. You're allowed time to heal."

Star looked into his earnest face. After all the lies and betrayals, what would he have done had he not had Damien at his side? How petty was he to still hold everything that'd happened against him?

"I know." His voice strained with the lie. Damien arched an eyebrow and Star glowered. "I do, even if I don't. What does the Bear want?"

"For you to show back up, for one," Damien answered lightly.

Star sighed, nodding. There was a lot unsaid between them, but he hadn't the energy to dredge it up. Instead, he walked to where Cal had slept through their exchange and nudged his ribs. Green eyes, so like Star's own, blinked up at him and his mouth opened in an obscenely wide yawn.

"Done?" Cal sat up. Seeing Damien, his grin doubled. "Hey!"

Damien chuckled, wrapping an arm around Star's neck. "Morning, Cal. Escaping chores, or here for the show?"

Cal flushed. "A little of both?"

Star snorted. He'd figured as much.

"Good lad." Damien chuckled.

"Did Da send you to find me?" Cal asked, suspicious, and the sudden wariness made Star want to laugh again. While the rest of the Bears put his hackles up, Cal's excitement made him easier to be around.

"Nah, he was looking for Star. I bet you could slip away again if you really wanted." Damien pulled Star closer and then dragged him along the path to the house. "I'm lucky Hender saw you two head this way. Otherwise, I'd still be wandering the grounds."

Star grimaced at the name, but Damien didn't seem to notice. "What do you think, Cal? Time to escape?"

In response, Cal took to their heels, apparently deciding it was better to face the Bear than flee.

"You really shouldn't have come out here alone," Damien said with strained levity.

"I was fine, Damien." And he was. Or would be, anyway, if he had any say in the matter.

"But you might not have been."

Cal watched their back and forth with obvious interest, which had Star wanting to both sigh and bark at him for space.

Instead he gritted his teeth, focusing on Damien. "I hardly see the need. I'm not a child, and I don't need you following me around. I've killed and I've kept my head on my neck this long."

Beresford was out in the yard waiting for them, a wagon hitched with a team of horses already chomping at their bits to be off.

"There you are, boys," he called before zeroing in on Cal. "So, the missing cub lumbers back, does he?"

Cal cringed, but more for show, Star thought. "I wanted to see Star practice."

Beresford nodded slowly. "Mm. And not nap in the grass, I bet." His eyes flicked up to where bits of mulch, grass, and other fragments of the earth had caught in those thick locks. Cal jerked a hand up, then grinned with not one ounce of repentance. Star found himself impressed by the gull.

Beresford just sighed. "Gavin is off in the field toward town. Make yourself useful, trouble."

And off Cal ran.

Star, meanwhile, steeled himself and sidled up alongside Beresford. "I was wondering about a hand of yours, Hender. Has he worked here long?" He felt Damien's sharp attention but didn't shift his own.

"He came on about fourteen, fifteen years ago," Beresford said, squinting in thought. "From somewhere north, I think. Not a talker, but he knows a lot about fishing for a cowhand. Did he bother you, son?"

Star lifted a shoulder. "Nothing like that. We spoke a few times, and I wondered if he might have known Ty."

Ty's name brought a flinch across Beresford's broad face. "Afraid not. Man came on after your mom passed."

Star frowned but nodded, ending the topic. "What was it you wanted?"

Beresford's wary expression served its own warning. "Actually, Damien collected you for Mae. I'm heading into town, but she wanted to talk to you."

Judging by Damien's expression, he hadn't known. Beresford left then, leaving Star to process the unexpected revelation.

Mae?

He'd barely thought the word and they'd arrived at the door. Star wished he could dig in his heels or find a good excuse to run. Too late to escape, Star straightened his back and entered the house.

CHAPTER

✹

TWENTY-ONE

The Bearson matriarch was easy enough to find. Her back to the kitchen door, Mae hummed as she tucked a strip of linen around a wooden bowl of freshly kneaded dough. Star forced himself to meet her eyes as she turned to them. His smile felt weak at best, and the one she returned was little better.

"Good morning, boys," she greeted.

"Beresford said you were looking for me?" Star's words came out as a question.

"I was hoping you'd take a walk with me."

Star couldn't find any signs of deception. Even so, his chest ached from the sudden tightness of his lungs. "Of course."

"I promise not to keep your young man long," Mae told Damien as she led Star back out into the morning sun. "Why don't you take a seat and have something to drink?"

Damien answered, though Star didn't catch it. The door closed a few steps later, separating them from Damien. Star struggled to think of something to say, but Mae, seemingly not bothered by the awkwardness, took his healing arm in a careful grip, patting his hand.

She smiled. "It must feel nice, having this back."

"Aye." He gave a sharp nod to Aric when he came out of the barn doors. Aric looked startled but didn't come their way.

Star let her lead, and she guided him away from the corral, off toward the low hills in the distance. They were walking in the direction of Bill's cabin, Star realized. "Cal said you visited Bill twice this week."

"Cal needs to worry more about his own matters and less about ours." Star flinched, wishing he hadn't mentioned it. Mae sighed before he could gather up an apology. "I did visit him. My brother isn't an easy man to forgive but he's still my blood."

Blood. Everything always came back to that.

"I want to show you something," she told him at last, releasing him and taking a step back. They were almost to the hills, now. He swallowed but stood straight, waiting.

She dipped her hand under the neckline of her paisley dress. When it reappeared, there was a small amber pendant dangling in her fingers. She pulled it off over her head.

"It has long been in my family." She lifted it between them so that the tear in the center could catch the light. He knew what he saw, had known as soon as the amber glinted under the sunlight, and not even the late-summer heat could burn off the responding chill.

Another one. He'd gone his life never seeing such, and now, within a moon, he'd known two. "Isn't it cursed?"

She shook her head, grabbing his arm and squeezing, ignoring how he flinched, or maybe too concerned to care. "No, dear. It belongs to my blood, always has. It's why I have my dreams. It guides me, giving them to me when I need to see. My ancestors never abused it, and it has never been stolen. It was a gift, and we've kept it as such. It has always been treasured as it should be, and so it's still sweet and safe. It's a gift from her child."

"Nothing of the sun or her child is sweet and safe." Star tried to pull his arm free, pain lacing his heart, but she clung with desperation. "Apparently, my parents had gifts, and they both died anyway."

She shook her head, her face filled with determination and belief. "No. It's a gift, Star, and so is the one in your blood. She *is* death, but she is also life, same as the moon. The punishments she wrought were for the thieving and greedy, and their intensity grew when people turned on those like us, doing so to spite her while claiming it was *for* her."

He stared, confusion twisting with horror as he listened. "My father never had a relic. If any of his people did, it was lost forever ago. All he had was the wind."

"No," she said, her voice soft. "Your people were different. Living relics. They were the amber and her tear ran in your blood. She made you free to be guided by the air and her hand, and loved that freedom it inspired."

Living relics. He'd never heard them described as such, but it made far too much sense.

"It's no less a curse." Star shook his head, unable to dislodge the idea. "Where was the wind when my father died? It never saved him."

The admission seared him. To lose Ty like that, and then to have her tell him they were gifted? He'd been his father's curse the same as they'd been the sun's. His eyes burned.

Mae's hand slid over his chin, gentle. "I dreamed of Sunny and Ty before I met them. My mother had just died, thrown from a horse the week before. I didn't feel gifted then either. All I wanted was my mother back. Still, I'd taken her relic and placed it over my own breast, as my uncle had directed. Then, there they were. The dreams, carrying a message to check the barn in the coming days for children needing safety. Did Ty ever tell you how his people were attacked?"

"A little. Bill told me the rest. After . . ." All he'd ever have was the story told from another mouth.

She sighed, small and pained. "We gave them clothes like ours, to replace their ruined ones that marked them as what they were, and hid them."

"I knew your family took them in." Star had nothing else to say about the rest of it. He still felt horror at what he'd heard, wondering how Ty had been brave enough to sit there, hiding the rifle he never moved without. How brave must his mother have been, too, to hold a knife and face them down?

"Yes. When I married, Bill was gone more often than not and our father no longer cared. It all came to me, so we pulled the holdings into Beresford's own. The cabin where Bill is staying?"

"My parents lived there. You saved them, and still my mother hurt you. Slept with your husband." Star closed his eyes. Choked. "And then my father stole me."

"Bear made his own choices," Mae said, firm. "Sunny loved him from the first time she saw him, but I don't think he ever saw her until she grew. As for her brother, she forced him to take you, Star."

"Bill told me how she killed herself," Star acknowledged, chilled and sickened. "That she held a gun to her chest and told Dad to take me. And he did."

Mae's voice gentled as she answered his unasked question. "Ty had left her there, time and again, when all she wanted was to be at his side. And when she took herself from him, what remained of her but you?"

A retched defeat weighed Star's mind. "How can you stand having me here or on any part of your property? Why don't you want me as far from your family as you can get me?" He was shaking again and took a step back, separating them. "Your dreams are your curse, but you're just too good to see it. They brought her to you, and now they've brought me."

Mae followed him step for step. "I don't regret our family taking them in, Star. It was right, and I would tell them my dream again."

"She hurt you."

"But not out of cruelty. Even I have to acknowledge that. There was a drive in her that was as terrifying as it was beautiful, and it drove her to love my Bear." The pain on her face rent Star's chest. Bitterness coated the words—an old hurt still buried deep—but before Star could apologize, Mae kept talking. "Bill and Ty would travel, on and on, and then come back in a handful of moons. They did this time and again, slipping away in the night."

"What about Sunny?"

"At first they both would sneak off, and Bill with them. But our families pressured Sunny to stay, saying it was too dangerous. So, when Ty pushed her for agreement, she lashed out as soon as he left, driving us all away. Isolating herself. That first time she remained behind was when Ty and Bill returned to save her."

"Save her?" Star asked.

"She was barely a woman, new to her sixteenth summer, when a handful of Hollowoods broke their word to Bay and found her here. Four men, descendants of the ones who'd killed the rest of their kind. They took her innocence, tortured her, and only Ty and Bill saved her life."

The horror had Star staring, sickened. Finn came back to him, then. He'd been the same age as his mother when it'd happened, though Finn hadn't intended to kill him. He felt acid in his throat and shivered, caught between remembered pain and heart-wrenching sympathy.

"How . . .?"

Mae shook her head. "That was Ty's story, and I've never been party. After that, though, I asked my Bear to keep a closer eye on her. We would ride out and visit, and while she welcomed him warmly, she was always cool with me. I started leaving the visits more to Bear, not wanting to spend so much time in her presence. I used Aric as my excuse. Then, her nineteenth year, she finally got what she wanted." She took up his arm again. "Come look at the water?"

He walked slowly, welcoming the momentary reprieve. He wanted to run as far as he could, find somewhere to rest and lick his wounds. Instead, they looked into the stream running over the glistening rocks, restless and beautiful, brown and cool.

"I never liked her." The words, which should have been cold or cruel, were devoid of either emotion. Instead, she delivered it as a fact. "I've blamed her all these years, but she made it hard for me to do anything else. Bill loved Ty like a brother, and I liked him enough. Sunny disliked most people from the start, of that I have no doubt.

"I rarely dream, but for a moon I dreamt of a furious and desperate Sunny pacing her cabin cage. I set them from my mind, upset with Bear, upset with her. I wish every day that I'd pieced together what those dreams had meant to warn. It wasn't until the night she killed herself that I saw more than her wild pacing. I woke, ran to the room where I'd forced Bear to sleep since his betrayal, and sent him rushing to her and their small babe."

She pulled back her skirts, kneeling to touch the water. He followed, trailing his fingertips through the flow. His chest ached and his head pounded from tension. If only the water could wash away his thoughts. How much had it cost her, admitting this?

"You sent him to her, though," Star managed to say. "To us. You tried to help."

"Not soon enough." A muscle in her jaw flexed. "I should have spoken to him. We hadn't been talking, not really. Those dreams told me she was unhappy, as I knew she had to be as she wasn't one to stay still. Seeing her hollowing, her weight falling away, I'd relished the proof she suffered, since I was also suffering." Her voice wavered on the last words. "She was so young, and I should have been kinder. Couldn't have been kinder, for how would I have known the need, young as I was too?"

There was so much pain tangled in his past. No wonder his father never shared, much as it still left him with a hollow ache. How hurt had his mother been, wanting and lonely, as free a spirit as Ty had been but without the means to flee?

Everyone kept calling her cold, cruel, but Ty had loved her, and he'd been merciless in his assessments of those in their life. He'd never have lied about her, not like that. Withheld, yes—he'd done that with a depth Star never could have guessed—but all these people only seemed to know a shadow of what his father had.

"They couldn't catch your father," Mae went on, oblivious to his thoughts. "It drove my husband mad. For years, he was lost to me. His mind was obsessed with getting you back. My dreams let me draw you, see you. I tried to figure out where you were from them, but they were always faded, tricky things. Still, I gave Bear the pictures and we paid for people to find you."

Her eyes were intent on the water. "Please, give us a chance." She turned her pained and pleading face his way. "Your father will show you the land he means to give you. I know you both must be hesitant, but he just wants to know you, and I want to see him at peace."

"I'll try." He meant it. He liked them all and, wonder of wonders, they seemed to like him. How long would it last? He didn't know, but he did know that he wanted to try anyway. Damien's concerns itched at his mind, reminders of the strengthened tension between them, but he forced the thoughts away.

"Thank you."

A stiffness fell away from her that he hadn't realized was there until it was gone. She lifted up a handful of water, letting it slip from her fist. Then she stood. "There's a dance marking the end of the moon. It'll be at our neighbors', the Crowsfields. You and Damien are invited. Knott and Ostra too."

Curiosity sparked in him. He'd heard of dances but never been to one. He expected Damien would enjoy getting out and socializing, and he didn't yet trust the safety of the Bear's territory.

"Do I have any choice?" He tried for a teasing tone that might have hit the mark.

"Of course not," she answered, smiling. "Damien, either. This will be good for you both."

There was a light breeze, comforting on his skin and carrying captive clouds on a leisurely race through the sky above. He could hear others a short distance off, yelling and laughing as they worked.

"Do you ever dream of anything that isn't . . ." *Heartbreaking*, he wanted to say. He chewed his lip, wishing he'd thought before opening his mouth.

"I do, dear. Just the one, but it's beautiful. I dream I'm walking down a steep, hidden path into a deep, bowl-shaped chasm." Her eyes grew distant. "Pine roots are holding its sides together, along with the path I'm on. I feel so much peace and longing when I walk there. I know I'm home when I get to the bottom, but I can't make it to where the waterfall pours from the cliff to fill the basin." She nodded. "Let's go back. Later, when Bear returns from town, maybe he can show you the land where you will hopefully be building."

They walked, the sun overhead and a breeze strong at their backs, urging them forward.

Back to Damien.

What curse, he wondered, would he be for *Damien*? And how was Star to convince him to stay?

As days passed, Damien's concerns didn't abate. Most of the hands were polite to their faces, but he couldn't shake the unease he'd felt since Bill's newest confession about Finn being a Hollowood. Most of his family tragedies circled that bloodline, and he hadn't known until recently the threat even existed. He wasn't quite ready to declare anyone else a threat yet, but neither was he willing to relax his watch. When he'd shared his feelings with Ostra and Knott, he'd found only agreement.

"They don't talk about the lad around us much," Knott had told him, "but they're a nice enough lot."

Ostra, a pensive look on her face, had worried Damien the most. "I can't get a read on a few of the quiet ones. Hender, for one, is uneasy and watchful in a way that keeps a soul on edge."

"Danger from that quarter?" Damien had asked, remembering Star asking Beresford about him.

Ostra and Knott had both shrugged. Damien didn't like not knowing.

Worries bit at him as he picked at breakfast that morning. So intent on them, he hardly paid attention to Beresford's awkward throat-clearing.

"There's a patch of land I want to give you boys to build on," he said, setting his cup of tea down. Startled, both of them looked up.

"Beresford," Mae chided, narrowing her eyes.

He lifted a hand. "No rush, lads. It's there *if* you choose."

Star sat straighter in his chair, eyes lit up. A thread of pain wormed its way through him. Star looked his age for once, free for the first time since Damien had carried him away from his father's body. Damien wished he could feel that same joy, but he couldn't forget the way the hands watched Star when his back was turned.

"We'd love to see it," Damien assured, since Star was obviously too tongue-tied to answer. He hid his disquiet, not wanting to insult their hosts. "Grateful as we are to you for giving us a room, we could do with a space of our own down the road, should we settle here. Thank you."

Mae gave a tight smile, and Beresford flushed. He turned soft eyes on Star. "It's near enough that we can be there in minutes if you need us, but it gives you plenty of privacy too. I'll take you for a ride out that way if you'd like?"

For years, Damien had longed to settle. Now that he had Star, he couldn't imagine a life without him, but so soon? He knew by the hungry eagerness on Star's face that he wanted the chance badly. Damien shoved his concerns down until later, watching his lover approach Bear, ready to be off.

The ride out was maybe five minutes by Star's calculation. They took a well-worn path through the field for most of the way, but turned when they neared low hills. They crested them, then rode a short distance more before Beresford came to a stop and dismounted. "This is the place."

They followed suit, Star feeling a thrill of excitement as he slid from his saddle. The reality of the offer crashed down on him as he took it in: a place he could call his.

"It's beautiful." He knelt to run his hands over a patch of wildflowers. Golden grass mixed with green in a sea that stretched far as the horizon, broken only by a little bubbling brook that curled down from the hills. Five minutes' ride from the bulk of his newfound family, and two from where Aric had built. People were all around him. "Thank you."

Damien sidled closer and wrapped an arm around his shoulders.

"We just want you happy." Beresford sounded so like his wife that it made Star's lips twitch. He clapped Star's shoulder, then Damien's, and laughed. "It might look pretty, but it'll take us all quite a bit of work. As soon as the harvest is through, come fall, we'll get everything arranged."

Damien nudged Star as Beresford mounted and turned his horse to face the direction of the homestead. "What is it?" Trust him to pick up on Star's unease.

He took up Clay's reins. "I'm going to see Bill." He swallowed a wince as the words put a stony frown on Beresford's face.

"I'll ride with you," Damien offered quickly.

"Then I'll see you at home," Beresford said. "Do you remember how to find him?" Star gestured the way, and Beresford's jaw worked before he nodded. "Ride safe, then." He tipped his hat and started off.

Star watched, trying to ignore the guilt that ate at him. It was hard not to talk about Bill. No matter how the Bears hated Bill, Star loved him. The joy of the morning faded as reality washed away the dream.

He looked to Damien, wondering at his silence. Damien turned under the weight of Star's eyes. Star admired his profile in the sunlight, knowing he loved him but not knowing how to breach the pain between them. He opened his mouth, not sure what would come out.

It was Damien, however, who spoke first. "Are you sure you want to consider staying?"

Star startled, searching his face. He hadn't thought Damien was looking to leave him. "I thought we might all stay. The five of us. We could have a home, a place where we belong." Somewhere they wouldn't have to fight to survive or sleep with an eye open.

"I'm not leaving you, Star." Damien eased the panicked weight that his first comment had caused. "We've only been here a short time. We should learn the lay of the land before making any final decisions that can't easily be undone."

Fair, even if Star wanted to argue. He forced himself to nod before the two of them mounted and set off. He focused on the land ahead of Clay, avoiding Damien's concerned gaze.

CHAPTER

※

TWENTY-TWO

"Jonnie would have liked it here," Knott said in his usual gruff tone.

"Aye," Damien agreed, looking out over the golden grass.

Ostra quirked an eyebrow. "Well?"

"They've offered us land. A place to build our own house. Star is excited, of course. I'm . . ." Damien trailed off, uncertain.

Ostra cut in before he could order what he was thinking into a sensible string of words. "Star just had every shred of his scant stability torn from under his feet. I'd expect him to either grab for something like this with both hands or run for the south. One of you has to think."

Not a question. As always, she got straight to his problem. Well, the part that didn't leave him feeling selfish.

"Bill told us Star's family was murdered near here," he said. "The survivors of those monsters tried to kill his mother. Bay's threats were all that kept them coming again. How is bringing him here supposed to keep him safe?"

Never mind his own reservations about settling somewhere so suddenly. He'd dreamed of a home, yes. That didn't make the gifting of one any less suspect.

"If they want him, how is settling anywhere else going to keep him safe?" Ostra pointed out. "Here there are numbers. There's a whole pack willing to fight for Star. We leave and it's just the four of us."

The truth of it twisted in his guts.

"It wouldn't be bad to have a place to call ours," Knott muttered, his eyes on the distant bluff. "Something built with our own hands."

For the first time since Bay's house, Damien let himself really think about the possibility. "But do we want that *here*?"

"If not, where else? When? The grave might come before tomorrow does."

Damien flinched, Jonnie's absence a pain none of them wanted to relive. Damien had too many lives on his shoulders as it was. How could he carry their loss too?

"Go find your lad." Ostra waved him off. "Leave us to our brief freedom."

Star had a restless night. It had been a few days since their visit to Bill, and things with Damien were still strained. Needing to burn off energy, he slipped from their bed shortly before dawn, dressed quietly, and took the stairs. He avoided the creakier steps and closed the front door on a whisper. From there, he made his way to the old fence for more practice.

Sunrise gilded already golden fields. He stretched a kink out of his muscles before taking up his knives. He didn't pay any mind when he first heard the riders, assuming them to be hands following after stray livestock. His throwing was better now but still not as it was.

When the horses sped up, heading for him, he finally stopped. His knives were gone but his dagger wasn't. As the riders leapt from their saddles, Star dropped to his knee, seizing his dagger and slicing at the calf before him. He shot his other leg out to kick the next closest man's knee.

There were only three, but even as the first limped and the second stumbled, he couldn't get the blade into the third before he launched, grabbing Star by his neck. Star turned his blade, going for the arm, but the stumbling man stopped it. Gagging, he tried to pry off the headlock, kicking out for anything he could reach.

A shot split the air.

"Let my brother go!"

Cal. The arm loosened, and Star sagged, breathing again. Looking up, he found Cal standing over them, face hard and gun held steady on one of the three assailants. But Star was still restrained by the stranger kneeling behind him, his legs splayed.

"You'd kill me over this creature?" The man's voice was hurt and angry. "After all these years I've worked for your family?"

"I have four more bullets loaded and ready. You know I can shoot, Roy, and he *is* my family."

Roy. The hand he'd met next to Hender. The arm dropped from Star's neck, and Star scrambled to his feet. He raised his dagger in front of him, moving until he could pull the throwing knives out of the blocks of wood. Cal barely blinked, gun trained and ready.

"We'll go, then, shall we?" Roy suggested.

"Don't move," Cal said. "I'm taking you back to Dad."

"Or you'll shoot us, lad?"

Joining Cal on the hill, Star looked them over carefully, then sniffed. "Drop your belts and get out of here."

"Star!" Cal exclaimed, angrily.

Star shook his head. "We can't murder them and they won't stay. If they leave those weapons, we should be fine."

Cal grabbed Star's arm. Wonder of all wonders, Star let him, taking comfort from his worry rather than finding it unnerving. They watched the men get on their horses and ride off.

"We need to head back and see Dad," Cal told him firmly.

He tugged on Star's arm and Star followed.

Having woken to find Star off wandering, Damien had planned to track him down only to be waved off by Cal. Chuckling, he let the kid have the job. Star liked Cal, and Damien enjoyed seeing the way Star lit up while dealing with him.

So, Damien leaned against the corral, stroking Ink's nose and chatting with Beresford while Aric lurked nearby. He and Beresford traded light talk, both more interested in the surrounding fields, and even Aric sprinkled a few comments into the mix.

The easy air between them died when Star and Cal came striding their way through the tall grass. It took Damien maybe two seconds to figure out something was wrong. Cal's face was a cold angry mask, and Star had that stubborn jut to his jaw that made Damien want to bury his head and cry.

Once they got the story out of them, Cal overeager and Star more like pulling teeth, Beresford's response was all it could possibly be.

"No wandering alone anymore!" he thundered.

Damien cringed. That was not the way to do it. Knott, who had drifted their way from the barn, gave Damien a commiserating look. Aric's vocal agreement with Beresford wasn't going to help.

"Sir—" Damien started.

Star overrode him. "I'm a man grown. I can watch myself!"

"Against multiple men with guns? What if Cal hadn't happened along?" Yep. There went that jaw, harder than ever. "And why the hell were they attacking you! *Roy* led them?"

Star's look shifted to a recalcitrant scowl. Damien moved closer, wanting to comfort him.

Beresford whirled on Aric. "Grab the horses. Damien, you stay—"

"This is my problem!" Star countered, furious.

"On my land. *My* son."

Damien could see on Star's face he wanted to say no and couldn't. He was almost trembling in suppressed fury.

"I'm coming with you," Star snarled. "We can waste time arguing or we can ride."

Star took off for his horse. Damien and Knott fell into step, letting Beresford bring up the rear. Was this mess somehow connected to Star's past?

"We have his back," Knott reminded Damien, voice quiet.

It ended up being a moot point, anyway. The trail led onto the road, and there was no way to track it from there. Too much foot and horse-traffic, no new rain.

"Roy," Beresford grumbled as they made their way back to the ranch. "Roy Fields. Man worked here almost fifteen years, and not a single complaint against him. Cal didn't know the others, he said? I'll talk to the men. Between Gavin and I, we'll unearth something to this."

But they didn't. No one was able or willing to put a name to anyone who might have attacked Star at Roy's side. Damien couldn't shake the feeling that there was a Hollowood hand to the matter, but no one else raised the name. Star just set his lips and refused to follow the line of talk, and Beresford insisted Bay's deal held. Frustrations, both.

Only Knott and Ostra agreed with him vocally. More and more, Damien wanted to drag Star out of the north. If they could talk, maybe he could turn Star's stubborn, bull-headed mind to the idea.

By the sun, he hoped he'd have the chance.

CHAPTER

※

TWENTY-THREE

"I'm still not sure about this dance," Beresford muttered, but it was clear he was losing steam.

Damien sighed in seeming agreement but didn't press Star any more than he already had. Star appreciated the break. Since they'd arrived, there wasn't much point in chewing over their worries. He graciously didn't point that out.

Lanterns sat on logs scattered around the yard, offering up light as the sun gave ground to the moon. Looking at the wood, Star mused that it was no wonder the Crowsfields had sent for Aric and Cal earlier that day. They'd have needed their strength to move them all.

"Have fun, lads." Beresford eyed a group of people chatting around a string of tapped barrels. With a heavy clap to both Star's and Damien's shoulders, he took off to join the crowd.

"You have any trouble, come get one of us," Gavin added firmly before following at his boss's heels.

Star looked questioningly at Damien, wondering what they were supposed to do now that he'd gotten his way.

Damien quirked his lips and shrugged. "I guess we have fun?"

At least he was starting to lose that brittle edge he'd carried since the attack. Star eyed the crowd in the expanse of field. Some sent discreet glances their way, ones that danced away from theirs.

Aric's face was flushed with drink as he jogged over to them. "Come meet the Crowsfields' son and daughter."

Star padded along at his brother's side, Damien a comforting presence at their back. Cal didn't seem to notice as they passed where he sat chatting with a handful of youngsters. Aric's steps were intent, and the strangers that noted Aric's progress seemed more amused than anything else. Star didn't miss that when those looks shifted to him and Damien they became less so.

A young woman met them near a table heavy with baked pastries and spiced pitchers. Aric took up her hand as soon as he came in reach. The man behind her, his hair the same shade of red as hers, crossed his wiry arms with a wide grin.

"Bess? Freddy?" Aric greeted them, his eyes only for Bess. "This is my brother, Star, and his partner, Damien."

The siblings nodded, their smiles the most welcoming Star had received outside his family.

"Welcome home, Star," Freddy said. "And nice to meet you, Damien."

Home sat heavy and double-edged on Star's heart. He managed a rough nod.

"I'm so glad you're here tonight," Bess said, taking the sting out of Freddy's unmeant wounding.

"Thank you," he told them. "It's a pleasure to meet you both."

After a time, Star and Damien wandered off, watching the revelry. Ostra and Knott arrived with a handful of others as the moon finally took command.

"Hiding?" Ostra teased.

Star shrugged, feeling foolish but not quite wrong. "We're enjoying ourselves."

"Of course."

"How went the rest of your day?" Damien asked, thankfully drawing Ostra's and Knott's amused gazes his way.

"Well enough," Knott said.

A ripple of sound, fingers testing strings, silenced whatever else he might have said. Ostra shot Damien a saucy grin and snagged Star's arm. Star, laughing in surprise, let her, relishing in the flow of the music and the playful energy as she led him into some easy steps. He cast her out in a spin as a rolling set of notes rose, catching her back in his arms easily and matching her step for step. Beresford, nearby, was dancing gently with Mae.

"Think you can get Knott to dance?" Star teased, throwing his head back toward where Damien and he were getting mugs of ale.

Ostra, not missing a beat, rolled her eyes. "If he knows best, you bet." She twisted, and he followed, switching roles so she could spin him. They came together again as the song ended.

She gave him a toothy smile, patted his shoulder, then stalked over to stand in front of Knott expectantly. Star slipped next to Damien, resting his chin on Damien's shoulder as they watched Knott follow Ostra.

"I guess he did know best." Star chuckled.

Damien cast him a questioning look, and Star grinned.

They managed to remain tucked away at the edge of the gathering, keeping out of the busy patches. Ostra and Knott danced, Aric and Bess nearby. Cal was still with his friends, heads bent together in some likely mischief. Eventually, Damien went to find drinks, only to be caught by Beresford and dragged into conversation.

It was nice, Star mused, to have some time to himself within sight of all the revelry. It was impossible to think when people pressed around him so close, wanting his attention or keeping him in sight. Even now Damien cast glances his way, as if he were a child likely to wander off.

"I'm amazed you dared return here."

Star startled, fingers itching for a knife. He caught himself before he grabbed one, narrowing his eyes. He hadn't heard anyone come into his space, too intent on his thoughts. "You've a problem with me," he growled.

"I do," came Hender's cold answer. "And I have since your whore of a mother and her cur of a brother destroyed everything."

Star stiffened. "You knew them?" Something about the man left Star uneasy. There was a familiarity in his features that Star couldn't place.

"Never met them. I've saved that pleasure for meeting you." Hender stalked off, heading to the horses.

Star stared after him, trying to make sense of the encounter. Nothing came together and, frustrated, he lurched forward. "Hold up!" Hender was on horseback but didn't ride off, glaring at Star with a hard look that prickled at his bone marrow. He grabbed the horse's reins, meeting Hender's cold gaze. "If you've a problem with me, then I want to hear the why of it."

The lantern light played over the sharp lines of Hender's face, casting shadow down his throat. "It's the cursed blood of you that I can't stand. Some men die and others get old. Deals rot faster than a life."

The prickle in Star's bones turned to ice and he let go, stepping back. He'd only heard that level of hatred coming from one throat, and that one was long in a shallow grave. *Hollowood?*

He watched Hender ride off, his wits stolen. It took too damn long for him to shake off the chill and seek out the man who called himself his father. Beresford had dragged Damien into a small crowd with visible joy. Damien, teeth set, was making nice.

Catching sight of Star as he approached, Beresford crowed, "My son!"

Star smiled weakly and traded small talk with the group. Beresford, like many of those around them, was already deep into his cups. No help there, then. Ostra came up and whisked Damien away, as she had with each of them at various points.

Taking the chance, Star faced his sire. "Is Bill coming tonight?" He might be able to give Star some idea where to start.

Beresford pressed his lips together, merriment tempered, but it was a red-headed man who spoke up. Mr. Crowsfield, Star figured, judging by the features he shared with his children.

"He was invited." His voice was as strained as the expressions on those surrounding them.

"We hoped to see him," Mae added with false cheer.

"Thank you." Star touched Beresford's arm, giving it a little squeeze. It brought the grin back to his sire's face.

When Damien joined him shortly after, smelling of ale and good, honest sweat, Star did his best to cover his unease. There was no point telling him anything until he understood it himself. "I'm going to Bill's for a visit."

Knott shot a look his way, eyebrow up.

"Right now?" Damien asked, the usual sharpness of his eyes blunted.

"I have questions."

"What questions?"

Star rolled his eyes. "I'll tell you later—you've my word. I want to see him first."

Damien nodded. "Okay, yeah, let me get Ink and Clay—"

"No." Star shook his head. "Stay here. Have fun. I'll meet you back at the house."

Damien didn't look like he was going to agree. Star felt his earlier frustrations return as Damien's frown deepened.

Thankfully, before they could enter into an argument Ostra came to his rescue. "Damien, come dance again and give Knott a chance for another drink."

Damien looked between them, still frowning, and followed where she led, leaving Star and Knott.

"Thank her for me?" Star turned for the horses.

He didn't make it a step before Knott's hand caught his arm. "I will. But not until we're both shut of whatever mess you're headed into."

Star swallowed a sigh and nodded. "Fine."

The ride to Bill's felt longer this time. Neither the cattle nor the odd hand on patrol sent more than a cursory glance their way.

Knott pulled up a short ways from the cabin and, drawing his gun, rested it over his lap. "You go visit. I'll wait here and keep watch."

"I doubt there's any actual trouble," Star pointed out. "You can come with me."

Knott shook his head. "All the same, I'd rather keep watch."

Star walked Clay to the cabin and slid from his saddle, taking one last deep, bracing breath. Bill, doubtless having heard their approach, stood on the porch. He leaned against the door, clothes dirty and hair a tangled, unkempt mat. Star could smell the sour of too much drink too often, but his eyes were clearer than they'd been on the last two visits.

His smile was sad. "Didn't expect anyone to drop by tonight, what with the dance."

"You talked to Mae," Star returned.

"Aye. I won't be seeing forgiveness from her any time soon but she's still my sister and I guess she still acknowledges it."

"I'm glad."

"Nice to see you had the sense to bring company, even if it isn't who I'd have expected." Bill raised a brow. "Aren't you supposed to be socializing with the local gawkers come to see the Bear's lost cub?"

Star gritted his teeth. "I was, up until one of Beresford's men had some hard words for me. I wonder if you knew him. I already know he doesn't like my mother or father." Fury crossed Bill's face. Drunk and angry meant danger, and Star caught Bill's arm. "I can look out for myself." He glared, meeting the rage with his own brand of stubbornness. "I just want to know more before I talk to the man again."

"Who is the son of a bitch?" Bill demanded.

"Your word you'll listen and leave me to it?"

Bill glowered. Curiosity apparently beat out anger. "Fine. Unless I have reason to act."

Star relaxed, letting Bill pull free. "Hender."

He'd hoped for a reaction, but Bill's brow furrowed. "I don't know that name. What did he say, exactly?"

Star's heart sank. He hesitated a moment, but he'd already given the name. If he didn't share, Bill might try tracking Hender down himself. "He called my mother a whore and said her brother was a cur. That deals rot."

That got the expected anger, but not all of it was for Hender.

"And you rode here? *Just the two of you?*" Bill roared. Star stared as Bill caught his arm this time. Bill's grip, hard enough to bruise, held to him as if it was all that kept Star there.

Damn it. Star forced himself to stay calm. Only years of being treated like a child held his temper in check. "I'm not as weak as you think. I've survived twenty years now."

"And not one of them on your own."

Star scowled, and Bill sighed. His hold eased. "I'm sorry, Star. It's likely Hender's mad over the mess with Beresford. His men love him, and they never would admit he's as susceptible to fault as the rest of us."

"After all this time?" Star pressed doubtfully. "I asked Beresford, but he said Hender came here after you guys were already gone. Why would he care what happened between my mother and the Bear?" None of it, especially Bill's nerves, made sense.

Bill narrowed his eyes. "You asked him? Tonight?"

Caught out, Star grimaced. "Days ago now. It isn't the first time Hender and I spoke, but he wasn't this threatening before, just rude."

No need to mention Roy or that mess. No one had told Bill, a fact for which he was grateful. As it was, Bill chewed over the newest information slowly, the worry on his face only strengthening.

"Be careful, aye, lad?" Bill waited until Star nodded.

CHAPTER

✴

TWENTY-FOUR

Star woke Damien and dragged him downstairs, finding Beresford and Aric waiting for him at the table. The cool tea and untouched plates set before them spoke of a hard waking. It was a shock to see Bill also there, plate empty and chair tipped back. How much of Bill's tension came from being at that table, and how much stemmed from their conversation last night? Regardless, it wasn't Star's concern at that moment.

"Where can I find Hender?" Star demanded. Bill made an aggravated sound that he ignored. "He and I had a conversation last night that I want to finish."

Beresford sighed. "Bill already told me about it, and I went to see him, but he took off sometime last night. Left his clothes, his things. When I asked Gavin, he'd been just as surprised. Said he'd thought better of Hender after all these years. I had too." His eyes narrowed. "And why didn't you tell me one of my men was bothering you?"

Star shrugged. "It wasn't anything worth mentioning."

Beresford scowled. "Anyone else says something, you're to come straight to me."

"Or me," Aric snapped, arms crossed and eyes as hard as his father's.

Star looked away. "His problem was with me, not either of you."

"And you're blood."

Blood. It always came down to that.

That night, Star finally brought it all up to Damien. Damien's answer was one that Star should have expected.

"Maybe settling here isn't the right idea. If people are going to hold a past you weren't part of over your head, we ought to consider moving on. Your family will still be here. Hell, we can visit. A new place with a fresh history to begin—mightn't that be the smarter idea?"

It'd made sense, but Star knew his own mind. He wanted what his newfound family offered. It was strange, rocky, and there was discomfort tangled up in his yearning, but he wasn't ready to give up.

Would that take away the chance he had with Damien? "I don't want to lose you."

"That's what I'm worried about. Staying here might not be good for our health. Hender might not stick to words next time. Same goes for Roy, or anyone else."

"I'm not weak," Star had growled.

"But you're not that strong, either. Not enough to always keep yourself safe."

The response had been a slap. "I'm going to bed."

Damien, for his part, had flinched as if it'd burned his tongue. "Sun and moon, Star, I'm sorry. I'm just worried."

Star had snorted, but when Damien had turned in with him, he'd let Damien pull him close. It was easier to pretend the world wasn't shattering when Damien's arms were around him, and it was too quiet to hear the cracks between their words.

CHAPTER

✹

TWENTY-FIVE

Two days after the dance, a message was delivered by the blacksmith's boy. A telegram had arrived in Ameson marked urgent: *Chuck—on way home.*

The urgency, Damien figured, was in the forewarning of Chuck's impending return.

"He'll be in a good rush," Beresford mused.

And, when Chuck arrived, that warning was well worth it.

"Where's your runt?" he demanded as soon as he rode close enough to yell.

Damien bit his lip to stop a laugh as Star, face wrinkled in displeasure, marched outside. Not willing to miss it, no matter how Chuck felt about him, Damien rushed after him. Mae, for her part, sighed and watched them go from where she'd been kneading bread.

Chuck had aged since last Damien had seen him, but that didn't take away from his presence. He glowered as he climbed off his horse's back. Stiff as he moved, there was no exhaustion in his eyes. "Star! Keep your ass where it can be found, got it? Gavin says you went out—"

"Uncle!" Beresford said, exasperated.

"—and got attacked all alone, and there will be none of that! No Bears get murdered on our watch, and certainly not on our own land!"

A mix of emotions played over Star's delicate face, as amusing as it was worrisome. Beresford looked like he'd swallowed something too large to choke back up.

"There has been trouble, and we're all taking care not to go out alone," Cal tried, ever the mediator. His face was mottled red. Star squinted at Cal suspiciously.

"There are people who still want that young fool dead! I don't care what you idiots say. He gets watched."

Damien cringed as Star's sharp green eyes fastened onto Chuck. "If they want me dead, then let them come see me! It's my business."

"And that's why you shouldn't be let loose," Chuck drawled. "See, nephew? If you've any sense, you'll keep the fool housebound."

"Let's get some water," Damien cut in. "How about you help your uncle inside, Cal? Star and I will get him something cold to drink from the well."

Judging by Star's face, he would rather beat Chuck with the tin buckets than fill them, but Damien counted it as a victory when Star went willingly enough. Beresford's voice carried as Damien dragged Star off, low and likely not complimentary. Cal, for his part, stayed behind as asked.

"Chuck's just worried." Damien filled the waiting bucket.

Star stood back, his handsome face still annoyed. "I can look after myself."

Damien refrained from pointing out how well that had been working. Instead he passed the bucket and filled a second one. "Let him grumble. I'm surprised he traveled so soon after being shot."

That took some of Star's anger away and replaced it with concern. They made it back inside. Star hadn't softened any, but at least he was being quiet.

"How is Wendy?" Damien asked Chuck.

Sprawled out in a seat at the table, Chuck boasted a bit more color on his face. "She's well. Getting things back together, I'd say. That man of hers isn't a whole lot of use, but they'll be fine."

Damien laughed despite himself and caught Star's lips twitch. "She's a good woman."

"They took great care of me. Wanted me to stay abed a bit longer, not that I'd let *that* happen at my age."

Mae carried over a bowl of stew and took a chair next to Chuck. The bread she'd been working on sat in a cloth-covered bowl, likely left to rise. Chuck thanked her heartily and dug in with a happy grunt.

"It would take a bullet to the skull to keep you there," Beresford commented. It seemed Star wasn't the only one still annoyed.

"I like it here." Star sat on their bed, watching as Damien buckled his belt. He planned to ride out and spend the morning with Knott and Ostra. He'd offered for Star to come along, but Star had begged off.

"It's a nice ranch." The stiffness of Damien's expression warned Star that there was more.

"Say what you mean." Star narrowed his eyes.

Damien sighed. "I can't shake the thought of how Roy attacked you, or how Hender cornered you at the dance."

He still wanted Star to reconsider staying, then.

"I want a home." He hadn't intended to sound so plaintive.

"Moon's tears, Star, you know I'd like to give you one. Why here, though? You've been threatened, and that sun-damned man might have done worse had Cal not stumbled on you! Thank the Moon he's so interested in you."

Star glared. "It was once. They caught me off-guard."

"Their catching you is enough to make me scared." Damien sat next to him. Star scowled but Damien, undaunted, slid an arm around his shoulders and pulled him close. "Ever since I met you, I've known you were capable. That doesn't change how I feel knowing you're in danger. Leaving doesn't mean you never see these people again, only that we put some space between us and this danger."

"You want me to run."

"I want *us* to run."

Us. Even with everything that had passed between them, Star craved that us.

"And if they attack because of me? And I'm not here?"

Damien stared at him, jaw firming. "They're more likely to be in danger because you're here."

He was right, not that Star would admit it.

"Ostra and Knott are waiting on you." He jerked free of Damien's arm and climbed to his feet.

Damien flinched. "Star, I don't mean to fight. I just want—"

Star knew what he wanted. He knew, too, that Damien had a point. That didn't make him have to listen.

"I'll be here when you get back."

Damien let it go, likely reading Star's stubborn face. "I'll be back by noon. Promise you'll be around?"

Star glared harder. "I'm a grown man. None of you seem to want to accept that, but I promise I am capable of keeping myself in one piece."

Damien visibly desired to say more, but Star took the win when he merely sighed. "At least let's not part on bad terms?"

Star pressed his lips together, turning away. Damien had the right of it but Star couldn't bring himself to answer. As soon as the door shut, he closed his eyes, counting. He waited long enough for Damien to saddle his horse and leave.

Then he headed out himself.

Star let his steps carry him without conscious thought. Now that his anger had cooled, shame creeped in. How much would Damien take before he left? They'd known each other such a short time, and the fresh, new heat that had flared between them had been changed after Ty's death.

Star wanted Damien, needed him, but what need did Damien have for *him*?

A shout cut through Star's thoughts as he crested the hill between the Bearson lands and the Crowsfields' property.

"Look what we have here!"

He slowed, then ice coated over him. He'd gone there out of spite and now was getting what he'd earned.

They'd walked up on him quietly, their guns pointed and their grins pleased. Star should have listened to Chuck and the others, he reflected as he glared at the approaching men.

"Lad, bring me my horse," Roy ordered, the apparent leader. The youngest of the crew broke off and ran for where Star saw mounts waiting down the hill. "I'd no idea it'd be this easy. We thought we'd have to ambush you. Here you are, instead, giving yourself to us."

Star lifted his chin and met gleeful eyes dead-on. "You look like Hender. I see it now that I know to look for a connection. That why you're here to see me?"

"My cousin," Roy answered agreeably.

"I guess he's more interested in getting other people to do his dirty work than in dirtying his own hands."

Roy's expression chilled. The boy approached, leading a horse. Roy dug rope from the saddlebags, twisted it over his arm, and headed Star's way. He chuckled as he neared, a cold sound. "I know your blood, boy. Your whore mother and her bastard brother killed Hender's father and my uncle. I'm not taking any chances. By getting rid of you, we'll clean the last of your rotting disease. That's what the earth wants."

Star jerked, mind flashing to the story of the damned tree. He stared, aghast. They *were* Hollowoods. There was no doubt anymore.

"Now you know who we are, eh?" Roy simpered, reading his expression correctly. "Think of all the horror of your existence: What your ma and uncle did to my family. For those, I want you buried alive. Hender would rather bury you back on our family land, but I know better. Man still thinks I'm the distraction while he gets the bait. We daren't try and take you that far alive. When he gets back, he'll see I was right. Give me your hands."

Bile rising in his throat, Star contemplated dying on his feet. Instead, he lifted his hands. He wished he'd been smarter. Wished, too, he hadn't let Damien leave without any kind words.

The bastard tied him tightly, taking no care how much the rope dug into skin. Star scowled, hiding his fear behind anger.

Roy smiled, patted the bound wrists, and turned. He wrapped one end of the rope around his saddle horn.

Star felt an even worse fear mounting as Roy continued by wrapping the trailing bit of rope around the horn of the saddle. Then he climbed back into the saddle.

"I'm looking forward to this," he explained, voice cruelly amused. "You're a wild animal, like the rest of your blood. I'll have the pleasure of purging it. If you can keep up, you'll get to live long enough to suffocate at the bottom of the hole we dug. If you can't, well, I'll have to hope you're conscious enough at the end to know when we start burying you."

He rode just fast enough that Star could keep his feet if he jogged. The rope pulled, soaking with blood as it cut deep. At first Star was weak with horror, but adrenaline kept him upright. He thought he knew when they crossed onto Crowsfield property, then he stumbled as the group changed direction.

It was a terrible relief when the mad dash finally ended. Star sagged, bound hands on his knees as he fought to gasp in air. A deep hole had been dug into the dirt, a pile of rubble alongside it ready to be thrown back in.

Roy jerked the rope, and Star sprawled onto the ground. "Get his feet tied! Use the end and keep it loose enough he's stretched out down there."

So saying, the bastard crouched by Star's head, probably thinking him worn to exhaustion. Star gathered what strength he could and threw his head forward, bashing it into his nose. Roy tumbled back, blood spraying. The other men pinned Star before he could do more damage. Roy leaned over him, warmth splattering his face. The eyes above that red-smeared nose were wild with anger. He backhanded Star, and Star's neck snapped to the side. His thoughts splashed apart, leaving only a dull ache and a wish to see Damien.

It hardly mattered what Star wanted, or what Roy did to him. The fight was won. Still, Star could at least take some delight in Roy's visibly broken nose before he died. He wished he hadn't been such a proud, stubborn fool.

"I'm going to enjoy this," Roy growled. He picked Star up, groaning with the strain. Before Star could do more than think of struggling, Roy threw him into the pit. Choking as air rushed from his lungs, Star fought waves of black. Shovelfuls of dirt were landing on him, driving the little breath he managed to regain back out. "You can rot in there. Let the sun have its own curse returned."

Each load of soil weighted down his body. Thrashing knocked some down, but only at first. Panic raced in his chest as it rose around his neck, his struggles exhausting him. His mouth and nose were full of damp dirt, and he couldn't blink enough out of his eyes.

"Your uncle did half my work for me, y'know." Roy's muscles bulged as he continued. "Your father buried that bastard Finn in the valley. That was a fine piece of work."

Even with his terror, confusion ignited. What did Finn have to do with anything?

Shots sounded over the bite of the shovels. Men dropped, one falling to sprawl across Star and crush his abused lungs. Blood ran thick from the man's chest. The rush of fear and hope burned.

"Son!"

Beresford leaned over the hole, his broad face strained but not pained. Star could hear Knott and Ostra behind him, barking at someone to sit and shut up if they didn't want to join their friends. Beresford grabbed him and pulled him out of the pit. Star choked, pressing his eyes tightly shut.

Beresford cut his wrists free before doing the same for his ankles. "Lad?"

Star wiped at his eyes. Blood covered his face, but at least he could see. "How'd you find me?"

"Cal saw you walking and started to follow. When you got taken, he ran to get help."

Cal. He should've expected that. The kid was practically a second shadow, and he'd saved him from Hender's men before.

"Thanks." Star shuddered.

A moan caught his ears. Turning, he found Roy still alive. Ostra stood over him with a gun trained to his head while Knott crouched next to her, a wad of shirt pressed to Roy's wound.

Knott looked like he'd rather be choking him with it, honestly. "Who are these bastard?"

"Roy is Hender's cousin," Star said. "The rest are with him, and he says Hender is around here still."

"Gavin will be by soon with more men." Beresford sounded furious. "I'll have them search the land."

Star got unsteadily to his feet. His legs were numb at first, as were his hands. Beresford made a move to catch him, but he shook his head. Stalking to where Roy lay, Star hunched down, rubbing his bleeding wrists. "What was this about? Will this be over now that you're through?"

Teeth bared and barely conscious, Roy whispered, "Told 'em where you are. And had others holding back. We'll get the last of you. I failed but Hender won't."

Star shook his head. "You'll be the one to rot." With all he'd learned of the Hollowoods, their desperate need for his death still didn't make sense.

Beresford rose to his feet. "Will he make the trip back?"

Knott's nose wrinkled. "He should."

Beresford clapped Star's shoulder, his big hand warm on Star's chilled skin, then moved to collect rope. He used it to bind Roy, ignoring his pained sounds. "Better safe than sorry. How are you, son?"

"Sorry," Star admitted, more embarrassed than anything as the last of his adrenaline and fear faded. It left behind an aching, weary sense of shame.

"We're just glad Cal caught you in time."

And thank the moon Cal hadn't tried to save him again. They both might have ended up in the shallow grave. The thought sobered Star. Damien had been right to say he was a threat to this family.

"Seems I owe him my life again," Star said. The taste of his almost-grave still tainted the air.

Gavin showed up soon with a wagon from the Crowsfields. "Cal is back at the ranch. I saw Sole riding that way, so I expect he'll meet us as soon as he hears what's afoot." He strode to where Roy lay in the dirt, sparing a quick glance for the bodies scattered around.

Gavin sneered. "Guess we're dragging this one back."

"Aye."

Beresford helped Gavin throw Roy into the back none too gently.

"It a problem if he bleeds out?" Gavin asked.

"I'd like some answers," Beresford said. "I'd also like his head."

"Guess we should get going, then. Kid?"

Star grimaced when he realized that was directed at him. With a scowl, he climbed into the wagon, glad enough to get a moment's rest. Better to ride than go on foot, even if it put him uncomfortably close to the unconscious man who'd have happily buried him alive.

Ostra and Knott followed on horseback as Beresford kept ahead, eyeing the land. It rankled Star that he'd needed to be saved again, but worse was the nausea of what had almost happened to him. He felt a bit better as they neared home, though it was a short-lived relief.

Aric came up on them, riding hard. "Dad! Thank the moon. *Ride*! It's Mom!"

Beresford cursed and took off, calling for the others to hurry.

"Go!" Star begged Ostra and Knott, the air locked in his lungs. "We'll be there soon."

Gavin's pinched, angry face bent over the reins. He urged the wagon to a speed bordering insensible, and they rattled violently over the ground. Star leaned forward, holding fast to the sides as the others rode off.

Roy had said that Hender had plans of his own. What had they *done*?

Gavin rumbled into the yard and pulled to a jerking, horse-startling stop near the barn. Star leapt from the wagon, his aching body rushing for the house. Pools of blood lay soaking into the soil, the bodies removed but the stains not yet covered with dirt.

Aric, standing in the dooryard with Ostra and Knott, fell to his heels. "I just rode into the yard. Found Mom unconscious on the ground, four of our hands dead."

Aric's words came out in a terrible rush that cut through Star, setting a twinge in his chest. This was on him, he knew. Mae was all right, but what of Cal? And *Damien*? Had he been there yet? If Gavin had seen him headed this way but they hadn't met him, where *was* he?

Star's long strides carried him into the parlor, where his body locked. Mae—face grave-pale and tear-marked—slumped against her husband. Beresford hugged her close, his face buried in her hair.

"Mom?" Aric edged nearer to her, looking nervous and worried.

She twisted to face them, the tremble in her hands visible. "They took Cal and Damien."

The ground shifted under Star's feet. Aric—how had he moved so quickly?—caught him before he could stumble. Pressed lips and angry eyes met his own.

"We need to ride after them." Star fought exhaustion after so many waves of fear-fueled adrenaline. He could hear the madness and desperation in his voice but didn't care. "It's my fault. Who is chasing them? We'll catch up."

Never mind that he wasn't sure he could sit in a saddle straight. They had to move *now*. Bill would find their trail, and they'd get them back safely. This couldn't end with more blood on Star's hands. Now, more than anything, he just wanted to see Damien. To apologize. To explain how sorry he was, sorry he hadn't listened.

Mae's thin arms wrapped around his neck. "No." She felt heavy, as if only pride kept her on her feet. "It wasn't your fault, Star, and you can't throw yourself at those monsters. We have people searching the trail, our own and the Crowsfields'."

"This *is* on me. They took from me on purpose."

She sighed. "We should have been more vigilant. Strangers rarely come to the house, and their wagon was heaped with hay. If Damien hadn't come when he did, they would've taken my baby alone." She shuddered, still not letting go. "He told them he'd trade himself for my son. They pretended to accept."

She hadn't had a dream, and so there'd been no forewarning. It'd failed her with her own child? Proof, Star felt, that it was his curse at its heart. One thing stood out, though. The pendant she always kept around her neck was missing.

"I'll bring them back," he vowed, squeezing her.

She lurched, giving his shoulders a rough shake. "You will stay right here while we contact the Sighted and send his people after the rest."

"I have to—"

"No," Beresford spoke up. "She's right. This isn't us mounting a blind attack. This is a trap, your man and Cal as bait. Hender wants you tearing off after them."

Star lifted his chin, glaring over Mae's shoulder. "They took Damien and my little brother."

Mae slid down onto the couch, her strength visibly spent. "So you'd throw your life away? And my baby's with it?"

That struck home. The room began spinning, and only Beresford, catching Star by the arm, kept him on his feet.

"I will go with you," Beresford promised. "We'll get them home safely. Right now, though? It isn't yet time. We need answers first. What can you do that the others cannot?"

"We went in blind once." Ostra's voice cut through the room from behind him, soft but steely. When had she entered? "Use this time and don't repeat mistakes."

Star found her eyes and recognized that same desperate need, but she hadn't left in a rash bid to catch up. The realization clenched a fist around Star's heart. He'd do right by her and Knott. Make this right, somehow, for the family that had taken him in only to be attacked.

"Sit," Beresford ordered firmly.

"We've gotten Roy settled. Take a second to clear your head," Ostra told him, adding support to Beresford's direction.

Exhaustion settled in fast, eating Star's reserves. He sank into a soft chair. "I should be doing something."

Beresford shook his head. "Relax, son. Get your breath, then you can come with me. We'll question Roy first."

Star could feel Beresford's need to act and knew it tempered only by the need to keep those he still held safe. He couldn't do both. Star took a deep breath, taking a minute to grab onto his raging thoughts and forcefully calm the drowning flood. What use was he if he went in panicked?

"Ready, now, lad?" Beresford asked.

Star steeled himself.

Beresford went straight out to the yard, his stride eating ground faster than Star's. Aric, tall as the man, kept pace. Knott came from the barn and met them.

"Where is that bastard who attacked my boy?" Beresford demanded, his face drawn with pain and fear.

"In the barn. Gavin is watching him at gunpoint."

"He awake yet?"

"No, but when he is, there will be answers."

"Get the Sighted," Beresford barked to Aric, who ran for the horses.

They entered the barn and found Hender's kinsman thrown into an unused stall.

"I'll take over until the Blade arrives," Beresford told Ostra.

It was Knott who answered first. "Ostra and I will join the rest in trying to find a trail. Gavin has already left to collect the Sighted."

"Send for us if you need us," Ostra ordered.

Star started to follow but Knott's hand stopped him. "They did this to get to you, lad. Leave the search to us and stay where there are more eyes."

A flash of anger sparked along his spine, quickly swallowed by chilly acceptance. The Blade would be on his way. There wasn't a lot of time for Star to ask questions. Lips pressed, he nodded once, hard. Knott squeezed his shoulder and turned away.

"We won't lose another one," Ostra promised, pressing a quick, startling kiss to Star's cheek before following Knott out.

"Be safe," he begged, and got a wave in reply.

Beresford crouched next to where one of his farm hands kept Roy at gunpoint. "What am I to do?"

Not entirely sure he expected an answer, Star offered one all the same. "It depends what Roy tells us. We need to know what's going on: what we face, where to find them, and why the hell they're so desperate. Hender can't be far, and maybe Ostra and Knott will ride back with word. But until we know . . ."

He let his sentence trail off, desperately hoping to hear horses pound into the yard and voices call that their family had been restored.

There was only a creak of joints as Beresford heaved to his feet. "We need Roy awake, then. Get a bucket of water from the pump."

Star fell to the task, relieved to have a job to focus on instead of wallowing in guilt and fear. It felt good to dump water on that pale, lax face and watch the flash of pain as Roy surged up, startled and gasping.

"Where were you supposed to meet Hender?" Star snapped, standing over him and glaring.

Reason returned to the man's eyes as they fastened on his face. A sneer was Roy's only answer. If he registered the gun still trained his way, and how could he *not*, he didn't show it.

Star opened his mouth, but the sound of approaching horses drifted through the walls.

"Go check who it is," Beresford ordered. "We'll keep watch."

Star slid up to a window and found Gavin riding next to a stranger with Aric bringing up the rear. One of the borrowed Crowsfield hands called a greeting, and Star left the barn to join them.

The Blade was a large, thick-necked man with a scarred face and a missing nose tip. He wore the thistle-tattoo of the Sighted Blades on his hands, and gave them a cursory look before dismounting.

"No question whose you are." He raised a bushy brow at the dirt on Star's clothes and skin. "Where's the man who tried to kill you?"

"In the barn." Star led the way, refusing to miss any of the coming interrogation.

Roy stirred at the sight of them. He hadn't moved more than an inch, likely unable to do so.

The Blade frowned, his expression empty. "You've taken a boy from my town."

Roy's eyes lit on his tattoos. A crooked grin cracked his ashy face. "He got one of the Bears, then." There was a sick glee in the words.

"And you'll tell us where to find Cal if you want to go to your hanging with all your pieces intact," Star declared.

"Steady," the Blade snapped, the word a growl. He shot Star a glare, then sent a second to Beresford before looking back at their captive. "Your son has the right idea, though."

"It doesn't matter what I say. They'll have switched to horses as soon as they could, and if you haven't tracked them yet, you won't. We had people with fresh mounts ready, and more of our people waiting when they make it home. You'll never catch them."

"Then what do you want?" the Blade demanded. "This insanity must have a purpose."

"A trade. The curse for the cub."

The Blade's lip twitched. "And where do we give this trade?"

"Ask Bay. The traitor's protection isn't as strong with us as it had been with the last generation."

Star flinched, his chest a throbbing mess of startled pain and doubtful fury. He threw himself onto his knees beside Roy, fisting his wet shirt. "Why are you all so damn driven to take me? If Hender'd wanted me dead, he could've shot me time and again!"

Roy sneered, madness burning bright. "Hender and the others want your blood shed over the roots of our tree. That's where the first of our killings happened. It's where the last one should. I figured it'd do as much good to dump you back in the earth that wants you and let it take your life. Guess it'll be that fool Hender who wins out."

"Tree! Dad said the same thing. What does a tree want with blood? Your people are going to kill my brother and my lover for some damn *tree*?"

"Easy," Bear soothed. "He wants you mad. Bastard is enjoying upsetting you."

A hollow laugh greeted the words. Star released Roy and let Beresford pull him to his feet.

"The lad asks the correct questions," the Blade said, frowning at the Hollowood. "If Hender is trying to lure him to a specific tree, then you obviously know where they're headed. Bay's is a good distance from here. Wouldn't your buddies rather pursue before the moon changes?"

Roy would say no more, not even with incentive.

"He believes in what he says," the Blade decided finally, face set. "I'll keep at him until his execution. Meanwhile, keep your hands searching. I'll send more to help."

Mae came out as the Blade tied Roy to a saddle. She stood on the front stoop, watching with hard eyes. She remained unsteady on her feet but her chin was high.

Beresford led Star aside, his face was gray and pained. "We'll get the boys back," Beresford assured him. "Aric is riding now to track the hands we sent. If they haven't lost the trail, he'll tell us rather than keep following the tracks."

"I can't stay here." Star's words shook. "Once we get them back, I need to go. I can't be a curse on you."

"And face them alone next time?" Beresford's voice was angry.

Star flinched but held his ground. "Did they ever bother you and yours before I came here?"

"Then we root them out," Beresford thundered. "I refuse to trade one child for the other, and there won't be rest for *any* of us until those monsters are gone from this land."

Star wanted to argue. Instead, he huffed. "I'm going to see Bill. He might be able to tell me what Roy meant about Bay."

Beresford sighed but nodded. "Let me come with you. I don't feel safe letting you out of sight."

Star hesitated, knowing of the resentment between the two men. Still, he agreed.

CHAPTER

☀

TWENTY-SIX

"The people who killed Dad's family," Star spit out as soon as Bill opened the door, "I need to know where they are. The bastards took Damien and Cal."

Bill swallowed hard. "What?"

Star filled him in, and his reaction was as violent as expected. The bottle in Bill's hand shattered as it slammed into the step.

"Sorry, kid." Bill sighed. "Fuck. Okay. Have a seat. We need to talk."

"There isn't time," Beresford argued, drawing Bill's wary eye.

Snarling something Star couldn't piece together, Bill grabbed the closest porch chair. He took Star's arm and guided him onto the hard wooden seat. "You take this time now or you'll have nothing *but* time in the grave."

He stalked inside, returning moments later with a handful of bottles. He passed them around before slumping down in his open doorway. He opened his with his teeth, then took a long pull.

"Well?" Beresford demanded. "My youngest is missing and every passing minute puts him in greater danger."

Bill muttered to himself, eyes never leaving Star's. "Hender Hollowood. Bay's hold really is dying."

"I know," Star snapped. "We need to go after them. Where would a Hollowood go? Do you know? Did Dad ever tell you?"

"This is tricky and hard to wrap a head around." Bill took a heavy drink from his bottle, and Star wanted nothing more than to grab it and dash it on the wood. Leave the glass to spill more blood over old floorboards.

"It doesn't matter why right now, Bill," Star said, more plaintive than he liked. "Cal and Damien need us." If he could get Damien back, he'd make things right.

Bill shook his head. "It matters."

Fine, but Star could hear it later. "If you don't know where to find them, then I'm riding to visit Bay. I want you with me. I can't stay here. I need to move."

Bill and Beresford both puffed up.

"You're safer—"

"You were almost *buried alive*—"

Star gritted his teeth. "You can join me, or you can stay right here, but I'm riding as soon as I throw my things together. Ostra and Knott will be at my back. They want Damien back as much as I do." He breathed hard. Forced himself to sound calmer. "Bill, they took your *nephew*. They took the man I love. I need to help."

"Fine," Bill relented. "I'll ride with you, but not to Bay. He told us long ago where to find his family, and I'll take you there."

Star choked on an angry cry, lurching for the horses. "Why didn't you say so?"

Beresford scowled, and his large hand closed like a vice around Star's wrist. "Can you even ride like that, Bill?"

"I can if you wait for morning. Supplies, a plan—that'll help."

"We can't wait that long," Star argued.

"As soon as the sun opens her eye and not a second after," Beresford promised, cutting past Star's protests. "Bill isn't well enough, and after the day you had, I don't want you riding off without at least a minute's sleep. For all we know, the others may still catch up with them."

But Star knew. He felt it deep in his chest. He hoped he was wrong.

"It's for the best," Bill muttered. "I'll give you a message for Mae to send tomorrow in town, and not waste a moment taking it there." He stumbled as he rose to get paper, and Beresford steadied him. The look he gave Bill wasn't forgiveness but it was acceptance.

A start.

CHAPTER

※

TWENTY-SEVEN

Star tucked close to Bill as they rode the next morning. Nightmares had chased him throughout the night, keeping any possible peace out of reach. One thing kept coming back to him: Finn, for there could be no other *bastard buried in the valley*.

"The Hollowoods knew Finn came here," he made himself share.

"How do you know?"

"Because Roy said as much." Star fought waves of fear and anger that wanted to pull him under. "They aren't going to live past this."

They traveled long into the evening. Their horses were all young, healthy stock, and were kept to a steady pace. They were almost to the Hollowoods' when they met up with Bay and his men. Though he'd always known Bay cared for him, seeing him there touched him.

There was, however, a reckoning behind the move that Star understood. He felt enough guilt himself to recognize another man's need to purge some of it. Steeling his nerve, Star rode up, meeting Bay's sharp eyes with a wan smile.

"It's good to see you whole and hale, lad," Bay greeted, "but I wish things weren't so dark."

"I'm damn glad to see you." Star swallowed. "Bill told me how you land in all this."

The lines on Bay's face deepened. "I'm so sorry, Star."

"It hurt to hear but I know you. Dad knew you. And you protected us all these years."

"Not in the end." Bay's bowed shoulders stooped. "They still got Ty, and now they're after you."

Regrets of his own burned Star's chest. "We made the choice to ride after Sam Hollowood, and that's who holds the blame for Dad's death. Not you, not anyone else."

"I just wish he'd sent word about Sam when it happened," Bay said with a sigh. The riders on his heels shifted in their saddles, looking away to grant their boss what privacy they could.

"He wanted it handled quietly." Bill pulled up alongside them, his face as drawn as Bay's. "I suggested it, but he was determined to go that route by ourselves."

"The stubborn fool."

"We should ride on." Beresford was looking ahead. "There'll be more time for discussion once we've made camp. Bay? There are few men I'd rather have at our backs."

Exhaustion did nothing to dull Damien's fury. Cal kept up a brave face, but his terror showed through the cracks. Damien kept an eye on him as they rode, hating that he couldn't help. Hender drove his men hard, his growled reminders of the pursuit on their heels as loud as the horses' hooves.

Chafing from the ropes binding Damien was a constant reminder of his failure. The men kept both him and Cal at gunpoint. Only the threat of a bullet to Cal kept Damien from striking that bastard Hender anyway. Said bastard slowed, leaving the road for a narrower path breaking through a thick swath of the forest.

"Almost home." Hender's lips twisted over a contented smirk. "Then you boys get to see your graves."

Cal's breath hitched and Damien choked on a snarl. There was no missing Hender's obvious pleasure at the reaction, and Damien's control broke.

"Seems to me I'll be seeing yours too," he snapped.

Hender bristled. "I only need one of you. Should I shoot you here and leave you on the path? Think your corpse would stay long enough for your whore to see it?"

Swallowing down icy bile, Damien sneered. "It still won't stop you from dying."

Hender pulled up short and yanked out his gun. Damien's teeth scraped together as Hender aimed it between Cal's terrified eyes. "Maybe I'll kill the kid. How would you like *that*?"

"Easy, kid," Damien murmured to Cal, wanting nothing more in that moment than to wrap his hands around Hender's thin neck and squeeze.

Terrified but brave, Cal didn't say a word. He was possibly too scared, but at least he didn't feed the madman's ego.

Hender holstered his gun and whipped back around. "It'll be more satisfying to kill all of you together."

Their company continued. The path narrowed, but the horses knew the way, perking up as they obviously neared whatever hell awaited the captives.

Damien saw the tree and couldn't stop staring.

The oak was black as old blood, its bark choking on hoary lichen and moss. The closer they came, the more apparent it was that patches of the tree had already died. It listed sideways, unsteady in its age, and the malformed branches grew sparse and mottled leaves.

"Beautiful, ain't it?" Hender purred, his voice curdling Damien's blood.

"It looks past its time."

"It still helps us. It's what brought me to your whore, after all. And what took Sam to your friend."

Hender seemed happy enough to talk, filling the air with filth as they pulled into the yard of a sprawling, paint-peeled house almost as past its prime as the tree.

As Damien and Cal were yanked from their saddles, Hender talked of how he and Sam were the last two to eat its acorns. Sam had left for his own ranch, claiming he and his son could take care of the matter, the same day Hender had ridden for the Bearsons' with his new name.

Hender chuckled, all good humor as he grabbed Cal and hauled him forward. Damien, almost trembling in fury, fell into step as the gun digging into his back shoved him into the house. Strangers watched as they passed, all wide grins or curled lips. There weren't many Hollowoods, Damien noted, but those he saw showed no remorse or doubt.

They were herded down into a damp-smelling cellar, and only after Damien let himself be bound anew did Hender continue his story.

"I thought the vision showing me Black Falls meant that bastard Star would come back eventually. I never would've guessed *this*." He yanked something familiar-but-not out of his pocket.

Cal stared at the relic with fury. "That's Mom's!"

Hender's fist clenched around the handle of his gun. "It ain't your mom's, kid. It's the earth's, and he'll be getting it back."

Damien leaned forward, determined to draw eyes off Cal. "I guess Sam wasn't the only murderer in the family. That's what this is about, aye? You're gearing up for a host of murders. It looks to me like the whole bunch of you needs to be put down."

It did its job. Hender whirled back on him. "Sam was a greedy fool. We all saw the burns on his arms after he burned your friend's homestead to the ground. Idiot claimed he'd lost the relic and thought us dumb enough to believe him. Nothing else but a fool attempt to use one would leave such a mess. We were all taught better. Never would've thought the selfish bastard would do any good. Then he killed one of the curs. Now I just have the one to cull."

Rage burned through Damien at the callous words. "You're madmen who killed women and children on account of a misshapen tree. What use is it? Are you all that stupid?"

The mad light in Hender's eyes told Damien he'd hit his mark. "It passes on what the land wants, and that's who we do this for."

"So you worship it? Because it grew ugly?"

"It grew that way after it tasted their blood," Hender growled. "The need did that to it! Your lover will get the end his mother and uncle should have, and it'll bring the tree back."

"So you think."

Hender leaned close, trembling. "We'll have our blood-letting beneath the tree. Those twins should have been the last, but they got away. *Twice*. And then she had *him*, spreading more poison. Now we're down to the end of their line again. His blood needs to be spilt over those roots. It *will* do what it should."

Damien sneered. "The damn thing will rot away before any of that crew let you hurt Star."

"No," Hender crowed, fury replaced by glee that was far, far worse. "Your whore will come here for you and his brother."

They made camp that night after a long, quiet ride. Ostra and Knott, returning separately and empty-handed, sat off to the side, leaning close in an intense discussion that Star wasn't quite brave enough to approach. Aric, having met up with them later again, had stepped away from camp, both to patrol the nearby land and to clear his head.

"I really am sorry I did this to your family," Star told Beresford, staying where he sat.

Looking up from his weary contemplation of the fire, Beresford shook his head hard. "No, son. These bastards are the curse." Worry had aged him.

Bay sank down alongside them from where he had been not-so-discreetly listening. "They should have been wiped out long ago. That my line is still orchestrating these sick schemes . . ." A sigh. "Not anymore, at least. Not after we leave their lands. I want every one of them in the ground."

"And then you start the cycle again," Star pointed out. It was like his father had always said when drinking: *"Rot gets deep. Sets in with weedy veins rooting down through madness."* He'd always talked about his worry it would get Star, conversations Ty had never remembered in the light of the sun.

Bay shook his head. "It isn't all of them, lad. Those like me left ages ago. I've kept track enough to know the youngest in that house is full-grown, yet unmarried. Most are older, and all of them will be gunning for our heads when they know we're there. Taking them out will be a mercy to the land."

Star closed his eyes, willing himself to accept it all. "How did you know to find us here?"

"I received a telegram from Bill saying what you were about. They broke their deal with me by coming down here and gunning for you, and I'll see them all dead for it."

"What is this all about? Bill told me what he knew, but that can't be all of it."

"It's an ugly tale."

"Roy almost succeeded in burying me alive. I've a right to know why."

Guilt crossed Bay's face. "I am so, so sorry, Star."

Star lifted his chin. "What could they possibly gain by killing all of us?"

Bay nodded. "I'll tell it to you, then, but you won't be happy for it." He sighed, looking down at his hands. "My family went after a young couple who broke away from your people to settle. They'd taken the name Scales and had three children. The whole thing started over land. Over sheep, of all the stupid—" Bitterness weighed his words. "My family wanted more grazing land. The best. The Scales refused to sell. They'd left their life for that sliver of their own.

"When they refused, the Hollowoods, then wearing the name Ram, stole their children. Carried them off into the woods. Stood them all around a tree, not for any reason other than it was deep in the woods and they wanted to save bullets."

Star cringed, his muscles clenched. "They killed them."

"Aye. Blood, from what the Hollowoods call 'the Son,' soaked into the roots. It liked it. Liked the water in it, though those madmen won't believe that. The tree grew thick. Fast." He shook his head. "So they brought more blood. Killed more. The Wind-whispers, still strong and nomadic, cottoned on, but they were too late. They stopped making temporary settlements, instead always living on the move and losing children as often as gaining.

"And while they died, the sick bastards dumped blood on those roots, and if prisoners were dragged to the north, then their bodies were buried around it. The tree kept growing, and the Rams changed their name to Hollowood, declared it their mission to feed it. They started to worship the twisted thing."

"*Why?*"

"Mad dogs, lad." Sneering over the words, Bay shook his head. "And madder to go. They started stealing relics. Some damn fool soaked the acorns off the tree and ate the meat. Had a vision where to find a relic and, when they followed, it was true. They drove your people from their territory, killed families to steal their amber baubles, and the only thankful part of the whole sickening mess is that they don't often get those cursed dreams. The less they can feed the poisoned thing, the less it shares."

Star clenched his jaw. "But that hasn't stopped their belief."

"No. Sun-damned fools, they've mired so long in filth that they won't see the wrong. They just keep telling each other they're right."

The others were gathered close, drawn by the story.

"The growth of the tree was a sign. A sign for rebirth. It was their job to throw those amber pendants to the tree. Their job to rid the earth of the ones who they said stole the Son's gifted blood."

Star shuddered. How many untold dead? Family he'd never gotten to meet and ancestors never given time to share their stories like his father had. "And in the end, Dad and I remained."

"Aye."

Beresford glared into the trees beyond the fire, his jaw working but no sound coming. Finally, he gathered himself enough to speak. "All for some stump."

"Thank you," Star told Bay. "Now at least I know the why."

When they went to their bedrolls, Star curled up tight, lonely and uncertain. Bay's story circled in his thoughts like a buzzard ready to pick over the carcass of his hope.

"Tomorrow we'll get them back," he vowed to the moon and his children.

They crept, slowly, within the borders of the Hollowoods' stolen territory. Theirs was an army, one Star was pleased to see could move well when the occasion demanded it. They'd left their horses back in a meadow, hobbled but saddled. They might need to make a quick dash, but he hoped not.

They slid stealthily through the woods, alert for any sign of an enemy guard. Aric kept to Star's back, and he understood in a way. Losing Cal had shaken all the Bears, and rather than blame him, they'd only seemed to grow more obsessed with keeping him in sight.

There were two men standing a short distance off, and another two up on a wooden platform, half-hidden in the foliage. Star pulled up, slinking low, and noted that those behind him instantly followed suit.

Aric and Knott approached those on the ground, slow and easy. Star watched, a knife in each hand. When they threw themselves onto the men's backs, Star moved, blades slicing through the air and lodging into unprotected throats. A shot of relief and pride stabbed through Star as both hit true.

They fell, and Star's muscles tensed, a new blade in each hand. He glanced towards Aric and Knott, sure the noise would bring an army down around their heads, but neither showed any sign of concern and no sounds came except those of the surrounding woods. He and the others slowly relaxed, drifting apart to cover more area.

For now, at least, they were unnoticed. With their numbers, staying that way was against them. Star hoped the others were doing as well as they closed in on their appointed targets. Bay, drawing on forty-year-old memories, had been as exact as could be expected. So far, things lined up nicely.

Soon they came to the clearing where the bastards' house sat. Near it, the rest of the forest cut away, and Star stumbled.

The tree.

Even at a distance he could see its gnarled, hunching, hulking size. It was the cause of centuries of bloodshed and horror. How much of his family's blood stained that surrounding ground?

He wanted to burn it. *Would* burn it, once they finished. He doubted anyone would stop him.

"Star." Aric slid next to him.

Star shook himself. Looked back to find Knott and Ostra waiting on him too. Ducking his head, he pressed on.

They came up behind the house, and there across the empty field Star saw the back stoop with its low, sloping roof. He just needed to wait for Bay's signal, then they'd climb up there—provided someone didn't shoot them first.

The signal came—a single shot that reverberated through the woods—and they moved. Heart in his throat, Star helped Knott boost Aric up onto the low steel roof, then Ostra. A cry went up inside that was answered out in the woods, those survivors still out there no doubt rushing their way. Seizing Aric's and Ostra's outstretched hands, Star took Knott's boost and clambered up. The sheets of metal were slick under his feet, but the easy grade of the roof helped them to keep their balance.

A few of Bay's crew broke from the trees as Star eased his way across the slippery surface, and silently wished Knott luck as the man joined those on the ground. Star heard shattering glass and cracking wood as windows and doors gave way beneath their assault. Hopefully most Hollowoods out in the woods were already dead. The next step's success depended on how many were left.

Aric and Star tried to open the windows to the second floor first. Ostra crouched at their backs, eyes roving and gun ready. The first was locked, and judging by Aric's frustrated breath, so was the second. Using the handle of a blade, Star shattered and cleared the glass. Any second, enemies could hear and pour into the room. Aric tried to push forward, no doubt intending to enter first, but Star moved before he could.

No one was there, though he could still hear fighting downstairs. Knives in hand, Star crept down the stairs, easing to where he could see. There was a door to a root cellar.

As he came down, two people ran up the steep cellar stairs, leaving Star exposed. He dropped one as he leapt back, and just in time. A shot splintered the wall panel behind where he'd crouched. Another unseen gun went off as he moved and the two Hollowoods lay where they'd fallen, one choking on blood and the other gone.

"Come on upstairs, old man," Bay bellowed from somewhere nearby, voice hard.

Old man? Star felt a flicker of confusion that only grew at the loud, bitter laugh that answered Bay's words.

"One old man is dead, Bay, and you'll be another at the end of this."

Star leapt down the last of the stairs and found Bay closing the distance to the cellar door. Ostra, hot on his heels, hissed an annoyed bark that he ignored.

"Hender!" Star yelled, anger rumbling beneath the name.

Another laugh from the bowels of the house, but no words.

"Hender, are ya?" Bay sneered. "So your grandfather died, the old bastard, and the agreement we made means nothing anymore?"

From the foot of the stairs, Star could see the bulk of their crew spread around, most standing near the stairway but others pressed to the windows, guns cocked and eyes watching. Judging by the bodies in the yard, Star doubted many Hollowood reinforcements would be on their way.

Beresford bulled through the tattered back door to join them. Heart thumping in his throat, Star took up post by Bay.

"The agreement never should've been made. We've a right to spill that cursed whoreson's blood, and I'll happily spill yours with it."

"This old buzzard isn't so easy to kill. You're a young pup who thinks he's a big man, but those stories they filled you with are naught but piss in the spoiled dirt. You gonna kill for it? Die for it?"

"He got my cousin killed. Same as the rest of his poisoned lot killed my dad. Blood, Bay. It's just me now. What'll you bastards do? What'll *I* do? Should I go ahead and shoot the two down here with me?"

Star growled and would have torn through the door had Ostra and Aric not seized him.

"And your line ended my family!" Star yelled, struggling against the relentless holds. "Give them back to me, you bastard! They have no part in any of your madness!"

Quiet, again. Star slumped, choking on the fury he couldn't act on. Aric loosened his grip but it didn't matter. Ostra held fast.

"Come get me, wind-bastard, or I'll put a bullet in your lover's brain. Then your brother's, and a last in my own."

Nothing could have kept Star from running then.

Ostra choked on a gasp as Star drove his elbow into her guts, freeing himself. She wasn't prepared for his going for her gun, and he stole it before diving forward into the low-ceilinged stairway.

In the end, it was that reckless, mindless, sense-stealing fury that undid Hender. Star raised the borrowed gun and curled a finger over the trigger as his eyes landed on Hender's twisted, snarling face. He squeezed.

Hender jerked his gun around and fired. The bullet grazed Star's head, its report striking his ears. He lurched backwards instinctively, head smashing into a support beam in his blind move and feet slipping from the too-narrow steps.

He hit the rough-packed dirt at the bottom of the stairs hard, blackness dancing with sparks across his eyes and the wind thrown from his lungs. For two heartbeats Star struggled, trying to right himself, waiting for the next bullet to bury itself in him. If he'd the breath, he would have laughed.

Everything he'd been through, and he'd die as Ty had always feared: at the hands of the ones who killed his world. But Star had come too far to let it be easy. Nose filled with the scent of rot, his right hand scrabbled in the dirt, searching blindly for the gun that had escaped him on impact.

Instead of a bullet, hands slammed into his skin. He hissed what little air he'd regained and tried a backward blow with his elbow, but when a large hand curled over his forearm, he finally recognized the voice ringing in his head. He stilled and strove to make out the words.

"—safe. It's over. Damn it, let me see where he hit you!"

Star let Aric manhandle him, the blackness over his vision falling away. He found two more blurry forms not far from them.

Fingers poked at the side of his head, stabbing him with pain. He ignored it and Aric both, instead squinting at the others.

The sight that came into slow focus finally eased his terror: his brother and lover, both alive and safe, if a little bruised. There were gags shoved into their mouth, but Cal's eyes were alight with relief.

Over. All of it.

"The fool's fine!" Aric hollered up the stairs. Then to Star, "Get your man loose. Cal, I have you. Thank the moon."

Aric released him, and Star practically fell onto Damien's knees as he fumbled with his gag. It took more effort than it should have to free the damn thing, but his shaking fingers did the job.

Damien's dry cough and husky laugh was music. "Damn good to see you."

Warmth seeped into Star's bones. Ducking his head, he pulled out a knife and went to work on his bound hands. As soon as he had them loose, Damien grabbed his wrists. The hold was weak, likely from too long immobile, but Star stilled all the same.

"Take a breath before you get my feet," Damien ordered. "By the sun, I thought you cracked your head in two."

Star steeled himself, then looked up. "I'm sorry."

Damien sighed. "Star. No." One of his hands slid gently through Star's hair. "You've an egg growing that'll feed a ranch. You need to take it easy."

"You're the one I'm worried about," Star fired back, pulling away to get Damien's ankles. He rubbed around where the binds had held, while Damien did the same to his wrists. Now that the danger had passed, the pressure that'd kept Star moving died. Limbs shaking, he shuddered under a wave of utter exhaustion.

Cal huddled against Aric, begging him to not forget something Hender carried in his pocket. It took a few repeats for Star to realize he was talking about Mae's relic.

They weren't alone for long. Feet pounded down the steps, and Beresford ran to Cal, yanking the boy up. Father embraced son, Beresford squeezing his cub as tears of relief covered his face.

A melancholic ache spread through Star's chest. A handful of moons ago, he hadn't known these men existed. He hadn't known what the Hollowoods had done to him, both by hand and by repercussion. Now the monsters were dead, but it didn't feel over.

Star stumbled upright, helping Damien rise in turn. Damien sagged, legs not yet ready, and Star hastened to keep him up as he found his feet. Then Damien's strong arms were around him, a welcome brace. He buried his face in Damien's neck and willed his head to settle.

The smell of old sweat and several days' dirt promised that Damien really was alive and healthy. Damien didn't complain of the blood soaking into his already filthy shirt, just held him. A heavy weight landed on his back, knocking him hard against Damien. They almost fell.

"I thought they'd kill you," Cal sobbed, clinging harder, "and it was my fault."

He shook his head as he patted Cal's arm, and almost regretted the move as the world pulsed again. Cal didn't let go, and were it not for Damien's shaky support, all of them might have ended up on the ground.

"It wouldn't have been your fault," Star assured him. The blame belonged with the dead. "You're safe now and we'll get you home. This nightmare is over."

Cal finally let go and Star gingerly turned to face him. Cal looked dead on his feet, but there were no signs of any pain.

"Did they hurt either of you?" he asked.

Cal's shaken head and Damien's quirked eyebrow almost brought Star down again with the weight of his relief.

He forced himself to look toward Hender, needing proof of death before he left. Hender, sprawled in his own blood and staring, looked nothing like the monster he had been, which was sad, somehow. Death revealed the human, Star supposed.

Damien took his arm, leading him away. Star released a long breath, reminding himself that they'd made it through to the end. Damien and Cal were fine; Hender and his men were gone. There'd be time to make things right.

They took the stairs slowly, the Bears tight together and Damien and Star at their heels. His head was settling but it all felt unreal. They passed the bodies in the halls, following their own bloody footsteps out into the field. The cleaner air hit his face, a welcome taste of life after the closed-in death.

Star stopped as the others, save Damien, kept moving. Something in his core told him it wasn't time yet to set the past aside. A soft breeze, barely enough to stir the hair not tacky with blood, rose from the corner of the field, urging him to turn, to look.

For a heartbeat Star stood there, startled and shaken. The present returned to him with a blow that rattled. The wind had never touched him before, not in that way, and yet the familiarity of its brush reached down into the hollow of his bones to warm them.

There were whispers beneath its breath, words he couldn't understand but that wrapped around him, cajoling and welcoming both. A tear dripped down Star's face as he stared at its urging to face the field around the house. He wiped the tear away, smearing the not-yet-dry blood and wishing the gesture could take the ache with it.

Curling his hand over Damien's, Star squeezed once, not looking his way. Then he walked through the wreckage and detritus of battle, led by that new-old touch, to stand below the tree that had taken a senseless act of violence and sent its consequences echoing through the land. The hollow beneath its heaving roots was black with shadow, but that was where he needed to go.

He crawled, digging hands into mulch and rot and shoving handful by handful out of his way. Webbing caught in his hair, a spider crawled down his neck and then up over his bandana, and still he dug. His head beat a reminder of its abuse and he ignored that too, intent on his search. Bone, rot, and a chain.

He picked that up gently, twisting his arm behind him to rest it outside the hollow. He kept searching.

"Star?"

Damien was beside him, peering in, concerned. Guilt bit at Star, but he shoved it back. There'd be time for rest later. "Search the roots for more."

Beresford joined too. They began a hesitant hunt as Star felt in the gaps beneath root, digging more, teeth gritted and jaw clenched against the need to gag at the scent.

Hands on hips hauled him out. Damien was looking at him, worried. "We found twenty, Star. The more we dig, the less I like it. Those roots are huge and deep, but it's old, and some are dead and rotting. You've a pile too. Don't make yourself one of the bones here. You haven't even let us see to your head."

Star reached for Damien's arm, stopped, his eyes locked on his bleeding fingers. He hadn't noticed the pain, too swallowed by the need to search. The others were using sticks to dig, he noted. Cal was kneeling next to him, bruises on his face and concern in his eyes. Cal, who was too young for any of the things he'd been through since Star came into his life.

The guilt he'd shoved away returned with a deep bite. "Let's get you and Cal home." The wind was gone again and his move was his own.

Damien brushed at the mess of Star's hair, the gentle scrape of his fingers grounding. "I'm not upset, Star, and neither is your little brother. But we are tired, and we aren't the only ones."

The relics they'd gathered lay in a pile, and Star stared at them, lost. So many lives shed over them, drawn by their amber-captured droplets from a spring terrible for its mistaken generosity.

"Here, lad."

Damien's hand fell to Star's shoulder as they both looked up to see Bill, sweat-damp blond hair streaked with dirt, holding out a leather sack.

"Thank you," Star said, so damn grateful he was okay. Damien took the bag with his own nod of thanks and rested it on the ground, open.

Star started filling it, his hands shaking. Damien helped as Bill hovered, shifting it as needed. Most of the others watched them work, not sure what to do. Ostra still dug, her gray-streaked auburn head bent to the task. When she came to them, she carried a longer, cylindrical piece that she put into the bag herself.

Star's eyes left his work, and he stared at the tree. How many people who shared his blood had died at its roots? It was over now, but too late to save so many. "What do you think will happen to it without the water in the relics?" The rough grate of his voice made him wince.

"Doesn't matter," Bay huffed, voice as forbidding as the look on his face. "My people and I are staying here and burning this hell down. Then I plan to dig deep to the bowels of the earth and get any last inch of stolen shit away."

Star closed his eyes. "Thank you."

Knott snorted, Ostra leaning close to rest her hand on his bandaged shoulder.

"Let's get shut of this sun-damned nightmare," Damien suggested.

Star couldn't agree more.

They made camp away from the sight of Hender's homestead, leaving the bodies of the enemies but bringing their own. The wounded rested as those able prepared the graves and put the lost to rest.

Bay had set his survivors to guard his once homestead, claiming the purge of the land for himself. "My people and I will watch after those who can't yet travel. You take care of that bag of yours. I'll deal with my blood."

Now, some slept while others, kept awake by either leftover nerves or an unwillingness to release their tension, waited as if for a sign. Cal was the first to pass out under the watchful eye of both his eldest brother and father. He deserved the rest, the poor lad.

Star leaned against Damien's side and squinted into the tree line, the shadows around the light of the watchfire too thick. His head hurt less, the wound cleaned and bandaged, but he couldn't relax. He continually imagined bodies prowling beyond their sight, leftovers of Hender's blood still hungry for trouble.

The air was soft on his face, no message in its touch. "I felt the wind today."

Damien shifted and Star loosed a grunt of discontent. He felt Damien's stare on him but didn't look away from the far edge of camp. There was more to say and he needed to lance it before anything else in this rotten place had a chance to fester.

"We've never talked about any of this," Star continued. "Not what's between us, not what happened at Wendy's." The words caught hard in his throat. "We haven't talked about what we plan. Not really. We've only talked at each other. And when he took you, I thought we'd never get to."

The heat of Damien's hand swallowed Star's own, his touch gentle as always. "I didn't think you were ready to talk." The laugh that followed was soft and bitter. "I'm not too sure I was, either."

Star clung to the tenuous line between them. "I want you."

Damien's face pressed into his neck, an easy nudge meant to slide skin together and feel close. "You've got me. That doesn't change what happened."

"We flew blind after Hollowood, and Dad died in payment. Part of me blamed you and it hurt. The rest blamed me." And still did, deep down.

Damien's thumb stroked over Star's knuckles, a calming comfort. "Only used to?"

"I stormed out in a fit the day you rode off to spend time with Knott and Ostra. It was childish of me, and because of that you and Cal went through hell." He hated himself for that childishness. Acknowledged, too, he had to forgive it if any of them were going to move forward.

"You couldn't know, Star."

Star shook his head, not letting himself get pulled from what he wanted to say. "I made the choice to follow when you rode after Hollowood, and Dad made his own choice to have our backs. I didn't want to face that. It hurt too damn much." Letting the pain go meant letting Ty go, twisted as it sounded. Star didn't say that part, but he understood it all the same.

"Star, you couldn't know," Damien repeated.

Star cut in before Damien could say any more. He had to get it out now or he never would. "The others stopped me when I tried for the same move with you and Cal. I'd have ridden after you blind, and you'd have ended up rotting with me if I'd managed to find you."

Damien could have taken offense at his words. Star was baring his soul and it wasn't pretty. Instead, he stayed steady at his side, no surprise or judgment on his face. "There were no right moves that day," Damien told him. "Letting Hollowood go would mean knowing he could come back for Wendy and her family at any time. By chasing him, we had no plan, no control."

Looking away from the fire-lit trees, Star eyed the others. Those not asleep were clustered in small groups, heads together and voices low enough not to carry. Star was grateful for the space they offered them.

His gaze fell to Knott and Ostra, curled close together. "Knott took a bullet today. It could have been him lost this time, and because of me."

"And I'd have buried a part of my heart today. Ostra and Knott rode with you here because they chose to, and that's what family does. It could have been any of us. Hender came dangerously close to taking you from me."

Damien's quiet, pained words washed the hesitation from Star's gut. He pushed forward into Damien's careful touch, ignoring the throb of pain and threatening pull to the stitches. "I'm sorry."

In the wake of the battle, Star could see where he'd been a fool. He would keep losing Ty time and again—each time a new question came up he'd never have answered or when he saw a sight he wanted to share with him and couldn't—but he'd never lose him as his father.

Damien answered slowly and with a pained sadness no one could fake. "So am I."

Star laughed bitterly. "What a pair." The hurt that had coiled in his chest and shadowed the air between them loosened its hold. He pressed his lips to Damien's chapped ones. There was no heat in it, just a welcome, quiet promise.

When they broke apart, Star shifted, leaning against Damien. He should keep watch on the trees, but instead his eyes slid shut. It had been a long day. A long *moon*.

Damien rested his chin against Star's head, the stubble scraping against Star's scalp and stirring his loose hair. "You've never felt the wind before today. What do you think it means?"

What had it been about? Maybe that he'd done what it wanted. He told Damien as much.

Damien nodded. "And if it calls again?"

Star, eyes still closed, focused on the warmth of Damien next to him. "If it does, I follow."

He shifted to brush a chaste kiss to Star's scalp. "We."

The certainty of it brought moisture to Star's eyes. He bit it back, not letting the comfort deter him from what he still needed to say. "You were right that we shouldn't stay with Beresford. If I hadn't insisted on it, none of this would have happened. And why stay at all if we might have to leave?"

The words were hard, and the loss they'd lead to harder. A home with the Bears had been a chance at a life together with a measure of peace, but it had been a selfish thing to try. Now the threat was gone, but it didn't lessen Star's guilt.

"No." Damien's answer shocked Star. "Knott and Ostra will be there to keep our place if we need to travel. A home means a place to come back to at the end of a trail. After how damn hard we fought to end this, I'd say the both of us earned that chance."

A sob caught in his throat. Star forced it back, blaming the aching in his head. "Might be you're right."

Damien buried his face into Star's hair, a soft rumble of affirmation lost in the black strands, and Star smiled.

CHAPTER TWENTY-EIGHT

A moon later, they finally made the journey back into the Scar.

Days before their leaving, Star had been shocked when Mae came to their room. Damien had stood back, uncertain, as Mae sat next to where Star was perched on their bed. She'd slipped the relic from around her neck and set it between them, looking at it and then him.

"Are you sure?" Star asked. He knew what those dreams had meant for her, both good and bad.

"Let me, please, dear," she said, patting his hand. "It dreams of its home. Maybe I can think of it as an old apology."

The sadness in her eyes was one he didn't know how to answer, and so he'd hugged her. She'd let him, and when they'd separated, she'd touched his chin, a half smile on trembling lips. "You're very like your fathers. Thank you for giving us a chance, and for helping to return my Cal."

She'd stood and left with a soft goodnight that Star had barely managed to return before the door closed on her back.

As they made camp a few nights before they would enter the sun's basin, Star looked over their party, wondering how things had come to this. He'd never thought he would willingly enter that hell with anyone besides his father.

Both of his brothers were there, along with his father. Chuck had opted to stay home and keep watch, stating that at least one Bear had to be around if something came up. Cal, the reckless lad, had to be watched closely, but he listened when Star called, which was nice. Not enough people listened to him.

Knott and Ostra had traveled to Wendy's before joining them.

Tonight they'd dug out a fire pit to cook a warm meal Aric had caught. Once they entered the Scar, there would be no fires.

Star leaned against Damien's side, watching the flickering of the flame and lost in thoughts. The curse was ended, he really believed that. Bay had sent word after he'd lanced his ancestors' land, and Star found himself certain that, finally, the last of the rot and decay would seep out of that wound in the north.

Damien's hand slid over his thigh, the heat seeping through Star's pants to warm his skin. It crept lower, callouses scratching lightly against denim and curling over where Star felt himself stirring, interested.

"Think there's still a man who'd like to sneak off?" Damien's voice against his ear sent a thrill through his chest.

Indeed there was.

Star studied their companions. Knott was determinedly keeping his head turned away from them, and Ostra, leaning against him as she talked, had a smirk twitching her lips. Cal might be some trouble, Star mused. Aric glanced his way, noticed Damien's hand, then clenched his jaw and pointedly turned back to Beresford.

Aric and Damien got along better now, thank the moon, but Star wasn't sure the tension between the two would ever fully fade. Still, Star also bet that Aric would never let their youngest brother slip off after them when he had suspicions what they were about.

Star stood up, dislodging Damien's hand only to grab it and tug.

They walked a short distance, and Star felt a sad little bit of nostalgic memory stir at the familiarity of it. Things had seemed so simple, then. Damien had been an interesting stranger, attractive and enticing. Lust was easy when he gave it its head. Love, that was harder.

When they were far enough away, Star stopped. He studied Damien, seeing the changes in him and recognizing how deeply he wanted the once-bountied in his heart.

"I'd challenge you to have me feel it—" Star chuckled tiredly "—but all I want is to go easy. Feel that you're alive."

"Same here," Damien admitted, swallowing a yawn. Damien sat and Star curled against him, undoing his belt and jeans and then sliding the belt off, but nothing more.

Damien reached down, sliding his hand into the loose front of Star's jeans. Star leaned back, head on Damien's shoulder, his own hand rubbing him over top the belted pants.

"We'll end up needing to wash the things," Damien pointed out, then sighed out a breath as Star worked him through the sturdy material.

"We won't finish in them," Star protested.

Still, neither of them were moving to stand or strip.

Instead, they nestled there together, content and patient. The pleasure they brought to each other was as quiet as they felt, and when they finally finished, pants damp with their release and tongues tangled in a lazy duel, it was nice.

They did end up having to wash their clothes in the stream and lay them out on the rocks to dry. That was fine too. The night was warm, even as summer was heading to its close.

Damien stood on a stony bank, water from the ocean pouring in to fill the deepest part of the Sun's Scar. The rock had been worn down over the last few centuries, smoothed and polished. A waterfall was far in the distance, beautiful and terrible both.

They'd entered far to the south, in a place Star had never crossed and that he doubted anyone else had, either. There had been no attacks the first two nights, neither from viper nor wraith.

"Where are they?" Star had wondered as they walked, sounding uneasy at the quiet.

"Who knows?" Damien hadn't felt any more comfortable with the change. The Bears had been watchful, though Cal had needed to be herded back time and again.

"What do you think happened to them?"

Damien gave it some thought. "Maybe the bag you carry."

"It's possible they feel it and think we're already theirs." But that didn't seem right.

Damien shook his head. That wasn't what he meant. "This mess started with those bastards and their hungry tree. Now they're gone, there is a chance things will get better. It might even be they're giving us that chance."

Damn it to the sun, he hoped so.

"It can't be a bad thing we're traveling safe," Beresford had added, having been listening closely. "We— *Cal!*"

Star had choked on a laugh and Damien, swallowing his own chuckle, had watched him lecture his son. Ostra and Knott had seemed to enjoy the show as much as they did.

Damien felt like those days were ages ago. The laughter was gone, all quiet in the face of Star's solemn approach to the water's edge.

One by one, Star reached into his sack and pulled out a pendant or charm. Threw it. There were many, most of them containing droplets of water, some with other bits of preserved treasure. Insects. Twigs.

Each hit the water with a ring of displacement. Then there came another toss. At last the bag was empty, and Star passed it to Cal. Damien wondered if Star knew there were tears on his face.

"Now what?" Star asked, seeming exhausted.

Damien curled his arm around Star's shoulders, nosing his chin. "Now we help your family with their harvest and prepare to build ourselves a home."

There, beneath the tears, was that sweet smile, a reflection of Star's core. This gift? Damien wasn't returning it. Star would stay his.

Dear Reader,

Thank you for reading Leona Bentley's *Guided by the Wind*!

We know your time is precious and you have many, many entertainment options, so it means a lot that you've chosen to spend your time reading. We really hope you enjoyed it.

We'd be honored if you'd consider posting a review—good or bad—on sites like **Amazon, Barnes & Noble, Kobo, Goodreads, Twitter, Facebook, Tumblr,** and your blog or website. We'd also be honored if you told your friends and family about this book. Word of mouth is a book's lifeblood!

For more information on upcoming releases, author interviews, blog tours, contests, giveaways, and more, please sign up for our weekly, spam-free newsletter and visit us around the web:

Newsletter: riptidepublishing.com/newsletter
Twitter: twitter.com/RiptideBooks
Facebook: facebook.com/RiptidePublishing
Goodreads: tinyurl.com/RiptideOnGoodreads
Tumblr: riptidepublishing.tumblr.com

Thank you so much for Reading the Rainbow!

RiptidePublishing.com

ALSO BY

☀

LEONA BENTLEY

Mosquito District
By the River Shore

ABOUT THE
AUTHOR

Leona Bentley grew up in the Canadian Maritimes. Autumn is her favorite time of year, and she can often be found drinking coffee late into the fall nights as she works on her newest stories.

You can find her at Goodreads, and her website is leonabentleynet.wordpress.com.

Enjoy more stories like
Guided by the Wind
at RiptidePublishing.com!

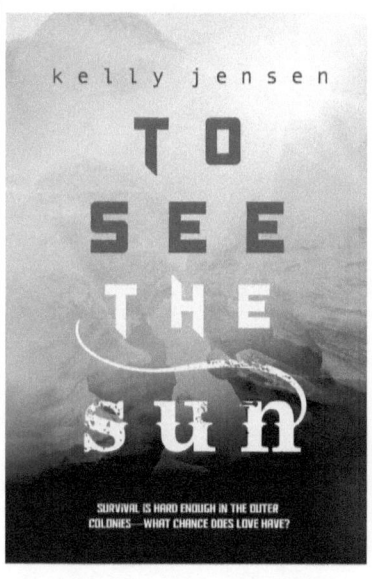